Praise for
A Strange and Stubborn Endurance

"Many a reader longing for a sense of homecoming in the realm of romantic fantasy will find it in *A Strange and Stubborn Endurance*."
—Jacqueline Carey, *New York Times* bestselling author of the Kushiel's Legacy series

"A satisfying balance of romance and action, with political intrigue that is both elaborate and plausible and rich, fascinating world-building."
—Malka Older, award-winning author

"I flew through this book and enjoyed every page of the journey. . . . I loved that this was a gripping political fantasy, but I loved even more that it was wrapped around a stubbornly kindhearted romance."
—Freya Marske, author of *A Marvellous Light*

"An emotionally gripping, delightful queer fantasy filled with political intrigue, family dynamics, and tender moments that will grab readers' hearts and minds."
—*Library Journal* (starred review)

"An absolute delight! A perfect balance of romance, fantasy politics, and a truly sinister murder plot. It put me in mind of *The Goblin Emperor* (earnest but wounded lead characters you can't help rooting for) and *Winter's Orbit* (queer marriage of convenience with deep SFF politics)."
—Olivia Waite, award-winning author

"Blending intrigue and queer romance, *A Strange and Stubborn Endurance* stitches together two cultures and reembroiders gender conventions. Meadows combines the personal and political through an elegant voice, and finds time for tender moments of healing."
—E. J. Beaton, author of *The Councillor*

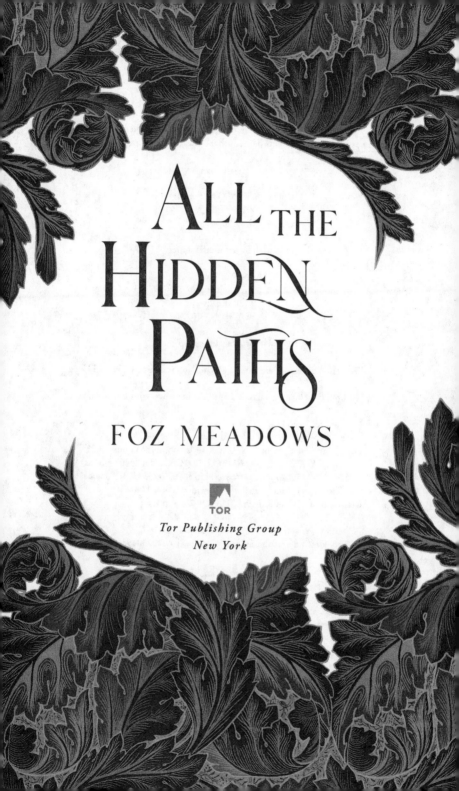

ALL THE HIDDEN PATHS

FOZ MEADOWS

TOR

Tor Publishing Group
New York

ALL THE HIDDEN PATHS

Map by Jennifer Hanover

A Tor Book
Published by Tom Doherty Associates / Tor Publishing Group
120 Broadway
New York, NY 10271

www.torpublishinggroup.com

Tor® is a registered trademark of Macmillan Publishing Group, LLC.

The Library of Congress has cataloged the hardcover edition as follows:

Names: Meadows, Foz, author.
Title: All the hidden paths / Foz Meadows.
Description: First edition. | New York : Tor Publishing Group, 2023.
Identifiers: LCCN 2023045862 (print) | LCCN 2023045863 (ebook) |
    ISBN 9781250829306 (hardcover) | ISBN 9781250829313 (ebook)
Subjects: LCSH: Fantasy fiction. | Romance fiction. | Novels.
Classification: LCC PR9639.4.M43 A78 2023 (print) |
    LCC PR9639.4.M43 (ebook) | DDC 823/.92—dc23
LC record available at https://lccn.loc.gov/2023045862
LC ebook record available at https://lccn.loc.gov/2023045863

ISBN 978-1-250-82932-0 (trade paperback)

Our books may be purchased in bulk for promotional, educational, or business use. Please contact your local bookseller or the Macmillan Corporate and Premium Sales Department at 1-800-221-7945, extension 5442, or by email at MacmillanSpecialMarkets@macmillan.com.

First Tor Paperback Edition: 2024

Printed in the United States of America

0 9 8 7 6 5 4 3 2 1

*For anyone who's ever come out
and wondered what comes next.*

Author's Note

All the Hidden Paths contains instances of dubious consent and undernegotiated kink.

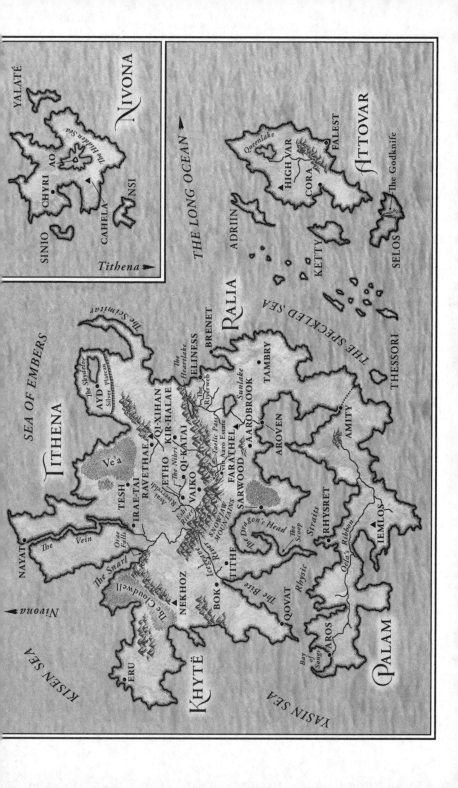

Six months, I'd been in Eliness; six sunfucking months of going unnoticed, working hard and drinking just enough to dull the sting of it, and all for nothing. Six months without so much as winking at another man, let alone screwing one, and Lord Sun knows there were men enough to be tempting. My office stood in sight of the docks, which teemed with strapping, broad-shouldered roughs, hauling cargo or doing whatever sailors do in port that isn't drinking or fucking, and there I sat, as celibate as an Attovari monk and twice as miserable. No men, nor any sociable vices that might lead to a lapse in judgement; I even drank alone, or on rare occasions with Yarrick, whom I wouldn't have fucked in a fit but who was, at least, reasonable company.

Six virtuous, miserable months, and still the Shade came for me anyway.

I'd just left work on a grim and drizzling evening when he materialised from the fog and blocked my path, sudden enough that I shrieked.

"Asrien bo Erat," he intoned. His voice was deep and mocking, and he omitted my title because he could, patrician features exuding superiority the way other men exude sweat. The rain turned the grey in his hair to silver, glinting in the low light. A hatefully handsome comeuppance.

"Lord Cato," I grit out, embarrassed and angry and fearful. "What a surprise."

"An unpleasant one, no doubt." Smiling thinly, he gestured ahead. "We will speak in private."

He set off for my lodgings unerringly and at speed, leaving me with my far shorter stride to struggle along in his wake. A less confident man would've kept his eye on me, worried I might flee; the Shade, however, had no such insecurities. Spymasters seldom do.

"As you know where I live," I said acidly, "I wonder you didn't wait for me there instead."

"I had business elsewhere. Your office was on my way."

He didn't deny that he could've broken in, had he wanted to. There was no point.

The drizzle had soaked me through by the time we reached my dingy rooms. The landlady, normally stationed in the central parlour, was nowhere to be seen as I unlocked my door and entered. The Shade watched, perversely amused as I shrugged out of my wet coat—his own was sturdy black wool, elegantly cut and far better suited to the time of year than my flimsy former finery. I claimed the only chair with a child's defiance, staring up at him with what little fire I could muster, but regretted it the instant he stepped forwards and loomed over me, his long features hard as iron.

"You speak Tithenai, do you not?"

I stared, waiting for him to continue. He didn't, and after several infuriating seconds, I realised he wanted me to answer.

"I do," I bit out. "You know I do. It's half my sunfucking job."

He twitched at the profanity, but otherwise remained impassive.

"Good," he said. "You will require the use of it."

A long pause followed.

"Yes?" I prompted eventually. "And?"

"In your . . . former circles," said Cato, the euphemism dripping with distaste, "did you ever encounter Velasin vin Aaro?"

The *vin* said he was gentry, but the Shade's apparent disdain for his title could've meant any number of things. I racked my brains and came up empty. "No. Or if I did, I never knew his name. Who is he? What's this all about?"

Again I waited. Again he said nothing. The Shade's pale lip

curled in a grimace, and all at once I realised that, whatever he was here to say, it disgusted him—and that could mean only one thing.

"Oh, I see." I leaned back in the chair, letting my legs sprawl open, grinning like I'd caught his eye at the kind of bar that wasn't supposed to exist in Ralia. "This is litai business, isn't it?"

Cato snarled, and I had half a second to bask in having unsettled him before he backhanded me for it. My head snapped to the right, and I laughed because I'd learned early that it was better to laugh at blows than cry from them. My ears rang as my top lip throbbed, and when I touched it, my fingertips came away bloody. I blinked through the resultant dizziness and stared at the hand he was flexing, open and shut, open and shut, like he wanted to wipe it clean but not where I could see him. As if admitting he found me repulsive would've meant showing weakness.

I snorted. As if I couldn't tell anyway.

"Velasin vin Aaro," said the Shade, continuing with pseudo-calm, "is the third son of Lord Varus vin Aaro, to whom His Majesty recently granted such lands and powers as formerly belonged to the traitor Lord Ennan vin Mica."

Now there was a name I recognised, as would most anyone in Ralia. I nodded grudging comprehension, still thumbing my split lip, and Cato continued.

"At the encouragement of King Markus, Lord Varus arranged a marriage between Velasin and a Tithenai noblewoman out of Qi-Katai, to help mend the rift vin Mica's banditry caused. But." And here he stopped, a look on his face like he'd bitten into a particularly sour quince. "Owing to some . . . indecorous behaviour on Velasin's part, the Tithenai envoy was made aware of his . . . unconventional preferences. And being Tithenai, their solution was to—offer him a groom, instead. Which offer he accepted, and which has now been formalised, *without* His Majesty's consultation."

It took a moment for the words to sink in, and when they did, a stupid grin spread across my face. My cut lip split wider and I didn't care, the sting of it nothing compared to the Shade's distaste.

"Oh, that's priceless!" I cackled. "A diplomatic litai marriage, and your lot have to eat it!"

A triumphal sneer crossed Cato's face, and too late I remembered why he was telling me this in the first place.

"We will not, as you say, be *eating it* for long." He leaned in close, and I shrank back without meaning to. "Because *you*, Asrien, will end it."

"Me?" I spluttered. "I'm no assassin—" But even as the words left my mouth, I knew that wasn't what he meant.

"Would that death were an option," the Shade said bitterly. "In this case, however, as Ralia's official, traditional stance on such unions is widely known, and as better relations with Tithena are genuinely desired"—*despite their perversity,* he didn't add, though his tone and scowl clearly implied it—"we have determined that even a seemingly accidental death would be laid at our feet, and however unpleasant the current situation is, we do not wish for a new diplomatic crisis. As such, we are taking a different route." His expression sharpened to a terrible smile. "You, Asrien, will go to Tithena. You will insinuate yourself into the confidence of Lord Velasin vin Aaro by whatever means necessary, and you will seduce him away from his . . . from Tiern Caethari Aeduria. Or, should that prove the more difficult option, seduce the tiern away from him. As a Ralian will be seen to be acting shamefully in either case, we do not especially care which of them you cozen."

He paused, his black eyes raking me with a coldly speculative look. "Although," he murmured, "looking as you do, you could easily pass for a Palamite." He smirked. "Or would it be more than passing? Your mother has always denied it, but—"

"I don't speak Palamish," I snapped, knowing my cheeks were flushed bright red and hating it even more than usual. Some Ralians might be light-haired or light-eyed or both, especially in the south, but even paired with plain brown eyes, my too-blond hair and too-pale skin spoke more of Palam or Attovar than Ralia, and nobody had ever let my mother or me forget it.

Least of all my father. Or, it seemed now, Lord Cato.

"A pity," said the Shade, savouring my discomfort like a good brandy. Then he shrugged. "Regardless, all that matters is that the marriage of Velasin and Caethari ends—and is seen to end—because of their inclinations, and not our intervention."

Feeling slightly hysterical, I asked, "And what if I end up married to one of them instead?"

"Don't be disgusting," Cato snapped. But then, after a moment, he muttered, "If that's what it takes, however . . . it would still be embarrassing, but the diplomatic union would be ended, and we'd have no need to formally acknowledge whatever broke it. But—" And here he paused, disdainful gaze flicking over me once more. "—I highly doubt it will come to that. Your value, such as it is, lies wholly in your usefulness as an instrument to your betters; beyond that, you bring nothing to anyone."

The worst thing was, he didn't say it to twist the knife, but as a bored statement of fact. It hurt in a way that made me harden, baring my teeth at him.

"Once I'm in Tithena, what's to stop me from doing as I please?"

"Two things," said the Shade, with deadly softness. "One, your beloved mother is still in a position to be ruined by your antics, should they be made public, and two—" He reached into his coat and withdrew a wicked knife, fitting the point beneath my chin and lifting, so that my head tipped up. "—there would be no diplomatic consequences to killing *you*."

The pressure on the knifepoint increased. I felt a sting, gulping as a thin trickle of blood ran down my bared throat. The Shade tracked its descent with idle curiosity, until it reached my collar and began to dampen the fabric there. Then he looked up again, holding my gaze for longer than was comfortable; long enough that my starved libido gave a jolt, like maybe he was about to lean across the blade and—

Sunfucking stars, I'd been in Eliness too long.

"You'd have to find me to kill me," I said, attempting bravado.

"One lone man who won't return to Ralia—that's a waste of the crown's resources, surely."

"You're right," said the Shade, and gently scraped the blade's edge against my throat, as if in parody of giving me a shave, though all this achieved was smearing the trickle of blood around. His mouth smiled, but his eyes were cold as week-old embers. "*You* would be hard to find. Your mother, however—"

"*Don't,*" I gasped, all bravery gone. "You can't, she's done nothing wrong, she's loyal to King Markus—"

"Accidents do happen," Lord Cato said softly, "and in any case, one might argue that producing a son like you is treason enough."

My chest felt suddenly inverted, fleshless ribs behind my naked heart. I valued few things in this world—stars knew, I cared little enough for myself, most days—but my mother . . .

"What if I fail?" I asked, and it came out a whisper.

"That will depend entirely upon the manner of your failure. Should your *native powers of seduction*"—the words dripped with loathing—"prove insufficient, there is an alternative." Lord Cato bared his teeth in what was almost, but not quite, a smile. "You see, there is *one* instance in which the death of Velasin vin Aaro would be deemed acceptable. As it stands, his former . . . *entanglement,* Killic vin Lato, pursued Velasin to Qi-Katai. On being rebuffed, he reacted violently, and Velasin killed him." Ugly relish coloured his tone. "As such, if Velasin were to be killed in turn by another jilted lover . . . well. You could almost call it poetic. And who could blame the crown for that?"

Brusque in victory, the Shade withdrew the knife, wiped the tip on my stinging cheek and resheathed it discreetly.

"Should you behave yourself," he went on, as mildly if we'd been discussing the weather over tea, "and provided you succeed in your mission in whatever capacity, you are free to remain in Tithena. We might even see our way to extending you a small stipend by way of recompense—though not, of course, if you engage in a public union with either Velasin or Caethari; or any other man, for that matter." His lip curled. "And, of course, your debts here will be erased."

"And my mother?"

"Your mother will come to no harm, provided you do as you're told."

I digested this, numbness spreading through me. There was no way out, and never had been. If Lord Cato had been some garden-variety blackmailer, I'd have feigned agreement, slipped out the second his back was turned and run home to get Mother on the next ship out of Ralia, and damned to the consequences. But I couldn't outrun a Shade. Named for the spectral guardians of the underworld, they were the crown's eyes and ears, spies and secret-stealers and hidden knives—and among their ranks, it was whispered, Lord Cato stood closer to the king than anyone but his own shadow.

Gulping, I asked, "How soon do I leave for Qi-Katai?"

"You don't," came the reply. "You're headed for Qi-Xihan."

I blinked at him, confused. "But you said—"

"Qi-Xihan is more swiftly reached from here," said the Shade, "but even if it wasn't, they'll be headed there soon enough. Besides which, you'll have more excuse to approach them in the capital, and your presence will seem . . . less coincidental, shall we say, if you arrive there first."

"What of my work here?" I asked—desperately, as I hardly liked it at the best of times. "What will you say to—"

"Asrien," said Lord Cato, and here he sounded almost amused. "I am a Shade in the king's employ. Do trust that I know what I'm doing."

I looked away and forced myself to swallow. "Yes, my lord."

"Good boy," he said, and smiled.

Part One

VELASIN

1

We'd been at Caethari's holdings in the Avai riverveldt just long enough for me to fall in love with them when the summons came. A courier rode in on a fine bay mare and handed the message to Cae in person, bowing from the saddle in one breath and departing in the next, her job done. A sense of foreboding tickled my neck as my husband broke the elaborate wax seal on the missive and unrolled its fine paper, frowning at the contents. I'd been happy enough for long enough—which is to say, for nearly three weeks—that I'd grown suspicious of my own felicity, and when Cae's mouth twisted in annoyance, some cynical part of me rejoiced in perverse vindication. *See?* it seemed to say. *We knew this couldn't last.*

"We're wanted in Qi-Xihan," said Cae. He swallowed, glancing at me. "Her Majesty Asa Ivadi Ruqai desires an audience."

Whatever crisis I'd been expecting, this wasn't it. I blinked at him. "What?"

"The asa wants to see us," Cae repeated. He shot me a look that was equal parts confused and frustrated. "She doesn't say why; only that we're to appear at our earliest convenience, which is a polite way of saying *as soon as is humanly possible,* and that this is her personal request."

I grimaced, thoughts whirling. "There must be trouble with Ralia over our marriage," I said. "Either King Markus objects, or one of his factions does, and we need to give an accounting of it all." I faltered. "That, or—the other thing."

My husband winced and looked away, leaving me to silently

curse myself. *The other thing,* I'd said, as though the deaths of Caethari's father and sister, the former at the latter's hands, was a sordid afterthought. The only reason he wasn't dressed all in black was in deference to the newness of our marriage: Tithenai custom held that to observe full mourning before a new couple's second and final marriage-gathering was bad luck. As such, Cae wore a dark lin edged with black and had wound black ribbons into his braid, but was otherwise dressed normally. My lin, too, was trimmed with black, and as my hair was yet too short for a proper Tithenai braid, I wore my matching ribbons bound around my wrists. Cae had tried to say it wasn't necessary—I'd scarcely known his father, while his sister's last act had been to take me hostage—but I'd ignored him and done it anyway. Honouring his grief seemed the very least I could do, under the circumstances.

I placed a hesitant hand on Cae's shoulder, relieved when he leaned into the touch.

"You needn't talk around it so," he said, raising his opposite hand to squeeze my fingers, this gentleness in contrast to the bitter scrape of his voice. "Call it what it is: Laecia's treachery."

"I'll call it whatever hurts you least."

"There is no *least hurt,* with a thing like this." And then, with a sigh, "I'm sorry, Vel. I shouldn't snap. It's just . . . I thought we'd have more time here."

"Me, too," I admitted, and took a moment to ache at the thought of leaving. When we'd first set out from Qi-Katai, I'd been apprehensive, worried that whatever rural charms Avai might offer would prove an insufficient sap to my fractious brain and urban predilections. What would it mean for my marriage if I couldn't find some means of self-occupation that neither endangered the pair of us nor drove Cae to distraction? The prospect of helping administer his holdings here was a potential lifeline, and one I was all too afraid would fray apart in my hands.

But the moment we'd ridden down the broad, paved drive to the main estate—the same drive in which we presently stood—I'd felt myself bewitched. It was calm in Avai, the sort of calm that sinks across your shoulders like a soft, cool fur and eases whatever tension you've been carrying. The scent of the Eshi River was everywhere—not acrid and foul, like so many city rivers come to be, marred by human refuse and the leavings of industry, but bright and clean. Birdsong cut through the elegant, curving branches of trees I'd never seen before, while neat fields and orchards in late-autumn hues of brown and russet patchworked the valleys between gentle, rolling hills. I'd found nature beautiful before, of course—I'm not made of stone—but Avai felt different.

Perhaps it was simply that my life, since leaving Farathel, had been one overwrought commotion after the next, such that the pretty quietude of this patch of Tithena was a balm I hadn't known I'd needed. Perhaps my tastes were maturing as I aged—and moons, but this recent span of weeks had certainly aged me!

Or perhaps I only felt what I did because of Caethari. For all that our marriage and acquaintance both were scarcely a month old, I had come to care for him as I'd cared for few others in my life. In the aftermath of his sister's betrayal, he'd confessed his love for me, and though I didn't yet trust that the depth of my feelings matched his own, the knowledge that he didn't expect direct reciprocation—that he was content for me to be as I was, at least for now—meant more than I could say. Avai mattered to him: was that why it mattered to me? I rubbed my beribboned wrists together, unsettled by the prospect.

"Wait," said Cae, suddenly. "There's a second page."

"A second page?"

"Or, not a page—there's something stuck, here—" He held up the letter and flipped it over, blunt nails scrabbling ineffectually at the edges. I watched him struggle for a moment, suppressing a smile at the peek of tongue protruding from his mouth, then took the paper from him. At first glance, it seemed a single, ordinary piece of stationery, albeit an expensive one; but at the top, where the broken wax seal had started to flake, a careful eye could just make out the leading edge of a second sheet stuck perfectly to the first. It was a technique I'd seen before, though not recently—for a brief time in Farathel, it had been all the rage to send secret, doubled missives like this—and so I knew the trick to prying it loose.

"Markel!" I called across the lawn, to where my dearest friend and ostensible servant was lazing contentedly on the grass, pretending to take no notice of us. "Can I borrow your letter-knife?"

"I've got a knife," Cae muttered not-quite-sulkily, indicating the leather-sheathed blade with its ring handle of polished jade that I'd given him as a marriage gift.

"I know," I said, and kissed his cheek to show I'd meant no slight. "But this calls for delicate work, and your blade isn't thin enough."

"Hmph."

Markel ambled over, one brow raised at the pair of us and a crooked grin on his face. He passed me the letter-knife handle-first, a flash of recognition in his eyes as he watched me slip it between the two pressed pages.

"Haven't seen this in a while," he signed—more slowly than was usual between us, partly in deference to the fact that Cae was still learning sign-speech, but also because he was using a new, syllable-based sign alphabet designed to spell out Tithenai words more easily, the better to enable more fluent communication with Cae. It was all Markel's development, something he'd shyly admitted to having worked on for a while, but which he'd altered to work with Tithenai more than Ralian, and in the fortnight since he'd introduced it to us, it had done wonders to improve Cae's confidence with signing.

I nodded absently, refocussing on the paper. The hidden sheet was thinner than I'd first assumed, like the finest rice paper, the edges sealed so neatly with adhesive that it was hard work not to tear it. Still, I managed in the end, and with a little *hah!* of triumph, I peeled away the second page and handed it to Cae.

He held it up to the sky, letting the wintry light illuminate the contents. Unlike the primary letter, this one was neither written in the neat, precise hand of a professional scribe nor inked in the customary black or blue. Instead, the writing was small and curlicue, difficult to make out, and written with an ink (if the term applied) that bleached instead of stained. The message was pale and indistinct even with the aid of direct sunlight: held normally, you could scarcely see it at all.

"It's in the asa's own hand," Cae said, startled. "She writes, 'I bid you travel discreetly. Observe the state of Tithena and report your findings to me.'"

"She wants us to *spy* for her?" I exclaimed.

"You needn't sound quite so delighted," Cae said dryly, "but yes." Carefully, he rerolled both pieces of paper. "Asa Ivadi is well-known to be fond of issuing private games and challenges to her subjects, like sending a hidden message to some noble or minister asking for their private observations. If they don't find it, she'll know them to be incurious and unobservant; if they do, their compliance tells her what they think is valuable information and how good they are—or not—at acquiring it."

"I like her already."

Cae snorted. "You would," he said. "This is much more your thing than mine."

That stung, though I was sure he hadn't meant it to. "We can always pretend we didn't find it, if you prefer."

"What? Of course not!" Cae looked at me, a worried furrow between his brows. I'd aimed to keep both my tone and expression neutral, but I mustn't have succeeded; that, or he was getting eerily good at reading me, for he promptly leaned in and kissed the corner of my mouth, so lightly that I shivered. "I'm sorry, Vel. That wasn't meant as a dig."

"I know," I said, flustered. I wasn't used to being so sweetly perceived, and it threw me off-balance. "It's me who ought to apologise, spoiling your good humour—"

"You haven't spoiled anything, saints!"

"I only meant—"

"I know what you meant, I just—"

Markel cut us off with a throaty noise of amusement, grinning from ear to ear. I flushed and ducked my head, smiling into the collar of my mourning lin. It was still a new and wonderful thing, to be bedding a man approved of by my oldest friend; almost as new and wonderful as the fact that, in Tithena, we could openly claim each other. In Ralia, the lifelong necessity of keeping my inclinations secret had sickened me like a slow cancer; here, we were two men married, and while ours had been a political match forged in unpleasant circumstances, I'd sooner have lopped off a hand than repudiated Cae.

"You're very married today," signed Markel. Before I could reply to that, he nodded his stubbled head to indicate the asa's letters. "Does this mean we're headed to Qi-Xihan?"

"It does," I said, "and immediately. Though if you'd rather stay here or return to Qi-Katai, I'd understand."

Markel favoured me with a withering look. "I'll go and see about packing," he signed, and strode off towards the main house with a sarcastic wave over his shoulder.

"Well," said Cae, after a moment. "That would seem to be settled, wouldn't it?"

"Quite decisively, yes."

He laughed and stepped closer, sliding an arm around my waist. "Look on the bright side. I'll get to show you the capital." He leaned in, kissing up my throat to my ear. "And the palace accommodations are *very* luxurious."

I made an involuntary sound and turned to face him, looping my arms around his neck with the closest approximation to coy ease I was capable of mustering. "Are they now," I said, and for an answer he kissed me properly, both hands on my hips as he drew us together. I melted into it, heart hammering with a mixture of new anticipation and old fear: I wasn't yet used to being intimate in public without risk of either discovery or censure, and so it yet felt illicitly thrilling to kiss my husband outdoors. Though Cae was, as I'd quickly learned, a consummate kisser; even in private, he left me dizzied and wanting.

All too soon, he broke away again, raising a hand to smooth his thumb across my cheek. I flushed as he brushed the stubble—I'd been lax with my grooming the past few days, not bothering to shave—and was on the brink of apology when he murmured, "It suits you, you know."

"What does?"

"This." He repeated the gesture, rubbing back and forth across the unshaven grain. "It makes you look rakish."

I scoffed to hide how flustered I was. "You're the rakish one, with your fine salt locks." I stroked the new silver at his temple, smiling around the lump in my throat that rose whenever I thought on how he'd acquired it. "Especially with your ribbons, the effect is quite piratical."

"Piratical?"

"Dashing, then."

"I can work with dashing," he said, and kissed me again—a light press of lips, but I deepened it greedily, pulling him close once more.

We had talked, my new husband and I, albeit somewhat awkwardly, about our mutual expectations around bedplay. Knowing his feelings to be deeper than my own, Cae had made it clear that he didn't want to pressure me; that he was, in fact, actively afraid of doing so. For this reason, he'd said, I should be the one to instigate things, at least for now, and in the moment, I'd been so overwhelmed by the consideration that I'd proceeded to do so eagerly. But volition is a tricky thing, and in the weeks since, my contrarian nature had reared its head: having struggled my whole romantic life in Ralia to play at seeming disaffected, to show less than I felt, now that I had express permission to do as I wished, I found myself holding back. What if Cae became bored with me? What if my need and greediness lost me his regard? *Or what if,* my insecurities whispered, *he's already tiring of you, and this is his way of slowing things down?*

I shoved the last thought aside as unworthy paranoia. Cae had been nothing but honest with me: it was I who struggled to navigate my desires. I knew how to want in secret, but wanting openly was something else altogether. Though I longed to lead Cae back inside and take him to bed, I made myself break the kiss instead. *Tonight,* I silently promised us both, working to marshal my scattered thoughts. The courier's arrival had knocked me off-balance, and it was only belatedly that I recalled why we'd come outdoors in the first place.

"What," I said, then stopped, flashing Cae a smile as I caught my breath. "What did you want to show me?"

"Show you?" he echoed, sounding as dazed as I felt.

"Before the courier came," I said. "You wanted to show me something."

"Oh!" Cae laughed, a little sheepishly. "I'd almost forgotten."

He started walking, leading me across the lawn at a leisurely pace. By Ralian standards, the lawn was a mess: not manicured in the slightest, but dotted everywhere with wildflowers, patches of clover and other plants I'd been taught to view as weeds. There was a similar lawn in the Aida back in Qi-Katai, though not so diverse in its floral offerings, and I'd initially wondered at its apparently unkempt state. It was only after we'd come to Avai that I tentatively brought the matter up with Cae, who laughed and told me that the plain grass lawns favoured by Ralian nobles were seen as useless in Tithena.

"What's the point?" he'd asked. "The wild plants feed the bees and birds, the rabbits and deer, and do the grass no harm; indeed, it takes more effort to water and hold the soil together without them. Blank lawns are a great big show of nothing."

I'd had no answer to that, though it went against everything I'd ever been taught about the aesthetics of horticulture. Two days later, Cae made me a daisy-crown from that very lawn and kissed me on the cheek, and whatever objections I might've had melted away like frost in sunlight.

Now, however, I realised we were taking a path away from the lawn and towards the stables. My stomach gave a familiar, grieving twist: though small against her other crimes, Laecia's murder of my beloved horse, Quip, still pained me. I worked hard not to show it—what was a horse, against Cae's loss of father and sister?—but I'd raised Quip from a foal, and images of his bloody end still found me in my dreams, along with the deaths of Killic, Laecia, Ren Adan, Tar Katvi and the former Tieren Halithar.

"I'll take no offence if it's not to your liking," Cae said suddenly, a mere ten paces from the stable door. He swallowed before continuing, and I was startled to realise that he was nervous. "But I thought—I hoped that it might suit you."

Inside, the scent and sound of horses was the most poignant sort of sense memory. I'd always loved riding, and was so preoccupied with my own feelings that, when Cae finally halted before an airy, spacious stall, it took me several astonished seconds to realise what was happening.

The stall was occupied by a fine-boned filly the colour of quicksilver, neat ears pricked with interest. She moved towards us, showing off the depth of her chest and her strong, lean legs; the proud way she held herself. Though her powerful quarters and tall build spoke to the finest courser bloodlines, the delicacy of her head and the high carriage of her tail suggested more than a drop of Nivonai dune-runner blood. Her mane and tail were white waterfalls shot with silver, while her pale grey coat showed bluish dapples where it caught the light.

She was utterly exquisite, and as I stared at her, she leaned her head over the railing and bumped her velvet nose against my shirt, whuffling curiously.

"Cae?" I asked shakily, one hand rising of its own accord to stroke the filly's cheek. "What is this?"

Softly, Cae replied, "She's yours, if you want her."

I stared at him, mouth dry. I've no idea what my face was doing, but whatever it was made Cae look aside, rubbing awkwardly at his arm.

"I know she can't replace Quip, not truly, and I'm sure you'll want to make your own choice at some point, but until then, I just thought . . . you need a horse. She's trained to saddle, but newly enough to learn your preferences, and—"

Whatever he'd been about to say was lost as I closed the distance between us and kissed him fiercely, a rushing in my ears as he reciprocated. When we finally broke apart, my heart was pounding.

"She's perfect," I rasped, chest tight as I met his gaze. My throat was full of words that refused to fall into order. Beyond what the filly must have cost—and moons, but that dunerunner blood must've made her costly!—the thoughtfulness of the gesture near undid me. In Ralia, it was always risky for men like myself to gift their lovers anything or to be so gifted in turn; the risk of discovery—or worse, of having such an item of sentiment used against you—was too high. But even when it came to my family, I was unaccustomed to receiving much in the way of gifts on occasions that usually merited them, let alone unprompted. I was not only a third son, but one whose relationships with my elder brothers had always been somewhat fractious and whose father had little love for festivities. The only other people to have ever put so much thought into presents for me were Markel and my long-dead mother, and even Markel, in keeping with the taboo nature of our friendship—servants and noblemen were not meant to interact as we did, let alone care for one another—tended to stick to small and subtle things.

The filly, though. For all that he was grieving the loss of so much more than a horse, Cae had not only noticed my feelings, but held them as significant; had gone out of his way to procure this most exquisite, beautiful remedy, and yet had done so without any expectation that I'd thank him for it.

"She's perfect," I said again, and hoped he heard what I didn't say: *You are perfect, too.* "I don't—I hardly know what to say." A child's eagerness rose in me, as when I'd been presented with my very first pony. "May I saddle her, take her out for a turn?"

"You don't need my permission, Vel," said Cae, but he was smiling at last, soft and well-pleased. "She's all yours."

Alight with anticipation, I hurried to the tack room and fetched saddle, blanket and bridle. The filly gave a low whicker as I hung the saddle over the edge of her stall, stepping back neatly as I let myself in. She turned her head side-on, looking at me with one large, round eye, then shook out her mane and snorted, as though, in her equine way, she found me amusing.

"Does she have a name?" I asked, settling the blanket across her withers.

"Not yet," said Cae, who was leaned back against a support beam with his arms crossed, watching me. "I thought you'd want to give her one yourself, assuming you liked her."

"I do. Very much." I swallowed around a sudden lump in my throat, hands resting on the saddle. A half-dozen potential names flashed through my mind, but one shone out above all others, perfect and irreproachable. "Gift," I said, fixing my gaze on the polished saddle leather. "That's what I'll call her."

"It suits," Cae said, and there was something so tender in the way he spoke that I didn't dare look at him. I focussed on saddling Gift instead, cheeks flushed as I checked and double-checked the girth—like Quip, she puffed out her chest at the first cinching, trying to trick me into leaving it loose—before turning to the bridle. I'd always favoured gentle bits, and was glad of that now as I coaxed the metal into her soft mouth. She whuffled slightly, tossing her head before consenting to lower it, neck arched as I settled the browband in place, then rolling the bit against her teeth as I secured the throatlatch.

As I led her out of the stall, Cae smiled at me and fell into step beside us.

"Am I permitted to watch you ride," he teased, "or would you two prefer to be alone?"

For an answer, I thwacked him across the arm with the reins. "You can stay if you behave," I said, both pleased and embarrassed.

Cae only laughed. "Whatever my husband commands."

As we headed outside, the crisp, cool air and pale autumn light made Gift's coat gleam like polished glass. She snorted again, bumping her head against me as if she, too, were eager to ride, and as I swung up into the saddle, I let out a burst of laughter. Gift danced beneath me, responsive as a silk ribbon caught in a breeze, and when I urged her forwards, she obeyed with a will.

The next hour passed in a blur of joy as Gift and I learned each other. She had her quirks, like pulling against the rein if called to turn at a canter, but nothing that time and patient training couldn't mend, and such minor defects were far outweighed by her graces. She was agile, clever and breathtakingly fast, her transitions as clean as her gait was smooth. Cae watched us with a pleasure to which he was wholly entitled, but all my attention was fixed on Gift. She was not Quip—would never be Quip—but that wasn't the point: she was herself, something wholly new and wonderful, and my heart sang with it.

I was just letting her cool down through a trot when, from the corner of my eye, I spied Markel waving from the other end of the lawn. Seeing he had my attention, he gestured over his shoulder. Surprised, I looked past him and recognised Ru Telitha, dismounting as she gave her horse's reins to a waiting servant. She was dressed for travel in a practical lin, undershirt and nara, her curly hair tied back in a Tithenai braid.

"Oh," said Cae, following my gaze. He tensed all over, swallowing hard. "That's unexpected."

I winced, my pulse ticking up in sympathy. In addition to being a friendly fellow scholar of languages and Markel's current paramour, Telitha was also the trusted right hand of Yasa Kithadi, Cae's grandmother. Her presence here was unlikely to be a purely social visit, and as I came down from my giddy high, I recalled the importance of Asa Ivadi's missive.

"Very," I said, dismounting Gift. Handing her off to a groom—I'd have to forgo the pleasure of brushing her down today—I hurried to Cae's side and, though still tentative about such displays in public, laced our fingers together.

"I'm sure it's nothing serious," I murmured, though I was sure of no such thing. "But if it is, we'll handle it."

Cae managed a watery smile before squaring his shoulders, face smoothing into what I'd come to think of as his soldier's mask: a sort of studied calm, more stern than blank, which gave away nothing of his thoughts. And yet, to my surprise, he didn't let go of my hand, but squeezed it marginally tighter, staying close as we walked to meet Telitha.

Markel fell into silent step beside us, his own happy expression dimming somewhat as he registered Cae's stoicism. He blinked, confused for all of a moment, then let out a breath of understanding, mouth twisted in a way that said he was annoyed at himself for missing the nonromantic significance of who had come, and why.

"Greetings!" said Telitha, executing a scholar's bow as we reached her. She winked at Markel from behind her black lacquer-framed glasses, but sobered as she faced Caethari. "Tiern, rest easy. I come bearing no grim news."

Cae's grip on me went briefly lax before tightening again. "And yet, I suspect, you are not come for purely personal reasons."

"Alas, no." Her pretty smile was apologetic. "Has the courier reached you yet? They sought you first in Qi-Katai, but of course you weren't there."

"They've come and gone a few hours back," I said, when Cae failed to answer. "Asa Ivadi has summoned us to Qi-Xihan."

Telitha sighed. "The yasa guessed as much. It's why she sent me. She wanted to give you this, to take with you." Reaching into a satchel slung across her body, she withdrew what looked like a jewellery box, sized for an ornate necklace. It was made of aging white leather stamped with curling gold patterns, and Cae flinched at the sight of it.

"No," he said, voice suddenly hoarse. "It's too soon. I don't want it."

The ru's expression was sad, but she didn't withdraw the box, and after a fraught, silent span of seconds, Cae dropped my hand and took it from her, fingers shaking as he flicked it open.

Inside was a circular metal disc bearing an unfamiliar symbol picked out in gold and enamel, its circumference engraved with words too small for me to read. There was also a small loop set at the top, as though it was meant to be worn on a chain or pin, but if such a matching piece had ever existed, it was missing now.

"What is it?" I asked.

Cae shut the box again, head bowed. "It's the seal of my grandmother's yaserate," he said, voice numb. "Bearing it officially makes me her heir."

2

The four of us dined that evening in one of the smaller, more private rooms available at the Avai estate. In the hours since Telitha's arrival, Cae had become withdrawn, retreating to our rooms and asking, in a soft, odd tone I'd never heard before, if he might have some time alone. I acquiesced, though I wanted nothing more than to stay with him, but when we reunited to eat, it didn't seem that the time apart had done him any good. I squeezed his leg beneath the table, and in response he managed only a flicker of smile that didn't reach his eyes.

Though the food was excellent, I found myself with little appetite. Markel and Telitha were signing together, keeping their hands low and discreet, their delight at seeing one another tempered by the terrible chasm of my husband's grief. He'd never aspired to inherit his grandmother's title, and unlike his elder sister Riya, who'd been officially confirmed as tierena of Qi-Katai in a modest ceremony shortly before we left for the riverveldt, he'd never thought of himself as a future political player, either. Yasa Kithadi Taedu's primary holdings were in Ravethae, a prosperous region close to Qi-Xihan, but she also held a confirmed—and, crucially, heritable—seat on the Conclave, which was responsible for overseeing certain aspects of governance both nationally and within the capital itself. The precise details of how she managed her responsibilities in absentia were opaque to me, but even had I known in full, it wouldn't have been relevant: once he inherited, it would be a long time before Cae was sufficiently established to do likewise, and before then, he would have to learn.

Abruptly, Cae said, "Ru Telitha. Has word come—that is, has there been any news of my mother?"

Wincing, Telitha lowered her hands and shook her head. "I'm sorry, tiern. No word."

"Ah," said Cae, softly. "I'd thought as much. No matter." He bowed his head, poking listlessly at his food.

In fact, it mattered a very great deal, though saying so would've only exposed the wound he was trying, however badly, to pretend was no wound at all. His mother, the former Tierena Inavi, had divorced his father more than a decade past, and was now remarried. One of the contractual conditions of their parting had been that only a child of her first marriage would be eligible to inherit the yaserate, and it was this uncertainty which had, in turn, led the late Tieren Halithar to prevaricate about naming his own successor to the tiercy. With primogeniture the legal default in cases where an heir wasn't named, as the eldest, Riya had been guaranteed an inheritance from whichever of her father or grandmother died first, leaving whoever lived longest to name their first-choice heir—but as both still wished for Riya to inherit *something,* and as they'd refused to discuss the matter, neither would risk naming their preferred candidate while the other lived, in case they each favoured a different child.

Tragically, it had turned out that Laecia was the preferred candidate of both Tieren Halithar and Yasa Kithadi, though she hadn't known it. After years of feeling herself discounted in favour of her siblings, she'd known new hope when her father arranged her betrothal to me—a diplomatic marriage meant to usher in a new era of trade between Tithena and Ralia. But when my preference for men was revealed, the alliance had shifted, sending me to marry Cae instead. Though nobody had meant it as a slight to Laecia, the loss had been one blow too many for her to bear. She'd schemed against my marriage, and when that scheming was unveiled, she'd snapped, her bloody actions culminating in the murder of her father and several others, and in the scrambling aftermath, she'd met her death at mine and Markel's hands.

By rights, Tierena Inavi ought to have been present for Laecia's funeral, if not Halithar's, to say nothing of offering comfort to Cae and Riya. But my mother-in-law could not be reached: as best Ru Daro, intelligencer to Clan Aeduria, had been able to establish, she and her new husband were currently sailing to Nivona, unreachable until or unless the message sent to inform them of the news was received by the Tithenai embassy there and passed to them on arrival.

Never having met Cae's mother and knowing little of her beyond her divorce and remarriage—options she would not have had in Ralia, where my marriage to another man was likewise a scandalous impossibility—it was, I knew, unfair of me to judge her. Nonetheless, having lost my own, beloved mother in childhood and being confronted daily with the depth of Cae's grief, it was hard not to resent her absence, however irrationally. What did I expect her to do—magically transport herself across an ocean and half a continent on the basis of news she was yet to receive?

And yet. *And yet.* I couldn't tell if I was being Ralian about the whole thing or if it was just a complex human yearning with no easy solution; either way, it pained me to see Cae hurting.

"I thought," said Telitha, after an awkward silence, "that I might, if you permitted it, accompany you on the first leg of your journey to Qi-Xihan—perhaps as far as Etho?"

Recalling the local maps over which I'd pored on first arriving at Avai, I placed Etho as a small town set just south of the point where the Nihri River forked away from the Eshi, catering to travellers passing between the riverveldt and the bigger roads heading north-east towards the capital, among other places. It was perhaps a three-day ride from Avai, and for a brief moment I wondered at Telitha's willingness to travel so far out of her way; but then I saw Markel smiling at her and understood at once.

"Of course," I said, when it became apparent that Cae wasn't going to answer. I touched him lightly to get his attention and he jolted in his seat, as startled as if I'd woken him from a dream.

"What?" he said—and then, coming back to the moment, "Oh. Yes. As Vel said."

The meal didn't last long after that. With the conversation stagnating, Markel and Telitha were keen to catch up more privately, and Cae was in no humour to detain them. As Cae went ahead to our rooms, I detoured by the kitchens to reassure the cook that my husband's poor appetite was no reflection on the quality of his work. I wasn't quite sure he believed me—the cook, I'd learned quickly, took such pride in serving his tiern that any uneaten food was counted a personal failure—but more than one of his juniors shot me grateful looks as I left, so I judged I'd done the right thing.

As I climbed the stairs to our chamber, I slowed my step, trying to think what I might do or say to ease Cae's heart, but when I reached the room itself, it was empty.

I stood a moment, flummoxed by my husband's absence. Where else would he have gone? Not to Markel and Telitha, and not towards the kitchens. He might've sought a sparring match with one of the guards, but as that would've required interaction, I considered it unlikely.

"The gardens, then," I muttered to the empty air. Whether alone or in company, Cae preferred to cope with frustration through movement; most likely, he'd be practicing combat patterns on the lawn or stalking about in a fit of restless energy.

As night fell, the estate's magelights flickered on, keeping the darkness at bay. In Qi-Katai, I'd only seen magelights used indoors, but at Avai, someone—either Cae himself or a steward conscious of his master's tastes—had thought to install them outside, too, bathing the lawn and the winding path through the gardens in a pale gold glow more reminiscent of dawn than fire. It made for a pretty sight, as though I were following a trail laid out by wisps in a children's tale.

I finally found Cae halted before a stand of smooth, grey-and-cream-barked trees whose name I didn't know, spaced to demarcate the curve of a pleasant cul-de-sac and hemmed in by a wall of flower-studded shrubbery. His posture was tense, hands clenching and unclenching where they hung at his sides, and he whipped around at the sound of my approach as if in fear of an ambush. I startled in turn, heart hammering at the sudden, unpleasant fear of having caught a stag at bay, but when Cae saw it was me, he slumped, and some of my tension ebbed.

"I'm sorry," he murmured, unable to meet my gaze. "I didn't mean to make you trek out after me."

What could I say? I wanted so badly to help, but words felt inadequate. Only time could ease such hurts as beset him; time and, perhaps, the arrival of his mother, though in truth I knew so little about their relationship that I couldn't rely on that, either. As my thoughts whirled uselessly, I stepped closer, my hand moving of its own accord to map the corded muscle of Cae's arm. I hadn't meant to tease, but his breathing hitched regardless, and all at once I remembered the silent promise I'd made earlier.

"Cae," I said, still struggling to find the right words, "you're not—you don't have to pretend you aren't upset."

Cae quirked an eyebrow. "This, coming from you?"

"It takes one to know one," I replied.

He snorted at that, then sighed, running a tired hand over his face. "I needed some air. I can't . . . I don't know how to react to any of this."

"Do you need to know? You speak as if there's some set and proper way you ought to be doing things, but there isn't."

The corner of his mouth twitched. "It might be easier, if there was."

"*Might*," I echoed, and dared to step closer, setting my free hand to his hip. I'd meant to try and lighten his mood, but all at once he lifted his head sufficiently to look out at me through his lashes—a new experience, as he was the taller of us—and there was something so nakedly vulnerable in the expression that I utterly lost my words.

Instead, I inhaled, then stuttered out, "You—you deserve good husbandry in this, from me. For you. What might I do?" I released his arm and grazed my thumb across the arc of his cheek. He jerked at the touch, pinning me with his deep brown gaze. "Whatever I can do for you, Cae, I will."

My husband's eyes flashed; he drew a shuddering breath and kissed me, both of us stepping back until I thumped up against the smooth trunk of one of the trees. Pinned between it and Cae, I was flooded with sensation, the desire I'd stifled earlier roaring back to life; and yet there was something plaintive to his passion, too, as though his mouth on mine was more plea than demand.

Eventually, Cae broke away panting, the golden glow of the magelights giving his eyes a febrile gleam. For two long seconds, neither of us spoke—and then, like one of his saints at their holy altars, he went to his knees before me, big hands sliding down my thighs in silent supplication.

"*Oh*," I breathed, arrested by the sight of him.

"May I?" he asked, and when I nodded, he leaned in and rubbed his cheek against my thigh—*like a cat scenting a doorpost,* part of me thought inanely, but any inappropriate laughter that might've been born from the comparison promptly died as he untied my nara, reverently thumbing my hips as he slid my smallclothes down. I'd been hard since his hands had started to roam as he kissed me; the sight of him now made my cock jerk. Cae stroked me once, his callused grip skating expertly along my length, and took me in his mouth.

I groaned, hips twitching as I fought the impulse to thrust into him. I braced one palm against the trunk, the other resting against the curve of his head, the silk of his braided hair. He pushed into the touch and looked up at me, contriving to nod just slightly around his mouthful, dark eyes sparking with hunger. He hadn't knelt for me before—nor I for him, in truth; I'd so far skirted that particular act without caring to examine the source of my hesitance—and in Ralia, my preferences had ensured I'd far more often given than received of it. As such, I had surprisingly little experience to draw upon as to how to proceed; or, more specifically, for how rough to be.

The thought sent a dizzying bolt of arousal through me, groin to throat. Twining my fingers in Cae's hair, I pushed in slowly as far as I dared, then drew back out again, all but the crown. His lips were plush and slick, soft-hot where they wrapped around me, sucking with obscene intent; I shuddered all over, lungs crushed up against my ribs, and slid inside once more, almost to the hilt.

A twig snapped in the darkness.

I froze, so deeply inside Cae's mouth that I must've stoppered his throat, and yet he didn't protest, continuing to grip my thighs, thumbs smoothing over the muscle as his fingers dug in for purchase. *We'll be caught,* I thought, old panic careening wildly through my veins—I'd been caught before, caught at my father's estate—he'd disown me—no, he'd already disowned me, but that had been Killic, not Caethari, Killic who'd forced—

I looked down at Cae, who hadn't moved, though his eyes were starting to water. I eased a little out of him and felt his throat convulse as he sucked in air, and for a horrid, wrenching moment, I was transported back to a different night, a different garden, bruising fingers on my jaw and a deadening ache in my heart.

Then Cae pulled off just far enough to say, with a strange, rasping urgency, "You can fuck my mouth, Vel, please—"

The memory's grip on me shattered, and in its place came a wildness that was equal parts defiance and desire. Avai was not Ralia; Cae was not Killic; here, I was in control. For an answer, I tightened my grip on Cae's hair, which had slackened during my episode, and thrust my cock into his mouth more forcefully than I ever had anyone's. He moaned around me, eyes fluttering shut as I tipped his head back and did as he wanted. My free hand found its way to his cheek, stroking with filthy wonder against the distending press of myself within him.

All thought fled: there was only pleasure and the chasing of it as Cae knelt, slack-jawed and soft-mouthed, lips ruddy with use.

Periodically he came up for air, coughing and gasping, only to swallow me down again within moments. Tension wound through me, thighs to sac to fingers; I trembled and arched against my own onrushing climax, my body trying to brace and thrust at the same time.

"Sweetheart," I gasped—in Ralian, my Tithenai lost to the darkness beyond the magelights. "Cae, I'm close, you can—I should—"

Cae's hands clamped around my wrists, preventing me from pulling away. His eyes were open once more, dark lashes thick with tears, and when he squeezed, I spent down his throat with a muffled cry, barely managing to keep upright. I staggered back as Cae let go, leaning once more against the tree as my breath came in shuddering gasps. My softening cock was still in his mouth; he gave one last, pointed suck and withdrew, leaning his forehead heavily against my thigh. Dazed as I was, it took me precious seconds to notice that he'd slipped a hand down to stroke himself, but before I could move to see to him, he came with a gasp, shoulders heaving as he mouthed the sweat from my skin.

For a moment, all was silent save for the soft breeze rustling the garden. Then Cae knelt back and smiled at me, and when he spoke, his voice was rough from my use of him, raw and wanton.

"Gods, that was good." He tucked himself away and did the same for me, kissing the cut of my hip before covering it once more beneath smallclothes and nara. "You're a marvel, Vel, truly."

I managed a breathless laugh. "I should be saying that, not you." The sentence started out Ralian, but I found my Tithenai by the end of it. "You did all the work."

"Depends on your definition," he countered, coming to his feet. He swayed alarmingly for a moment, almost as if drugged, then put his hot, used mouth on mine and kissed me. I chased the taste of myself on his tongue, though unurgently; we were languorous together, syrup-slow and sticky. We swayed away from the tree as if moving to music, Cae's face pressed to my clavicle.

"I need to lie down," he mumbled, though there was a twist of laugh to the words that said he was pleased about it.

"Let's, then," I said, feeling hardly more capable.

Cae kissed my neck for an answer, and together we stumbled back through the gardens, alternately laughing and shushing each other like errant children out after curfew. I felt a pang of shameful panic as we approached the house—anyone who saw us would surely know what we'd been up to—but as friends and servants alike were evidently occupied elsewhere, we encountered no one.

Safe in the privacy of our chambers, we shucked our clothes on wobbly legs and stumbled into the washroom, getting in each other's way as we managed our exhausted, perfunctory ablutions. As Cae began to quieten, so did I, and by the time we extinguished the lights and fell naked into bed, our conversation had faltered.

"Good night," Cae mumbled into my shoulder. He followed the words with a brush of lips, then rolled over with a groan, taking the warm, muscular arm slung over my stomach with him. The lack of contact left me feeling strangely bereft, though I wasn't sure why: the same thing happened most nights.

"Sleep well," I replied. The words felt faint on my tongue, coloured by the secondhand aftertaste of my own spend, lingering even after I'd rinsed my mouth. Cae made no reply, which wasn't unusual, either; he had a soldier's knack for falling asleep in moments. But though I was tired from the same endeavours, my body refused to follow him into sleep. I lay in the dark, thoughts massing and spreading like ink poured into water, a growing coldness creeping into my limbs.

What Cae and I had done was outside my experience—not the act itself, but the roughness with which I'd indulged in a less-accustomed role. I ought to have had no doubts as to whether my husband had enjoyed himself, not least because Cae had asked it of me, and yet I felt a stirring of unease. Unbidden, I thought again of Killic, his fingers digging into my jaw. The memory was enough to make me break out in a sweat. Had he succeeded that night, I had no doubt he would've withheld his usual courtesies, and the idea that I'd acted now as he'd meant to then sent sickness roiling through me.

It's not the same, I thought frantically—it couldn't be, or consent meant nothing. And yet it frightened me, to think that I'd chased my pleasure so aggressively now, when I never had before. The day he'd appeared at the Aida, Killic had excused his assault of me by claiming he'd been carried away; that he'd thought it no different to things we'd done before. I hadn't believed him then, but a worm of doubt began to burrow into me: had I not been carried away with Cae? Killic's spectre had hung so sharply overhead, if only for a moment, that I'd indulged myself in a way I never had before. That Cae had wanted and enjoyed it ought to have been all the comfort I needed, and yet I felt sick with myself. Cae's pleasure wasn't the issue; mine was. I didn't like that I'd liked it; that I'd acted without thought, spurred on by ugly memories that had no business dictating how I treated anyone, let alone Caethari.

What sort of husband are you? a viperous part of me whispered. *He deserves better. Sweeter. Someone who can love him back, not just use and take.*

I squeezed my eyes shut against my hammering thoughts, but they wouldn't dissipate, growing louder and louder until I'd twisted myself into a knot of misery.

It was a long time before I slept.

3

I woke the next day to an empty bed and what I would've thought
was a hangover, if not for the fact that I'd barely drunk at dinner.
My panic of the night before had dulled to a nascent ache, throbbing within me like a second, queasy heartbeat as I registered Cae's
absence. I sat up, blinking blearily. He wasn't in our chambers, and
the door to the washroom was open, with no telltale sound of water
or off-key humming to suggest he was using it anyway.

"Don't," I told myself, massaging my temples. "Just—don't."

I rose, washed and dressed, recalling only halfway through the
process that we'd be setting out for Qi-Xihan at some point, and
that I ought to prepare accordingly. The events of the previous day
felt half a dream, the idea that I'd used Cae's mouth in the gardens
as absurd a prospect as him gifting me a ludicrously expensive horse.
Perhaps I would go downstairs and find it all a hallucination. More
likely, I'd fallen so far into my cups at dinner that my wretched
brain had made the whole thing up to cover for absent memories of
having danced on the table or challenged Cae to a duel.

The reality of Telitha's arrival, however, could not be wished away.
Asa Ivadi had summoned us, and with that summons had come Cae's
unwelcome receipt of an honour he'd never coveted and certainly
didn't want. My phantom hangover pulsed once more as I recalled
his unhappiness at being named his grandmother's formal heir, the
vacant grief that had plagued him through dinner—and all at once,
a new anxiety gripped my throat and squeezed.

Cae hadn't been himself last night. Had I taken advantage of
him?

The thought was so horrifying, I almost stopped breathing. I sat down hard on the bed as my vision tunnelled, hands gripping my knees as Killic's excuses ran through my head like poison: *rough play, caught up in the moment, clearly enjoying yourself.* All of it applied. I could no longer remember Cae's enthusiasm; only the terror of having inflicted on him what Killic had tried to do to me. Some desperate, rational part of me tried to advocate for calm, for common sense, but it was drowned out by the rest. The uncertainty of it, the fact that I didn't know for sure—that there was any room to doubt at all—felt as good as a confirmation of my vileness.

"Vel?"

I barely registered the voice, flinching like a startled deer when Cae's hand fell on my shoulder. I stared at him, struggling to process his presence, then blurted out, "Last night. I hurt you. Did I hurt you? I'm sorry, I'm so—I'm sorry Cae, I—"

"Velasin—"

"You weren't yourself, and I just—I didn't even—"

"*Velasin.*" Cae gripped me gently by the shoulders and gave a little shake, brow crinkled with confusion. "Vel, where's this coming from? Last night was good. You were wonderful. Exactly what I needed." He hesitated, scanning me with worried eyes for long enough that a look of horror crept into them. "Unless . . . oh, fucking saints—did you not want—I should've asked, I—"

"*No!*" I burst out, appalled by the idea that Cae would blame himself. "Not, I mean—I did want it, you didn't—it's *me,* I've never done something like that, and now I don't—I thought—"

My voice had risen, panicked and shrill; I was struggling to breathe. Cae looked frightened for all of a moment, and then something clicked within him. He let out a whoosh of breath and embraced me, curling a warm, possessive hand around the nape of my neck.

"Oh, Vel," he murmured. "Sweetheart, I'm sorry. Having someone be rough with me like that, when I'm thinking too hard or feeling too much, it . . . I don't know how to explain, but it calms me down. Makes everything simpler." He let out a shaky sound, not quite a laugh. "And it feels good, too, for me. You can—if you want, when we see him next—you can ask Liran about it. He did it for me sometimes—"

"*I'm not Liran.*"

The words burst from me with ugly force; I pulled out of Cae's embrace, hot all over with embarrassment and anger at the look of shock on his face. I'd never been jealous of Liran before—I liked him greatly, even—but the precedent of his competence and beauty as Cae's former lover was still intimidating, and hearing myself compared to him at such a moment, in such a way, was like being doused with ice water.

I wrenched myself upright, fully intending to storm out of the room—it's what I'd always done in the past, when a lovers' spat became too overwhelming to continue—but only made it halfway to the door before Cae's voice, unbearably lost and small, stopped me in my tracks.

"I'm sorry."

I froze, heart thundering in my ears. I turned jerkily, slowly, and my treacherous gaze caught on the mourning ribbons wound through his braid.

My husband was grieving a loss whose depth I could scarcely comprehend, and still he bent for me; still he tried. What kind of man would I be, to deal him yet more pain?

All at once, the fury went out of me, leaving behind a monstrous exhaustion.

"Forgive me," I said, stepping back towards him. He was still perched on the edge of the bed; I hesitated, then knelt beside him, pressing my forehead to the curve of his knee. "You've wed a feral thing, I'm afraid. I have no civilisation."

"Velasin—"

"No," I said, as softly as I could. "No, don't take this on yourself.

You've enough to bear already." He flinched, and I set my hands on his leg, struggling for penitence as I looked up at him. "I'm being difficult. I don't mean to, it's just—this is new, for me."

"What is?" asked Cae, sounding oddly light-headed.

"Cohabitation. I've never—I've argued with lovers before, but I've never had to share space with them while it was happening. Either it blew over in an instant, or we stayed apart for a while until things cooled down. I've never had to talk things out before."

"Never?" Cae asked.

I let out an odd little laugh. "Being with other men in Ralia is like building sandcastles: no matter what you do, you can't withstand the sea. What's the point in finessing something you're not allowed to keep? It hurts so much more to try when you know it can't go anywhere. So here I am, starting fights out of nothing with no idea what to do next."

"It's not nothing," Cae said, resting one of his hands on mine. "If what we did upset you—"

"It didn't," I said, then looked away. "Well. It didn't at the time. It's only that after . . ." My words trailed off, shame curdling in my belly. Cae knew about Killic, and yet it felt impossible to explain to him how those memories had tangled me up, made me fear and doubt myself. In daylight, with Cae manifestly unharmed by anything other than my own neuroses, it felt absurd, for all that I'd been running myself in circles about it just seconds before he walked in. But then, that was the real problem: my perpetually fractious brain, picking at the slightest bit of contentment like a schoolboy with a scab, compelled to reopen the wound beneath for the sake of something to do.

"Do you regret it, then?" Cae asked, swallowing. "What we did?"

Neither of us breathed as I considered my answer. Like a wave, the fear and guilt I'd been wrestling with rose up within me—only to crest and break beneath the warmth of Cae's touch, the reality of his presence.

"No," I said, exhaling hard. "No, I don't."

Cae's shoulders sagged with relief. "Nor do I," he said, "though I should've taken better care of you afterwards. And I shouldn't—just now, I shouldn't have brought up Liran, not like that."

"I overreacted," I said, trembling slightly at the admission, mostly from making it at all, but partly because I worried it wasn't true. I'd chosen to trust in Cae's good intentions towards me, but how much could that count for, when I'd been such a poor judge of character in the past? Shaking these thoughts away, I added, "And it does help, knowing you've wanted it before."

Cae gave a tired smile, then bent and kissed my forehead.

"We're both new to husbandry," he said, leaning back. "It would be stranger, I think, if we were savants at it."

That startled a laugh from me, and for the first time that morning, I felt like myself.

"Well then," I said, rising to my feet. "As I'm quite done being dramatic, I ought to see what Markel is up to. Or have you already spoken to him?"

"I have, as it happens," Cae replied, standing in turn. "He sent me up to see when he could start packing your things."

"That would be Markel's delicate way of telling me to get out of bed," I said dryly.

It was Cae's turn to laugh at that, and the sound of it warmed me like mulled wine on a cold night.

Daring to link my arm through his, I drew him out of our chambers and down to the lower floor of the building, where we promptly ran into Markel coming the other way. Though my friend was habitually discreet about his romantic affairs, there was still a certain glow to him that spoke of a pleasant evening spent in Telitha's company. I stifled a smirk; my first instinct was to tease him, but as I had no wish to be teased in turn, I turned the expression into a smile, removed my arm from Cae's and said, "Look, I'm up!"

"Wonders will never cease," signed Markel. "Do you want to sort your clothes, leave some of them here?"

I considered a moment, then shook my head. "No. We might as

well take it all. I didn't pack for a trip to court—who knows what we'll end up needing?"

"Farathel games," signed Markel, his smile taking on a sharpish gleam.

"Farathel games," I echoed, and felt my heart thump with treacherous excitement.

Turning to Cae, Markel signed more slowly, "Shall I pack for you, too?"

It took Cae a moment to parse the request, but when he did, he made a surprised, pleased noise and nodded. "That's kind of you, Markel—yes, please, I'd appreciate it. And as Vel said, there's no need to sort anything." He signed along in clumsy tandem to his spoken words, the better to help himself practice.

With an approving nod, Markel moved on, leaving us to continue through the estate. Feeling my stomach rumble, I steered us towards the main dining room, where the cook—presumably galvanised by his self-professed failure the night before—was almost desperate to feed us breakfast. Cae looked slightly startled by his fervency, though as I soon gathered he'd declined to eat twice already that morning, I was less surprised.

"Such a harsh master," I teased him, as we sat down to await the promised spread. "Distressing your poor cook so. What would Ren Valiu think?"

Cae gaped at me like an ornamental fish awaiting breadcrumbs, his expression so comical that I couldn't help but laugh.

"Ren Valiu doesn't ambush me," Cae muttered finally, but softened when the cook returned with a tray of steaming jidha, a pitcher of khai and a platter of pork-and-pear fritters. We wolfed into the meal with unfeigned enthusiasm—I was yet to encounter any Tithenai food I didn't like, and my not-a-hangover had rendered me starving besides—and before long there was nothing left but empty plates and the cook's proud satisfaction.

With our bellies full and after a quick discussion, we parted ways, Cae to inform the estate's steward of our intent to leave, and me to see to the horses. Despite the circumstances, I was eager to visit Gift, who whuffled into my palm and let me pet her keen, velvety ears when I arrived. Coming from Qi-Katai, we'd only brought one packhorse between the three of us, and no spare mounts: the trip had been a leisurely one, and we'd seen no need to overburden ourselves. Venturing forth to Qi-Xihan, however, was a very different prospect: aside from being a far longer journey, we'd be travelling faster, which meant more stress on the horses under load. It also occurred to me that, unprepared for court as we were, we might well end up making various purchases en route, which would also have to be carried.

After a brief conference with the head groom, I settled on adding an extra packhorse and a spare mount to our train, the former a sturdy black gelding and the latter a neat roan mare. I didn't truly expect to need so many horses, but I reasoned it was better to be prepared for either misfortune or future excess baggage now—and to pay a little extra for stabling along the way as insurance—rather than potentially incurring the far greater cost of a new mount, should the need arise. The groom inquired about tack and fodder, how much of each I might like to take and of what kind, and before I knew it, I'd spent a pleasant hour surrounded by the familiar scents of the stables.

When I finally extricated myself, I took a moment to bask in the late-morning sun, breathing in the clean, cool air of Avai. I already knew I'd miss the place, but the prospect of seeing Qi-Xihan, despite the circumstances, was a genuinely exciting one.

"Tiern Velasin?"

I turned and smiled at Telitha, who'd managed to get quite close without my noticing. Like Markel, she, too, looked especially well, dark eyes aglow behind her spectacles and kinky curls loose in a sun-kissed, leonine halo.

"Good morning," I said. "Did you rest well?"

"Exceptionally," she said, grinning.

"I'm very glad to hear it. We'll be happy to have you along the next few days, especially Markel."

"My thanks for allowing it." She ducked her head, pleased, and I felt a sudden rush of fondness for her. I hadn't met many of Markel's paramours before—but then, none had been especially serious. Moons knew, I had little enough experience with amicable relationships between men and women of any sort, let alone love matches, but there was something about Telitha that made me feel an anxious mix of pride and hope. Perhaps it was simply that I liked her, which was novel in and of itself. With the notable exception of my Ralian friend Aline, I'd had few chances to socialise equitably with women before, and it had almost never been on my own terms.

I thought briefly of Lady Sine, my father's new wife, and the kindness she'd shown me when I first left for Tithena. We barely knew each other, but all at once, the notion that I might never see her again felt like a personal loss. And then there was her son, my new little half-brother Jarien—who might he grow up to be?

"Before I left Qi-Katai," said Telitha, jolting me out of my reverie, "Yasa Kithadi asked that I pass on a warning to you. It's nothing dire," she added, seeing my startled response to this, "but she said to tell you—and this is a direct quote—that in Qi-Xihan, you'll have more things to worry about than what your husband inherits."

I took a moment to digest this. "I don't suppose," I asked carefully, "the yasa specified what things, specifically, I ought to worry about?"

"She did not," said Telitha, eyes dancing with borrowed mischief. "I believe she wants you to figure it out yourself. Oh! Though she did also want me to give you this."

Reaching into her pocket, she withdrew a small object and placed it in my hand. On examination, it proved to be a sleeping creature I didn't recognise, carved from a single piece of carnelian.

It was curled in a catlike posture, chin on its paws, but it wasn't a cat; it was more solid than that, with tufted cheeks, rounded ears, and subtle scoring on the face and tail to indicate stripes.

I looked at Telitha. "I don't understand."

"It's a reseko," said Telitha helpfully. "A sort of little bear-cat that lives in trees in the mountains. They're native to Tithena, though they're rare this far south. They're considered tricksters, which makes them sacred to Ruya."

"And?" I said, after a moment.

"And what?"

"And why is Yasa Kithadi giving me one?"

"For luck, I think," said Telitha. "Though it's probably also a hint."

I made a disgusted face. Telitha laughed.

"I'm sorry!" she said, throwing up her hands. "Don't shoot the messenger! You know what she's like." And indeed, I did: Yasa Kithadi Taedu was sharp and tempestuous by turns, but also fond of games—a trait, I noted with chagrin, that she and Asa Ivadi appeared to share.

Accepting my fate with a sigh, I tucked the little reseko into my pocket. "Thank you, then, I suppose. And your mistress. Though I would've preferred a straightforward message."

"You'll figure it out," said Telitha kindly. "And really, you should be honoured. If the yasa didn't approve of you, she wouldn't have given you any clues at all."

And with that disconcerting thought to warm me, I went in search of my husband.

4

We embarked within the next hour—me, Caethari, Markel, Telitha, two packhorses and one spare, with Markel leading the latter three in a docile string behind him. Cae affected joviality as the estate vanished from sight, but his left hand strayed frequently to the pocket in which he kept the yaserate's seal, a physical reminder of his unwanted inheritance. The third time I saw him do it, I flashed him a look of concern, but he shook his head in response and laughed at something Telitha said, making clear his determination to focus on the positive, or at least the present.

Perhaps selfishly, I was all too glad to do so: Gift danced beneath me like a harnessed breeze, and once we joined the broad, smooth river road that would, in due course, take us to Etho, I couldn't resist the chance to test her. Letting out a whoop, I heeled my filly into a gallop and dashed off ahead of the others, wind whistling in my ears. Distantly, I was aware of Cae yelling after me, but the exhilaration of riding was such that I didn't slow. Gift's gait was as steady and silken as her coat, even at speed; the Eshi River rushed alongside us as if in a race, and drifts of autumn leaves swirled through the air as our passage disturbed them. I laughed aloud for the joy of it, and I didn't rein Gift in until she began to slow of her own accord.

As we came to a halt, I patted her sweaty neck, taking in the scenery. To the right was a stand of manicured trees, carefully pruned of undergrowth and overhanging branches, while to the left, the river ran on below its rocky banks. Though not particularly fierce, this part of the Eshi frothed and foamed around a series of boulders, sending rainbow-edged mist into the air. Dismounting Gift, I led her off the road and over to a scenic outcrop, feeling something peaceful settle within me as I watched the water flow.

I was still there when the others caught up to us, Cae leading at a laboured canter so as not to get too far ahead of Markel, who was burdened by the extra horses, and Telitha, who was keeping pace with him. I felt a sheepish pang at having abandoned them so abruptly, but couldn't bring myself to regret my ride.

"I'm sorry," I said, as Cae drew up. I smiled at him, biting my lip in a show of contrition. "If you didn't want me to go gallivanting off, you should've bought me a less perfect horse."

Cae didn't answer, a distant look on his face. My stomach clenched, and as I struggled for something to say, he asked, in a strained voice, "Was it a pleasant ride?"

"Yes," I answered, compelled to honesty. I swallowed hard, mis-liking his bleak expression. "But Cae—"

"Then perhaps I should try it, too," he said, and without waiting for an answer, he kicked Alik, his chestnut gelding, forwards and galloped off as abruptly as I must've done, leaving the rest of us gawking in his wake.

A cold, gnawing uncertainty pooled in my core and began to chew its way upwards. I'd thought the morning's conversation had fixed things between us, but I realised too late that the mending had all been on Cae's part: I'd done nothing but create problems and then abandon him to go larking off at the start of a journey he didn't want to make in the first place.

Wretchedly, I turned to Markel and signed, "Should I chase af-ter him?"

Markel hesitated a moment, then shook his head. "Give him space," he signed back. "We'll reach him soon enough."

I remounted Gift and, heart sinking, pointed her back down the road. With Markel and Telitha signing together behind me, my thoughts swung wildly between fear and self-castigation. What did

I know of loss? I didn't know how to help him, and if all I could do was make things worse, then what use was I as a husband, let alone anything else?

So mired was I in these thoughts that, when we finally did catch up with Cae, I didn't immediately notice. He was on foot, leading Alik by hand, and when I drew tentatively level with him, he flashed me a weary look.

"Walking helps," he said, gaze flicking back to the road. "I'd hoped riding might, too, but it's not the same."

Mouth dry, I said, "I can lead Alik for you, if you like."

Cae faltered at that, then came to a halt. For a horrible moment, I thought he was going to snap at me, but all he did was sigh and nod.

"Thank you," he murmured, passing me Alik's reins.

"Of course. Any time."

A tiny smile flitted across Cae's mouth, there and gone like a glimmer of light on water. I clung to the memory of it as he squared his big, broad shoulders and set off again, trudging along like a pilgrim in search of penitence.

We kept on like that for the rest of the day, with Cae alternating between the road and the saddle. I restrained myself from any further excursions, occasionally chatting with Markel and Telitha, but more often facilitating conversation between them. Telitha had proved a quick study of Markel's signs, but like Cae, she was still learning, and I helped things along by teaching her the new shorthand Tithenai alphabet Markel had developed, as it was easier for her to hear the rules explained aloud in a language she already spoke. Cae, by contrast, said little to any of us. Though the act of walking did seem to improve his mood, he was more indrawn than ever, and while I knew what troubled him, it didn't stop my paranoia insisting that I'd managed to make things worse.

We rested that night at a small wayside inn. In deference to Asa Ivadi's challenge to travel discreetly and report our findings, we didn't announce ourselves as tierns of Qi-Katai, but rather neglected to correct our host's assumption that we were travelling scholars—

an assumption she made, not wholly inaccurately, after seeing
Markel and Telitha talk in signs, though had Cae been wearing a
sword at his hip, she might've thought differently. He'd brought
one, of course, a plain and functional thing, but it was bundled up
in its scabbard on one of the packhorses for this leg of the journey,
as the riverveldt was safe, and Cae had no wish to attract attention. Still, he carried the jade-handled knife I'd given him at his
belt, and when the innkeeper showed us in, I'll admit that I was
tickled to be addressed as ru, though aware that I hadn't earned
it. Dinner was quiet, but some of the day's tension ebbed with the
application of good food, and soon enough we adjourned to a pair
of simple rooms, our bellies full of fresh river-fish cooked with herbs
and spring onions.

As he slid beneath the covers that night, Cae kissed my shoulder,
nose brushing briefly against the bone. I froze, not having expected
it after the day we'd had and, in light of the previous evening, uncertain of how to respond. I knew what I wanted, but not what to
do about it, and after a moment, Cae rolled away without a word.

I lay awake for a long time after, cursing my cowardice.

Dawn brought with it a mist so thick, it might as well have
been drizzle. Weak, pinkish light struggled to limn the silver-
clogged air ahead of us, and it had rained overnight, too, leaving
the road treacherous in places, alternately muddy and half-frozen.
Under these conditions and with visibility so poor, Cae opted to
stay ahorse until well after midday, not wanting to risk his quick,
thought-clearing pace on ground he could neither trust nor see. We
moved slowly, letting the horses pick their way forwards, and were
eventually rewarded when the sun came out, allowing us to shed
the cloaks we'd donned that morning. Even so, the road remained
rucked and muddy, such that none of us suggested trying to make
up for lost time with a faster pace.

"We might end up camping by the roadside tonight," said Cae,
sounding unduly pleased about it.

I opened my mouth to make a sour retort, then bit it back,

forcing myself to be grateful he'd found something to be cheerful about.

"Are we equipped for that?" I asked instead, directing the question more towards Markel than my husband.

Markel grinned at me, knowing full well my feelings on sleeping outdoors. "We've bedrolls, but no tents," he signed. "I did consider packing some, but we're not going into the wilderness, and they take up a lot of room."

"Bedrolls are better than nothing," I muttered, trying very hard not to sound churlish.

"I've always liked sleeping outside," Cae said. "Even after the bear—"

He broke off, a terrible look on his face. He turned his head away, and all I could think to do was give him the courtesy of silence. As a youth, Cae had fought and killed a rabid bear, his flank still marked by the terrible rake of its claws. It was a long-running joke between them for Riya to say, *I liked you better before the bear*—and for Laecia, who'd been youngest of all, to protest their private humour.

But Laecia was dead.

Too late, I realised how hard Cae had worked these last few weeks to keep his grief at bay. He'd still been clearly in mourning, but I saw now with a sudden, wretched clarity that the receipt of his grandmother's seal and our summons to Qi-Xihan had broken whatever control he'd had over the depths of his loss. It made my skin prickle and heat with a mix of shame and panic: shame, that I hadn't noticed sooner and done something to ease it; panic, that I was a poor source of comfort at the best of times and here utterly out of my depth.

Had we been in private, I might have ventured to touch his arm or speak unguarded, but in public—even with an audience consisting only of Markel and Telitha—I was unable to do either. We'd kissed where people could see us, and that was still new and dangerous enough to set my pulse racing; to speak of our private feelings—for me to act, as my frustratingly Ralian sense of things continued to insist was the case, as a wife showing care to his husband—would've taken more courage than I presently possessed.

What came out of my mouth instead was, "Are we likely to see any bears near here? Telitha says that reseko keep to the mountains, but their bigger cousins must roam further afield, surely."

A piercingly awkward silence followed. One of the horses snorted. Sweat broke out on the nape of my neck; I didn't dare turn to look at Markel, but I could feel his judgement skewering my back like the tines of a pitchfork. Then:

"We might, actually," said Cae—his voice syrup-slow, as if he'd been woken from a dream. "There's plenty of fish in the Eshi, and there's always a few who venture into our farmlands to eat and hunt before they go into hibernation. Not that they always stop at fish, of course."

"Of course," I said faintly. "Bears can be quite troublesome, rabid or otherwise." And then, because I'd evidently taken complete leave of my senses and Markel wasn't close enough to stop me, "I never saw any bears near Aarobrook when I was growing up, but my grandfather used to swear blind that, when he was young, one wandered in at the end of spring and got roaring drunk on fermented plums that hadn't been cleared from the orchard. It terrorised the whole estate for an hour, roaming around and bellowing for whatever it is bears want when they're drunk, ate three of our chickens, then fell asleep in the fountain."

"In the *fountain*?"

"Yes, the one in the courtyard. Grandfather wanted to kill it, he said, but the fountain gets its water from a shared source, and his own father didn't want it fouled, and it's bad luck to kill a sleeping bear in any case. So they trussed it up by the paws like a game carcass, wrapped it in a sack and had a couple of plough horses drag it out to the forest on a travois. Or at least, that was the plan; the bear woke up halfway there and started trying to escape. The horses spooked and bolted, the travois came loose from the harness and the sack came loose from the travois, and then the bear chewed its way out because nobody had been brave enough to muzzle it. Or fool enough, Grandfather always said, given that they'd have had to untie it again once they let it go." I snorted. "In the end, though, the bear was too dizzy and drunk to do much of anything but roar and lumber away, but all the men still scrambled up the nearest tree until it was gone. They found the horses the next day, and nobody ever saw the bear again."

"Bears can climb trees," said Cae, after a moment. "Why would they try and hide in one?"

"Sheer panic?" I offered, sympathising immensely with the sentiment.

Cae made a soft noise that was very nearly laughter. "Your grandfather sounds like a character."

"Very much so," I said. "He was a younger son, like me; he was never meant to inherit, but his older brothers predeceased him, and so he ended up stuck with the family responsibility. He died when I was still young, but he left a big impression."

"How so?" Cae asked, and so I found myself launching into another of Grandfather's stories, about the time a friend's favourite horse took ill and died while under his care, and how he'd hunted high and low to find an identical beast with which to replace it—which he eventually did, and his friend never the wiser. Cae listened as I prattled on, and mile by mile, his mood thawed as steadily as the frozen ground, until he was chuckling along and interjecting with tales of his own as cheerfully as if he'd never faltered.

By nightfall, we were still several hours shy of reaching the inn marked on Telitha's map. Had I been travelling alone, I'd have pressed on—it was a clear, crisp evening, and the road had vastly improved since morning—but given his enthusiasm, I bowed to Cae's suggestion of a night spent under the stars. We pitched camp in a clearing just beyond sight of the road, the horses tethered to trees and our bedrolls arranged around the campfire, two pairs on either side. Mercifully, it didn't rain, though the wind from the river was chill and certain small, biting insects decided to make a feast of me. We toasted chewy bread and baked some pears in the fire to eat with goat's cheese, which went very well indeed with a bottle of crisp white wine that Markel had been savvy enough to purchase the previous day, and insects notwithstanding, it was so pleasant that I was almost minded to think camping not so bad, after all.

Until, of course, it was time to turn in, at which point Markel and I realised simultaneously that we'd be bedding down with our respective romantic partners while in sight and sound of each other. We both froze, our horrified gazes locked across the fire in a mutual parody of Ralian embarrassment while Cae and Telitha, politely oblivious to our awkwardness, prepared our beds.

"We will not speak of this," Markel signed fiercely at me.

"Never," I signed back in fervent agreement.

Markel nodded briskly and turned away to Telitha, leaving me to do the same with Cae. Instantly, my mouth went dry: in the time I'd been preoccupied with Markel, my husband had stripped unashamedly down to his smallclothes.

"Won't," I began aloud, then faltered, needing to swallow before I could continue. "Won't you be cold like that?"

"I always feel colder, sleeping fully clothed," he admitted, with an odd little duck of his head. He crouched down, fussing with our blankets. "It's not—I know that sounds strange, but it's true. For me, at least." He glanced at me and then down again, looking oddly flushed; or perhaps it was only the firelight. "It's something about how the air gets trapped against my skin, different parts being different temperatures. It's less comfortable, somehow."

"Oh," I said. "And do you, ah . . . when you're with your re-vetha—"

"No, no!" He laughed awkwardly, pulling the mourning ribbons from his braid. "At least, not when we're not on duty. Nairi would skin me alive. It's just that—oh." He went abruptly still. "Would you rather I stay dressed?"

"Please don't," I blurted.

Relaxing once more, Cae nodded, but made no move to get into bed. Shoving down my aching awareness of Markel and Telitha and trying not to stare at my husband, I shed my own boots, my coat and lin and even, after a moment's hesitation, my undershirt, leaving me bare-chested in the moonlight. Banded Coria—or Zo's Heart, as she was known in Tithena—was waxing near to full, while little gold Riva and rosy Asha—here called Ruya's Eye and Ayla's Hand—were on the wane, as though their section of sky was winking. I shivered in the evening chill and, before I could lose my nerve, lay down on my bedroll and slid beneath the blankets, only belatedly remembering to remove the mourning ribbons from my wrists.

After a moment's hesitation, Cae joined me, and had he not been making such a sincere effort to give me space, I might've laughed at how carefully he did so.

"You needn't fear," I murmured, daring to brush my knuckles against his shoulder. "I've no objection to proximity."

Cae let out a small sigh of relief. There was a moment of silence as we settled ourselves, tucking the blanket beneath our feet and rearranging our respective limbs, until we ended up cuddled together, Cae's arm wrapped around my waist, his chest against my back. The intimacy of it made my heart pound. His skin was hot on mine, a startling contrast to the cold night air on my face and neck, and I wondered if he really was right about bare skin being warmer.

"Is this all right?" Cae murmured, quiet enough not to carry across the fire.

"It is," I whispered back, too cowardly to say *of course, yes, please* or *I wish you'd do this every night.*

His arm tightened pleasantly around me. I could feel his breath on the nape of my neck, the barest brush of his mouth. Mortifyingly, given that we weren't alone, I realised I was half-hard. I made a terrible little noise in my throat and might've done something extremely foolish, like press my arse back to feel if Cae was anywhere near as affected as me, when all at once, the ground shook.

My yelp of shock was drowned out by the panicked stamping and whinnying of the horses. I felt like I was five years old again, curled in a ball on my mattress as my older brothers, Revic and Nathian, jumped around me like hellions. It was a poor comparison, but the closest one I could make to the bizarre sensation, as though the earth were horseflesh twitching angrily to rid itself of biting flies—and then, just as suddenly as it had started, it stopped.

"The fire!" Telitha exclaimed. As I sat up, she leapt to her feet, grabbed a sturdy branch, and began to poke the burning wood back into configuration, keeping the flames from spreading to the grass. I watched her with dazed fascination, only dimly aware of Markel rising to soothe the agitated horses, who were still snorting and prancing and pulling against their tethers.

"What," I said, voice shaking rather less than the ground had done, "was that?"

"An earthquake," said Cae, who demonstrably hadn't gone anywhere, and yet whose voice by my ear was nonetheless startling enough to make me jump. "An early one for the season, but nothing to worry about." He paused, and I realised rather belatedly that he'd sat up beside me, one big, warm hand curled around my waist. "Do you not have them in Ralia?"

"Not that I've ever experienced," I said faintly. I'd read about earthquakes before—had possibly even known, in the back of my mind, that they happened in Tithena—but experiencing one was a different thing altogether. I turned, blinking at my husband in the firelight, and managed to process the rest of his explanation. "Do earthquakes have a season?"

"We get more of them in winter," Cae said, almost apologetically. "Nobody's quite sure why, though the mages of Ruya's Order and the university scholars have theories about it. Something about the way ice expands underground? I can't remember the details."

I made a noise of what I hoped was polite interest and turned my gaze back to the fire, which Telitha had managed to get under control. She flashed me a smile and returned to her bedroll, holding one side of the blankets open for Markel, who'd evidently finished with the horses, too. I watched him climb in beside her in a vacant daze before remembering to be embarrassed for the both of us, at which point I dropped my mortified gaze to the grass.

"You're trembling," Cae murmured. The hand on my waist gave a gentle squeeze, drawing me back down beside him. I acquiesced without meaning to, heart pounding as I found myself back in my husband's embrace.

The fire crackled softly as the wind stirred. One of the horses snorted, pawing at the earth, before subsiding again. I felt wide awake, as alive to what had just happened as I was to Cae's touch, and with no idea how I was meant to fall asleep under such circumstances, I found myself uttering a request I hadn't made since childhood:

"Tell me a story?"

Cae huffed a laugh against my shoulder. "Truly?"

"Truly."

"Hm." His lips burred against my bare skin. Cae shifted against me, then fell silent for long enough that I began to feel anxious. I was on the brink of saying it didn't matter when, in a low, soft voice, he spoke again.

"When we were children, Riya was scared of earthquakes. Even though she's the eldest, whenever we felt one, she'd come running into my room to hide beneath the covers. She always pretended it was for my sake, like she was the one comforting me, but I figured it out eventually. But Laecia—" and here he let out a little choked noise, his grip on me tightening, "—she was never scared. She loved the power of them, the way things shook, and maybe that would've changed if we'd ever had a big one, like the quake that shattered Samiruq, but we only ever had tremors."

He paused, breathing softly against me. I pressed back against him, which was all the comfort I could think to offer. The crackle of the fire filled our silence. Then:

"The year before our mother left, Laecia finally realised how much they frightened Riya. And I thought, when it happened—Ri was fourteen by then, Laecia only seven—that Laecia would tease her for it, because she was so . . . even then, she was so eager to prove herself brave and clever; to be the most grown-up of all of us. But instead—instead, she marched up to Riya on the first day of winter and said, *Don't worry! I'm going to catch an earthquake in a jar for you, so you don't have to be scared.* And the way she said it . . . I don't know. It was a child's confidence in the impossible, but still, you could almost believe her."

Cae fell quiet again. I felt him shift, and then he pressed his forehead to the knobs of my spine, bowed as if in penitence.

"Riya and I were outside when the first quake came that year. When it stopped, we went looking for Laecia. We found her passed out on the floor of her room, surrounded by bits of broken glass. She wasn't badly hurt, but she never talked about catching quakes again." He swallowed. "At the time, we thought she'd just fallen and hit her head, but now . . . now, I think that was where her magic started. She tried to syphon power from the quake somehow, or touch its source, the way only a child would think to do, and the backlash exploded her jar." And then, voice twisting with pain, "If I'd only noticed—"

"Shh," I said, and turned within his arms, so that I could hold him, too. "Don't do that. Don't punish yourself."

"Why not?" Cae said, hurt twisting his voice. "Who else deserves it?"

I do. An ugly chill washed through me. It was my desperate plan that had led to Laecia's death, and Markel's hand that had wielded the weapon. I wouldn't have thought it possible for my silent body to communicate these thoughts, and yet somehow they did; Cae tensed around me and rasped, "Saints, Vel, I didn't mean *you*. What she'd done, what she was going to do—you didn't have any choice, and nor did Markel."

"If I'm not to blame, then neither are you," I said, trying very firmly to mean it. I sought his hand where it was wrapped around me and squeezed his fingers, burrowing against his warmth as a gust of cold air whipped by. And then, because I was too cowardly to continue the conversation, for all that I'd started it, "Good night, Cae."

For an answer, he kissed my temple. With predictable ease, I felt his body go lax and his breathing settle within short order, but I lay awake for a long time afterwards, staring up at distant stars that gleamed like broken glass.

5

We arrived in Etho a day later than planned, but in the afternoon rather than the evening, which almost made up for it. There'd been no more earthquakes on the rest of the journey; Cae and Telitha had both assured me that they seldom came close together, and yet my brain persisted in tricking me, inventing phantom tremors for me to jump at. Cae made a face whenever he caught me doing it like he was holding back laughter, while I, in turn, pretended not to have noticed. We'd been dancing around each other since the morning we woke cuddled by the embers of the fire, sleepily aroused, bodies moving together of their own accord, until the bubble-bursting moment when we'd remembered where we were, and why, and with whom, and sprang apart like cats splashed with wash-water.

Though not quite the tension of a few weeks past, our current détente was cousin to it still. What little equanimity we'd found in the wake of Laecia's death and during our stay at Avai had vanished on the road. Married or not, we were both still damnably new to each other, and there were some conversations it was simply impossible to have in front of an audience. Markel was dearer to me than my brothers had ever been, and Telitha, though a new acquaintance, was someone I'd swiftly grown to trust; even so, their presence made it impossible to discuss our wants, and by the time we had a moment alone, we'd both of us lost the nerve.

So when, after we'd secured a pair of rooms for ourselves and stabling for the horses at a large, prosperous-looking inn, Telitha immediately suggested that we split up to take in such sights as Etho

offered—she and Markel going one way, Cae and I another—I
ought to have been delighted. Instead, and despite my ready agreement, a terrible anxiousness stole over me the second our friends
were out of sight. We hadn't spoken again of Laecia or what we'd
done in the gardens, and it gnawed at me. I barely knew how to
argue with a lover, let alone negotiate the thornier, more subtle
intricacies of sharing a life with someone, and every time I remembered my own uncertainties, Cae's grief and my part in both, I felt
a chasm open behind my ribs.

"So," I ventured, when Markel and Telitha had waved goodbye
and vanished around a corner. "Ah, that is, I—"

"Would you like to get some food?" Cae asked, almost desperately.

"*Yes,*" I said, with far more fervour than the offer warranted.
"Yes, that sounds wonderful."

Barely a week prior, the interlude that followed would've been
blissful: Cae and I together, elbows brushing as we explored the
marketplace, admiring wares and remarking on the scenery as we
shared a packet of fried, savoury cakes purchased from a grandfa-
therly vendor, both of us working to keep the conversation light
and meaningless. Instead, I began to feel like I was slowly going
mad. Caethari was *right there,* smiling in the crisp autumn light,
and yet wholly inaccessible.

Inevitably, evening fell, necessitating a return to our lodgings
and the company of our companions. Part of me was grateful; with
Markel and Telitha present, I could once more pretend that our inability to have a real conversation was due to a lack of privacy, and
not our mutual ineptitude. The rest of me, however, was strangely
exhausted, and as our reunited quartet entered the inn's bustling
common room and beelined for the sole unoccupied table, I had
the sudden urge to be alone.

Social creature that I was, a desire for solitude seldom boded
well for my state of mind. Shoving my insecurities aside, I sat down
beside Markel, leaving Cae to claim the opposite seat, and forced
myself to be pleasant as Telitha asked about our afternoon.

That Markel didn't immediately register my false cheer, as he ordinarily would've done, was due less to my discretion and more to his ongoing preoccupation with Telitha. For all that she was steering the conversation, the pair of them were grinning stupidly across the table at each other, blushing in a way that suggested they'd spent their afternoon far more pleasurably—and more intimately—than Cae and I had ours. An unpleasant pang of jealousy soured my stomach. I didn't want to begrudge my friends their happiness nor Markel his independence, especially not with Telitha so soon due to return to Qi-Katai, but all at once, I realised how much I'd come to rely on his tacit understanding of my moods. It was Markel's deft touch on the tiller of my feelings that kept me on anything even vaguely resembling an even keel—into what reeds and rapids would I drift without his guidance?

"Excuse me," said an unfamiliar voice, bursting the melancholy bubble of my thoughts, "but might we share your table? It's getting crowded, and we'd rather not go elsewhere."

I turned, and found myself looking at a short, handsomely fat woman with sparkling eyes, warm brown skin and straight black hair cut in a style I'd hitherto only seen worn by men, which was to say, shorn short at the sides but longer on top, slicked dashingly back with oil. There was something about her that felt, if not exactly familiar, then somehow compelling; I didn't know why, but I set it aside to examine later. Beside her stood an imposingly tall, broad-shouldered man with a long, crooked nose and a startlingly soft mouth; he acknowledged my scrutiny with a dip of his chin, but otherwise remained silent.

"Of course," I said, all too glad of the distraction, and shuffled up a space, prompting everyone else to do likewise.

Introductions were made in short order: the woman, who ended up alongside Cae, was Qarrah, while her companion, who somehow squeezed himself in next to me, was Orin. It was notable that they gave neither titles nor clan-names, but as we'd made the same omissions in continued deference to Asa Ivadi's instructions, I didn't find it suspicious.

"Where are you travelling, ren?" Cae asked politely.

Qarrah stretched her elbows out on the table. "Oh, here and there. We were up in Irae-Tai for a bit, then took a detour over the river border into Khytë when we were coming south, and now, who knows? We're layscouts," she added, seeing my look of confusion.

The word was vaguely familiar, but I couldn't quite place it. "Layscouts?"

"They're employed by merchant houses and some nobles to investigate trade routes and track shifts in buying and selling, that sort of thing," said Cae, coming to my rescue. "They make new contacts, find new roads and generally seek out new trade opportunities."

"Which means, practically speaking, a lot of time spent trekking through the middle of nowhere interspersed with occasional violence," Qarrah explained, eyes twinkling. "Mostly from obstreperous wildlife—silk chamois in particular are territorial little sods—but also from sabotaging competitors, bandits and anyone else your prying questions might rub the wrong way."

I blinked, impressed. "That sounds like dangerous work!"

"It is," she replied—and then added thoughtfully, "though it might be less so, if Tithena had a watchtower network to her name." I nodded agreement; a similar question had been raised among Ralia's nobles not long ago, but as I was pretending to be Tithenai, I could hardly say so. "Even on the main roads," Qarrah continued, "there's long stretches where you're utterly on your own if something goes wrong, and even though we can look after ourselves"—she gestured between herself and Orin—"there's plenty of times we've skirted a band of louts set to shake down travellers with no way to pass a warning."

"Is that common?" I asked, remembering the attack at Vaiko; I'd speared a man through with a pitchfork there, and shuddered at the prospect of a repeat encounter.

"No, no!" Qarrah waved her hands. "Gods, don't let me put you off your travels—stick to the main roads and you'll likely be safe as stone. But getting about as much as we do, well; that's a different matter. Not that I'm complaining, of course—I like my job! But if you're privy to any good merchant gossip, I'd take it as a kindness if you passed it along." So saying, she grinned. She had a good face for grinning: round and small, with full apple cheeks to frame her broad, flat nose, and despite myself, I found I was grinning back.

Clicking his fingers to get my attention, Markel signed, "You should tell her about the Taelic Pass reopening."

Before I could raise my hands to reply, Qarrah broke in with, "What's this about the pass?"

All of us stared at her. "Ren," I said aloud, trying to keep the surprise from my voice, "you know sign-speech?"

"Eh," said Qarrah, making a so-so gesture with her hand. Eyes twinkling, she caught Markel's eye and offered him a knowing smile. "I've met enough Attovari sailors to have picked up dribs and drabs. But why do you use it? You don't look Attovari, and I mean that as a compliment."

"I'm mute," signed Markel. "We needed a way to talk, so Velasin researched it, and the two of us learned together."

Qarrah's brows rose. "That sounds like quite a story! But, I suspect, a personal one, so don't feel the need to tell it now." She grinned again. "I'd rather hear about the pass."

I'd liked her before then, but the easy joviality with which she handled the moment cemented it for me. Even so, I floundered at the realisation that answering would involve either lying outright about our identities, rather than by omission, or else divulging them belatedly, and therefore awkwardly.

It was Telitha who rescued me. "There's been a diplomatic marriage between Clan Aeduria in Qi-Katai and the Ralian noble family that now holds the other side of the pass. It's new yet—and scandalous for the Ralians, as it's two men who've married—but that's all the more reason for them to want trade to resume, to make it worth it."

Qarrah whistled. "Now, that *is* news, and news worth having!" She reached across the table and gave her companion a jovial thwack on the arm. "You hear that, Orin? If we'd stayed in Khytë like you wanted, we'd have missed a trick!"

Orin grunted in what sounded like grudging agreement. Qarrah slapped the table, beaming at us. "Drinks! My shout, as you've managed to justify my detour with a single tale—no, no, I'll get it, you stay here." And before we could protest, she extricated herself and headed for the bar.

"Qarrah is . . . an experience," said Orin. It was the first time he'd spoken, and I was surprised by how light his voice was, given the size of him. "She means well."

"If she brings me a drink, she can mean however she wants," quipped Cae. We all chuckled, but there was a tightness at the corners of his eyes that said he'd found the afternoon as draining as I had.

Before it had time to worsen, however, Qarrah returned with both the drinks and a server to tell us what was available for dinner, and all conversation was swiftly curtailed in favour of ordering. As at the last inn, there was a lot of fish on offer, and my stomach growled in anticipation of sampling it. As the server left, Qarrah launched into a tale about getting lost in the mountains in Khytë and being harassed by some unusually aggressive wild goats, which soon had all of us chuckling. She was one of those people with the easy knack of taking control of a group, not to exclude or dictate, but to set everyone at ease, and under the circumstances, I was immensely glad of it.

By the time the food arrived, we were all in a newly convivial mood and set to eating with a will. Though simpler than the excellent fare produced by the Aida's cook, Ren Valiu—or, indeed, by her anxious counterpart at the Avai estate—the inn's food was nonetheless memorable, the steamed fish simmered with chives, shallots and something I didn't recognise, thin slices of a pinkish fruit that was almost citric while still being slightly sweet. Cooked, the texture was already meltingly soft; after soaking in the light, buttery sauce, it was divine.

"They're called rosefruit," said Cae, seeing my interest. "Do you not have them in Ralia?"

"Not that I've ever encountered," I replied.

"Ralian cooks don't like them, in my experience," said Qarrah, gesturing with her kip. "The flavour's too light for most dark meat and it clashes with those heavy, creamy sauces they like for white meat."

"True," I said ruefully. And then, after a moment's thought, "Though it would work well in ladies' cordials, I think."

"Huh." Qarrah's brows rose slightly. "D'you know, I think you're right. Huh!" She set her kip down and clapped her hands, grinning. "You're just a hotbed of trade ideas, aren't you?"

"We do our best," signed Markel.

Qarrah barked with laughter.

We were nearing the end of the meal when Telitha announced her intention to shout us all another round. Cae tried to protest, but she waved him off with a quiet smile and stood, heading to the bar. Qarrah watched her go, an appreciative light in her eyes, but it wasn't until Telitha returned with a tray of drinks and set about distributing them that the nature of Qarrah's appreciation became clear to me.

"You know," she said, leaning forwards and speaking solely to Telitha, a slight smile on her lips, "if you were amenable, I'd be happy to buy you another one later, once we've a little more privacy."

Telitha laughed, surprised and pleased, but shook her head as she sat. "I'm flattered, ren, but I'm spoken for." So saying, she touched Markel lightly on the wrist, and he smiled at her in response.

"Ah, too bad!" said Qarrah, leaning back in her seat with a dramatic grin. "I'm always too late, it seems."

"You have good taste," signed Markel, smiling.

Qarrah laughed aloud and raised her glass to him. "As do you, ren."

With that, she kicked Orin lightly under the table, prompting him aloud to stop being a lump and contribute some conversation; they bickered back and forth for a moment, and then he obliged her, telling another story of their travels that began with Qarrah getting outrageously drunk and trying to fight a donkey. He had a wry, flat delivery that soon had everyone laughing—everyone but me, because I was frozen, rooted in the moment where Qarrah had propositioned Telitha openly, and been rejected, and nothing bad had come of it, and nobody thought it remarkable.

Too late, I realised I'd felt drawn to Qarrah because, on some level, I'd recognised her as being like me—a person who preferred their own sex to the opposite—though as I'd rarely met women who fell into that category, let alone so openly, I hadn't understood it right away. An ungainly feeling buzzed beneath my skin, persistent and edged with a kind of sadness that made my throat ache. I couldn't comprehend myself; I'd never felt this way about Riya, who was married to a woman, or by the other couples like myself and Cae to whom I'd been introduced, albeit briefly, in Qi-Katai. Moons, I'd even seen Liran flirt with a man before, and it hadn't caught me about the ribs like this. Why was I so undone by Qarrah's openness?

Because it is open, a part of me whispered. *Because it's what we've never had.*

My hands clenched in my lap; I stared at them, appalled as they began to shake. It made no sense: I was *married* to Caethari! Never mind the kisses we'd shared in public as a couple—we'd even kissed at our marriage-gathering, in front of an audience gathered for the purpose!

But you never had this: the freedom to try a brazen approach where anyone might see. To spot a handsome man at a bar and ask him to tarry with you without fear of violence or scorn or worse; to speak where it didn't matter who overheard.

The realisation rocked through me like a punch. I cared deeply for Cae—wanted very much, in fact, for our marriage to be a successful one—and yet the loss of something I'd never known to want, so certain it was impossible, was like looking down and finding I was suddenly missing a finger.

All at once, the delicious meal I'd eaten sat leaden in my stomach. I felt foolish, trapped, shame scratching against my skin from the inside out, and without meaning to, I stood abruptly, jerking away from the table.

"I don't feel well," I mumbled, trying and failing to forestall any concern, and lurched towards the doors.

Outside, the night air was sharp and cool, a welcome relief against my overheated cheeks. Moving in a daze, I walked around the side of the inn to the stables and leaned heavily against the rear wall, not knowing what to make of myself. Of all the things to have upset me in the past week, this was surely the most ridiculous; I gulped in air and stared at the stars, blinking against the absurdity of tears.

I'd been there maybe a minute when Caethari found me. He approached at a fast walk, visibly tense, but relaxed when he saw that I was, if not completely well, then at least not actually suffering.

"I'm sorry," I said, before he could get a word out. "I don't—something queer came over me, and—"

Cae stepped in and kissed me almost desperately, cradling my jaw with one big, rough palm. We'd neither of us shaved for days: his stubble rasped against mine, and I grabbed his lin to steady myself as I kissed back, not understanding his urgency but needing—suddenly, fiercely—to share in it.

My back hit the stable wall with a *thump*. Cae's mouth slipped off mine for just long enough that a gasp escaped, though whether from him or me, I couldn't tell; and then he was on me again, or I was on him, hands roaming with ragged fervour. There was something wildly adolescent about it—not just our mutual desperation and the speed with which it had built, but the fumbling, needy awareness that came from having no true privacy, yet being too caught up to seek some.

Cae's thick thigh found a welcome place between my own; I

made an embarrassing noise and rutted against it, a maddening, teasing friction. I felt his cock against my hip, but didn't dare to take him in hand, not even through our clothes. A distant part of me was equal parts aroused by and fearful of the threat of discovery, but in the moment, all that mattered was his mouth, his hands, the places where we touched.

A door banged open somewhere nearby, followed by a burst of drunken laughter. It jarred me back into my senses, and I shoved Cae away before I knew what I was doing, the action guided by instinct, though my hands retained a shaky grip on his lin.

"Sorry," I gasped. My mouth felt pleasantly used, my whole body aching with arousal. "Sorry, I didn't mean—"

"It's all right," said Cae. He looked dazed, and for a hopeful moment I thought we might resume; then he closed his callused hands over mine and squeezed, just once, before letting go, my grip releasing as he stepped away. Jerkily, he said, "I came to see—to get you. If, I thought . . . you didn't finish your drink."

"I'm fine," I said—reflexively, stupidly, as it was no answer to anything he'd just said. "I wanted some air." And then, because I could think of no other excuse, "I must be tired."

"We can go up, if you like. To the room."

"That would—yes. Please." I swallowed, flushed and awkward and wanting stupidly to grab him back, to resume what we'd been doing before my paranoia ruined it, but not knowing how to keep from making a fool of myself. "Will you come, too?"

"Would you like me to?"

"I'd—I don't want to pull you from company, but if you'd like—"

"I would," said Cae, and my heart gave a hopeful thump.

As we went back inside, I was so preoccupied with trying to straighten my clothes that, all unknowing, I crashed into someone coming the other way. With my head down, I didn't get a look at them; all I heard was a low, angry grunt as the impact jarred my shoulder. Mortified, I stammered out my apologies, but whoever it was didn't deign to reply; only made a disdainful noise and let their shoulder clip me again as they passed by, this time on purpose.

"Hey!" Caethari called after them, outraged, but the stranger—I'd thought them male, but couldn't be sure—ignored us both, stalking off towards the stables without so much as a backwards glance. Cae made to follow them, but though a childish part of me disliked the thought of such a person anywhere near Gift, I stayed my husband's arm and shook my head.

"Don't bother. Anyway, it was my fault for not looking where I was going."

"That's still no excuse for rudeness," Cae grumbled, but let the matter be.

Returning briefly to our companions, we made our excuses and headed upstairs. The inn was three stories tall, and the two rooms we'd booked were on the top, on opposite sides of a central hallway. There was also a shared bathing chamber at the far end of the floor; I'd forgotten about it until I caught sight of the sign, and then suddenly all I could think of was getting clean.

"You go first," said Cae, lips twitching as he followed my line of sight, and I felt a surge of affection for him.

With all the earlier tensions, both pleasant and fraught, apparently dissolved between us, the rest of the evening passed easily. I washed and even managed a shave; I'd likely have a shadow again by midday, but my not-beard was starting to itch in a way I hated, and I didn't trust myself to remember to shave in the morning. When it was Cae's turn, I sent our road-worn things to be laundered in-house, stripped down to a clean pair of smallclothes, and collapsed into bed. I'd slept on softer mattresses, but I was wearier than I'd realised; having only thought to close my eyes for a moment, I drifted off, rousing for a brief, bleary instant when Cae returned before, at his murmured assurances, collapsing into true sleep.

My dreams were shapeless at first, but soon a strange restlessness crept into them, as though I were tossing and turning but unable, quite, to wake. My dream-self coughed, and so did my body, coughing over and over until I broke out of sleep completely. Why was I coughing?

Beside me, Cae made a raspy, choking noise. Something nearby was crackling, the air far hotter than it ought to have been, and all at once, my senses came alive.

Smoke.

The inn was on fire.

"Cae!" I rasped, sitting upright—or trying to, at least; I coughed again, doubling over as smoke racked my lungs and stung my eyes to watering. I bent towards him, shaking his shoulder frantically. "Cae, wake up!"

He lurched upright, dazed and hacking as he tried to speak; our struggling eyes met through the wreathing smoke, and then we both scrambled to our feet. He was in just a hipwrap, I in only my smallclothes, but for once, I was too frightened to care about modesty. Flames danced in all but one of the windows, the beams overhead creaking ominously—the roof must've caught, I realised with a jolt—but our room wasn't yet alight. I grabbed the nearest bag and headed for the door, trying feebly to shield my nose and mouth with my arm, but Cae grabbed my bicep and stopped me.

"Wait!" he rasped. As I watched, confused and terrified, he grabbed a lin—his or mine, I wasn't sure—tore it in half and doused the cloth with water from the ewer on his nightstand, proceeding to wrap the wet cloth around his nose and mouth. Then he did the same with me, knotting the impromptu shield behind my head; the smoke still clawed my stinging eyes, but it helped to ease my breathing. I thought we'd go then, but instead he grabbed up the bag I'd rescued, snatched its companion from the dresser, went to the one window not yet alight, eased it open with surprising care, and threw our things out into the dark. I shook as I watched him, head spinning from fear and smoke—could we get out that way, too? Reflexively, I turned to seek Markel's opinion, and only then remembered that he and Telitha were in a different room.

Fear froze my heart. "The others!" I gasped, moving to tug Cae's arm—he'd clearly been assessing the window as an escape option, but he startled at my touch, eyes going wide above the cloth. "Markel and Telitha, we have to get them!"

Cae swore and nodded. "Keep behind me," he grit out, coughing again behind his mask. He approached the door warily, setting his knuckles to the wood before snatching them back again. He paused, then repeated the gesture more slowly, letting the contact stand for a good two seconds. From there, he hovered his palm over the handle—testing for heat, I realised belatedly—before finally cracking the door open, peering through the slit at the hall beyond.

When he moved, I followed him, unprepared for the wave of crisping heat that rolled towards us. The hallway was burning at one end, the flames spreading fast along the ceiling, smoke already thick. Cae strode towards the neighbouring room, but just as he raised his hand to knock, the door swung open, revealing a frightened Markel and Telitha. Both were red-eyed and coughing, but my heart clenched to see them alive.

"We need to get everyone out!" croaked Telitha, gesturing to the other doors. Before anyone could reply, the burning roof gave an ominous groan, followed by a splintering crack—one of the central beams was breaking, threatening to fall, while beneath our feet, the boards were growing hot, scorching our bare feet.

We all froze, just for a heartbeat—and then Markel was moving, running up one side of the hall to bang on every door, while Cae, a second behind him, did the same on the opposite side. It took them both towards the bathing chamber, away from the thicker smoke and flickering flames that billowed from the stairs.

As Cae and Markel hurried back, the roof groaned again; I had just enough time to see two doors crack open, their terrified occupants fleeing into the hall, before I was hustled towards the burning stairwell, my husband's grip tight on my arm.

"Fuck," Cae swore, as we saw what lay before us. The stairs were a tunnel of fire, burning on the roof, the walls, even the bannisters, smoke pouring up from between the slats. When he spoke again, his voice was a coughing rasp. "One at a time; everyone hold some-one else. Test each step before you put your weight on it, but try to move quickly. Go!"

He took the lead, towing me behind him; Markel gripped my other arm, and behind him came Telitha. The stairs creaked and burned beneath us; fire reached out like biting tendrils, scoring our hair and clothes, though none of us was truly dressed. The descent felt endless, not least because I'd somehow forgotten we had two floors to go down instead of one. The inn's middle floor was burning fiercely, and I flinched to hear a crash and a scream from an unseen room as we reached the second set of stairs, which soon proved to be more treacherous than the first. Twice, a stair broke when Cae set foot on it—the second time, he almost fell through the gap, saved only by my hauling on him, Markel hauling on me and Telitha hauling on Markel, giving Cae a precious chance to brace his hands on the wall.

We finally emerged into the common room—the place where we'd eaten such a companionable meal only hours past—and it was nothing but smoke and fire, choking and hot and terrible. As we crossed the floor, a heavy beam fell beside us, throwing up a shower of sparks and a gust of flames. I screamed, or would've done if my throat weren't raw; Cae dragged me on, and somehow we made it to the entrance, banging open the unlatched door and stumbling into the night, where we found ourselves in a crowd of fellow escapees, all doubled over gasping and coughing, rubbing at smoke-reddened eyes. I ripped off my makeshift mask, sucking in air as the four of us staggered away from the inn, the cobblestones shockingly cold on my scalded feet. Moans of pain and jagged crying overlaid the crackle of the burning inn, cut through with snippets of conversation:

"—kitchen must've caught, that whole side went up like tinder—"

"—not sure where—"

"—wardens will be here soon, they must've seen—"

"—gods, she was right behind me, I swear—"

"—get everyone to safety—"

"—won't stand much longer—"

"Velasin!"

I jerked at this last, whirling in the semi-dark with Cae still gripping my arm, and found myself face-to-face with a soot-smeared Qarrah, Orin a looming shadow at her shoulder.

"Moons," I croaked, "I'm glad you got out!"

"And you lot, too." The whites of her eyes gleamed wildly. She reached out, then hissed and snatched her hand away, flipping it to gesture at me. "You're burned!"

"I am?" I said, just as Cae tugged me to face him—he'd taken his mask off, too, a part of me noted distantly—and asked, "You are?"

"I don't know?" I said, heart hammering all over again. I couldn't tell; even without my watering eyes, it was dark and we had no mirror, and if I was in pain—or if I should've been, rather—I couldn't yet feel it.

"You both are," Qarrah said. "Not surprising, given you've no clothes, but—" she stepped closer, keen gaze raking us in the smoky light, "—it doesn't look too serious."

Something brushed my arm. I jumped, shaky at the contact, before realising it was Markel, coming to stand beside me, Telitha still clinging to his arm. He signed something to Qarrah, but I didn't catch it. In response, she nodded and clapped him on the shoulder, and I was on the verge of asking what he'd said when a loud cry went up, drawing all our attention.

At first, I didn't see what was wrong; then I caught the word *horses* and realised, with a sickening lurch, that the stables had caught alight, the wooden roof and hayloft burning with terrifying speed.

The horses.

Gift.

All at once, I was back in the Aida's stables, kneeling in a pool of blood by the butchered body of Quip, whom I'd raised from a foal. A horse screamed, high and shrill and eerie, and something within me snapped. I'd already lost Quip to an ugly death; I couldn't bear to lose Gift, too. I lunged forwards, moving instinctively, only to be brought up short by Cae's grip on my wrist. I turned and stared at him, panicked in the dark.

"Gift," I said, hearing the shake in my voice, "let me go, I have to get her out—"

"Vel, no!" Cae tightened his hold, tugging me back towards him. "The wardens are coming, they'll get the horses—"

"*I have to save her!*" The words came out a shriek; a distant part of me knew I was lost to reason, but my senses were full of remembered blood and a sweet bay head with dead, staring eyes. I fought Cae's restraint, wrestling to get away, but he was stronger. Cursing, he grappled me back against his chest, his free arm barred around my waist; I twisted in his hold, trying futilely to break it, but he only held me tighter.

"Vel, please! You can't go in there, you can't—"

"I can! I have to! Let me *go!*"

"I'm not going to let you kill yourself over a fucking horse!"

I stamped down on his foot, bare heel to bare instep; Cae swore furiously, but didn't relent. His grip on my wrist squeezed tighter, wrangling it up behind my back to try and stop my thrashing—

A garden at night. Killic, twisting my arm behind me, grabbing my hand to make me bring him off—

Terror of a whole new kind shot through me: a bodily, fearful panic instilled by past violence. It no longer mattered that Cae was the person holding me, nor that he was trying to save my idiot skin from doing something dangerous; Killic's spectre blocked him out, more powerful than even my memories of Quip, his echo swollen with fear of the fire, fear for those I cared for, fear of Gift's death. It wasn't the first time I'd flinched from Cae's touch on account of what I'd been through, but before, it had always been plain to Cae what was happening and why; now, though, he knew only that I was fighting his hold to try and run into the very same danger we'd just escaped, and even when I began to beg, he held firm.

"*Please,*" I gasped, tears streaking my cheeks as I writhed and fought him, "please, no, please, please stop, *please*—" I let out a desperate, throaty noise, too lost to animal panic to explain what I needed, as rational as a wild thing snared. The firmness of his grip on my arm, the iron hug of his embrace, the press of his chest against my back, the zinging bursts of pain as my burns made themselves known, even the distant terror of fire—all of it conspired with the dark, the smoke and the noise to throw me back through time, until I was once more trapped in my father's garden, Killic making use of me as my life fell apart and the fists of my will banged helplessly on the walls of my frozen body. I wept and begged and fought Cae's hold until my throat was raw; until something vital in me snapped, and I lost what little awareness I'd had until that point, uncomprehending of anything beyond the loop of remembered terror in which I'd trapped myself. It was only when I began to let out broken, hiccupping sobs, my legs going out from under me, that Cae loosened his hold to let me down, and by then, it was too late: I fell to my knees and curled into a quivering ball, my eyes squeezed shut, arms curled around my head.

"Vel?" Cae asked, voice shaky and hoarse. "Vel, what—?"

He touched me and I flinched as though stabbed, locking up on myself like a pillbug. I was breathing too fast and far too shallow, already dizzy from smoke and fear, ears ringing as if my head were underwater. I hardly knew what was happening; only that it hurt, my racing heart seconds from collapse.

"Oh gods," Cae whispered. "Oh gods, Vel—"

I shuddered and passed out.

Part Two

CAETHARI

6

Years ago, when Cae was not yet fully a man, he'd been sent in pursuit of a small group of bandits harrying a community at the farthest edges of Qi-Katai's jurisdiction. Young and still cocky from his fateful run-in with the rabid bear, he'd judged that surprise would be of more use than numbers, and taken just two soldiers along to hunt the criminals under cover of darkness. He'd thought the bandits would be easy prey, disorganised and apt to surrender when faced with trained professionals, but much like the bear, they'd proven to be dangerous when cornered. The resulting fight was short and brutal: the bandits had fought to the death rather than be captured, and in the process, their leader dealt a gruesome wound to one of Cae's soldiers, a veteran named Mauri. Cae had killed the man a stroke later, but not in time to stop Mauri's guts from spilling open, her lung from being punctured. Wounds she'd taken protecting him.

The bandit camp was out in the hills; the nearest medical aid, however, was back in the township with the rest of Cae's people. Unable to move Mauri, he'd sent his remaining soldier to fetch the healer at all speed; Marui's wounds were bad, but if they could be tended in time, not necessarily fatal. The soldier had gone, and Cae had sat with Mauri in the iron-scented dark, trying to keep her insides where they ought to be, offering what comfort he could—but all the while, she'd been in agony, blood bubbling on her lips with every breath, her slippery innards pulsing against his grip. Mauri had been staunch and strong, but long before help could possibly have arrived, she started to plead for a swift, clean end—for Cae to give her battlefield mercy.

Shaking, desperate, Cae had refused, telling her over and over that she could live, that the healer would save her, not because he knew so with any certainty, but because he'd been a green boy still, and could no more have killed a comrade, even one dying in pain, than sprouted wings.

And Mauri had died, in the end, first lapsing into unconsciousness, then finally breathing her last a good half-hour before the healer arrived on a lathered horse, too late to ever have saved her. Guilt at her death—because he'd been reckless and underprepared; because she'd taken a blow meant for him; because he hadn't granted her that final, begged-for reprieve from pain—had dogged Cae for years afterwards, even as he'd done his best to learn from it; to be a better leader, a better man. He'd made mistakes since, but none that had pierced his conscience as keenly as Mauri's dying.

Until now.

It didn't matter that Cae had only wanted to keep his husband safe: the instant Vel started begging and pleading, voice twisting out of bloody-minded determination and into unbridled fear, he should've known that something was wrong. That Cae himself—like Markel, like Telitha; like everyone who'd fled in the inn—had been addled, injured and panicked was, he considered bitterly, no excuse. Of all people, he should've been able keep his wits in a crisis, let alone remembered that being grabbed a certain way could set Vel to reliving Killic's assault. His terror at the prospect of losing his husband—of losing *Vel,* the man for whom he'd already lost both father and sister, a grief so fresh it was yet to stop bleeding—had overridden everything else, insisting that releasing him could only end in death.

Not until Vel lay weeping on the cobbles did Cae comprehend the monstrousness of what he'd done.

Breathing harshly, he stumbled away from Vel's fallen body, leaving Markel and Telitha to try and coax his husband back into something resembling consciousness. Bile rose in Cae's throat; short of assaulting Vel, the very thought of which made him retch, he couldn't imagine a worse thing to have done to him. His traitor hands shook, and for a strange, dislocated moment, Cae imagined cutting them off, as if that might somehow sever him from the hurt they'd caused. *What sort of man are you?*

Distantly, he was aware of Qarrah speaking, trying to get his attention, but Cae shrugged her off, hardly noticing when she and Orin vanished into the crowd. He stared at Velasin for as long as he could stand it, which was precisely as long as it took for Vel to look up and see him staring. Cae backed away in a lurch of grief, unable to meet Vel's gaze. He made it to an alley, braced his arms against the wall and hung his head down until the world stopped spinning. He wanted a sword, wanted something to hit, but absent either option, he wanted to *move*—how else to make sense of himself, except through use?

Amidst thoughts spinning like broken gears, he remembered throwing their things from the third-floor window. Assuming they hadn't been scavenged by some fast-fingered stranger or caught fire along with the inn, they ought to still be recoverable. It was a thin scrap of purpose to cling to, but as sick and shamed as he felt, Cae grasped it with both hands as an excuse to act. Striding back into the crowd, he passed by Vel and the others, making sure they were still where he'd left them, but didn't stop. Etho's wardens had arrived to try and control the blazing inn: they'd brought a water wagon, but from what Cae could see, as the structure was already nearing collapse, priority was given to stopping the fire's spread.

He'd had some fire training himself, along with the rest of his revetha back in Qi-Katai, as disaster relief was one of the foremost duties for which they might be called upon. He'd used that training to help get Vel and the others out safely, but though some reckless, desperate part of him wanted to join the wardens and aid in their work, seeking a greater respite in greater action, he forced himself to focus on reclaiming their things instead. *You as good as broke Vel to keep him away from the stables,* he inwardly snarled at himself. *The least you could do is not be a fucking hypocrite by running straight back to the flames.*

Close enough now for his eyes to smart anew from the smoke, Cae pulled his makeshift mask back over his nose and mouth and warily skirted the burning building. The walls and roof were fully alight, bright tongues of fire licking into the dark. The fact that the inn sat on its own, large plot of land instead of directly abutting the neighbouring structures boded well for the wardens and their efforts at containment, but the ground alongside the building was all bare earth, not cobbled stone, and while it was mostly dirt, there was still enough grass to prove potentially hazardous. A few spot fires had already caught; Cae skirted them carefully, scanning the ground, and was finally rewarded by the sight of their bags, tangled in an ungainly spill a bare arm's length from the encroaching flames.

Working quickly, Cae gathered up everything he could see. The tiny stirring of relief he felt on finding the jade-handled knife Vel had given him vanished when, in the next instant, he found the box containing his grandmother's seal. He stared at it for a fraught, pointless moment, half wishing it had been destroyed, half hating himself for wishing so, before resuming his salvage, shoving loose articles into bags regardless of whether they were his or Vel's and coughing all the while. His heart, his lungs: his whole chest hurt. Easier to blame it all on the smoke, for now. Easier to shove clothes into bags than worry if he'd irreparably broken a marriage that had barely even begun, and which—his thoughts were only too keen to remind him—his husband had been forced to in the first place.

A sudden icy panic twined between Cae's ribs, a chilling counterpoint to the fire's radiant heat. What felt like years ago now, when they'd first discussed the practicalities of wedded life, Vel had promised Cae that, should he ever opt for divorce, if Cae was good enough to let him go, then Velasin would register no fault against him. But could that still hold true now, after what Cae had done?

Heart pounding, he shoved the thought aside and forced himself to make his way back to Vel and the others through what was fast becoming a thronging crowd. Awakened by the commotion, the nearby residents of Etho had come to join it, partly to spectate on the unfolding chaos, but mostly to make sure that the blaze wouldn't spread to their homes. There were enough new people milling about that Cae was briefly lost, certain that he'd returned to where he'd left Vel and the others yet unable, despite staring wildly about, to find them.

A strong hand clapped his arm, suddenly enough that, if he hadn't been so focussed on keeping hold of their rescued possessions, he would've dropped them in shock.

"They've moved," said Qarrah, giving Cae's arm a squeeze before releasing him. He stared at her, uncomprehending.

"Moved on from Etho?" he asked—stupidly, given the context, but he couldn't seem to marshal his thoughts beyond the fact that he'd done something terrible, and Velasin ought to want to leave him for it.

"Moved to the roadside, over here," said Qarrah, not unkindly, and proceeded to shepherd him there as if he were a particularly dim-witted lamb separated from its ewe.

Sure enough, once they broke through a milling knot of people to the far edge of the street, there was Vel, sitting on the curb with his head on his knees and his arms around his shins, shivering as Telitha crouched beside him, murmuring into his ear with a hand on his shoulder. Cae dropped his armful of salvaged possessions and stared in an agony of guilt, heart thumping awkwardly. He tried to think of what he could possibly say or do that would constitute an apology, not knowing where to even begin—and then Markel appeared in front of him, as furious as Cae had ever seen him.

Markel glared at him for long enough that Cae's nape began to prickle with sweat, before none-too-gently grabbing his arm and hauling him over to the spill of yellow light beneath a nearby streetlamp, the better to make his hands visible.

"You *left him*!" Markel signed sharply. "Why? Why did you do that? Holding him back, I understand that, but to *leave*?"

"I—" Cae began, a terrible iciness spreading through him, and before he could finish the rest of the sentence, his knees went out like they hadn't since the last time he'd been stabbed. He crumpled with a truly embarrassing lack of grace, half grabbing at Markel's lin on the way down; that steadied him, but still he was left kneeling, staring up at Markel with exhausted, bewildering grief.

"I'm sorry," Cae rasped, throat suddenly tight. "I didn't—I thought—it didn't seem right to touch him again. How could I touch him again?" He let out a noise that was perilously close to a sob and, without meaning to, tipped forwards, resting his head against Markel's thigh in penitence.

A gentle hand settled on his head. Struggling to master himself, Cae sucked in air and rocked back on his heels, reluctantly looking up. He'd feared more anger, but Markel's expression was almost sad as he signed slowly, "You aren't upset with him?"

"What?" Cae stared at him. "What? Why would I be?"

"It's what he fears most," Markel signed. "That all of what he is will prove too much; that you'll tire of him."

"He said that?"

Markel's mouth twitched, the almost-smile a little sad and a lot fond. "He didn't have to."

Cae sat with that a moment, fingers twitching by his sides. "What can I do?" he asked at last.

"Right now?"

"To start with."

"Right now, you can sit with him."

"I can do that," Cae whispered. "I can—yes. All right."

As woozily as if he were drunk, he swayed to his feet, nodded his thanks to Markel and made his way over to Vel. At his approach, Telitha looked up, exchanged a worried look over Cae's shoulder with Markel and then moved aside without a word, an anxious look on her face.

Trembling, Cae sat down beside his husband and tried not to burst into sudden, hysterical laughter at the belated realisation that they were both still practically naked, Vel in his smallclothes and Cae in his hipwrap. The impulse died, however, when he saw the state of Velasin's skin: up close and with the streetlamp's aid, the burns Qarrah had mentioned were all too visible, livid reddish streaks on his arms and ribs where the fire had caught him. He tracked them with his eyes, stomach churning with the desire to soothe, to touch, to do anything that might make his husband feel better—but what right did Cae have to any of that, if Vel no longer wanted him? Despite what Markel had said, his own fears were not so easily assuaged.

"I'm so sorry," Cae croaked, not knowing what else to say. "Vel, I—"

"Don't." His husband's voice was barely a whisper, and yet Cae flinched as if he'd shouted. "Please. Just—don't."

I love you, Cae thought desperately, wanting it to mean something but knowing, in that moment, that it didn't. "What can I do?" he asked, shakily.

Velasin was silent for a long moment. "Clothes," he said finally. "Bring me clothes. If you—please." This last half-swallowed, accompanied by a darting side glance upwards. Had Cae been standing, this would've been enough to fell him: Vel's hooded, gold-grey eyes were reddened with smoke and weeping, yet still so soft that Cae was pierced all over again.

"I can do that," Cae said, and didn't quite scramble to obey, recalling only once he was up that, having gone to the trouble of rescuing them, he'd then proceeded to drop their possessions in the street. A terrible panic seized him as he darted forwards—what if they'd been lost or stolen? what if they were ruined?—before he realised that Telitha, may she live a hundred years in perfect health, had had the good sense to take over where he'd left off, gathering up their sooty, fallen things and setting them in order.

She looked up at Cae's approach, her expression profoundly weary. There were ashy streaks on her cheeks, throat and spectacles, her hair was in total disarray and her clothes scorched in places, but otherwise, she looked mercifully unharmed.

"Thank you," Cae said, nodding to the bags in her lap. "I— thank you."

Telitha quirked a small, rueful smile. "It's a good thing I didn't have that much with me; I doubt that any of it will be salvageable, now."

Cae winced, feeling obscurely guilty for having managed to save his and Vel's possessions but not those of their friends. "Can you, ah—I need clothes, for Velasin. And for me, too," he added belatedly. "Do you mind if I—?"

Wordlessly, Telitha made space for him beside her. Fumble-fingered, Cae pawed through their things, wincing at every smear of soot or grime he left on the fabric, until he had two pairs of nara, two undershirts, two lins and, for himself, a pair of smallclothes, as he could hardly wear the hipwrap in lieu of them. With studied politeness, Telitha looked away as he dressed himself, returning quietly to the work of repacking the bags as Cae took the clothes to Velasin.

His husband looked up at his approach, eyes widening slightly as Cae held out the rucked and crumpled things, as though he thought he'd sent Cae on an impossible mission—and perhaps he had, Cae thought with an uneasy jolt. Snatching the clothes with a mumbled *thanks,* Vel began hurriedly to dress, prompting Cae to stand guard over him. They were both still lamentably barefoot on the increasingly cold ground—he hadn't thought to save their boots—but it was better than nothing.

"I'm done now," Vel said quietly. Cae turned, heart in his throat. There was a smudge of ash high on Vel's left cheekbone, and his unbound hair was wild. The undershirt Cae had given him must've been one of Cae's own, as it was clearly too big on Velasin, the long sleeves draping down over his hands.

He was beautiful.

The night dragged on like a dying horse stuck in its traces. Nobody moved or even spoke, the four of them not-quite-huddled together as the wardens dealt with the fire and such members of the crowd as had homes to go to retreated back indoors. At one point, the town healers, who'd evidently been circulating through the crowds since the very start of the disaster, made their way over to their little group and examined them all, using charms to clear their throats and lungs of smoke and clever glass artifex wands to cleanse and draw the heat from their burns. They looked as exhausted as Cae felt, but smiled wearily when he had the presence of mind to grab for their bags, locate his purse and pay them for their services.

Not long after that, Qarrah appeared by Cae's side like a stocky ghost, making him jump.

"We've got your horses," she said without preamble. "Or we will do soon, if you come with me. Orin's waiting with them now, over there." She tipped her chin back the way she'd come.

At the word *horses,* Velasin jerked like a poorly made puppet and lurched to his feet. "They're alive?" he croaked, and Cae cursed himself for eight kinds of a fool for not having thought to investigate that earlier.

"Alive and well," Qarrah confirmed. "When the stable caught, some of the wardens went in and got them out, then had the bright idea to track down the ostlers, so's there'd be someone around to vouch for who owned which mounts. Tack will have to wait till morning—they've got that part of the fire out, but nobody wants to poke around under an unstable roof in the dark if they can avoid it—but the horses are the main thing. Orin's got ours already, but you need to come and identify yourself before they'll hand yours over."

Velasin moved so fast he almost tripped on the cobbles, scrambling in the direction Qarrah had pointed. Cae hurried after him, as did Qarrah, Markel and Telitha, until they arrived in an open lot in the next street over—a place where itinerant market tents were usually set up—and found a handful of people working to corral a number of agitated horses. Speaking frantically with the nearest ostler, Vel pushed into the herd and then let out a cry as he located Gift. Cae followed more slowly, arriving in time to see his husband fling his arms around the filly's neck and bury his face in her mane.

Forcing himself to look away, he caught the attention of the ostler, a kem in thir fifties who, to Cae's immense relief, remembered their party, and was only too happy to relinquish their string of horses.

"What a night," thei muttered over and over, as thei led Cae and Markel through the herd to unhitch their beasts. "What a night, what a wretched bad night!"

In the time it took them to collect the rest of the horses, Velasin was able to compose himself, leading Gift out to stand by Qarrah, Orin and their two horses just as Cae had begun to worry about extracting him.

"Well then," said Telitha, in the bracingly cheerful tones of the truly exhausted. "Where to now?"

Qarrah exchanged a glance with Orin, then said, "We've sorted some lodgings nearby—it's a barn, not exactly luxurious, but there's a roof and wash-water and it won't be on fire, and the owner said we're welcome to bring along anyone else who's been stranded, so—"

"Gods, that sounds *wonderful*," Cae said fervently. "Lead on, will you?"

So Qarrah did, the lot of them and their horses trudging wearily through the streets. Vel kept apart from everyone else, even Markel, one hand fisted in Gift's silvery mane, his shoulders tightly hunched. Cae ached for him; wanted nothing more than to pull him aside and comfort him until Vel cracked a smile, or at least didn't look so miserable. It was like they'd gone back weeks in time, before Vel had started to warm to him, and yet it was even worse than that, because instead of fear and unfamiliarity, it was Cae's own actions that had frozen things between them.

The barn, when they reached it, was a simple, two-storey structure on the edge of Etho, set close to a lovingly maintained house on a fenced-in property, a single lantern burning in the neat front window. Two cows lowed in startlement at their arrival, setting off the braying of a donkey and an indignant bleating of goats, but when the interlopers proved not to be dangerous, the resident animals settled down again. As the barn itself had limited space for four-legged occupants, Vel, Markel and Orin went to hobble their small herd of horses out in the yard, leaving Cae, Qarrah and Telitha to pick out sleeping spots.

"Me'n Orin will stay by the door," said Qarrah, gesturing to either side of the posts. "It's what we always do in places like this. The owners left us some blankets out back." Without waiting for an answer, she rolled her shoulders and went in search of them.

Telitha glanced around, clearly less familiar with barns as sleeping places. All at once, Cae's throat tightened: he couldn't imagine Vel would want to share a blanket with him, even assuming Qarrah found enough to go around.

"Telitha—" he began, not sure what he was asking for, only to be forestalled by a shake of her head.

"Markel's going to sleep with him," she said. "Not, I mean—not sleep *with* him, sleep with him. Share his bed. Keep him company."

Cae exhaled and nodded, a mix of frustration and disappointment knotted in his throat.

"That . . . that makes sense," he forced himself to say, refusing to acknowledge the undercurrent of jealousy that accompanied the prospect of his husband sleeping with another man, albeit platonically. Even when his sisters—he shied away from naming Laecia in his thoughts, though a terrible pang still racked him with the remembrance—had speculated about the nature of Velasin and Markel's relationship, Cae had never felt threatened by it. In fact, between Cae and Vel, it was Cae that Markel had kissed; admittedly only as part of the traditional game of temptations at their marriage-gathering, but kissed nonetheless. (And it had been a good kiss, too, though under the present circumstances, it felt vaguely treacherous to admit as much.) And Telitha, who was Markel's current paramour, was clearly unbothered, having turned away from Cae to climb the ladder up to the hayloft. Really, what grounds did he have to feel upset about anything?

Before Cae could formulate an answer to his own question, Vel came back in with Orin and Markel, his expression obscured by the soft, dark waves of his unbound hair. Cae wanted to say something, anything, to ease things between them, but before he could think of where to start, Qarrah returned with the blankets, tossing one to Orin before handing two to Markel and one to Cae, a sympathetic look in her eyes.

With a synchronicity born of long practice, Qarrah and Orin settled themselves in their chosen spots on either side of the door, leaving Markel to usher Velasin up to the hayloft. Cae waited a moment to follow them, heart thudding in his chest. The hayloft was small and, true to purpose, quite full of hay; nonetheless, Telitha had managed to clear some space between the bales for the four of them. Velasin was already curled up on a blanket to the far left, bracketed in by Markel; Telitha came next, which left Cae to take the discomfortingly small space to her right. He left as much of a gap between them as he could, a part of him wondering hysterically how much more awkward the arrangement might've been, had Vel still wanted to sleep with him—it hadn't escaped him, the night they'd camped out on the road, how Ralian Vel and Markel had been about being seen with their partners—and yet he would've preferred it a thousand times over to their current state of tension.

"Good night," he murmured—to all of them, but to Velasin especially. Markel turned and signed a weary "You, too," in response, while Telitha's reply was swallowed by a yawn.

Velasin said nothing.

Cae lay down on the hard, rough boards and tugged the blanket over him. Stray pieces of hay dug into his arms and neck, but he lacked the energy to clear them away. He felt cold and sad and heavy, like a sack of mud left out overnight.

Please, he hoped—not praying, exactly, but wishing with all the fervour his exhausted heart could muster—*please let things be better in the morning.* Things often were, if only because you'd had the benefit of a night's rest to reset your brain and such bodily functions as frayed without sleep. There was a chance, however small, that all would be well again on waking.

Cae shut his eyes, the false hope flickering out like a rain-damped candlewick.

He didn't know how to fix this.

7

D awn found them all exhausted from the night's events, as wrung-out and filthy as dishrags. The sun was risen by the time Cae hauled his aching, stiff-limbed body into a sitting position, blinking in the grey light. He propped his back against a haybale, aware that he felt ghastly but not quite remembering why. It was the sort of churning, greasily amorphous shame that usually meant he'd drunk too much the night before and done something stupid, but when he glanced across and saw Telitha, Markel and Velasin all huddled up in their makeshift beds, the pang that went through him was worse than anything he'd ever felt from too much drink. His companions had shifted in the night: Telitha hugged Markel's back, the two of them curved together like spoons in a drawer, while Velasin, whose meagre blanket had fallen off, was balled up like a runty kitten, half-burrowed into the nearest haybale.

Move. I need to move. And yet he was rooted to the spot, obsessively cataloguing the unhappy scrunch of Velasin's brow, the pale, ashy cast to his olive skin, his messy, straw-strewn hair. Vel hadn't looked so unkempt since the day he'd first arrived in Qi-Katai, heartsick and hurting from the same hidden wounds Cae's idiocy of the night before had ripped open again, and after weeks of marriage, Cae knew that, for all his husband was loath to complain about anything real, he hated feeling unclean.

A bath, he thought desperately, coming to his feet. *I'll get him a bath.*

Careful not to disturb the sleepers, Cae shinned down from the hayloft and into the main barn, where he was gratified and yet oddly unsurprised to find that Qarrah and Orin were already awake. After exchanging murmured greetings, he explained his mission. In response, Qarrah led him over to the farmhouse, introduced him to the stocky, sensible woman in charge of it and bartered the loan of her washtub and heatstone and the promise of breakfast for a price which, to Qarrah's annoyance and the woman's clear approval, Cae refused to haggle over. While he returned to the barn and dug out his purse, Orin and Qarrah brought the tub around to the pump and set about filling it, leaving Cae, once he'd paid, with nothing to do but shift awkwardly from foot to foot as Orin worked the pump.

Cae's thoughts spun in desperate search of ways to make himself useful. Could he have their clothes laundered? Regretfully, he was forced to admit that there wasn't enough time, nor would there be much point in trekking back to the ruined inn and seeing if any of the possessions they'd left behind were salvageable. Frustrated, he kicked his heel against the packed dirt of the yard—then froze, recalling all at once that neither he nor Vel had any boots. That was something he could do, surely: go into town and get boots for the pair of them, and maybe even some clothes that weren't smeared with ash.

He was on the brink of striding off to do just that when Qarrah appeared in front of him, one brow raised. "If you're thinking of going anywhere, I'd consider bathing first," she said, giving him a deservedly unfavourable once-over. "Especially if you're planning on buying anything. If I know merchants—and I do, that being my job—the canny ones will've already figured out that anyone who lost their belongings last night while being flush enough to stay at that inn in the first place is an easy mark, desperate for whatever they've got to sell and—" the raised eyebrow became even more judgemental, "—ill-equipped to haggle for it."

"And?" said Cae, far ruder than he'd usually be. The longer he stood still, the more his body itched for motion. "I have plenty of money—"

"—but don't yet know what else you might need to spend it on," Qarrah said firmly. "What if all your tack burned up in the stables? Unless you're planning to walk wherever you're headed, you'll need saddles more than boots. Be patient," she added, this last a tad more gently. "Nobody else is awake yet, and the tub's near full. You could scrub your clothes a bit, too."

Cae opened his mouth. Shut it. Swallowed hard and said, half-mumbled, "Vel should go first."

"Ayla's tits," Qarrah muttered, not unkindly. "You dumb besotted lug, is that what all this is about?"

Cae jerked his head up, cheeks burning. "You don't understand—"

"Easy, easy!" Qarrah put up her hands and waited as Cae calmed. "It's been a rough night all around, I meant no offence."

"Sorry. I just—" Cae tried and failed to keep the pleading out of his voice. "—I need something to *do*."

"You're as bad as Orin," Qarrah grumbled. Sighing, she laced her hands behind her head and stared at the sky a moment. "All right. How's this—I'll guard the bath for your beloved while you go see what's happened to your tack; you hardly need to be clean for *that*. Though I suggest you take at least one horse to carry back whatever's left."

Cae fell on the suggestion with all the fevered gratitude of a starving man on a loaf of bread, and soon departed with a pack-horse on a lead rope, filled with sharp, clean focus as he headed towards the inn.

For Cae, doing something was always better than doing nothing. Introspection was not his friend at the best of times; in the wake of his father's murder and his sister's death, it had swiftly proved unbearable. As such, the project of doing right by Vel—of wooing him, watching him, trying to anticipate his needs—had fast become the cornerstone of Cae's personal equilibrium. He'd thrown himself into tracking down the perfect horse to serve in Quip's stead, not just because Vel deserved the best, but because it was preoccupying. Focussing on what he could do for Velasin was both right and safe: right, because Vel had been betrothed against his will, which made it Cae's responsibility to make their marriage a working partnership, something his husband would want to remain in; safe, because it was the only way to act on his own desires without being monstrously selfish. Propositioning Vel in the garden at Avai had been an exception to this, and all that had done was panic Vel further. Even so, a greedy, desirous part of Cae kept turning the memory over and over in his thoughts: how good it had felt to kneel, the all-encompassing, mind-clearing pleasure of Vel's sweet cock in his throat.

Cae wanted to kneel for Vel again, or Vel to kneel for him; could barely look on the warm, smooth column of Velasin's throat without yearning to see it patterned with marks in the shape of his mouth. He wanted to slide between Vel's thighs and stay there; wanted to lick him open until he was begging for Cae to fill him up and make him wetter still; wanted Vel to shove him down and ride him ragged; wanted those lean, clever fingers to stretch him open at both ends until his head was empty and his cock was spent.

Left unchecked, Cae's wanting would drown them both, and so he contained and channelled those wants like a river diverted through dams and locks—or at least, he had done, until Asa Ivadi's missive had flung them out of his carefully curated plans and towards Qi-Xihan. The road was not distraction enough from everything Cae was trying to ignore, and now he'd done exactly what he feared the most and inflicted yet more pain on his husband. That Cae still wanted—horribly, achingly, viscerally—to take Vel to bed and stay there until the world went away felt newly grotesque, and yet he could no more stamp out his desires than pluck the moons from the sky.

Every day since Laecia's betrayal, Cae had woken aching with grief and guilt that were growing harder to set aside. His sister was a murderer; she'd killed their father and been killed in turn, but her death brought no justice to anyone. There was only numbness, a creeping pain that said it was somehow all his fault; that if he'd only loved her better, known her more, understood how much magic mattered to her—how much she wanted from life, and what she was prepared to do to get it—things never would have come to this. The day they'd stumbled unwittingly into Laecia's alliance with Ren Adan, Vel had wanted to flee—what if Cae had heeded him then? They'd caught Laecia by surprise; if they'd run for the street instead of staying inside to talk—if she hadn't had time to steel herself to using her magic—how different might things be now?

Those and other, sharper questions circled Cae's thoughts like vultures above a dying beast, readying their talons. But Cae had trained as a soldier; he knew how to keep his guard up. Though part of him had braced for a difficult errand, in the end, the process was surprisingly swift: true to Qarrah's report and with the notable exception of the roof, the stables remained largely whole. The wardens had made fast work of clearing them, and the ostlers had a system in place for knowing which belongings went with which patrons. Aside from being ashy and a little charred in places, all their gear was intact, including their camping equipment, the bulk of Markel's personal possessions and every other practical thing they'd locked away with the saddles instead of bringing inside.

Until it was returned to him, Cae hadn't realised how much they'd been in danger of losing, and tipped both ostlers and wardens extravagantly for its safe return. It took a bit more doing to get everything originally meant for seven mounts onto the back of one, but it was the kind of challenge he welcomed, and eventually, both he and the horse were ready for the return journey, laden like a pair of tinker's mules.

By the time they made it back to the farm, Cae was ferociously hungry, and could only nod wordless gratitude at Orin when, on seeing him arrive, the taciturn man took the reins of his horse, cocked a thumb towards the barn and said, "Go eat breakfast. I'll take care of this."

It was only when Cae strode into the barn that he realised—or remembered, rather—that Vel would be there, too; Vel, who'd barely spoken a word to him since falling from Cae's grasp.

Cae froze up on the threshold like a wagon whose wheels were jammed, staring uselessly at the barn's interior. An upturned crate had been dragged out to serve as a table, on which rested a pitcher of fresh milk and six clay cups, baked eggs with peppers and goat's cheese, and a tray of steaming bread rolls. Four mismatched stools were spaced around the crate, three of them occupied by Telitha, Markel and Velasin, while Qarrah leaned against the wall, chewing meditatively on a roll.

Cae's stomach rumbled. The obvious thing to do was to take the spare stool—presumably vacated by Orin—but that would mean sitting next to Velasin, who would be within his rights not to want Cae within a hundred yards of him, let alone so close—

Vel glanced up, eyes widening as they latched on Cae, who was helpless not to look back. Vel's unbound hair was damp, a few drying tendrils stuck to his throat and jaw. He was still washed out with exhaustion, and there were dark bags under his hooded eyes, but his lips were full and ruddy, partially in contrast to his unusual pallor but mostly as if he'd been biting them (Cae wanted to bite them), and his undershirt, worn without a lin, skewed open at the throat, revealing its water-sheened hollow. He was damp all over, Cae realised, enough that the undershirt was sticking to him, the white fabric gleaming translucent where it pressed against his skin, and yet it hung loose at the wrists, slewing high on one shoulder while all but falling off the other—

"That's my shirt," Cae blurted stupidly, the realisation hitting him low in the gut.

Velasin flushed—that beautiful, dusky blush that ran from neck to navel. "I'm sorry," he said, voice low; he dropped his gaze, hands twitching against the fabric. "I can change it—"

"Please don't," said Cae, aware he sounded desperate but not able, quite, to regret it. He swallowed, taking half a step forwards, and all at once became conscious that, while Telitha, Markel and

Qarrah were courteously pretending not to listen, they were none-theless an audience. "I—Vel. Can we speak? Outside?"

"Of course," said Velasin, after a beat. He rose shakily, lean body silhouetted within the too-big shirt—his nara, at least, appeared to be his own, a fitted blue pair designed to be tucked into rid-ing boots, though his feet were bare—and made his way to Cae, who was so arrested by the sight that it took him an embarrassing two seconds to recall that he, too, was meant to move. Ears and neck burning, he turned on his heel and headed outside, away from where Orin was sorting the tack and towards the washtub.

Cae stared down at the water as they came to a halt, acutely aware of Vel's presence at his elbow. He hadn't cared before about being filthy, but felt a sudden, unaccustomed pang of self-consciousness about it now. The feeling lodged in his breastbone like an oily, unpopped bubble as he sucked in breath and turned to face his husband.

"I'm sorry—"

They both stopped, equally startled, for both of them had spo-ken, the doubled words overlapping in an eerie-awkward sync. Cae felt as if he'd been boxed about the ears, or possibly as if he were drunk. He stared at Velasin, bewildered anxiety skittering up his throat like a half-swallowed spider as his husband's face closed over.

"You've—what? Vel, you don't—you have nothing to apolo-gise for, it's—it was me, I was—I grabbed you like that, I can't—I should've known better, I shouldn't have—"

"Do not," said Vel, with such a note of quiet, angry command that Cae's mouth snapped shut, a reflexive shiver running up his spine, "condescend to me in this." His jaw worked soundlessly for a moment, fists clenched by his sides, and when he spoke again, it was with a measured, halting vehemence, as though each word were snaring its barbs on his tongue. "I am acutely aware of my failings in this matter. I behaved like a child, but that doesn't mean you must coddle me like one."

Stricken, Cae tried to reach for him. "Vel—"

"No." His husband stepped back to avoid Cae's touch, throat bobbing as he swallowed; Cae tracked the motion helplessly even as the rejection seared him, hand falling dead to his side. "No, Caethari. I am—I have been—I have already imposed too deeply on your good nature, but no more. Not for this." He looked away, face cast in a woundingly handsome profile, and said quietly, bitterly, "Haven't I cost you enough already?"

Cae's throat dried up like a river in drought. He wanted to deny it, wanted to offer whatever comfort would melt the rigid unhappiness from Velasin's posture, but suddenly his thoughts were full up with the memory of Laecia bursting their father's heart in his chest, blood weeping from his eyes; of Laecia screaming, consumed by fire as Markel's arrow pierced her through the head. *It's not his fault,* Cae yelled within his thoughts, *Vel didn't ask for any of this, it was Laecia's doing—*

But would it have happened without him? asked the treacherous, aching voice of Cae's squashed-down grief. Not just grief, he realised a heartbeat later, but anger, too; and hurt, at Vel's rejection of him. Cae tried to wrestle it out of himself—it wasn't Velasin's fault; he was entitled to keep his distance—but all the while, something spiked and ugly was rising within him, refusing his efforts to swallow it down, so that what finally spilled from his mouth was, "What is it you want from me?"

The words came out raw. For a moment, Vel's eyes flashed with something like shock, or possibly sympathy; then his face shuttered again, a practiced mask whose polite neutrality made Cae want to scream, and before Vel could answer, Cae found himself barrelling on with, "I know you didn't choose me, or us, or any of this. I know I'm not what you wanted, but I'm trying—I'm trying so *fucking* hard, Vel, and I can't—what is it I'm doing wrong?" That plaintive note was back in his voice, and this time, it made him wince with an embarrassment that didn't even have the decency to render him mute. "What else can I do? What else should I be doing?"

"Nothing," said Velasin, the single word brittle and clipped.

"This is not—" he abruptly slipped into Ralian, the way he only did when he was overwhelmed or truly upset, "—my failings are not a puzzle you can finesse into nonexistence. I am as I am, and I'm sorry for both our sakes to have such burdensome neuroses—"

"*You are not a fucking burden!*" Cae shouted. Frustration boiled within him; he had the maddening sense that they were somehow having two different conversations, which made him want to grab Vel's shoulders and shake him until some sense fell out. For a moment, the desire was so strong that his hands twitched abortively upwards; seeing this, alarm flashed over Vel's face, and Cae stepped back as if he'd been struck, abruptly sick and furious with it. "You're not a burden," he said again—more calmly, he hoped, though his voice strained with the effort. "And last night was not your fault."

The edge of Vel's smile was sharp enough to cut. "You saying that doesn't make it true."

"No, you're right. The fact that it's true makes it true."

The smile slipped away, replaced by something nearer to anger. "Stop it, Cae."

"I won't."

"I told you, I won't be coddled—"

"You think this is coddling?"

"I think I'm sick of being pitied!"

"Pity?" Cae ran a frustrated hand through his hair. "What's wrong with you, that you can't tell the difference between care and pity?"

Velasin stilled. "You know exactly what's wrong with me."

Cae swore. "I didn't mean it like that—"

"Maybe not, but it's the first honest thing you've said today."

Hot and cold anger washed through Cae, a ripple of ugly sensation. "I am not a *liar.*"

"You're delusional," Vel snapped, two bright spots of colour staining his cheeks. "Everybody lies."

"You certainly do," snarled Cae, "and to nobody more than yourself!"

Vel jerked as if he'd been slapped. "What's that supposed to mean?"

Cae hardly knew, except that some part of him evidently did, because what came out in answer was, "You think you're alone in suffering; that all your hurts make you monstrous beyond sympathy, and in that hurt, you bite and snap at anyone trying to help you like a stray with a broken leg. Meanwhile, I've lost my father, my sister, and now I'm being dragged into my grandmother's mess, and still you're picking a fight with me for the crime of caring about you! I am so *fucking* tired," Cae rasped, and was horrified to feel the warning heat of tears behind his eyes. He blinked them back furiously, swallowing and swallowing around what felt like a whole throatful of thorns, until he regained control of himself. "I don't want to fight with you, Vel, least of all about this." He pinched the bridge of his nose, ashamed and drained and wishing—deeply, fervently—for a comprehensible enemy he could swing a sword at, instead of these treacherous verbal battles that sprang up from nowhere and stung like nettle-rash. "Please. I thought at least—had we not agreed to be friends?"

"We did," Vel whispered. He looked pale now, though Cae was so overwrought himself that he didn't know at what point during his outburst it had happened. "I—I'm sorry, Cae."

Whatever fight was left in Cae went out of him in a rush. "Vel—"

"Thank you, for recovering our things. We should—I should go and saddle the horses. Don't want to overstay our welcome." He managed a tremulous smile that didn't meet his eyes. "You should wash up. You did so much last night, and I didn't—" his breathing hitched awfully, "—moons, I never even thanked you for getting us out of there, did I?"

"You don't need to thank me—"

"Thank you," said Vel, and before Cae could stop him, he slipped in under his guard and brushed a fleeting kiss against his cheek. Dumbstruck, Cae almost didn't react in time, with the result that Vel was already moving away when Cae grabbed his waist to reel him back in again. For half a heartbeat, he wasn't sure what he'd meant to do; then Vel's gaze dropped to his mouth, lingering just a fraction too long to be incidental, and Cae was helpless not to kiss him about it. Vel let out a little shocked noise that tapered into a whine as their mouths pressed together—lightly at first, Cae conscious that Vel might pull away, but deepening when he didn't. When Vel kissed back, it was with a sudden, shocking fervour, dizzying Cae with the effort of keeping pace. He squeezed Vel's hips, hands stroking up along his flanks as Vel's fingers laced together around the nape of Cae's neck, and for a brief, exquisite instant, everything felt right.

Then Vel pulled away with a stuttered gasp, his fingertips leaving sparks in their wake as they skittered across Cae's shoulders. They stared at each other, Cae in a daze and Vel with an expression on his face that Cae couldn't begin to interpret. For several seconds, neither of them spoke. Then:

"Good!" Vel said—in Ralian, his voice higher than usual. "That's—thank you. Yes. I'll just—horses. Good." And before Cae could parse what any of this meant, Vel turned on his heel and hurried away to . . . wherever the horses were, presumably, leaving Cae half-hard and achingly confused.

"What," he whispered, touching two fingertips to his bottom lip. "*What.*"

The only answer came from a nanny-goat hitched to a nearby fence, whose unexpected bleat was so loud that Cae jumped half a foot in the air in shock, not having known she was there. Recovering somewhat, he glared at the goat. The goat stared back impassively with eerie yellow goat-eyes, made a sort of hissing noise and bleated again before returning her attention to a tempting clump of grass.

Feeling more than a little insane, Cae walked to the washtub, knelt down beside it, dunked his head in the water and screamed, producing a rush of bubbles. This made him feel marginally better, and so he stripped off his filthy clothes, clambered awkwardly in—the tub was not quite big enough for a man of his proportions, but he could sit with his knees scrunched up—and set about scrubbing himself with punishing vigour. He was still doing this when Qarrah reappeared; her brows shot up to her hairline, and Cae, who was ordinarily deeply unembarrassed by incidental nudity, startled so wildly that he almost capsized the tub.

"Well," said Qarrah. "I suppose that answers that question."

What question? Cae pointedly didn't ask. Instead, he ventured, "I don't suppose you could bring me one of my bags, would you? And possibly a towel? I didn't quite think this through." He smiled his most charming smile, or tried to; under the circumstances, it doubtless fell a bit flat. Qarrah gave him a searching look that was rather reminiscent of the goat's, then rolled her eyes.

"You're lucky I'm a soft touch," she said, and proved it by bringing him not only what he'd requested, but also his second-best pair of boots, which had evidently been packed with the rest of their gear in the stables; Cae was slightly embarrassed to realise he'd forgotten about them completely.

"Thank you," he said, and dressed himself within short order, whereupon Qarrah, with all the finely honed instincts of a prize sheepdog, herded him back towards the impromptu breakfast table, standing over him sternly until he had some milk and eggs and bread—all of which were extremely good, if no longer quite as warm as they'd been. By the time he was done, he felt more human than he had at any point since he'd woken to find the inn on fire, and all at once, he became belatedly conscious of how much they all owed to Qarrah and Orin, without whose intercession they probably would've spent the night on the roadside and the morning in cold, tired panic. Certainly, there wouldn't have been half so fine a breakfast, and Cae said as much as he rambled out his thanks.

Qarrah only laughed and clapped him on the shoulder.

"It works out an even trade, really," she said with a grin. "Looking after you lot gave us something useful to do; me'n Orin would've probably thrown our backs out wrestling over who had the warmer blanket otherwise."

"Where are you headed next?" Cae asked. "If you're headed north—"

Qarrah gave a regretful shake of her head. "Sorry," she said. "North is where we came from, or north-west, if you're being technical. We'll probably head for the border; maybe do some snouting about for trade opportunities in Qi-Katai, now the Ralian border's opening up again."

"Really?" said Telitha, materialising as if from thin air. To Cae's relief, he wasn't alone in his startlement at her sudden appearance; Qarrah jumped, too, and looked instantly cross about it. "When are you headed out?"

"Not long after you, I'd imagine," Qarrah answered. "Why do you ask?"

Telitha bit her lip. "It's just—if it's not too much trouble, could I ride with you? I'm headed back myself, and after last night . . ." Her voice trailed away.

Qarrah blinked in surprise. "You're not headed to Qi-Xihan?"

"Oh!" said Telitha. "No, no, I was just—I came to see Markel off, but I've duties to get back to." She hesitated, looking as uncertain as Cae had ever seen her. "I understand if you'd rather not, but—"

Qarrah scoffed, cutting her off. "Don't be ridiculous. Of course you can ride with us!"

As Telitha and Qarrah fell into conversation, Cae felt absurdly blindsided. In all the uproar, he'd somehow forgotten that Telitha was only coming with them as far as Etho. He felt a strange pang at the forthcoming loss; he liked Telitha, and even if he hadn't, he felt increasingly awkward about travelling alone with Vel and Markel when he hardly knew what his husband thought of him. He liked Markel, too, but his friendship with Vel predated Vel's marriage to Cae by a solid decade; if said marriage was unsettled, there was no question as to whose side Markel would take.

And things *were* unsettled, Cae realised with a lurch. For all that they'd argued, relented and reached some sort of equanimity—for all the desperate heat of that last, plundered kiss—he still didn't know how things stood between them. It perturbed him, that they'd ended with Vel apologising when Cae was ultimately the one at fault; and yet he wasn't sure that the apology had been fully unmerited, either. It was all a maddening snarl of uncertainty, and as he contemplated the distance they had yet to travel to Qi-Xihan, Cae's heart sank to think that unravelling it might take a similar length of time, or—saints!—even longer.

Cae smiled grimly, sighed, and squared himself to the task.

If nothing else, he was good at moving forwards.

8

They departed the farmstead within the hour, riding together as far as the main road before Telitha, Qarrah and Orin turned back towards Avai, leaving Cae, Vel and Markel, once they'd said their goodbyes—quite passionately, in the case of Markel and Telitha—to carry on north. They didn't talk aloud or in signs, Markel because he was mourning his lover's departure, and Cae and Vel because—well. For any number of reasons.

More than once that morning, they passed or were passed by fellow survivors of the burning inn, distinguished as such by their weary expressions and scorched belongings. Far too belatedly, Cae realised he didn't know if there'd been any deaths. He might've asked the wardens when he'd reclaimed their tack, but he'd been too preoccupied; the question simply hadn't occurred to him, and now it was too late. His ignorance bred a squirming guilt, the feeling sharp enough that he broke their self-imposed silence to say, "How many died, I wonder?"

"Ten," said Vel, softly. "Though they only found nine bodies; it's presumed there must be nothing left of the tenth."

Cae startled, not having expected an answer. The pit in his stomach deepened. "Ten?"

Vel nodded but didn't look at him, his fingers twined in Gift's silvery mane. "We had it from the farmwife while you were getting the saddles; she was up before us and heard it in town. Ten deaths, the wardens said: three patrons—or four, including the one whose body was unrecoverable—two maids, an undercook, the barman, an ostler and the boy who swept the stairs."

"Oh," said Cae, bleakly.

They fell silent again, the plodding of the horses a slow, rhythmic counterpoint to the building churn of the Eshi as they headed downhill from the higher ground on which Etho was built. The river would fork soon, the main flow twisting away north-west while its smaller tributary, the Nihri, turned south-east, to wend and narrow before vanishing (mostly) underground in the wetlands southwest of Qi-Katai. Cae knew this, not because he'd spent much time studying the map, which was now in Markel's keeping, but from past experience. A decade ago, heavy spring rains had caused both the Eshi and Nihri to burst their banks, flooding the surrounding farmlands, and as certain of them fell within Qi-Katai's jurisdiction, Cae's revetha had been dispatched to aid in disaster relief. His abiding memory was of wet, cold muck that stank strongly of bloated livestock and rotten grain, not the pleasant, late-autumn morning through which they were currently riding, and as such, he tried to take some pleasure from his surroundings.

After hours spent riding down the gentle, occasionally twisting incline, the road rose again, so that their first view of the river-fork came as they crested the subsequent rise. To their left, the Eshi churned with the onset of rocks and rapids, the water a cheerful roar as it galloped away from them, while directly ahead, the slimmer, calmer Nihri blocked their path, a shining silver ribbon laid across the land. The ferry station was off to the right, capitalising on the fact that the Nihri was narrower at its start, while the ferry itself—a broad, sturdy flatboat guided by a rope across the river and steered by pole—was just returning from the far bank.

Obliged to wait, they dismounted and ambled over to the station, a neat, two-room building set just back of a well-maintained jetty, complete with a trough and hitching-post. As the horses drank, Cae felt wistful about the prospect of lunch, but only briefly; no sooner had the thought occurred than Vel and Markel produced a meal from their saddlebags. It was the same bread they'd had at breakfast, along with some ham and hard-boiled eggs, cold and plain but nonetheless good, and Cae was slightly ashamed to realise they must've bought it from the farmwife while he'd been preoccupied. It was something he ought to have thought of, and while he was grateful to have the meal regardless, he mentally chastised himself for the lapse, his mental voice sounding eerily like Nairi's.

By the time they'd finished eating, the flatboat was just pulling into dock, bearing two merchants, two donkeys and a stout, strong-looking woman with a heavily laden basket hoisted on her back. Cae watched the disembarkation with idle interest: the ferry was manned by a man and woman whose powerful shoulders, weathered brown skin and strikingly identical features marked them as siblings rather than spouses, the pair moving with practiced ease. Unlike other such craft that Cae had seen, the flatboat had no central cabin or roofed structure: though fenced in with railings on all four sides, the boat was otherwise completely open, designed to carry the largest amount of horses and cargo with minimum obstruction. The gangplank lay flat on the deck until it was needed, a wooden board sturdy and broad enough that neither donkey baulked at the transition to the jetty, and just like that, the passengers were on their way, sparing little more than a glance for the newcomers.

"Welcome!" said the sister, grinning as she waved them over. "Passage for three, yes?"

"That's right," said Cae.

"Excellent! I'm Amra, and this is my brother, Emas." She cocked a thumb over her shoulder, and Emas, who was coiling a rope on deck, looked up to give them a wave. "Passage is four seroi per person, plus one extra for each additional horse, though we do sometimes take trade in lieu of coin! Payment up front, a smooth ride guaranteed." She beamed at them.

Nodding, Cae pulled out his purse and paid.

"My thanks," said Amra, flashing a grateful smile as she tucked the coins into her leather belt-pouch. The stitching gleamed blue as she cinched it tight, signalling the presence of some clever charm or cantrip to protect against theft. Nor did it escape Cae's notice, as Emas approached to help load the horses onto the boat, that both siblings were armed, albeit discreetly: a short, thick cosh hung from Amra's belt, while Emas carried a sheathed knife. Intellectually, he knew, such precautions made sense—even in a prosperous, well-travelled area such as this, ferries and those who worked them were vulnerable to predation—but all the same, a frisson of unease ran up his spine. His sword was still bundled away on one of the packhorses; had he been less distracted that morning, he might've thought to buckle it at his hip, and resolved to do so once they'd crossed the river.

Gift pranced nervously as she walked down the gangplank, slender ears laid back along her head at the unfamiliar rolling of the flatboat. Vel petted and soothed her as Emas brought the other horses aboard, and Cae, who felt rather in need of some soothing himself, stared pointedly down at the water while telling himself he wasn't remotely jealous of a *horse*.

With Vel's attention firmly elsewhere, Markel sidled up next to him, one eyebrow raised. "Are things well between you?" he signed discreetly.

Flushing, Cae snuck a glance over his shoulder to confirm Vel's preoccupation before signing back, "I hope so." He hesitated, then added, "He confuses me. I'm afraid to do the wrong thing, but I don't know what that is, and I'm not sure he knows what he wants from me, either."

Markel snorted. "That sounds about right."

In the scant time since Cae had first committed to learning Markel's signs, he'd worked at it with the same intense focus he'd once brought to studying swordplay, but even with daily practice, there were limits to how quickly he could learn. Markel's shorthand sign alphabet, which he'd modified to better work with Tithenai, had proven a godsend, enabling him to sign with a rough degree of fluency while still learning. Not even Vel had known about the project before Markel brought it up, though he'd been astonished and delighted as he translated Markel's explanation of it aloud: a desire to make basic sign easier, so that more people could learn a little and still communicate effectively.

Sign-speech, he said, originated in Attovar, which nation's alphabet was almost identical the Ralian one, and it was this alphabet that Cae had originally learned as a way to spell out words he didn't know. Communicating letter by letter was slow and cumbersome in any language, but the Attovari-Ralian alphabet was particularly poorly suited to spelling Tithenai words, and once Markel had realised this, he'd tweaked his invented system to account for it.

The basis of the thing was an expanded alphabet, including unique signs for common syllable sounds and letter pairings, as well as a way to pair vowels and consonants within the same sign, the reading order determined by which hand was used for which part, with modifying gestures to indicate things like plurals and doubled letters. Truthfully, Cae didn't understand the formal linguistic underpinnings of it all, though Vel had tried to explain it to him—he'd been writing it all down at the time, so beautifully flushed with enthusiasm that it was a miracle Cae recalled anything else—but the practical upshot was that, after some trial and error, several days of hard work and when combined with an exhaustively drilled set of existing signs for basic terms, he and Markel could now communicate with far more ease than previously. Long-term, of course, it was still better to know the full language, but for now, he was exceedingly glad to be able not just to talk to Markel, but to hear him.

In the present, Markel chewed his lip, considering. Hesitantly, he signed, "I can't tell you what to do; I can only ask that you keep being patient with him. He's never known someone like you, and whenever he's uncertain about something he wants, he ties himself up in knots over it."

"He's not the only one," Cae muttered, unable to suppress a tiny thrill of hope at the idea of *something he wants.*

Markel flashed him a sympathetic look, softened with a grin

made more boyish than usual by the fact that, at some point that morning, he'd taken the time to shave. Cae, who hadn't, felt suddenly aware of his own dark stubble, and was about to venture an inane comment to that effect when Amra called out, "Casting off!"

The deck rocked slightly beneath their feet as they moved away from the jetty. Amra poled the flatboat into the river and Emas hauled them along the rope, helping to keep the ferry on a set course. The synchronicity between the siblings was compelling to watch: Emas timed each pull to match the deep push of Amra's pole, so that the craft moved smoothly and slowly forwards.

As Gift finally grew accustomed to these strange new circumstances, Vel let her be and came to stand beside Markel. It would've been a simple thing to stay, but Cae abruptly lost his nerve and hurried back to check on his own horse, a highly unnecessary action as Alik, unlike Gift, was completely unfazed by the boat, head down as he contemplated whether the planking was edible. Still, Cae stroked his neck and checked the girth—it was, of course, fine—before finally taking a deep, steadying breath and resuming his spot at the front rail, this time alongside Vel rather than Markel, but with a cautious gap left between them.

Vel glanced at him, bit his lip, then looked back out at the Nihri. Cae felt like he'd been doused with cold water. The strength of his desire for Vel kept taking him aback; he wanted so much that it made his whole body feel awkward and somehow off-balance, the way it hadn't since he was thirteen or so, as if his hands were useless, oversized paws at the end of his wrists. It had been struggle enough since their marriage, but after what he'd done last night, he didn't deserve his fantasies, no matter what Vel said. He wanted to move, hands itching for the jade-handled knife at his belt. If he'd only been able to fling it at a target, or at least to flip it from hand to hand . . . but there were no targets on the ferry, and while it was years since he'd dropped a knife, in his present state, he didn't trust himself not to fumble the blade straight into the saints-cursed river.

Talk to him, Cae told himself, as Markel moved away to take his turn with the horses. *Say something! Anything!* But all he could think of was their abortive kiss outside the barn that morning, and nothing about it made him want to *talk*.

In desperate search for inspiration, he stared at the far bank, which was rapidly drawing closer; in the time he'd spent introspecting, the practiced efforts of Emas and Amra had brought them just past the midway point of the Nihri. The station and jetty on the far side were perfect mirrors of their counterparts, appearing equally neat and well-maintained. There was a flattish, slightly sandy loading area beyond the jetty, and then the road began again, framed on both sides by the same tall, still-canopied trees that extended right to the riverbank—

Something flashed in the foliage, a bright incongruity against the red and orange leaves. For a moment, Cae thought he'd confused himself, that it was light on the water or river-spray catching the sun, but then he saw it again: a tiny wink of reflective brightness that had no business being where it was.

A strange, honeyed sensation crept over him, as though time had slowed for him alone. As if from a distance, he recalled his earlier awareness of the vulnerability of ferries, the arms the siblings carried and the absence of his sword, Qarrah's talk of bandits and watchtowers; remembered, too, that Laecia and her co-conspirator Ren Adan had initially tried to have Vel killed with a crossbow. And then he moved—impulsively, instinctively, just as his body had yearned to do since the moment he'd stepped on the ferry— and lunged towards Vel, grappling him around the shoulders and flinging them both to the deck.

Something clipped Cae's left ear as he fell, a whistling sharpness almost lost in Vel's frightened yelp, the thud of their bodies hitting the wood; and then he felt the warm trickle of blood down his neck, and knew with chilling certainty that he'd been right.

"Ware archer!" Cae bellowed, rising to his knees as he hauled Vel away from the railing. For a terrifying moment, he thought Vel might panic again, but instead he moved with alacrity, scrambling onto his rear and letting Cae move him aside. Cae curled himself around Vel, aiming to set his back to the water in lieu of a shield, and grunted when a second arrow thudded into the meat of his shoulder.

"No no no no, Cae, fuck!" Vel swore, gripping Cae's lin with both hands and trying to drag him vaguely towards the centre of the flatboat, which, to the immense credit of the siblings, was not only still moving forwards, but doing so at a faster clip than previously.

"Stay down!" Amra called grimly, exerting herself to greater effort as Emas matched her stroke for stroke. "We're sitting ducks on the water!"

A third arrow whizzed by, this one missing Cae and Vel by a hairsbreadth. Cae had just enough time to think that their burst of speed had fouled the archer's aim before Vel, who'd been muttering in low, indecipherable panic, yelled out, "Markel! The gangplank!"

Shoulder throbbing, Cae whipped his head around to watch as Markel hauled up the broad, flat gangplank and bore it over to them, thumping it down on the long edge and then propping it up at an angle to serve as a makeshift shield. He was just in time: no sooner had he tipped it back than a fourth arrow drove itself so far into the wood that the head protruded from the other side, a bare handspan from Cae's forehead.

Cae stared at Vel, who was still clutching his lin, a manic look on his face. "They can't have you," Vel hissed fiercely, giving Cae a little shake. "They *cannot have you,* do you hear me?"

"They won't," said Cae, and dared to set one of his hands over Vel's two, squeezing gently. And then, because this felt an important point, "But Vel, they were aiming at you, too."

Velasin paled, but whatever he might've said was cut off by a cry of pain from Emas; an arrow had sprouted in his leg, but even as he dropped to one knee, he didn't lose his grip on the rope, continuing to haul them across with bloody-minded determination.

Cae's thoughts, frozen until that moment, whirred into action. Five shots, not in a flurry but spaced to suggest a single archer, a theory backed up by the single gleam he'd seen in the trees. Which meant that, once they docked—if they docked—and their assailant was still aloft, whoever it was would be trapped, with no clean way to escape: a scenario that any competent bandit would much prefer to avoid. Sucking in air, Cae dared a peek over the top of the gangplank and, sure enough, caught a flash of motion in the trees, as of a person descending at speed.

"They're running," he said, pitching his voice to carry to the siblings but not—he hoped—to their attacker. Gritting his teeth, he reached across his body, snapped the shaft of the arrow in his shoulder in half, and readied himself to run.

"Docking!" Amra called, hoarse with exhaustion, and before either Vel or Markel could stop him, Cae leapt to his feet, drew the jade-handled knife from its sheath, ran across the deck and leapt to the jetty. Pelting down the weathered boards to the loading area, he was just in time to see a brown-clad stranger with a bow and quiver over their shoulders leap into the saddle of a horse left hidden in the trees. Snapping the reins violently against the animal's neck, they urged it into a gallop; Cae shouted and briefly gave chase, but even as he pulled his arm back for a knife-throw, he knew it was too late. He was forced to stop, glaring at the retreating cloud of dust kicked up in the bandit's wake.

Furious, he turned and jogged back to the ferry, and arrived to find the boat tied up and the gangplank laid out—still with the arrow sticking from its edge—as Amra, her undershirt dark with sweat, cradled her brother's head in her lap.

"I've been shot before," said Emas, wincing an attempt at a smile. "I'll be fine."

"I couldn't catch them," Cae said, throat tight with failure.

"You were on foot," Vel said, coming to stand in front of him. His expression was tense with worry, gaze fixated on the arrow-stump still protruding from Cae's shoulder. He raised a hand, half-extended as if he wanted to touch, then let it drop. "You could hardly have run down a horse."

"If I'd had the sense to grab Alik and ride straight after him—"

"—then you'd have been an idiot," Vel said bluntly. "First, you're injured; second, you would've lost nearly as much time as we already have getting mounted on land, with no way to know if whoever that was had left the road or hidden while you went past them; third, you'd be leaving the rest of us behind; and fourth, no."

Cae's lips twitched. "No?"

"No," Vel said firmly. And then he swallowed, a horrible look of guilt on his face, and reached up to touch the stinging nick in Cae's ear, a fleeting brush of his fingertip against the tacky blood. "They already came far closer than I'd like."

Cae didn't know what to say to that, and was mercifully saved from having to reply by the snorting of the horses, which prompted a flushing Vel to duck his head and hurry back onto the flatboat, the better to help Markel unload them.

"How far is the next town?" he asked Amra, carefully leading Gift onto the jetty. Whatever nerves the filly had felt on boarding evidently didn't extent to arrows, and she disembarked calmly, uncaring of human drama.

"Just a few miles down the road," Amra replied. She bit her lip. "There's a healer there, but I can't leave the ferry untended—if you could send them on to us when you arrive—"

"We can take Emas there," Cae said gently. "He can ride one of the packhorses. Can't he?" he added, flashing a hopeful glance at first Vel and then Markel, who knew more about the arrangement of their luggage.

"It's the least we can do," Vel said. He was speaking to Amra, but his gaze was on Cae, only flicking to her at the last minute. "After all you both did to get us ashore."

"I'd appreciate that," said Amra. A look of worry crossed her face. "Though . . . what if whoever that was tries again further on? Bandits don't usually work alone; there could be more waiting to pick you off."

"I don't think that's likely," Cae said, seeing Velasin flinch. "I mean . . . it's possible, but if they had numbers, it would've been better tactically to ambush us here, before we had time to mount up." He frowned.

"I suppose that makes sense," Amra said, looking worriedly at her brother. "Like Emas said, we've dealt with bandits before, but not recently. They normally target merchant convoys, not random travellers."

Markel clicked his fingers twice: his polite request to talk. Though Amra didn't know what it meant, she turned to face him, expectant, as did everyone else; even Emas lifted his head to see.

As Markel signed, Vel translated aloud. "Markel says, he doesn't think this was a bandit attack, though it was meant to look like one." His voice shook slightly. "He thinks we'll be fine on the road, but that, wherever we stay the night, we should take turns keeping watch and—" he faltered, "—beware of further attacks."

The realisation hit Cae like a numbing fist to the stomach. He stared at Vel, who stared back in helpless dismay. The archer had targeted *them*, only shooting Emas once they'd taken refuge behind the gangplank. Their assailant wasn't a bandit, but an assassin.

Someone was trying to kill them.

9

The afternoon passed in a blur of pain and tension. Though Cae took the precaution of reclaiming his sword and was, despite the reassurances he'd made to Amra and Velasin, half-prepared to be attacked once they left the ferry, they made it to the next town without incident. The local healer, a short, stocky man whose braided beard reached almost to his feet, took one look at Emas and ordered him inside to lie down, the better to have the damage assessed; Cae's shoulder, by contrast, he dealt with smartly, pulling out the arrowhead and the embedded fabric both with a murmured charm and a practiced flick of his wrist. He hummed and poked at the wound to be sure, used a combination of magic and alcohol to clean it—the latter stung considerably more than the former; Cae grit his teeth to keep from hissing at the sharp, burning pain—and then wrapped it in a clean bandage. The nick in Cae's ear he healed almost as an afterthought, accepting Vel's coin for his services with a brisk, efficient nod before going back into his home to tend to Emas.

With their duty to the ferryman discharged, they consulted Markel's map and agreed to push on to the next small hamlet, believing they could make it before dark. They rode faster than usual, alternating between a canter over the flattest stretches of road and walking in between, the three of them acutely aware of the threat of ambush. They didn't discuss their assailant or the reason they'd been targeted, though Cae felt grimly conscious of his grandmother's seal. After everything that had happened since Velasin's arrival in Tithena, it felt only logical that some unknown faction was willing to kill for control of his grandmother's yaserate, though the prospect was so depressing that Cae lacked the will to speculate as to their identities.

Laecia would've known exactly who stood to inherit in the event of both their deaths with Riya already raised to the tierency, but Laecia was dead. The thought punched through him more surely than the arrow had, a grief that refused to go away. He'd never wanted to play these games; would he ever be free of them now?

The next town, when they reached it, was little more than a cluster of buildings around an open square with a public well. They spent the night in a lone, small wayhouse, all three of them crammed in the one room. This would've been awkward had Cae and Vel been sharing a bed, but as it was, the accommodations were almost full up, and they had to settle for three cots all in a row. As crowded as this arrangement was, at least the beds were more comfortable than the hayloft, though Cae couldn't decide whether he was relieved or frustrated to be denied the kind of privacy in which he and Vel might've managed a meaningful conversation, assuming he'd possessed either the energy or courage required to start one.

As they'd agreed to keep watch for safety's sake, Cae volunteered himself for the middle shift, which was always the least sought-after, on the basis that he, unlike Vel and Markel, was used to it. Neither man put up more than a token resistance to this suggestion, and so Cae lay down, ignoring the dull ache in his healing shoulder, as Vel took the first watch. Lying there in the dark, it prickled his neck to think of his husband sitting awake a mere arm's length away, yet somehow as unreachable as if he'd flown to the moons. That Vel had absolved him of his actions the night before ought to have brought some relief and reassurance, but all Cae felt was increased guilt, that Vel instead blamed himself. Their argument by the barn played on a loop in his head, showing him every better thing he could've said and done, the ways he might've comforted Vel instead of snapping at him, and yet the same spark of anger that had got him into trouble in the first place refused to fully extinguish itself, even after everything. He just wanted things to be *simple,* and now someone was trying to kill them, *again,* but once they made it to Qi-Xihan (*assuming we make it to Qi-Xihan,* some inner voice snarked) his only reward would be more and greater problems.

Not a reward, he told himself bitterly. *A punishment, for failing Laecia.*

When Cae did finally sleep, he at least slept well, his turbulent thoughts smoothed out by exhaustion. No would-be assassins menaced them during the night, and while they were all a little groggy, nobody complained. With food purchased and their lodgings paid for, Markel proceeded to give their tack and bags a far more thorough once-over than usual, paying particular attention to the girths, reins and straps. While sensible, the precaution set Cae's pulse racing, and although everything was eventually shown to be in good order, the tension lingered for hours after.

"Can we really be sure we're being targeted?" Vel asked at one point, sounding a little as if he were trying to convince himself and a lot as if he knew the endeavour was futile. "Coincidences do happen. We might have just been unlucky—the fire an accident, the archer an overly ambitious bandit wanting to rob the ferry."

"Perhaps," Cae allowed. "The fire, that's one thing; we might never know. But the ferry . . . if it was a robbery, why shoot when we were still so far from land? Why aim at you and me first, instead of Amra and Emas?"

Vel sighed. "I know. And even if it is some bizarre bad luck, it still makes sense to take precautions. It's just—" he made a frustrated noise, raking his hand through his hair, "—I hate that I'm still causing you this kind of trouble."

It took Cae a moment to parse that, let alone reply to it; his attention had snagged on Vel's wrists, or more particularly on the black mourning ribbons tied around them. Had Vel been wearing them yesterday? He didn't remember, and with a lurch of shame, Cae realised that he'd failed to beribbon his own braid for the last two days. He'd packed a mourning lin—knew that the ribbons, too, were somewhere among his possessions—but all at once, his grief felt disconnected from such visual courtesies. What use was wearing black? It didn't change anything. His sister, his father—they'd both still be dead, and though he'd never questioned the custom before, it suddenly felt absurd that a colour could signify anything, mean anything real, against the enormity of such a loss.

Too late, Cae realised Vel was still waiting for a reply, hunched self-consciously in the saddle, and winced when he recalled which remark he'd left hanging.

"It's not your fault," he said—hurriedly, though the rush came too late; it was clear Vel didn't believe him. "Truly, Vel. What proof do we have that they're here on your account? Far more likely that it's to do with Lae—with my grandmother's inheritance. Again."

He couldn't stop the bitterness from seeping into the words. This time, it was Vel who winced. They both fell silent, and might've remained stewing in their respective miseries for who knows how long without the intervention of Markel, who snapped his fingers to get their attention and then signed, big and exaggerated, "Personally, I think it's my fault, for being too handsome."

That roused a snort of unwilling laughter from Cae and a wry grin from Vel. Markel rolled his eyes, looking pleased with himself, and they continued in a slightly more cheerful silence.

Wary of their mystery assailant, they pushed on through evening for the safety of the next small town instead of camping by the roadside, only to end up once more sleeping three to a room—not for lack of space, but because, as they still intended to keep watch, it was the only configuration that made sense.

It suddenly occurred to Cae that, unless they somehow caught the assassin, they'd likely be doing this all the way to Qi-Xihan, and said as much out loud before he could stop himself. Though aiming for cheerful, his tone landed just north of gloomy; Markel's response was to freeze in place, while Vel looked stricken.

"I suppose so," he echoed. He stared at the bed he and Cae were to share, then glanced across to Markel's pallet, which was set against the far wall, a flush working its way up his neck. Cae was briefly overwhelmed by the urge to set his mouth to Velasin's pulse-point and suck a bruise there, which desire he firmly suppressed as Markel and Vel shared one of their silent yet deeply expressive looks. This one, he knew, meant mutual embarrassment about one of them sharing a bed with a partner where the other could see, and while it hadn't bothered him before, Cae felt a brief, irrational flare of hurt at being considered embarrassing by his husband. It didn't help, either, that sharing rooms meant no private space in which he and Vel could talk; or do more than talk, for that matter, assuming Vel had been amenable and Cae had deserved it. Possibly it was some strange reaction to grief on Cae's part, his body trying to process loss by fuelling him with a desire for life, but he felt helplessly aroused by Vel at the best of times, and despite everything, it was only getting stronger.

Vel chose this moment to remove his undershirt, revealing a tempting expanse of smooth, leanly muscled skin. Cae turned quickly to face the wall, willing his body to calmness as he stripped down to his smallclothes. Any other time, he might've changed into a hipwrap, but that would've felt like one step too many under the current circumstances.

When they were all as clean and comfortable as they were able to get, Vel set himself up to take first watch by ensconcing himself in the room's only chair, leaving Cae to lie down in bed alone.

"Good night," Vel said, addressing the room at large. Markel made a rough, sleepy noise and rolled over on his pallet, face to the wall, leaving Cae to echo softly, "Good night."

It felt like he'd barely sunk into dreaming when Vel woke him again. His hand on Cae's bare shoulder was warm, and for a sleepy, lurching moment, Cae forgot the tension between them—forgot that his husband hadn't been sharing his bed till that point—and smiled at him, reaching to draw Vel down. Their mouths brushed, a soft, sweet press of lips, until Vel broke the kiss and blurted, "Cae, it's your watch."

Cae froze, reality crashing down on him like a poorly built wall. "Oh," he rasped, voice rough from more than sleep. His palm was still curled around Vel's shoulder, his cock half-hard beneath the sheets. For an awkward moment, they hung together, touching in the dark, until Vel let out a short, strained laugh and eased himself upright.

"Sorry," Cae murmured, donning a robe against the night's chill.

"It's fine," Vel said quickly, crawling into bed without making eye contact.

Cae wished, briefly and vehemently, for the assassin to burst in through the door so he'd have the excuse to fight someone. When this didn't happen, he sighed and took up his spot in the chair—still warm from Vel's occupancy of it, with Cae's sword left within easy reach—and began his watch.

Though an ugly part of Cae was spoiling for a fight, the hours of his watch ticked by and nothing happened. Eventually, he woke Markel for his shift, taking care not to disturb his husband as he returned to their now-shared bed. Vel's face was lax with sleep, the fan of his lashes dark against his cheeks in the low, yellow candlelight, hair curled gently against ear and throat. Just the sight of him made Cae ache; it was painful to be so close and yet so far.

And so it went the next day and the day after that, the three of them sharing a room to better keep watch through the night. Living and travelling with his revetha, Cae was used to having no privacy, but the lack of it now, with his husband, when he so badly wanted to ease things between them, was like a slow form of torture. By the fifth day, he felt scraped thin enough to suggest that perhaps they were being unnecessarily cautious. Vel and Markel, equally unhappy with the arrangements, had agreed—only for them to wake the next morning and find the girth on Gift's saddle near torn through. The sabotage was clearly deliberate, but also well-disguised, with a clear, weak adhesive used to make the strap appear whole at a casual glance. If not for Markel's compulsive vigilance, they might've missed it, which would've proved disastrous when, later that morning, a series of loud, shrieking-roaring noises spooked the horses to a gallop on a twisty, rocky downhill stretch of road, as if they were being pursued by monsters. Even Vel was hard-pressed to keep his seat under those conditions; if the broken girth hadn't been found and replaced, he would've been flung down the boulder-strewn hillside the first time Gift broke and reared.

By the time they outran the terrible noises and reached ground that was sufficiently safe and level for them to stop and settle the horses, they were all deeply shaken. Cae didn't know whether he hugged Vel or Vel hugged him, only that, within seconds of dismounting, he had his husband wrapped in his arms, heart pounding with fear.

"Well," Vel croaked in Ralian, voice cracking with a poor attempt at laughter, "at least now we know it's me they're after." He was shaking like a rabbit; Cae held him and kissed his hair, unable to speak through the sudden, appalling tightness in his chest. If Markel hadn't noticed the girth—if Gift had flung him anyway—

Eventually, Markel clicked his fingers and signed that the longer they stayed where they were, the more time they gave the assassin to catch up with them. Letting go of Velasin was only slightly easier than lopping off one of his own arms, but Cae had done it, the three of them pushing on as far and as fast as the terrain and horses allowed. None of them spoke about the fact that Vel was evidently the one being targeted, though as Cae could think of little else, he assumed the same was true of the others, too. He went back and forth with it like a dog with a bone: had the saboteur really known which saddle was Vel's? Had they made a mistake? Or didn't it matter which of them was harmed—only that one of them was? Each possibility was disturbing for different reasons, but as Cae could do nothing about any of them for the moment, he shoved them ruthlessly aside. Once they made it safely to Qi-Xihan, or at the very least to Ravethae, then there'd be space enough to consider motives: until then, they could only do what they'd been doing.

The inn in which they stayed that night was rowdy with customers, and none of them got much sleep regardless of which watch they took, alive to every shout and creak and crash.

Three days later, the calendar ticked over from Noha, the last month of autumn, to Osu, the first month of winter. At any other time of year, they would've at least had the compensation of riding through lush, beautiful surrounds—this was Tithena's breadbasket, home to the rich fields and orchards that kept both tenants and landowners well-fed and prosperous—but now, the scenery was stark, bare branches and unsown fields. The lowlands didn't see much snow and especially not so early in the season, but the wind became increasingly chill and the rain more frequent the farther they travelled. There was even another small earthquake, a rippling tremor that set the horses to snorting as the land began to slope up again; Cae wasn't usually fazed by them, but after so many half-slept nights and the constant anxiety of their unknown pursuer, he couldn't help but startle.

And always, there was the fear of further attack. Though the threat hung over them constantly, it was rare that they could bring themselves to discuss it; nonetheless, it seemed clear that the assassin was, at least for now, determined to make Vel's death—or Cae's, whichever of them they were after—look accidental, which ruled out certain more pugilistic approaches. This lowered the risk of ambush, as did the fact that, so far, their adversary seemed to be working alone; and yet the incident at the ferry meant they couldn't fully discount the possibility of attack by "bandits," either. Whenever they traversed a stretch of road with plenty of cover to either side, or passed between hills or under bluffs, or went around a blind turning, Cae's sword-hand itched. His hand strayed often to both his sword and the ring-hilt of the jade-handled throwing knife Vel had given him, but for all their vigilance—or perhaps because of it—no attack was forthcoming.

Two days out from Ravethae, they had to cross the Sihae River, which was too deep to be easily forded and too fast-flowing for a ferry. In the distant past, armies attempting to march on Qi-Xihan had often faltered at the Sihae when defenders burned its bridges, but in these more peaceful times, there were several to choose from. The one before them hung several feet above the frothing water, the rope and wood construction narrow enough that they'd have to cross single file. There was, Cae knew, a bigger, sturdier bridge a few miles north-west of their current position, built to accommodate the main flow of trade from Irae-Tai, but it had been drizzling since dawn and despite the waterproofing of his travelling coat, he was sodden and damp with chill, his temper frayed from yet another fruitless second watch. For the first time since they'd left Avai, he found himself in a hurry, not just to press onwards, but to reach their destination—specifically his grandmother's holdings, whose security might finally ensure a full night's sleep. Vel and Markel were in a similar temper, and he didn't blame them. Nobody wanted to take the longer route, and so here they were.

As they lined up to cross, Vel took the lead, coaxing a dubious Gift towards the bridge with gentle pats and murmurs of encouragement. The filly was nervous, one ear swivelled sideways, the other laid back, head jerking up as she eyed the river with deep equine scepticism. She set one hoof on the planking, then another—then baulked, snorting as she threw her weight onto her haunches. Vel tried to urge her on, but she wouldn't go, stepping backwards rather than forwards. Cursing, Vel dismounted and tried to lead her across on foot, but Gift let out a shrill whinny and dug in, refusing to proceed.

As the rain beat down harder, Cae grit his teeth against the urge to shout. Gift was young and spirited and hadn't much liked the ferry, either; it was hardly surprising that she'd taken issue with the bridge. Nor could he fault Vel's management of her, accomplished horseman that he was; it was just that he was tired and cold and desperately short on patience, and every moment Gift spent fighting the bridle was another spent sitting pointlessly in the rain.

The thudding drum of approaching hoofbeats hit Cae like a slap.

His hand went instantly to his sword-hilt, his whole body primed for the attack he'd been anticipating for days—but it was only a trio of noblemen on three equally fine-boned coursers, laughing despite the weather as they pulled up to wait their turn. Or noble youths, really; up close, Cae didn't think any of them could be older than twenty, and that was being generous.

Wiping rain from his eyes, Vel sighed and tugged Gift away from the bridge.

"You first, rens," he said respectfully, executing a half-bow. Gesturing to Gift, he added, "It's her first bridge, and she isn't much pleased with it."

The lead rider, a striking olive-skinned youth with curly brown hair too short for braiding, laughed. "My thanks, ren," he said, and cheerfully heeled his own mount, a neat bay gelding, forwards onto the bridge, his companions following close behind.

Vel sighed wryly, patting Gift's muzzle. "Well," he said, "at least we know *some* horses can cross h—"

A terrible groaning sound cut him off. The bridge seemed to shake itself, twisting and writhing as if to buck off its passengers, and then, with a horrific *snap!*, the ropes tore free, or perhaps just tore, dumping all three riders and mounts into the water. Horses and men alike screamed in terror, heads and hooves flailing against the rush of the Sihae. The shock of it froze Cae for all of two seconds— and in that interminable span of time, Vel dropped Gift's reins, kicked his boots off, flung his coat aside and dove into the river.

10

"Vel!" Cae yelled, almost falling from the saddle in his haste to dismount. He ripped his own coat off, swearing as he exchanged a terrified look with Markel, who was equally rooted in place. "Mind the horses!" Cae shouted at him, and had just enough time to register Markel's horrified expression as he, too, wrenched his own boots off, unbuckled his sword-belt, staggered to the bank and launched himself into the water before either of them could think to talk him out of it.

The Sihae hit like an icy punch, so cold he briefly forgot how to swim. The current was strong, too strong—there was no question of fighting it. As his head broke the surface, a chill of fear went through him as he realised how far from the bridge he'd already been towed—and saints, where was Vel? A smack of water hit him in the eyes, and when he cleared it, fighting to move across the river, he saw that the fallen bridge was still attached to its moorings at the far bank, creating a perilous ladder to safety. No sooner had he realised this than he saw his husband, one arm looped through a knot of ropes that had once been the bridge's handrail, the other wrapped around the chest of the curly-haired nobleman, working desperately to keep both their heads above water. The youth's horse was nowhere to be seen, but a shrieking, kicking palfrey flailed two bodylengths away from him, her terrified rider still struggling to free his foot from the stirrup, while the third youth was clinging desperately to the tail-end of the collapsed bridge, his black gelding fully submerged except for his head, one terrified eye rolling wide and white as the water swept him away.

Just like that, Cae's training kicked in, overriding the part of him that was terrified for Vel. Swimming with the current, he made for the youth and the thrashing horse. The palfrey's hooves beat dangerously close to his head, one catching him a glancing blow to the shoulder, but the cold was such that Cae barely felt it, all his energy focussed on grabbing the nobleman, kicking fiercely as he took hold of him under the arms.

"Kick your boot off!" Cae shouted, coughing as rain and the river rushed into his mouth. He didn't know if the youth heard him, but he hauled back anyway, trying to pull them both across the current towards the trailing bridge. There was a horrific, sodden moment where the boy didn't move, and then he sobbed and bucked and came free, the force of his expulsion helping to push them both backwards. Cae pulled and kicked and fought, the freezing water an iron band around his chest, and then his leading arm hit wood. With a choking cry, he grabbed the remains of the bridge and clung on, working to hook his arm through the gap the way Vel had done. Even so, it was still a struggle to keep afloat: the wood was buoyant, but the river was fast and the weight of five people was working to drag it under.

"Climb up!" Cae shouted, struggling to make himself heard. "Climb to the bank!"

In his arms, the rescued youth sobbed an affirmative and grabbed for the bridge, relieving Cae of some of his burden. Exhaustedly, Cae started to haul himself upwards, hand over sodden, cold-numbed hand, fighting the current every step of the way. He allowed himself a single backwards glance—just enough to see that the youth he'd grabbed and the third boy, too, were grimly pulling themselves to safety—and then fixed his attention forwards again, where Vel was still desperately clutching the curly-haired youth, unable to move while bearing his weight. Cae didn't understand why at first, but as he drew closer, he realised the nobleman was unconscious. A bleeding gash on his forehead suggested that he, like Cae, had been struck by a flailing hoof, albeit more severely; without Vel's hold on him, he would've drowned.

Water roared in his ears, an agony of sound. He didn't know how long it took him to scale the ladder to Vel's position, only that it felt like years. Vel was terrifyingly pale, shaking with cold and exhaustion, but managed a grim smile at the sight of Cae.

"Go past us!" Vel gasped out, nodding his head towards the far bank, which was now almost within reach, the current having pulled the bridge straight at the same time they'd been climbing it. "Get ashore and haul us in!"

Cae considered this, then shook his head. "I won't have the strength," he shouted back. "Too much weight!" He hesitated, then swore and said, "Get him on my back!"

"I'll help!" croaked a wretched voice from behind, and suddenly the youth Cae had rescued was there, helping Vel drape the unconscious boy over Cae's shoulders, held in place by the press of Cae's left bicep across his limp arms. As the now-unencumbered Vel finally began to move forwards, there was a moment where the added weight combined with Cae's own lack of motion sank his head beneath the water; then he rallied, kicking fiercely to lift them both up, and began once more to haul himself on, the other two youths sobbing on his heels.

After what felt like a thousand years but was likely only minutes, they reached the bank. A shivering, shaking Vel had already hauled himself up between the sturdy posts set to anchor the bridge on that side, but though he must've been out of strength, he still reached down to help pull the unconscious youth from Cae's shoulders, dragging him up with a weak, triumphant cry. Then came Cae, arms trembling from the exertion; Vel grabbed at him too, cold fingers digging into his lin as he pulled him close. As Cae struggled, gasping and coughing, onto dry land, he had just enough energy to move away from the edge before collapsing onto Vel, face buried in his neck. He ached all over with cold, heart thundering, but all he felt was relief. Eyes falling shut, he pressed his mouth to Vel's bare skin and, without quite meaning to, sucked gently against his pulse-point, the fluttering *beat-beat-beat* against his tongue crowding out the taste of river-water. Shakily, Vel dug his hands into the sodden mass of his hair and stayed there, holding Cae's head in place, all the while making a throaty little *uh-uh* noise caught somewhere between gasping and laughter. Had Cae been any less frozen and wrung-out, it would've driven him crazy; as it was, he could only groan and squeeze Vel's shoulders.

Behind them, there was a slapping sound as the two remaining noblemen made it onto the bank. Cae laved a gentle kiss against the mark he'd surely left on Vel's throat, lingered a moment, then braced his weight on his palms to push himself to his knees. The world spun briefly around him; he grit his teeth and blinked until it steadied. It was still raining, he realised distantly, an unremitting drizzle ensuring that none of them could get dry without getting indoors.

"Th-thank you," croaked the nearest youth, arms wrapped around himself as he shivered violently. He was slender and delicate, with huge dark eyes and warm brown skin turned ashy with shock and cold. "Saints, oh saints, we nearly died—Ethin!" This last a gasp as he caught sight of his curly-haired companion, who was still lying insensate on the ground. Cae felt briefly guilty about not having attended to him immediately, then realised not even a minute had passed since he'd scrambled out of the Sihae. The delicate youth knee-walked over to his injured companion, whose freckled, olive-brown skin was blanching pale, and frantically shook his arm. "Ethin!"

"Oh gods," moaned the third, a shorter, stocky youth with the classically Tithenai combination of bronze-gold skin and straight black hair. "Oh gods, Yara, is he—is he—"

"He's alive," said Vel, who'd taken this long to sway upright and enter the conversation. He cut a glance at Cae, then scrubbed his hands through his sodden hair, shoving it out of his eyes, and added, "Took a nasty kick to the head, though. He needs a healer."

"The horses!" The delicate boy—Yara, evidently—jerked his head up, eyes wide with horror. "Oh saints, the *horses*—"

"Maybe they'll find their own way out downriver," said Cae, trying to inject a note of hope into the proceedings.

The stocky youth shot him a grateful look before moving to put an arm around the delicate boy's—Yara's—shoulders. "Don't worry about them now," he said to his friend, crowding in to stare worriedly down at the still-unconscious Ethin. "He's more important. One thing at a time, isn't that what you're always telling us?"

Yara made a sound that was not quite laughter. "One thing at a time," he said weakly.

All at once, Velasin startled to his feet. "*Fuck,*" he swore. "Markel!" And then, waving his arms and yelling across the river, "Markel! We're all right!"

Turning, Cae saw Markel on the other side of the Sihae, staring with a terrified intensity that carried across the distance. He still had all their horses, but would have to travel at least six miles to get to where they were now, and that was assuming there was an easy path from the next bridge down to their current part of the bank, which Cae didn't know for sure. The enormity of it was sobering: he and Vel needed warmth and dry clothes fast, but all their things were with Markel.

Vel seemed to be having the same realisation; he swore again and looked at Cae, teeth chattering as he hugged himself against the rain. He seemed to think for a moment, then whirled to the stocky youth and asked, "How far to the next town? The next house, even? What's closest this side of the river?"

The boy looked briefly taken aback, then blurted, "There's a little village about a mile on, called Riverwatch. We can get help there."

"All right," said Vel, "and can you get there easily from the other road?"

The boy blinked at him, nonplussed. "What other road?"

Vel gestured frantically at the river. "The other road! From the other bridge, the big one, further up that way—"

"Oh!" The boy nodded; his teeth, too, were chattering. "Yes, yes, there's a—a little road, one that comes back this way—I think it's signposted—"

"Thank you," said Vel, and promptly turned back to the river, waving once more to get Markel's attention. Once he had it, he began to sign, his gestures big and slow to compensate for the distance. "Markel! There's a village a mile on called Riverwatch. You can reach it from a little road once you cross the big bridge; we'll all go there now, all right?"

"What if I get there before you?" Markel signed back.

"Just go to the wayhouse or inn or tavern, whatever they have," Vel replied, "and we'll find you!"

"All right!" Markel signed—and then, pointedly directing his hands at Cae, "Is Velasin hurt?"

Clumsily, fingers aching with cold, Cae signed back, "I don't think so!"

Markel nodded. Hesitated a moment, then gathered up their clothes and boots and shoved them roughly into saddlebags; he hesitated over Cae's sword, then buckled it to his own waist. Grabbing Gift's and Alik's reins, he attached them both to the same string as the packhorses and their spare mount, swung back onto his sorrel mare, Grace, and set off towards the next bridge at a fast trot.

"Fuck," Vel said, more weakly than before. He swayed on his feet, and Cae was beside him in an instant, curling an arm around his ribs and taking his weight. Vel leaned against him gratefully, letting out a faint chuckle. "I'm beginning to think Qarrah was right about the watchtowers. How can the bridge get fixed if nobody knows it's down?" And then, lifting his head, "Are you all right?"

Cae's shoulder chose this moment to remind him that actually, he'd been kicked by a horse in almost the same place he'd recently taken an arrow. It was throbbing fiercely, a bone-deep ache that likely foreshadowed a truly spectacular bruise, but he didn't think the wound had reopened, and so he nodded. "I'm fine. That boy, though—"

They both turned to look. Ethin was still unconscious, but though he was breathing, his pallor and unresponsiveness were deeply worrying. Head injuries were difficult, dangerous things even without being dunked in a river, and with a sinking heart, Cae realised that, of the four of them, the other three likely weren't strong enough to carry the boy deadweight.

"I'll take him," Cae said, his shoulder silently protesting at the prospect. He shoved the pain away and focussed on the task at hand, walking over to the three rescued youths. One by one, he pointed at them, wanting to make sure he had their names right. "Ethin. Yara. And—?" He left the question hanging, staring pointedly at the stockier boy, who promptly shot to his feet.

"I'm Irias," he said, wiping rainwater out of his eyes. "Ciet Irias Atho, and these are Ciet Yarasil Ekkou and Tiern Ethin Talae." He straightened his back, trying very hard not to look like he was shaking, and said, "We owe you our lives."

"It's the least we could do," said Vel exhaustedly. "You wouldn't have been in danger if not for us." He cocked a tired thumb towards the river. "Someone's been trying to kill me for the past two weeks; they must've seen us coming and sawed through the bridge-ropes, hoping we'd go in. If my horse hadn't baulked—"

"Zo's *balls*," whispered Ciet Irias, both awed and terrified. He whipped his head around, looking for hidden assailants. "Will they, I mean—are we still in danger?"

Wearily, Vel shook his head. "I don't think so. Whoever it is, they want it to look like an accident." He laughed darkly. "That, and I don't think they'd have been fool enough to cut the bridge on that side and then try crossing themselves, so assuming they're still around, there's likely a river between us and them." And then he blanched, the impact of his own words hitting him hard enough that he slipped into Ralian, turning to stare frantically at Cae. "Markel," he breathed, looking half as if he wanted to leap back in the Sihae and swim to his friend. "Cae, they could go after Markel—"

"Easy," Cae said, raising his hands to squeeze Vel's shoulders. "Markel can take care of himself, and in any case, he's not the one they're after."

Vel slumped. "I suppose so," he rasped, recalling his Tithenai halfway through the sentence. "If anything happens to him—"

"It won't," Cae said, firmly. And then, in an effort to lighten the mood, "As our young friend here said, one thing at a time. Let's get to Riverwatch first, hmm?"

"All right," said Vel—and then, after taking a deep breath, "All right." He stepped away from Cae, rubbing yet more rainwater out of his eyes.

"But who *are* you both?" Ciet Yarasil cried, still clutching Tiern Ethin's arm. "And why is somebody trying to kill you?"

"I'm Tiern Caethari Aeduria," said Cae, "and this is my husband, Tiern Velasin." He managed a lopsided grin. "As for why anyone wants him dead—well, that's a long story, and one that can wait until we're all safely inside. Until then—" he stepped forwards, crouching down beside the unconscious young tiern, "—let's get your friend some help."

With Ciet Irias's enthusiastic assistance, they once more managed to load Tiern Ethin onto Cae's back. Shoulder throbbing, Cae jogged him into position—he had to lean forwards slightly, or else his passenger would topple off backwards—and held on as if he were taking the tiern on a pigaback ride, the two young ciets hovering on either side in case their friend fell. With the rain beating down more steadily, they set off for Riverwatch: an aching, frozen march. The road was flat and well-maintained, the going straight: under ordinary circumstances, it wouldn't have taken Cae more than fifteen minutes to reach the village. But burdened as he was, cold and tired and accompanied in any case by three other souls who lacked his soldier's conditioning, it was easily a half-hour before they caught sight of a small, respectable-looking inn on the edge of the village square.

Ciet Yarasil, who'd been crying quietly for almost the whole walk, let out a sob of joy and, briefly reinvigorated, went pelting forwards, yelling for help, with the result that they arrived at the inn amidst a crowd of curious onlookers.

"The bridge collapsed!" the boy kept saying, an edge of hysteria to his voice. "It collapsed, we fell, and Ethin is hurt—a healer, we need a healer, please!"

Murmurs of shock and alarm went up at the news about the bridge. The villagers moved with alacrity, and between one blink and the next—or possibly more than that; Cae's vision had been greying at the edges for the last few minutes—they were brought inside and hustled towards the fireplace.

The instant Tiern Ethin's weight was lifted from his back, Cae's knees buckled; had Vel not been there to guide him, he would've fallen to the floor. Vision swimming, he briefly lost all sense of what was going on around him, and was startled to come to and find he was halfway up the stairs, Vel's arm a guiding warmth around his waist.

"Vel?" he croaked.

"Shh," said Vel, "it's all right, we're nearly there—"

Cae blacked out on his feet again. The next thing he knew, he was slumped on a stool by a smaller fireplace in what looked to be a private room, an unfamiliar kem looking on as a pair of serving boys rushed to fill a wooden tub with water.

"Warm, now," said the kem, shooting a stern look at one of the boys. "Warm, not hot! If they have hot right out of the cold, it'll do more harm than good."

"Vel should go first," Cae mumbled—and then, lifting his head to try and find his husband, "Velasin?"

"I'm here," said a voice from his other side, a little exasperated and a lot fond, "and no, I'm not going first, because I didn't just haul an unconscious stranger a mile through the rain—" He broke off abruptly, at which point Cae realised that Vel, who'd evidently unbuttoned his lin for him, had just pulled aside his undershirt and seen the bruise on his shoulder. "Cae," said Vel, voice audibly pained, "you said you were fine!"

"I am fine," Cae said, with as much dignity as he could muster. Raising a hand, he gestured at what was, indeed, a truly spectacular bruise. "See? It's not even bleeding!"

Vel put his face in his hands and said something unintelligible in Ralian. When he was done, he looked up, switched back to Tithenai and said to the kem, "Please, when the healer is done with the young tiern, would you mind asking her to come and see us?"

"I'll do that," said the kem, and promptly left the room.

As the servants scurried to fill the tub, Cae sat meekly as Velasin undressed him down to his smallclothes, apparently too annoyed—or possibly just too worried—to care about the presence of others. Only then did Cae grab his husband's hands, which had been flitting around him for the past five minutes, and squeeze them between his palms, looking up at him anxiously. Though Vel had stripped out of his lin and wet socks, he was otherwise still dressed in his sodden things and, despite the blazing fire, shivering noticeably. Cae looked him up and down, a sudden lump in his throat.

"Your feet," he said suddenly. "All this way, we walked barefoot— are your feet all right?"

Vel made an odd little choking noise. "My feet?" he said, incredulous. "You're worried about my *feet?*"

"Why wouldn't I be?"

Vel had no answer to that. Instead, he watched as the last bucket of water was emptied into the tub, waited until the boys were gone and the door safely shut, then slung an arm around Cae's waist and helped him—somewhat unnecessarily, now that Cae had had a moment to recover—over to the bath. His chill, nimble fingers tugged Cae's wet smallclothes away, a process which involved Vel kneeling to drag them down his thighs. Cae stared at his husband in a daze, recalling only belatedly that the point of this activity was for him to get *into* the tub. He did so awkwardly: it was really too small for a grown man, let alone one of his size, but the instant he sat down, his knees sticking up like round, bronzed hills, he groaned in relief as the warm water eased his chills.

"Here," said Vel softly, coming to kneel behind him. "Let me."

Reaching into the bath with a wooden dipper, he poured a stream of water over Cae's head. His ears and nose stung fiercely for a moment; then the heat began to sink in, and he sighed again, eyes falling closed of their own accord. "Thank you," he murmured.

"Of course," said Vel. Another dip; another stream of water. When it was done, he felt Vel tugging at the end of his sodden braid, undoing it to finger-comb through his hair. The intimacy of it was such that suddenly, Cae was wide awake. He gripped the edges of the tub and stared at the ceiling, willing his cock to stay uninvolved. Though the warm air in the room was helping, Vel's breath still hitched with cold in a way that made Cae ache.

"I'm sorry," Vel said suddenly, the words a bare puff of air against Cae's ear.

Cae fought back a shiver that had nothing to do with the temperature. "For what?"

"For nearly getting you killed, again." He made an odd little sound, a hurt noise masquerading as laughter. "I seem to have a knack for it."

"Vel." Cae half turned in the tub and grabbed his husband's hands. "This wasn't your fault. Whoever is after us, whoever cut the bridge—"

"Yes, yes," said Vel, waspishly embarrassed as he drew his hands back, pushing at Cae's head until he turned around and let him go on with straightening out his hair. "You keep saying that, but it doesn't make me any less ill-omened, and the fact is that you're not going to talk my guilt away, even with those big soft eyes of yours."

Cae's heart gave a hopeful twist. "I have big soft eyes?"

"You know godsdamn well you do," Vel huffed, "as both Liran and Riya have warned me that you use them to your unscrupulous advantage."

"Maybe so," said Cae, "but it's nice to hear you say it."

Just for a heartbeat, Vel's hands stilled in their combing. "Anyway," he said, the words coming out on a slightly hurried inhale, "at least we saved those boys."

"You did, you mean," said Cae. "If you hadn't jumped in first, I'm not sure I would've thought to."

"Of course you would've!"

"No, I mean it. I'm not quick like you, Vel—I didn't realise we could use the bridge to save them until I was already in the water."

"Neither did I."

Cae froze. Slowly, he turned back around in the tub, and this time Vel didn't stop him, meeting his gaze with a guilty look that hadn't had time to convert itself into something more convincing, a light flush rising on his chilled cheeks.

"What do you mean, *neither did I.*" Cae stared at his husband, an incredulous lump rising in his throat. Just for a moment, his gaze caught on the thumb-smudge mark his mouth had left on Vel's throat, plum-dark and lovely, before flicking back up to those beautiful gold-grey eyes. "Velasin," he said, and the word came out wrecked. "You didn't—why would you do that? Why would you risk yourself like that?"

Vel gave a shrug whose attempt at airiness was belied by the way he stared studiedly over Cae's shoulder. "Because," he said lightly, "as soon as the bridge went, I knew I was meant to have fallen in. What sort of man would I be if I let them die in my place without even trying to save them?"

"You self-sacrificing little idiot," Cae said, and kissed him desperately, leaning half out of the tub as he drew Vel in with a hand around the back of his neck. Vel gasped against his mouth and kissed back, biting and urgent, hands coming up to grip Cae's shoulders. His fingers dug into the blooming bruise; Cae hissed in pain, but chased Vel's mouth when he pulled away, solving the problem by grabbing blindly for the offending hand and twining their fingers together. Heat suffused him, cock stirring beneath the water; there was barely room for one man in the tub, let alone two, but he was still on the brink of trying to haul Vel in with him when the door to their room banged open. Vel sprang back liked a miscreant child caught stealing sweets; dizzied, Cae looked up and realised, with commingled relief and irritation, that the newcomer was Markel.

Scrambling to his feet, Vel stumbled forwards and embraced his friend, who hugged him back fiercely. Cae looked away, a discomforting sense of loss roiling through his chest. He quashed it firmly; Markel had ridden six or seven miles at a pace, in the rain, while leading five horses, in order to reach them quickly, and did not deserve to be met with unfounded jealousy. Oblivious to Cae's inner turmoil, Markel's eyes widened as he looked past Vel and registered the bruise on Cae's shoulder.

"Are you well?" he signed, coming close enough to include Cae in the conversation without compromising what little privacy the tub afforded him.

"I'm fine," Cae replied—aloud, as he'd submerged his fingers in the blissfully warm water, the skin tingling painfully as they thawed. The arousal he'd felt moments earlier was gone again, replaced by a creeping lassitude that blurred the edges of his concentration. "Did Gift give you any trouble at the other bridge?"

Markel shook his head, signing a lengthy answer that Cae failed to catch, having blinked too long at the outset. At his look of incomprehension, Vel said aloud, "The other bridge was firm stone, Markel says; Gift didn't give it a second glance. Clever as she is, he thinks she must've sensed that something was wrong with the rope bridge, which is why she wouldn't cross it." He gulped, looking slightly overwhelmed. "She saved our lives."

"And then we dove in anyway," Cae said, smiling to ensure there was no sting in it. His eyes began to slip shut again; he shook his head, struggling to keep awake, but he was utterly wrung-out, the combination of the fire and warm water making him drowsy.

Seeing this, Markel glanced between them and signed, "I should see to the horses and bring your clean things up. You two get settled in."

"Many thanks," said Cae, voice cracking on a yawn.

Executing a half-bow in Cae's direction, Markel clapped Vel on the shoulder and left, the door shutting softly behind him. Blinking heavily, Cae forced himself to stand and groped around for a towel, eventually finding one on a warming rack in front of the fire.

"Your turn," he said to Vel, gesturing towards the tub.

Vel hesitated. "Cae—"

"You need to get warm. Please," Cae added, rubbing the warm towel over his face. "I promise I won't—" he yawned again, listing towards the bed in the corner, "—won't make a nuisance of myself."

He collapsed on the mattress, burrowing under the blanket with mole-like determination, and any reply Vel might've made was lost to a haze of sleep. He woke briefly to the sensation of a healer's touch, some charm or cantrip prickling through his bruised shoulder, then a different tingle as his sinuses were cleared, but it was a muzzy consciousness, easily banished.

When he finally woke again—properly, this time—the fire had burned down to embers, the room silvered with predawn light. Cae had all of three seconds to become aware of and marvel at the warmth of Velasin cuddled up against his flank before, a beat later, registering the quiet silhouette of Markel, sat in a chair by the fireplace, keeping his customary third watch.

As Cae lifted his head, their eyes met in the dim light. Easing himself carefully upright so as not to wake Velasin, Cae tentatively signed, "How long did I sleep?"

"It was afternoon when we got here, and now it's nearly dawn," Markel signed back. "So, eleven hours? Something like that. You clearly needed it." And then, nodding towards the bedside table, "You should eat. Velasin saved you dinner."

Turning, Cae found a plate of cold shrimp and noodle fritters and fell on it ravenously, washing it down with a pitcher of water. When he was done, he realised clean clothes were laid out for him on a nearby chair and, as Markel politely looked away, he rose and dressed himself, suppressing the ache that ran through him on leaving Vel alone in bed.

With nothing else to do and feeling somewhat awkward about it, he came and sat opposite Markel by the dying fire, staring at the embers.

A gentle click startled him from his reverie. When he looked up,

Markel signed, "I know it's been hard for you, to have me sharing your rooms." Cae froze up a little at this, but forced himself to relax as Markel continued. "Under the circumstances, I'm not sure what else we could've done, but I wanted to apologise anyway."

"That's not—" Cae began aloud, then winced, not wanting to wake Velasin, and went on in signs, "You don't have to. It's not your fault."

"I interrupted you earlier," Markel pointed out.

Cae hesitated, feeling uncomfortable. He'd been annoyed at the time, but didn't like to think that Markel had picked up on it, nor did he want to lie outright. After a moment, he signed, "You did, but it was necessary. We needed to know you were here, Velasin especially."

Uncertainty flickered on Markel's face. "About that," he signed. "None of us have had space to talk, but I suspect Velasin's been hiding behind my presence, at least to some extent. He's still tangled up about what happened in Etho, and with everything that's happened since, I think the knots have only grown worse."

Cae nodded, heart sinking. He'd suspected as much, so it shouldn't have stung, and yet he couldn't help but feel hurt, that his husband wanted space. "I don't know what to do," he signed helplessly. "I don't want him to think I'm pushing him away, but I don't want to pressure him, either."

Markel nodded understanding. "I wish I could advise you, but what you and he have, it's not like any relationship he's ever had before. It's not just that you're married; it's that he's never had to—" he paused, hands stalled as he tried to conjure the right words, "—negotiate with a partner. If there was ever an argument or an uncertainty, either he'd wait to be wooed back or things would just end."

"And what happened if he was the one who owed an apology?"

Markel raised an eyebrow, lips quirked with amusement. "Bold of you to assume he's ever been wrong."

Cae let out an unexpected burst of laughter, then promptly stifled it, casting a guilty glance at the bed. All at once, it felt wrong to be talking about his husband like this, especially with him in the same room, and something of the emotion must've shown on his face, for Markel's expression sobered, too.

"I know you care for him," Markel signed. "When he dove in the river, you dove in, too. I just—" He shook his head, frustrated, then let out a sigh. "I just wish things could be easy for him. For you. For both of you."

"Me, too," said Cae, and might have ventured more, had Vel not chosen that moment to stir. Heart turning over in his chest, Cae rose from his chair and went to the bedside, watching as Vel blinked sleepily awake. Love and anxiety clawed his throat in equal measure. Soon, they'd be in Ravethae, and after that, Qi-Xihan. Cae struggled with politics at the best of times; he'd visited the royal court before and never once felt anything but uneasy about it. In the back of his mind, he knew that their adventures on the road would have far greater repercussions than he'd yet allowed himself to contemplate, but just as he'd done since Etho, he refused to think about it. Being named heir to the yaserate was a problem he didn't know how to face, for all that it was rushing towards him with the dumb inevitability of waves against the shore—but for now, in this moment, there were smaller problems he could solve, and he clung to them desperately.

"Breakfast!" he said aloud. "I'll go and get us some."

He fled the room before Vel's eyes were open.

Part Three

VELASIN

11

We rode out of Riverwatch when dawn was barely a suggestion of warmth in the chilly, bruise-coloured sky. Markel and I had forgone an overnight vigil during Cae's convalescence, partly because neither of us was accustomed to taking the long, unpleasant second watch, which Cae had always insisted on claiming for himself, but mostly because the lack of sleep had started to leave us frayed. With Cae passed out, it hadn't been long before Markel and I had followed suit, and while Markel still rose early, the result was that, despite the hour, we were better rested than we'd been in weeks.

I regretted that there'd been no time to check on the youths we'd rescued before leaving, but it was a small loss in the scheme of things, and anyway, I had bigger problems to worry about. As embarrassing as it had been to share my husband's bed with Markel in the room, I was acutely conscious of the fact that, once we arrived at Yasa Kithadi's holdings in Ravethae, our shared vigil would no longer be necessary, which meant I'd have to face Caethari alone. Ever since Etho, I'd struggled to suppress the memory of my appalling conduct the night of the fire: how Cae had been forced to restrain me, and how that restraint had, through no fault of my husband's, led me to believe myself so besieged that I'd lost all sense, collapsing in an insensate fit of tears. On waking the next morning, my shame was such that I'd nearly lost my stomach over it. Occasional flinching was one thing, but the way I'd screamed and thrashed at Cae for the crime of saving me from myself was quite another—and then, to make things worse, I'd gone and picked a stupid, self-sabotaging fight with him, culminating in a blow not remotely lessened by the fact that I both deserved and had actively goaded him to it: Cae's look of exhausted pity as he said, *Had we not agreed to be friends?*

Just recalling it made my chest hurt. *Friends.* Friendship was the compromise we'd made when I'd first come to Tithena: an agreement to try and make our marriage work despite the absence of love, before our feelings—or Cae's, at least—had come to encompass it. Deep down, a part of me had always feared that Cae's love would fade, should I take too long to reciprocate, and yet the dagger of it twisted no less deeply for being foreseen. I didn't doubt that he cared for me still—he was too good a man to do otherwise—and as we'd agreed that marital friendship could encompass *casual intimacy* and *the possibility of comfort,* as Cae had put it what felt like a thousand years ago now, it didn't feel contradictory that he continued to kiss me, especially in the aftermath of yet another failed attempt on my life. The fact was, I had far more experience with being desired physically than I did with being cared for, and as we'd proved to be thrillingly compatible in the brief window of time before I'd ruined things—and as both of us were healthy men who found pleasure in sex—it felt only natural that we might continue doing so.

Indeed, my apprehension around finally being alone with Cae was equalled only by my desire for him: as much as it ached to know what I'd lost, I feared more the prospect of going untouched; of the little Cae still felt for me degrading into indifference. And the cold truth was, for all that I didn't yet love him, I cared for my husband fiercely. I wanted him to want me, and after endless days spent sharing a bed with no possibility of indulging one another, my body was primed to answer the simplest, most innocent of touches with a rush of lust and longing. The whole situation was so unbearably frustrating, I could've screamed—but as doing so would've only disgraced me further, I had no recourse but silence.

As the day drew on and my thoughts slowly turned from self-recrimination to more practical matters, I was forced to acknowledge that I had no idea what to expect from the royal court at Qi-Xihan. Twice since Etho, I'd hesitantly tried to broach the subject of court politics with Cae, but each time he'd pled ignorance, a haunted look on his face at the reminder that he was now his grandmother's heir, and I'd found myself unable to push. Partly this was due to guilt, to say nothing of an inherent reticence to add to Cae's burdens, but there was also an element of embarrassment: despite what I'd learned on the fly about Tithenai law and custom during the first weeks of my engagement, there were still gaping holes in my knowledge of how the nation was governed, and I didn't like to admit the depths of my ignorance. Before we left for Avai, Yasa Kithadi had quietly offered to give me some civics lessons "once things have calmed down a bit"—meaning, when the immediate mourning period for the former tieren and Laecia had passed—but as that was yet to happen, I had little to fall back on.

As such, I'd fallen into the habit of painting the Tithenai capital with Farathel's colours, and that could be a fatal mistake for any number of reasons. I had no desire to garner through ignorance more enemies than I currently possessed, and that meant knowing what I was heading towards. I didn't want to upset my husband, but I'd let the matter lie for as long as I could, and so I steeled myself to the task. On both previous occasions, I'd asked about Qi-Xihan's politics using broad-brush questions—*what's the general sentiment towards Ralia?* and *what do the courtiers think of Asa Ivadi?*—and as that had been unsuccessful, I tried a different angle of approach.

"Caethari," I asked, breaking a long stretch of silence, "what should I expect from Qi-Xihan?"

My husband startled a little at the question, which wasn't surprising; not being privy to my train of thought, to him, the query had come out of nowhere.

"In what sense?" he answered guardedly.

"In every sense. What is the court like? What level of formality am I to expect?" I forced a laugh, gesturing to our travel-worn clothes. "I assume we'll be underdressed on arrival, but how different is the fashion from that in Qi-Katai, and how much does it matter? Is the culture one of gossip or honesty? I know that we'll be representing your grandmother—" he winced at the reminder as I forced myself to plough on, "—but what does that mean, in terms of her alliances? Is Clan Taedu well-liked? Is Clan Aeduria known there, or can we expect to be nonentities on that count? How are things done?"

"Ah," said Cae, when my flow of questions finally ran to an end. He stared pointedly at Alik's mane, and I thought he might be gathering himself to answer, but the seconds ticked by and his expression remained lost. Eventually, without looking up, he said, "It's not . . . I'm not good at this sort of thing, Vel. I don't mean to deprive you of information, but I'm not—I was never—" He let out a short, angry laugh as he clenched the reins. "There's a reason I never aspired to inherit the yaserate. I—" He inhaled heavily, shaking his head, and briefly shut his eyes. When he opened them again, he said, in slow, drawn tones, "I believe the fashion is different, but it's never been my main preoccupation, and in any case, I've not visited in long enough that it's likely changed from whatever I remember. Clan Taedu is . . . prominent, but I've no idea how perception of it has shifted with my grandmother's stay in Qi-Katai. I would call the court formal, but as I have little patience with formality, I don't know what that's worth to you, or how it compares to your time in Farathel. Clan Aeduria is known there, and I suspect . . . I suspect *will* be known, because of what Lae—because of recent events, but as for the court culture, beyond Asa Ivadi's penchant for games and gathering information, I've never paid much attention. I've never had to," he finished softly, shoulders slumped in something like despair.

A pang of self-hatred went through me to have so distressed my husband, and yet I felt a flare of frustration, too. I didn't want to walk into Qi-Xihan blind, but as Cae clearly didn't want to discuss the matter—and as, in fairness, his knowledge genuinely appeared to be both limited and out of date for my purposes—that left me no recourse but to figure things out on my own. That Asa Ivadi had sanctioned our diplomatic union did nothing to tell me how that decision was viewed by her court at large, nor had I any true sense of the factions within the upper reaches of Tithenai politics. The Ralian ambassador, whom I'd met at the former Tieren Halithar's funeral, ought to have been a useful source of information, given his proximity to the betrothal negotiations, but at the time, he'd been more concerned with the potential ramifications of Killic's death at my hands, to say nothing of being mildly scandalised by the fact that I'd married a Tithenai man in the first place. Had the asa's missive reached us when we'd still been in Qi-Katai, I'd have gone straight to Yasa Kithadi, or possibly Keletha; as it hadn't, I ought to have asked Telitha before we'd reached Etho, and yet I'd been so preoccupied with Cae, and Telitha so preoccupied with Markel, that I couldn't conjure a retroactive starting point for such a conversation.

None of these thoughts were helpful in the moment, however, and so I forcibly set them aside. "Thank you," I said instead to Cae, gentling my tone and earning a tired, lacklustre smile for my efforts. I suppressed a wince, wondering frantically whether it was better to keep silent or pick a new topic of conversation, but dithered for so long that in the end, I made the decision by accident. Nobody spoke again for some time, and we kept on through the uneventful landscape until we finally reached the large, prosperous wayhouse that was to be our final stop before Ravethae. It was just past dusk when we arrived, the moonlight bright and clear. With only a few more hours of riding over good roads to go before we reached the estate, we might easily have pressed on, but it was clear that Cae wanted one more night with which to brace himself, and so I made no argument.

While keeping my usual watch that night, I found myself turning the little carnelian reseko figurine Yasa Kithadi had given me over and over in my hands, thumb smoothing against the carved stone. Telitha had said the creature was a trickster, though the gift itself likely represented a hint—but a hint to what? An ugly notion bloomed across my thoughts like mould: had the yasa known about my would-be assassin? I sat a moment with this nauseating possibility, then swiftly dismissed it out of hand. Even had she borne me sufficient enmity to either contract my death herself or passively allow my murder, after everything she'd endured in search of an heir to the yaserate, I didn't believe that she'd knowingly endanger Cae. I was paranoid enough already without indulging in wild speculation about the few people in my life who cared if I lived or died, but weeks of pursuit had worn me thin.

No. My own private suspicion, which I'd nursed since the incident with Gift's saddle, was far more likely: that the Ralian crown, embarrassed by my marriage to a man but unwilling to risk a diplomatic incident by publicly disavowing the tie it represented, wished for me to die in a purported accident. I'd declined to share this theory with my husband or Markel, not wishing to worry them—or, in the case of Cae, to add to his anxieties about being heir to the yaserate—and was doing my best not to dwell on it. But as I sat awake, Cae sleeping soundly in the borrowed bed we were yet to share, grief and rage swam up out of nowhere to sting my eyes with tears.

Ever since I'd understood that my preferences lay exclusively with men, I'd known that, in the eyes of my home nation, I was a wrong thing, deviant and forbidden. I'd known, too, that compared to others in similar situations—to metem folk like my friend Aline, or women who preferred women, or to anyone in the same boots as mine but without the money and status I'd used to shield myself—I was lucky. In Farathel, I'd had a circle of fellow litai, and though we'd banded together largely due to proximity and shared inclinations rather than any real mutual interests, providing more a sense of shared camaraderie than true friendship, still I'd had my deeper bonds with Markel and Aline—and with Killic, I'd believed, though thinking of him now made me ache in a different way. I'd walked my own sort of knife's edge, but I'd not had to contend with poverty or such social and legal conventions as curtailed the lives of Ralian women, and until that fateful betrothal to Laecia, I'd never been pressured to marry. My life had been one of risk and secrecy, but also of noble privilege. I hadn't liked to think myself invested in the latter, but thinking that my home nation might be seeking my death—that my rank had proved to be no protection at all from the crime of my existence—brought on a terrible choking helplessness, where rage became despair became shame became rage again.

How much pain and suffering might have been averted, if I'd never taken Killic into the gardens at my father's house? If I'd sent him away without giving him either the chance or desire to help himself to me, what then? He might still have followed me to Tithena, and perhaps he'd have acted appallingly there, too, had I married Laecia; or maybe he'd never have come at all, if his actions hadn't exposed us both. That felt more likely, and after everything, it shouldn't have stung, but there was a savage sort of bitterness in thinking that the man who'd cheated on me, raped me, attempted to blackmail me and who'd then tried to kill Caethari had still cared so much more for himself that, despite his protestations of love and apology, he'd never have pursued me while he still had a life to return to.

I squeezed the reseko figurine hard, the little tree-bear's ears digging into my palm. Married to Laecia, I'd still have come to know Cae; perhaps even to lust for him from a distance. What might Laecia have thought of that, had she noticed? And for how long might she have tolerated my refusal to bed her? Or—and this was a thought I'd never entertained before, such that I didn't initially know what to make of it—might she have eventually forced me, as Killic had done? I froze where I sat, staring blankly at the far wall. More than once in the aftermath of Killic's abuse, I'd thought that, if I'd still been destined for Laecia, I'd at least have had nothing to fear on that count, but was it really true? Ralian convention held rape to be a purely male crime, but though my countrymen were wrong on so many other points, I'd never thought to question that particular certainty. And yet I hadn't fought back against Killic, and like most men of my class, I'd been taught the fundamental abhorrence of raising my hand to a woman. If Laecia had bullied and insisted, would I have submitted? And if so, what difference would there have been, really, between her actions and Killic's?

The thought unsettled me, and as I glanced at Cae's sleeping form, I felt an odd flash of guilt, as if my morbid speculations were somehow dishonouring his sister's memory. That Laecia had stooped to murder didn't mean she'd have forced herself on me, and yet I couldn't forget her insistence that a husband who wouldn't bed his spouse was pointless and undesirable, either. How many Ralian wives lay with their husbands, I wondered, not due to physical violence, but because they were berated and cajoled into it, made subject to expectation? And if words could be used in place of force, then was it truly impossible that other Ralian men were likewise ill-used by their wives, regardless of whether they shared my inclinations?

I shook my head, disquieted by my thoughts, and returned my attention to the little reseko, trying to puzzle out why I'd been given it. But though I studied it from every possible angle, nothing came to me, and by the time the guttering candle signalled that I was due to wake Cae for his watch, I'd exhaustedly given the whole thing up as a poor joke on Yasa Kithadi's part—a parting prank to flummox her Ralian grandson-in-law.

Across the room on his pallet, Markel sighed in his sleep and rolled to face the wall, settling into deeper repose. Silently, I shed my things and prepared to climb in next to Cae, heart aching at the sight of him. His long braid was sleep-loosened, stray hairs catching on the stubble shading his handsome jaw, his long, dark lashes incongruously soft against the sharp curve of his cheek. His brow was furrowed faintly, as if he were frowning in his dreams; I wanted to place my thumb there and smooth it flat—and would've done, had I not lost the right. His bronze skin gleamed faintly golden in the candlelight, highlighting the well-defined musculature of his shoulders and arms, the sweet lines of throat and collarbone. I wanted to strip completely naked and rub against him like a cat; instead, I kept my smallclothes on and space between us on the mattress, squeezing his bicep lightly as I murmured his name to wake him.

"Wha?" Cae mumbled sleepily—and then, coming awake all at once, "Oh. Right. My watch." He cracked a yawn and grinned at me, the expression goofily soft, but before I could do something needy and foolish like pull him back down beside me, he'd swung his legs over the edge of the bed—I ogled him shamelessly, arrested as always by the sight of such a powerful man wearing nothing but a simple hipwrap, gaze tracking the flex of muscles across his back and arse—and risen, padding over to the chair.

"Goodnight, Cae," I whispered, and pressed my helpless face to the pillow.

12

Cae's mood was dark the next day, a glowering unease that raised the hairs on my neck. I wanted to comfort him, but didn't know how, and so devolved into aimless chatter about the scenery, my prattle so inane that at one point, Markel caught my eye and slowly shook his head. I faltered into merciful silence after that, but a little farther on, as we finally crested the lengthy hill up which we'd been riding, Cae called a halt and gestured stiffly at the tableau laid out before us.

"Ravethae," he said.

For a moment, I didn't comprehend him. "Which part?"

"All of it," he said, softly. "As far as to the mountains and the city's edge." And then, more quietly still, "When we came here as children, this was where my mother always placed the southern boundary. Right here, on this hill."

I froze in the saddle, staring dumbly. From our vantage point, the land splayed out before us was a vast expanse of farms and villages, woods and orchards, streams and ponds and who knew what else. To the north, the looming shadow of mountains brooded over what lay below; to the east, I could just make out the vast, high walls of Qi-Xihan, gleaming against the encircling peaks. But westward, the land went on and on, an endless strip of territory blurring against the horizon. I swallowed hard. My father's elevation had granted him lands and holdings that encompassed at least one small village occupied by his farmer-tenants, but this was a different scale altogether. Intellectually, I'd known that a Tithenai yaserate was roughly equivalent to a Ralian dukedom, but seeing it brought home to me the nature of Cae's elevation more sharply than anything else had.

"It's . . . so much," I said, inadequately.

Cae gave a tight little nod and heeled Alik forwards. "The main estate isn't far now," he said. "We should be there in time for lunch."

Anxiety and anticipation warred within me as we rode on. I felt hyperaware of our surroundings, not because I was braced for the assassin to try once more—although that possibility remained a lurking constant in the back of my mind—but because every tree, every orchard, every bridge over every streambed we passed would one day belong to Cae.

And then I saw the estate.

Despite the pale light and the stark framing of the newly bare trees that lined the drive leading up to the main lawn, the building was imposingly beautiful. It was easily three times bigger than the manor at Avai, and yet it didn't look grandiose, at least not to my eyes. I was still learning my way around Tithenai architecture, and as such had no sense of how old it was, to which traditions of design it might've belonged, but even so, I could tell it was expensive. The amount of glass alone was proof of that: on approach, I counted four stained-glass windows, each one an exquisite work of abstract, coiling colour. These were interspersed across the face of the building, which was itself built with at least three different kinds of stone—one a pale, reddish pink, one white, one silvery grey—mortared into geometric patterns.

Off to the side, I could see what looked like a truly impressive stable as well as some other outbuildings, but before I could properly catalogue them, I was distracted by the approach of a tall, graceful kem down the main drive. Thei were dressed in what I took to be Clan Taedu's livery, resembling as it did the red-and-grey uniforms of those in the Aida sworn to Yasa Kithadi's personal service, thir white-grey locs worn up in a braided coil that emphasised the elegant length of thir neck. Thei smiled as we dismounted, eyes crinkling at the edges, and offered us a short, welcoming bow.

"Yaseran Caethari, Tiern Velasin, Ren Markel—it's a pleasure to have you here. I am Ru Merit Kiso, the yasa's steward."

"Ru Merit, please," Cae said, "I would—I would much prefer to be called tiern than yaseran."

Ru Merit's expression turned apologetic. "The yasa's missive said you'd say as much. She also said to tell you to get used to it; that hiding from a title will not make it go away, and that I ought to help you acclimate to it."

"The yasa's missive?" Cae echoed, surprised. "You've heard from my grandmother, then?"

Ru Merit laughed. "Of course! We've waited years for her to choose an heir—do you think she wouldn't write us the moment it happened? Everything has been prepared, both here and at the house in Qi-Xihan, though I'd be surprised if you spend much time at the latter; it's far more likely Asa Ivadi will invite you to stay at court."

Cae looked so poleaxed, I might've teased him for it under different circumstances. As it was, it surprised me to realise that my husband hadn't anticipated his grandmother's actions. I'd assumed from the outset that Yasa Kithadi would've set her own plans for us in motion, but hadn't bothered to dwell on what they might be, partly because I'd been too mired in my own problems, but mostly because I knew we'd find out on arrival anyway.

"I can see I've caught you unawares," Ru Merit said—wryly, but not unkindly. Thei had a light, raspy voice that reminded me a little of a cat's purr, and so it felt strangely apropos when, at just that moment, a round, self-possessed little calico came trotting up to us, meowed loudly and proceeded to weave in and out of Ru Merit's legs. Utterly unfazed by this, Ru Merit crouched down, scooped up the cat and draped it around thir shoulders like a stole before continuing, "If Ren Markel would be good enough to take your mounts to the stable—" Thei nodded politely in Markel's direction, and I startled slightly to realise that he'd already taken hold of Gift's and Alik's reins in addition to all the others in anticipation of doing just that. "—I'll show you both inside."

All of us stared. Ru Merit blinked, nonplussed, before finally registering what we were looking at.

"Ah," thei said, flustered. Thir skin was too dark to show much of a blush, but thei dipped thir head and spread thir hands in a sort of amused embarrassment. "Forgive me. I'm a soft touch when it comes to cats—of which the estate has plenty—and in the yasa's absence, we've rather gotten used to indulging them." Thei touched the calico lightly between her ears. "This is Spoons."

"*Spoons?*" I asked, failing to keep the note of incredulity from my voice.

With great dignity, Ru Merit said, "She liked to sleep in ladles as a kitten."

Cae made a little coughing noise that sounded suspiciously like stifled laughter. I snuck a smiling glance at him and he grinned back, and just for a moment, things between us felt right and good, as if I'd never broken them. Then Ru Merit let out an *ahem!*, returning us to the moment, and said, "Is there anything else you'd like explained before we go in?"

I caught Markel's eye, the way I always did when the two of us entered a new place, to silently ask if he wanted his muteness conveyed to Ru Merit. He nodded yes, and so I turned back to thim and gave my usual spiel, explaining that he understood Tithenai—a fact which, of necessity, we'd ceased to keep secret—and carried a slate and pen with which to make himself understood to those who didn't speak his signs.

Ru Merit looked first surprised, then thoughtful. "Of course," thei said. "Thank you for informing me, but I believe it should pose no problem." And then, speaking directly to Markel, "Should any of my staff treat you disrespectfully in this regard, please let me know."

Now it was my and Markel's turn to look surprised. Though his muteness had so far been treated with less disdain in Tithena than Ralia, it still tended to catch us both off guard when those in a position of power acknowledged him directly. Markel recovered sufficiently enough to nod, offering Ru Merit a polite bow before leading the horses away. Ru Merit waited a moment, then led on towards the main building, all while maintaining the sort of neat, effortless aplomb that ought to have been undermined by having a cat across thir shoulders, let alone one named Spoons. As I matched my stride to thirs, I found myself staring at the little calico, who appeared to be in no danger of falling from her seemingly precarious perch. Sensing my scrutiny, Spoons blinked at me and yawned, as if I were a tiresome petitioner in the court of life, and I found myself biting back laughter.

If possible, the estate's interior was even more impressive than the outside had led me to expect. The marble floor of the entrance hall swam with coloured light from the stained-glass window set above the main doors, creating a sense of walking into an unreal place. Ru Merit proceeded to lead us upstairs through airy, spacious halls adorned with treasures—paintings, tapestries, sculptures, masks—while keeping up a pleasant, informative patter about such details as where the kitchens were (ground floor, north wing), the number of staff (reduced from full capacity in the yasa's absence, but still considerable), and the uses to which the many and various closed rooms had traditionally been put. For the first time, I appreciated the enormity of Yasa Kithadi's decision to stay so long in Qi-Katai: though Ru Merit was clearly a competent steward, for such a grand estate to have remained socially dormant for so long would've been no small thing in Ralia, and I suspected the same was true here.

Beside me, Cae was silent; his jaw was tight, but his eyes were overwhelmed. Before I could second-guess myself, I reached across and took his hand, squeezing gently. I'd intended a brief contact, but Cae tangled our fingers together and squeezed back hard, flashing me a look that was five parts gratitude to three parts heat. It ran through me like lightning, followed by the inevitable mix of shame and desire. A sliver of doubt pierced my thoughts: what if he loved me still, my fears since Etho unfounded? Moons knew, it would hardly be the first time I'd assumed the worst and been wrong where Cae was concerned. It was an awful thought, compelling and terrifying in equal measure: I wished it to be so, and yet the idea that Cae's regard was something I still retained—and could therefore still potentially lose—induced its own kind of anxiety.

I swallowed hard, my husband's hand burning against my own. If my behaviour in Etho hadn't been sufficient to kill Cae's affections, then I must surely be walking the proverbial tightrope, liable to fall with a single wrong step—

"And here are your chambers," Ru Merit said, gesturing to a pair of wooden doors carved with an alternating motif of stags and snowcats. Entering, thei said, "You'll forgive the presumption, but Yasa Kithadi sent us your measurements and had new clothes commissioned for you both, which you'll find in the cl—"

Thei broke off abruptly, coming to a halt. I was momentarily confused, until I tracked thir gaze to the sizeable bed set against the far wall, on which was seated a plump black cat with a white bib and paws.

"And who is this?" asked Cae. It was the first time he'd spoken since we'd come inside, and I felt a rush of relief at the amusement in his tone.

"That would be Son of Spoons," Ru Merit said dryly.

"Ah," said Cae, in slightly strangled tones. "Of course. Naturally."

Ru Merit sighed. "He must've snuck in behind one of the servants. We do try to keep the cats out of the bedrooms, but they have a way of getting in regardless."

Thei moved to shoo Son of Spoons away, but Cae stopped thim with a shake of his head. "Leave him be," he said. "He seems a pleasant fellow, and in any case, he was here first. What right do I have to evict him?"

"As you wish, yaseran," said Ru Merit. Thir tone was even, but thei looked quietly pleased. Turning back to the closet, which took up the whole left-hand wall, thei continued, "Now, as I was saying, we've had new clothes made up for you according to what's currently in fashion at court—nothing too outré, but nonetheless sufficiently in season to impress." Thei glanced at Cae and added, with unexpected gentleness, "We've had nothing made in mourning, but if you wished to have any black added, that can be arranged."

"That's . . . that won't be necessary," Cae said, clearly caught off guard. Unconsciously, his hand went to his braid, which conspicuously lacked the black mourning ribbon he'd once worn. It was yet another thing we hadn't talked about, for all that I'd stopped wearing my own ribbons as soon as I'd noticed his change in habit. "I thank you, though."

Nodding, Ru Merit opened the closet doors, revealing a wall of fabrics in a variety of colours and cuts. Rather than walk us through each piece one by one, however, thei merely indicated which half contained Cae's things and which my own.

"We'll have your existing clothes laundered, of course," thei went on, "and I imagine you'll want to wash up soon, too. Your private bathing room is through there"—thei gestured towards a door at the opposite end of the room to the closet—"but there's also quite a large bath on the ground floor that connects to the atrium garden, deep enough to swim in; the yasa's grandfather liked to be surrounded by plants as he bathed, so he had it built especially. Even if you don't plan to use it yourselves, it's a lovely instalment."

"I'm sure it is," I said, surprised such a thing existed. And then, mentally kicking myself for having taken so long to ask this particular question, "Where will Markel be staying?"

"There's a servants' suite opposite this one," Ru Merit replied. "Yasa Kithadi indicated in her letter that he normally resides in your shared apartments at the Aida, so we assumed proximity here would be desired."

"It is, thank you," I said, oddly relieved. After so many nights together in one room, it would've felt strange to have Markel so far away—and just like that, I recalled the reason for our recent sleeping arrangements, which I'd somehow managed to set out of mind for just long enough that recalling it tightened my ribs.

Swallowing, I said, "Ru Merit, you should know—the whole way here, someone's been trying to kill me. I don't know what security the estate has, but they should be alerted."

For half a second, Ru Merit's eyes went wide with shock; then thei smoothed thir face into a calm, professional mask. "We keep no soldiers here, tiern, but our staff are both vigilant and capable. Tell me what to expect."

With grim necessity, I laid out what had befallen us since Etho—the fire, the attack at the ferry, Gift's sabotaged girth, the broken bridge—as well as the precautions we'd taken against further attacks. I omitted only my own suspicions as to who, exactly, was behind the violence, though I did point out their desire to make my death seem accidental; after all, I had no proof, and didn't care to worry my husband unduly. Cae chimed in at various points to add his own observations; I'd let go of his hand at some point after entering our new chambers, but he took it up again as we spoke, thumb stroking soothing lines across my knuckles. I shivered at the contact and, with the story done, fell silent, awaiting Ru Merit's verdict.

Finally, thei spoke. "That is all . . . very troubling, tiern. I'm immensely relieved that you made it here in one piece; rest assured, the staff will be instructed to take every possible precaution, and I'll insist that a watch is kept."

"My thanks, ru," I said, sighing with unfeigned relief. "It has been—well. You can imagine."

Ru Merit nodded, which motion had the effect of finally bestirring Spoons from her spot on the steward's shoulders. Yawning widely, the little calico stretched her paws, braced her rear quarters against Ru Merit's neck and pounced neatly to the floor. Oddly mesmerised, I watched as Spoons approached our bed and leapt up onto the covers alongside her eponymous offspring. Son of Spoons made a small, inquisitive chirping noise and flopped over sideways, submitting to having his ears washed by his mother. Never having spent much time with cats before—my experience of them had been largely restricted to dockside strays, agile mousers and haughty stable-cats, none of whom had ever paid me much attention—I was at a loss to explain the sudden surge of affection I felt for the pair before me. Perhaps it was simply that I'd reached the end of a long and extremely fraught journey, but in that moment, I could easily have fought my would-be assassin barehanded to ensure the continued happiness of Spoons and Son of Spoons.

"One more thing, before I leave you to get settled in," said Ru Merit, dragging my attention away from the cats. "With your permission"—thir gaze flicked meaningfully to Cae—"there's someone I'd like to invite to dine with us this evening—or two someones, really. The first is Ciet Nevan Ori, and the second is his companion, a young Ralian expatriate who's been spending time at court. Assuming you wish to prepare yourselves before your meeting with Asa Ivadi, they can far better apprise you of the lay of the land than I. Do I have your permission?"

At the mention of the name *Ori,* Cae went very still. Carefully, he asked, "Is this ciet any relation to—?"

"Yes," said Ru Merit, oddly sombre. "His younger brother."

"Ah," said Cae.

I looked back and forth between them, waiting for a clue that didn't come. Clearly, I was missing something. "Whose younger brother?" I asked.

Cae sighed. "Cieten Vesu Ori's," he replied. "My mother's husband. Which I suppose makes him my uncle by marriage, although we've never met."

"He wasn't at their marriage-gathering?" I asked, intrigued despite myself. I knew precious little about the former Tierena Inavi—now presumably Cietena Inavi, if her new husband was a cieten—as the subject of her remarriage was a sensitive one for Cae.

"He might've been," Cae replied, "but I wasn't. I was serving with my revetha then, and in honesty, I was glad to have the excuse to stay away." He ducked his head, a little shamefaced at his past self, then draw a breath and said to Ru Merit, "Invite them.

If nothing else, he might know where, when . . . if my mother can be reached."

"Of course, yaseran," thei said. "I'll see to it right away."

With that, thei bowed, cast a final glance at the cats on the bed and exited our chamber, the doors shutting softly behind thim. It was the first time Cae and I had been properly alone together in what felt like forever, and my skin prickled all over with the sudden awareness of privacy. In that moment, some feral, desirous part of me wanted nothing more than to strip Cae naked, throw him to the bed and ride him ragged, but though my hands twitched with the urge to grab, I forced myself to stillness. Apart from anything else, I told myself sternly, we had no oil to hand, to say nothing of the likelihood of Markel once again interrupting us or the pair of cats on the mattress.

Instead, I took a deep breath and stepped away. "Unless you'd prefer to go first," I said, nodding towards the bathroom, "I plan to be in there for quite some time."

A smile flitted across Cae's handsome face. "By all means," he said. "Though if you toss me out your clothes, I'll have them laundered with everything else."

Madness overtook me then, or possibly just desire. I'd never considered myself a tease, but rather than answer Cae aloud, I found myself undressing, watching his eyes grow wide as I slowly stripped off my road-worn things, discarding them on the floor. As I pulled off my undershirt, his breathing hitched; as I lowered my nara, mine did. His gaze on me was a heated, tangible thing, and when I finally discarded my smallclothes, I felt dizzyingly wanton.

Flushed from neck to navel, I turned and sauntered towards the bathroom, pretending to a confidence I didn't remotely feel. I'd half expected Cae to come after me, but when he didn't, I wasn't sure whether I was relieved or disappointed. I waited for a moment, half-hard from the thrill of my own antics, and studied the room itself, which featured a similar layout to those at the Aida and the Avai estate. Seeing there was a shower, I let out a small moan: baths were an enjoyable indulgence under the right circumstances, but after—I did some quick mental arithmetic—nineteen days on the road, I craved a means of getting clean that didn't leave me sitting in dirty water, and where truly clean clothes would be available afterwards.

As I stepped under the hot spray, I tried to clear my mind for the first time in the nearly three weeks since we'd left Avai, but found it impossible. I still didn't know what I was walking into, and I silently promised myself that, if the evening's conversation did nothing to remedy my ignorance, I'd swallow my pride and ask Ru Merit to tell me whatever thei could. I felt a dull flash of frustration at Cae, that I'd been reduced to such tactics, but shoved it firmly aside as uncharitable. Nineteen days of travel should've been a luxurious stretch of time in which to learn about my destination, and yet I'd failed to do so: regardless of Cae's reticence, I could've pushed more, found ways to get him to open up, and yet I hadn't. Why was that?

I lingered on the question as I soaped my arms, then stopped, skin prickling with goosebumps as I realised the answer. Hunted as we'd been, the truth was that trying to force the issue with Cae would've felt like squabbling over a boiling pot while the house was on fire. On some level, ever since Etho and the ferry attack, I'd assumed I was going to die before we made it this far; that my would-be assassin would succeed.

I swayed, leaning heavily against the shower wall, my chest tight. For as long as I'd known of my preference for men, I'd understood myself as a kind of slowly unfolding tragedy. I might fuck and dally and even love in secret, but there could be no true future in any of it, not really. Being openly married to Cae felt surreal at the best of times, as though I was perpetually one wrong move away from ruining everything. So when I'd learned of the assassin, a part of me had simply accepted it as inevitable—the universe course-correcting against the possibility of my happiness—and I, without even realising, had resigned myself to it.

Inhaling sharply, I swayed upright, head bowed under the spray, and quietly resolved to be more than a tragedy. My future wasn't set in stone: despite everything, we'd finally made it to Ravethae, alive and whole, and tomorrow, we'd venture to Qi-Xihan. All I could do between now and then was eat, rest and ready myself as best I could, and if there were still important conversations that Caethari and I were yet to have—well. At least there was nothing else here to complicate things.

13

reshly washed, rested and dressed in our new finery, Cae and I headed down to dinner. Markel was elsewhere, eating with the servants, which left me feeling rather as if I were missing a limb. His presence at dinner, I'd learned, would've been a noteworthy breach of convention, and as such, he'd convinced me not to insist on his inclusion. Though I'd ultimately agreed with his reasoning, the necessity of it still left a sour taste in my mouth: evidently, the court culture of Qi-Xihan was more formal than what I'd grown used to in Qi-Katai, and I experienced my first true flash of homesickness for the familiarity of the Aida.

"You look wonderful," Cae murmured, misinterpreting my nervousness, though not without reason; I'd spent the last hour or so fretting over my choice of clothes, a little overwhelmed by the range of options. I'd struggled to decide between a fitted grey and green halik—something I desperately wanted to wear, but which was still sufficiently feminine by Ralian standards that I was struggling to work myself up to doing so in public—and my eventual outfit, a dark blue, asymmetrically cut lin embroidered with silver over a pair of silver nara embroidered with dark blue, their cut so loose and flowing that it was almost like wearing a skirt, except that they tucked into a butter-soft pair of black boots, also newly provided. In addition to its slanting hem, the lin had only one full-length sleeve, exposing the tight black undershirt I'd paired it with on the left-hand side. My hair was loose, my eyes lined with kohl, my jaw shaved to a faint, deliberate stubble, and I'd accentuated the whole look with a pair of silver and sapphire drop earrings. It was the most myself I'd felt in some time, and yet I trembled, not only from Markel's absence, but because one of the expected guests was Ralian, and I didn't know what he'd expect from me.

"Thank you," I replied, a little flustered. "You do, too." Cae's own outfit was simple but striking: a clean white undershirt paired with fitted brown nara and a neat red lin embroidered with yellow and orange flowers. He wore a gold ring in his one pierced ear and had, to my delight, coiled and pinned his braided hair into an artful knot at the back of his head. My fingers had itched to perform the braiding for him, but though the request had danced on the tip of my tongue, in the end, I'd proved myself too cowardly to ask.

"I'm glad you like it," he said, stroking self-consciously at the lin.

I like you, I thought, and had to work so hard at not blurting it out that I almost fell down the stairs.

Sensibly, Ru Merit had arranged for us to eat in one of the smaller dining rooms, with everyone to meet and mingle beforehand in an adjourning parlour. Hearing the murmur of voices, I straightened my posture as we entered, hoping fervently that I wouldn't embarrass myself or Cae at any point in the next few hours.

"Yaseran Caethari, Tiern Velasin!" Ru Merit greeted us warmly. Thei, too, had changed thir clothes, no longer wearing livery but a red silk halik patterned with white cats over black nara. This transformation would've taken me by surprise, had Cae not forewarned me of it; as Ru Merit was acting tonight as Yasa Kithadi's ambassador in a social (rather than purely functional) context, thei were expected to dress more elaborately. As such a thing was unheard of in Ralia, I'd filed this information away as yet another vital detail as to how Tithenai class distinctions worked. "This is Ciet Nevan Ori and his companion, Lord Asrien bo Erat."

Thei gestured to each man as thei spoke, and I found myself staring, arrested by the strange pairing before me. Ciet Nevan was a shortish, pleasant-looking man in his middle forties, not quite nondescript, but not truly handsome, either. The most striking thing about him was his dark grey eyes, though less for their own sake than by virtue of being accented by a slim pair of tortoiseshell-framed spectacles. His colouring was classically Tithenai, his build neither soft nor muscular behind a dark brown lin, the heavy, lustrous silk printed—somewhat incongruously, given his overall demeanor—with snarling tigers.

Lord Asrien, by contrast, looked younger than me, and was short enough besides that, even in his conspicuously well-heeled boots, his head barely reached past my shoulder. His skin was so fair and his hair so golden that he could easily have passed for Attovari or Palamish, but his eyes were a bright, warm brown and—I inhaled sharply—dusted with a faint sheen of shimmering powder across the lids. His small ears were pierced with dangling gold earrings, his other features a compelling mix of sharpness and delicacy, and his pink lips were quirked in a knowing, slightly foxish smile. He was also—tellingly, from my perspective—wearing a halik, as I had feared to do: it was spring green, made of a soft, expensive-looking fabric I didn't recognise, embroidered with a chasing pattern of autumn leaves, slit to the hips and worn over a silk orange undershirt whose fitted sleeves fluttered open at the wrists, paired with an equally orange, equally fitted pair of nara tucked into his knee-high brown boots.

To my Farathel instincts, he read as litai, and specifically as the kind of youth that older litai might call a berry, meaning: small, tartly sweet and ripe for the plucking. The term had applied to me once—possibly it still did, at least where Cae was concerned—and as we drew closer to Ciet Nevan and Lord Asrien, I felt a little frisson of electricity, a thrill between anticipation and danger.

The four of us introduced ourselves with a minimum of awkwardness, though I startled a little when Lord Asrien shook my hand, as I hadn't been expecting it. He smiled coyly up at me, fingers lingering ever so slightly before he pulled away. In Farathel, I would've understood it as part of a subtle dance designed to hint flirtatiously at shared inclinations, but in the present context, I hardly knew what to make of it. Lord Asrien knew I was married to Cae, which made me both a litai and unavailable; and to a Ralian eye, he was already clearly signalling his own preferences through his choice of clothes and makeup. So were the touch and glance the result of long-standing habit, or a calculated choice? When he did the same in greeting Cae, I charitably opted to assume the former, as the latter alternative was rather more disconcerting.

"I'm sorry we've had to meet under the shadow of such circumstances," said Ciet Nevan, with just a touch of unctuousness. He flashed Cae an apologetic look. "Please believe me, were I able to reach your mother and Vesu, I'd contact them in a heartbeat, but as it stands—"

"It's not your fault," Cae said hurriedly. He swallowed hard, striving to keep his tone light. "Do you know when they're scheduled to reach Nivona?"

Ciet Nevan spread his hands. "They may already be there, but that's no guarantee they've received my message. Their plan was to stop at Nsi before progressing to the mainland, and even then, the main Tithenai embassy is inland, in Cahela. And they've always been spontaneous travellers; even if the embassy sends messengers of their own to try and find them, there's no guarantee they'll be where they'd said they'd be." He sighed, rubbing ruefully at his chin. "I'm truly sorry, yaseran."

"It's all right," Cae said quietly. "I knew it wasn't . . . well. Anyway." He forced a smile, turning his attention to our other guest. "Lord Asrien, have you been in Tithena long?"

"Not long at all!" replied Lord Asrien, eyes twinkling. "Just under a month, I believe." His Tithenai was good; a little clipped in places as he searched for a word, but smoothly accented. He turned his attention to me and added, "Tiern Velasin, you've no idea how thrilled I am to meet you, especially given my own reasons for leaving Ralia." A shadow flicked across his features, there and gone, and a lurch of fearful sympathy went through me. I didn't know what—or possibly who—he was fleeing from, but I knew what

Ralia was to men like us, and that was enough. Before I could say anything, however, he brightened again, gesturing at a plush set of couches. "But please, let's sit! Ru Merit—" he flashed thim a boyish grin, "—I do believe you mentioned something about a Nayati wine?"

"I did indeed," said Ru Merit, and with the ice broken, thei set about serving us. I was deeply grateful for the alcohol and accidentally gulped my first sip; the wine was fresh and crisp without being watery, and I struggled to swallow slowly, the better to savour it without looking an oaf. While I was busy not choking, however, the others were moving, and my brief indecision resulted in Ciet Nevan opting to share a couch with Cae, leaving me with Lord Asrien. I was flustered enough that I couldn't think of a sufficiently witty, delicate way to fix things, and so could only answer Cae's slightly panicked gaze with an apologetic grimace.

"You needn't look quite so frightened," Lord Asrien said in Ralian, smiling mischievously as he took his seat. He angled himself towards me, one hand resting lightly on my knee, and a bolt of— heat? unease?—went through me at the contact. "I only bite under very specific circumstances."

"Lord Asrien—"

"Please, just Asrien. We need not stand on formality here."

"Lord—" I bit back the title and forced myself to accept the offer of informality. "Asrien. I—" And then I stopped, having forgotten whatever it was I'd been going to say to him.

The hand on my knee withdrew, and his smile changed, becoming gentler, more genuine. "I'm sorry," he said, the words soft. "I'm being a bit too much, aren't I? And here I promised myself I'd be on my best behaviour." A thread of sadness snaked through the words, and I mentally chastised myself for being so standoffish.

"It's all right," I said, and allowed some of my more private feelings to seep into my voice. "Being here, it's . . . it can be overwhelming, can't it? Wonderful, but so much."

"Exactly that," said Asrien. He laced his fingers together and sighed, his earrings swaying slightly with the motion. "It's not that litai play no games here; it's that they're different games, and I don't yet know the rules, which is disconcerting. I'm used to being *good* at this." The mischievous smile returned. "Or bad, as the situation calls for."

I laughed despite myself. "What do you do in Qi-Xihan?" I asked, which felt a safer question than how he'd come to be here in the first place.

Asrien's lips twitched. "This and that." His gaze flicked meaningfully to Ciet Nevan. "Him, on occasion. Oh, but I'm not aspiring to be your new uncle by marriage!" he added at my look of surprise. "Though Nevan is tempting enough in certain respects. It's more just—hm. Sampling the wares, shall we say?"

I managed a chuckle, though my whole body was fizzing strangely. There was something about discussing such things in Ralian, with a Ralian, and yet in an open context—my husband and Asrien's lover just feet away, Ru Merit hovering by their couch—that evoked the same queer yearning I'd felt on meeting Qarrah; that indescribable sense that here was a freedom I ought to have had all my life, but was only now discovering.

"Have you had any chance to do likewise?" asked Asrien, propping his chin on his hand.

"Do what?"

"Sampling." He flicked his gaze to Cae, who was deep in conversation with Ciet Nevan, and appraised him with an appreciative up-and-down. "Not that your yaseran renders any obvious cause for complaint."

Without meaning to, I raised a hand to the not-quite-a-lovebite Cae had left on my throat during our escapade at the river. Asrien tracked the motion and smirked significantly, making me flush. "It's—he's very—I have not *sampled,* but Cae—I am quite content," I stammered, more awkward than I'd been the first time a handsome man had propositioned me at a Farathel litai gathering.

"I'll *bet* you are," Asrien purred.

The conversation was abruptly too much, brushing far too close to too many things I wished not to discuss, and so I changed the topic, seizing the opportunity to gather some much-needed information. "Do you have any sense of how my—how Cae's and my marriage is being received at court, in terms of the alliance?" I asked. "In Qi-Xihan, I mean, not Farathel."

"*Well*," said Asrien, grinning conspiratorially and leaning in close, "as best I can tell, there's three main factions. One, naturally, views the whole thing as an outrage and an insult, on account of Ralia being a nation of untrustworthy, uncivilised malcontents who let a perfectly good trade route fall to ruin out of spite. Unsurprisingly, that's led by General Naza Karai, who holds the Iron Chair." He looked at me like I ought to know who that was and what it meant, and I felt a flash of angry shame to realise that I didn't. This must've shown on my face, for Asrien's brows shot up in surprise. Smirking very slightly, he said, "Your husband hasn't explained it?"

"No," I bit out, trying very hard not to feel slighted by Asrien, resentful towards Cae or unduly angry with myself. "Why don't you enlighten me?"

With what was either genuine contrition or a very good impression of it, Asrien proceeded to do so. "All right. The Conclave is the governing body in Tithena, the asa's hands and eyes. It's made up of sixteen seats, called chairs—seventeen, if you count Asa Ivadi's, though she mostly serves as the tiebreaker if the others deadlock. Six chairs, like the one your yaseran's grandmother holds—" he gave a cheeky nod towards Cae, now conversing with Ru Merit as well as Ciet Nevan, "—are all inherited, belonging to great nobles of the realm. Collectively, those are called the Circlet, because of course they are." He snorted with amusement. "Of the other ten chairs, half are appointments made by the reigning monarch, which means they do most of the work—diplomacy, agriculture, education, public works, public health." He ticked these off on his fingers like a schoolboy reciting a lesson. "Together, they're called the Heart. The other five, called the Will, are elected positions—one each for the temples, the judicate, the guilds, the military and, as a somewhat novel addition, the people. And of course, each chair has a name—the Iron Chair belongs to the military, for instance, while Clan Taedu holds the Jade Chair."

"What are the others?" I asked, and Asrien promptly rattled off the full list, looking pleased to have an excuse to display his learning. I took a moment to digest it all, parsing the implications in reference to his original comment, then said, "So the army, or at least its representative, is anti-Ralian." I exhaled hard to hide the unease this stirred in me; it was never pleasant to learn that one had enemies, especially powerful, well-armed ones. *I am not a tragedy.* "As you say, I suppose that makes sense."

"Quite," Asrien deadpanned. "As I understand it, the general hasn't held the Iron Chair for long, and was elected in large part because his predecessor, who counselled against war with Ralia in response to vin Mica's predations, was held by his peers to have been weak and ineffective. I haven't met him myself, but now that you're here, I'm sure the opportunity will present itself sooner or later." He rolled his eyes. "Apparently, even the Tithenai military council isn't immune to electing a big strong man who's bad at politics to do an expressly political job because muscles and skill at arms should be a universal form of competence. Do you know, he wasn't even a general before this? The title comes with the job; he's really just a *commander.*"

Suppressing the sudden urge to flee upstairs and hide beneath the bedcovers, I said quickly, "And the other two factions?"

"One wants better relations with Ralia, but dislikes the current approach as represented by you, partly because they've long since written the Taelic Pass off as a lost cause and look to lose money to their competitors if it reopens, but also because, well. You married a man, and Ralia doesn't like that, which means your being here might do more harm than good in the long run. Not my words!" he added quickly. "I'm just repeating what I've heard."

"I know," I said—and I did, though the truth still stung. I cast my mind back over what he'd told me and made an educated guess. "So that faction . . . it's led by the guild representative?"

"Clever boy," said Asrien approvingly, though I was surely his elder. "Specifically, by Ren Calo Adaas, who sits the Bronze Chair. Which leaves us with the final group, who likes you and wants this all to work, led by the Velvet Chair, Ru Kisian Faez, who's in charge of foreign affairs."

Faez. The clan-name was familiar, though it took me a moment to place it. Then it clicked: Ru Liran Faez was Caethari's former lover and a man I quite liked, though the circumstances were such that we'd yet to spend much time together. An odd frisson went through me at the connection: were the two related? It could've been a coincidence, but the suspicious part of me doubted it, and I resolved to ask Cae about it later.

"As for opinions within the court itself," said Asrien, "they run the gamut. Nobody has met you yet, but there are plenty of rumours about certain recent events in Qi-Katai." He smiled sharkishly. "I don't suppose you'd care to give me the details?"

I most certainly would not. "And what's the court like?" I asked instead—quickly, before he could warm to this new theme.

Asrien quirked an amused brow, fully aware of my gambit. "Compared to Farathel, you mean?" he said, indulging me.

"Just so."

"It's . . . different. And yet very much the same." He fluttered a hand, as if to indicate the whole of Tithena. "I've not met the asa personally—only glimpsed her from a distance—but she rules in truth, absolutely, not like Queen Erisa—or at least, not the way it's recorded, at any rate."

I nodded at this; Queen Erisa had ruled Ralia roughly a hundred and fifty years ago after being widowed early in her marriage. Though she'd eventually been succeeded by her son, she'd held power in her own right long past the point where he'd gained his majority, only stepping aside as his ostensible regent when various factions made it clear that a woman on the throne would no longer be tolerated.

Recalling the story prompted me to ask, "Is Asa Ivadi married, do you know? I'd assumed she must be, but I'm not actually sure."

Asrien's expression did something complicated. For the second time since we'd started talking and with a sort of scandalised delight, he said, "Your husband didn't tell you?"

I grit my teeth. "It never really came up."

"Oh, well." Asrien leaned in, grinning conspiratorially. "She *was* married, once, and she has two heirs by the former asan, but twenty years ago, he was caught forcing himself on one of her courtiers, so Asa Ivadi appointed herself the wronged woman's champion, challenged him to a duel and killed him over it—and in full view of the court, too, so no one could claim foul play! Can you even imagine?"

All at once, my hands felt tacky with Killic's blood, and I heard again the wet, horrible noise Cae's jade-handled knife had made as I punched it into his heart. Waves of cold rushed through me, and as if from underwater, I heard myself say, "How extraordinary." Blinking, I pinched down hard on the webbing between my thumb and forefinger, once on each hand, until the bruising ache brought me back to myself sufficiently to ask, "What must her heirs think of it?"

"I'm told it's something of a taboo subject with them, as you can imagine." Asrien leaned back, either ignoring or oblivious to my change in mood, and laughed. "Not that I've met them, of course, though I'll confess to being curious about the asarai." Something almost wistful flashed in Asrien's expression as he said this, there and gone like the flicker of a bird's wing seen through leaves. As cold and distant as I felt, I couldn't interpret it in the moment; nonetheless, some studious part of me tucked it away for later consideration, if only because I hadn't realised that one of the asa's children was kem.

"I've heard thir fashion sense is simply *divine*," Asrien continued, "which must truly be something, given the standards in Qi-Xihan!"

He laughed brightly, gesturing to his own attire. "Can you imagine me wearing this in Farathel? I'd be whipped through the streets!"

I came to my feet without meaning to, abruptly incapable of continuing the conversation. My head was full up with thoughts of Killic—his branding, death and assault of me featured prominently, but a slew of other, more complicated memories were in there, too, including a number of occasions on which he'd either scoffed at or fretted over my use of jewellery and cosmetics. *You'll make a spectacle of yourself,* he'd said once—scathingly, but in the next breath he'd gripped my hand, apologised and begged me not to endanger myself for the sake of fashion, and even with the terrible power of hindsight, I couldn't view his worry then as anything but sincere. Maybe he'd only feared that my exposure would threaten him, too, but either way, he hadn't been wrong.

I stared down at Asrien, whose pretty mouth hung open in shock at my odd behaviour—looked at his beautiful outfit and the obvious care he'd taken to adorn himself—and felt a sort of aching, unfathomable grief rip through me for all the different versions of ourselves we might have been, were our homeland other than what it was. Perhaps even Killic—

"Excuse me," I croaked out, and strode away to the other side of the room, halting only when there was nowhere left to go. I inhaled sharply, gripping the sill of the window before which I found myself, staring past my own unbearable reflection at the twilit grounds. I felt cold and strange and alien, my thoughts a jumble of remembered violence and self-recriminating confusion.

"I apologise for Asri," said a voice by my shoulder.

I jumped, though I hadn't meant to, and found myself looking at Ciet Nevan. "It wasn't his fault," I managed, embarrassed to have been caught sulking.

The ciet chuckled. "My young companion has many skills, but tact isn't always among them." Tone softening, he added, "Your husband has just been telling me about what you endured on your journey here. I can't imagine any of it has left you with much patience for socialising. Please, if at any point you wish to retire and send us early to bed, I promise I won't be the least offended."

It was a tiny courtesy in the scheme of things, but in that moment, I felt it deeply—so much so that I felt a flash of guilt at my initial assessment of him. I fumbled out an awkward thanks, which Ciet Nevan waved off with a smile before inquiring as to whether I had any interest in Tithenai art. It was an unexpected change of topic, but a safe one and therefore welcome. I expressed some curiosity, and he proceeded to explain the origins of certain pieces around the room. Steadily, my chilly dissociation began to thaw, leaving me feeling somewhat human again. My jaw unclenched, and as I returned to myself, I looked on Ciet Nevan with gratitude. Though lacking either the boisterous affability I associated with avuncular men or the self-important authority of paternal ones, his manner was somehow reminiscent of the two in combination: a sort of calm, inquisitive friendliness, neither grating nor boastful, that helped to set me at ease.

By the time Ru Merit politely interrupted to call us to dinner, I was quite relaxed. Casting around the room, I located Cae, who'd evidently been talking to Asrien, and headed over to him.

"Hungry?" I asked, our elbows brushing together as we headed for the dining room.

"I suppose," said Cae. There was something off about his tone, and he must've known it, for in the next breath he forced a smile and said, "Sorry. I think I'm wearier than I realised."

"That's hardly surprising," I said, suppressing a flash of guilt. I'd left him alone to pursue my own conversations, knowing full well his apprehension around being here. Had Asrien upset him somehow, or was it simply the situation? Recalling Ciet Nevan's offer, I added, "If you want to go up at any point, just tell me."

His smile became a fraction more genuine. "I'll keep that in mind."

We sat down to eat, the mood slightly strained. Ru Merit claimed the head of the table, with Cae and me opposite Ciet Nevan and

Asrien. I nudged Cae's foot beneath the table, hoping to convey some measure of solidarity, but though he pressed back, he didn't meet my gaze, too busy toying with his kip. My stomach clenched as the food was brought out, but unsettled as I felt, I was also hungry: our long, anxious journey had had a winnowing effect, and when Cae fell ravenously on his own meal, any compunctions I might've had about doing likewise vanished.

As was common in Tithena, the various dishes were served all at once instead of in courses, allowing the diners to pick and choose as their tastes dictated. I started off with a bowl of fragrant, savoury soup, the golden broth gleaming with oil and rich with a mix of fish, green onion, wild garlic and noodles. After that came several types of dumplings, meltingly soft spiced goat with field rice and a hot plum sauce, and a dish I hadn't had before that Ru Merit said was known locally as pig-leaves: absurdly thin slices of grilled pork marinated with a mix of honey, wine and sesame, layered between equally thin cuts of apple, pear and roast peppers coated with goat's cheese, all held together with tiny skewers. They were utterly divine, so much so that I transferred several to Cae's plate on general principle: everything else might be horrible, but food at least was something we could both enjoy.

There was little talk throughout the meal, and what there was passed mainly between Ru Merit and our guests, with Cae and me only contributing the odd word here or there. When the meal was finally done, however, and a carafe of sweet pink wine was brought to serve in place of dessert, talk inevitably turned to our forthcoming appearance at court.

"The asa likely knows by now that you've arrived," said Ciet Nevan—gently, for which I was grateful, as Cae's grip reflexively tightened on his wineglass. "If not because she's been keeping an eye on the roads, then from my coming here. As such, I expect she'll hold an open court tomorrow in anticipation of seeing you."

"Open court?" I asked.

"As distinct from a closed court, which is by invitation only," the ciet explained. "Though really, you could get away with calling it a salon. The asa presides and various courtiers attend, sometimes to make petitions or by the asa's request, if she wants to speak to them publicly, but otherwise, it's mostly an excuse to gather and be seen—though in this case, of course, your arrival is likely to be the main event." He hesitated, gauging Cae's reaction, then added, "If you like, as Ru Merit has been kind enough to extend thir hospitality overnight, we'd be happy to escort you there."

Cae processed this, then managed a stiff nod. "That would be much appreciated," he said.

Belatedly, I recalled the asa's hidden missive instructing us to observe what we could and report to her. A cold sweat prickled the back of my neck: what could we possibly say on that account that might satisfy her? My thoughts raced, combing through everything we'd seen and done since leaving Avai, searching for relevant details like a tardy schoolboy pawing through his notes ahead of a quiz. Surely there was something I could say of use—

"And of course," said Ciet Nevan, "she may want to discuss the issue of Velasin being your heir to the yaserate."

Everything seemed to freeze.

"I'm sorry," I said faintly, feeling rather as if I'd been struck about the ribs with a whip of ice. "I'm his *what*?"

"His heir presumptive," Ciet Nevan repeated, brow furrowed in puzzlement as he looked between Cae and me. "Am I mistaken? I wasn't aware of Caethari having any preexisting beneficiaries, and your marriage is thus far childless, which means that, in the event of his death, you inherit his estate. Is the law not the same in Ralia? Oh, I suppose it wouldn't be," he added in the same breath, head tilting as he considered it. "Because your women can't—well. Do most things, as I understand it, but in particular can't inherit a man's title."

"Not unless there are no male heirs, and the crown grants the lady's petition to continue her family line—which it won't, if there's a younger male in line but yet to reach his majority," Asrien interjected. "Or if she's pregnant with a legitimate child that *might* be male."

Ciet Nevan wrinkled his nose, as if at a peculiar fishy smell. "Just so," he said. "In Tithena, however—"

"But I *can't* be Cae's heir!" I exclaimed—a little too loudly, if the ciet's startlement was anything to go by. "Not to the yaserate, surely; not when it means a seat on the Conclave! How can I be in line to inherit a thing that isn't yet his? If anything happened to him"—a lump rose in my throat at the prospect—"wouldn't the choice of heir revert to the yasa?"

Ciet Nevan blinked, then flicked his gaze to Cae. "Do you have your grandmother's seal?"

Cae nodded stiffly. Satisfied, Ciet Nevan nodded and turned back to me. "Well, that settles it. Caethari is her official heir, which means that, even should he predecease the yasa—an unpleasant prospect, I admit, but a relevant hypothetical in this instance— the status of heir would pass to you." At my look of shock, he said, "The law was changed, oh, some three hundred years ago, after an incident where it was retroactively proved that a powerful yasan had murdered his younger brother, the previous heir, so that their mother would bestow him the inheritance instead. It caused quite a scandal, and so the reigning asan decreed that, among the great clans, once an official heir was chosen, that inheritance became part of their estate, so to speak, and therefore heritable by their own heir in the event of their death, rather than reverting to the existing title-holder to bestow again. As her own spouse predeceased her some years ago and with Inavi out of the running, had Yasa Kithadi died without naming Caethari, the title would've fallen by default to Tiera—sorry, to *Tierena* Riya—as her eldest grand-child—oh." He came to an abrupt silence, presumably recalling why and how Riya had come by her new title. He grimaced, clearly embarrassed, and finished hurriedly by saying, "In any case, as an officially bestowed inheritance is heritable, you are your husband's heir."

There was too little air in the room; I felt like I might pass out. Desperately, I said, "But that doesn't make *sense*. I've no blood ties to Clan Taedu—I'm not even Tithenai!"

"The first part isn't a problem," Ru Merit said, coming to Ciet Nevan's rescue. "After all, it's not uncommon for noble heirs to be adopted, or else conceived with the help of Zo's Sons or Ayla's Daughters—you've heard of them, I take it?"

I nodded dumbly; the topic had come up in the first days of Cae's and my marriage, though I hadn't expected to have it revisited quite so soon. Zo's Sons and Ayla's Daughters were temple-sworn dedicates who, should the need arise and usually (though not exclusively) with the aid of magic, might sire or carry children for couples who, for whatever reason, were unable to get one between themselves.

Couples like Cae and I.

"So," Ru Merit went on, "the lack of blood ties isn't what matters—and technically, legally, nor should the fact that you're Ralian. But. Well." Thei offered up a sympathetic smile, gesturing broadly to the world beyond the walls. "We live in unusual times. And it's been, oh, decades since a foreign spouse was in direct line to inherit a yaserate."

The frantically spinning wheel of my thoughts came screeching to a halt. Cold washed over me, top to toe, and when I turned to look at Cae, I felt like an ill-carved marionette, all unsanded wood and sharp angles.

"You knew," I said, disbelieving. "You knew I was your heir—your heir to *this*—and you didn't tell me?"

Cae stiffened. "You knew I was my grandmother's heir, and that I didn't want it. Wasn't that enough?"

The rebuke stung—I'd done a poor job of supporting him, I knew that—but still I couldn't stop myself from snapping, "Someone has been trying to *murder* me, Cae! And all the way here I've wondered why, and now I learn I'm in line for a fucking *yaserate*? For a seat on the fucking *Conclave*?"

Cae's handsome face turned ashen. "Gods," he whispered. "Oh gods, it never even occurred to me."

"Of course it didn't!" I shouted. I was shaking again, my throat a tangle of thorns. "Because you won't talk about any of this! I'm trying to help you, trying to get us through—" I gestured wildly to indicate the estate, his inheritance, all of it. "—but there's only so much I can do if you won't tell me what's going on!"

"You think it's *easy*?" Cae shot back. He banged his fist on the table, the sudden thump loud enough that I flinched, and rose sharply to his feet. "I didn't ask for any of this," he said, voice wretched with grief and anger. "This is Laecia's doing, all of it. She did this to us. To you. To *me*. So take it up with her."

And with that, he kicked his chair aside and strode furiously from the room.

For several stunned seconds, no one said anything; I sat dumbly in place, skin heating with mortification. If speaking intimately to a partner while in the company of friends was still painfully new and difficult for me, then fighting with one before strangers was utterly beyond my experience. I felt exposed, ashamed and panicked with no idea what to do next; how any graceful salvage could be made of the situation. I took a reflexive, too-fast gulp of that lovely wine, now tacky and oversweet in my mouth, and stood on legs as trembly as a fawn's.

"Thank you for your company," I stammered out. "I'm sorry, I—we are both overtired. We mean no offence."

"It's all right," said Ciet Nevan. He sounded so understanding; I didn't deserve it, and yet my eyes stung madly. "We'll see you both in the morning."

"Sleep well," added Asrien, so sweetly you could almost miss the barb in his feline smile.

I flinched, stammered something approximating thanks for the meal in Ru Merit's direction and lurched away towards our rooms. I felt unpleasantly like I was drunk, head throbbing and pulse racing, my stomach awash with nerves, not only from the public confrontation, but in anticipation of catching up with Cae. We'd argued before—most notably at Etho, the memory still sharp with guilt—but he'd never stormed off like this in apparent anger.

See? some vicious part of me whispered. *You were always bound to drive him away sooner or later. Who needs an assassin for tragedy?*

Swallowing my fears, I hastened on towards our room, only to hesitate before the door. If Cae was inside, I'd have to talk to him; if he wasn't, I'd worry about where he was.

Just do it, I told myself firmly, and entered.

There was Cae, stripped of his finery and with his braid un-pinned, clad in a pair of plain nara, an old undershirt and his travel-worn boots, his sword and scabbard belted to his waist. He whirled at the sound of my entry, the two of us staring at each other like rabbits caught in a farmer's lanternlight.

"Where are you going?" I asked, heart pounding.

"The armoury," Cae said. "I want to run some combat patterns."

I nodded. Motion soothed him, I knew that, and he'd had pre-cious little chance to keep his form up on the road. But I didn't want him to go, not yet. I had questions to ask.

"The Velvet Chair, Ru Kisian Faez," I said, edging forwards a step. "Asrien said he's leading the faction that wants our marriage to work. Is he—"

Cae shut his eyes, a weary hand scrubbing across his face. "Li-ran's cousin," he grit out. "Or second cousin, I can never remember which. But yes." His hand dropped down, eyes snapping open once more. "And no, I wasn't keeping that from you on purpose; I forgot. I've never even met the man, and Liran's only mentioned him once or twice."

My head whirled with a blizzard of implications. "But he's— Cae, he's *why we're married.* For all we know, the alliance was his idea! And he's Liran's cousin—what if that's not a coincidence?"

Caethari laughed, a harsh, ugly bark. "You say that like you were never betrothed to Laecia."

I froze, whatever I'd been about to say dying on my tongue. I *had* forgotten that, somehow, if only briefly. An indignant, obstreperous part of me insisted that the connection could still matter; that Clan Aeduria might well have come to the Velvet Chair's attention as an alliance prospect thanks to Liran's former relationship with Cae, but even if it was true, did it really matter? Cae had done nothing wrong, least of all kept secrets from me. Why did I keep assuming the worst?

"It's just," I began, and stopped again. I swallowed hard, my mouth full up with words I didn't know how to say. I wanted to do as Cae had done back at Avai, at Etho—apologise first, to show him the care and humility he'd always shown to me—but it was surprisingly hard, the hurt and anger still churning away inside me, yet somehow coexisting with a desire to pull him close. I sought his gaze, and for a miracle held it. He looked . . . tired was an under-statement. Worn down. Eroded. Lost. His parting words about Laecia came back to me, echoed in the slip I'd made—the fact that I'd forgotten my connection to her, even for an instant—and I felt all over again the enormity of what he'd lost on my account: A father. A sister. His chosen place in the world.

The chance to choose his husband.

My heart sank. What sort of selfish thing was I, to fault him for not having told me I was his heir? My knowing would've changed nothing, except that I would've had more to fret about. I hated that we'd argued where people could see us, and some ugly, sharp-edged part of me wanted to yell at him for it, as though the fight hadn't been my fault in the first place, but I swallowed it down, struggling to do better, *be* better.

"Caethari, I—"

"Do you want a child?" Cae asked abruptly, cutting me off.

I faltered, my mouth falling open. "What?"

"A child," Cae repeated. "Do you want one?"

I tamped down hard on an urge to laugh hysterically. "What, *now*?"

"It would solve our problem," Cae said. His voice was hollow, so exhausted that it had circled back around from anger to blank disaffection. "If we had a child, they'd be my heir, not you."

I did laugh at that, the sound jagged and choked. "A child would solve *nothing*," I spat, advancing on him, "because the problem, as ever, is *me*, not anything you've done or failed to do." I felt light-headed as I reached him, one hand moving unconsciously to smooth the rumpled fabric of his shirt, though even then, I was far from unmoved by the musculature beneath it. He inhaled sharply, but didn't push me away; and I, coward that I was, kept my gaze fixed on his throat, the better to avoid his eyes. "I am a poor sort of man in many respects, but I will not foist on an innocent child a burden I fear to lift myself. And I am afraid of this one, I can admit it. But that is no more your fault than anything to do with this inheritance." I took a deep breath. "I'm sorry, Cae. Truly."

My husband made a small, hurt noise, as if I'd punched him somewhere tender. "I don't know what to do with you in these moments, Vel," he said, voice rough. "I truly don't." His hands gripped my shoulders, hard enough that it was my turn to gasp; I looked up and saw wildness in his eyes. "You pull away, draw close, step back. You make me hope. You *dizzy* me," he rasped, and dropped his hands, setting space between us. "But I can't make your mind up for you. And what I need, right now—gods! What I need is air." He ran both hands over his head, eyes briefly falling shut. "I need *air*," he murmured again, and promptly sidestepped me, striding out of our suite in presumable search of a patch of sky under which to wield his sword.

Leaving me alone, my heart a clenched fist throbbing in my chest.

14

Shakily, I moved to the bed and sat down on it, staring at nothing. I didn't know what had just happened, not really; only that whatever fault existed between us was, as ever, mine. Cae was so good, and yet I kept hurting him, over and over, until even my kindness cut.

Something soft butted against my hand. I looked down, and there was Spoons, purring as she set her paws to my thigh and started kneading.

"Oh," I said, stupidly. "Oh."

I began to cry; softly at first, and then in deep, wrenching sobs that doubled me over, clutching my own stomach. All the fear and anxiety I'd stored up over our journey, the tension from dinner; everything came pouring out of me in a great, wrenching rush, until I could scarcely breathe for tears.

The next thing I knew, Markel was there, seated beside me and squeezing my hand. I looked up at him, wet-eyed and startled; I had no idea how long he'd been there or when he'd come in, and yet I was desperately grateful for his presence.

"What is it?" he signed—low down, where I could see it. "What's happened?"

"Nothing," I replied aloud, then shook my head, straightening as I reverted to signs, which were always easier in moments of distress. "Nothing, except it turns out I'm Cae's heir to the yaserate—I know, it's absurd, but Tithenai law is absurd—and I picked a stupid fight with him for not telling me about it, and I keep *hurting* him, Markel, even when I don't mean to. Why am I like this?" Voice rasping, I echoed that final query aloud, in Ralian. "Why am I *like* this?"

Markel made a considering noise. "Do you want the short answer or the long one?"

I laughed despite myself, smacking him over the shoulder even as I hiccupped, still crying. "Stop it!"

"So you don't want an answer?"

"I want to be *better*," I said, and without conscious volition, I let myself slump sideways over Markel's lap, my damp face pressed to the bedsheets as Spoons, not the least deterred by my antics, walked up onto my now-horizontal hip and settled herself there, anchored in place like a small, fluffy ship.

Markel sighed and rubbed my back, the way he'd often done when we were younger. I let the contact soothe me, and eventually, when I'd stopped crying, I rolled over—much to the displeasure of Spoons, who made an indignant noise at being forced to relocate once more—so that my head was in his lap.

"What do you want me to say?" he asked, his hands above my face. "I could say that he's terrible or that you are, but either would be a lie, and it wouldn't help. You're married. You're hurting. It's hard. What do I know about it?" He hesitated, smiling slightly as he smoothed my hair out of my eyes. "As for being heir to a yaserate . . . well. You already knew you'd hold the same rank when Caethari inherited. Why does it make such a difference?"

I blinked at him. "What?"

Markel stared down at me, frowning. "Don't tell me you hadn't realised."

I sat up beside him, flustered. After a moment, I said aloud, "I don't think I'd been letting myself think that far ahead. Cae doesn't want this inheritance, and he's already seen enough death. Why make it worse by thinking about what happens when his grandmother dies?"

Markel raised a slightly judgemental eyebrow. "And yet learning you were his heir upset you?"

"Yes, but that's different!" I exclaimed. "Marrying into a title is one thing, but holding it in my own right is—what?" I broke off, my chain of thought disrupted by the sight of Markel hiding his face in hands. He shook with silent laughter, but when he looked at me again, his expression was serious.

"Velasin," he signed, "for someone so smart, you can be uniquely dense at times. You keep thinking of yourself as Caethari's wife in the Ralian sense, which you already know is wrong, but because of how Ralian wives are treated, you've been assuming, too, that your title and authority are less than his here, because you married in. But they're not, and *you're* not. Haven't you noticed? You'll be a yasan in your own right one day, and I know—" he paused, holding a hand palm-out to forestall my response, "—I know you've always said you're allergic to being responsible, but that was, again, in *Ralia,* where responsibility meant taking a wife, and you don't have to do that here, because you already have a husband. So." He took a deep breath, steadying his hands. "As your friend, I think what you really need to be asking yourself is, are you actually capable of managing a yaserate, knowing you're married to someone who doesn't want to? Because I think you could be."

I gaped at him. "What?"

"You like having projects," Markel signed. "More than like, you *need* them, or you start to go peculiar, and what bigger project is there than to manage this sort of territory? You care about people, you notice things, and we both know you're savvy at politics. The only real issue is being a Ralian in Tithena and not knowing how things work, but the way I see it, assuming nothing untoward befalls Yasa Kithadi, you've years still before Cae inherits—why not use that time to learn what you'll have to do next?" More gently, he added, "I like Caethari very much, but we both know this isn't his forte; you keep fretting over how to be a good husband to him, but all you need to do is what he can't, which I think you'd be good at."

I sat in stunned silence for several seconds, digesting all this. Moons, but I'd been an idiot! Markel was right, and while I ought to have been used to the phenomenon by now, in this instance, it set my heart pounding. Back in Qi-Katai, when Cae and I had first talked about what our marriage would mean for me in a practical, occupational sense, the answer had been, more or less, that I could do what I wished. As we'd had more pressing matters to deal with both then and since, I'd not paused to give it a second thought. But running a yaserate . . . I swallowed, unable to share Markel's faith in my abilities. With no false modesty, I was the third son of a minor lord, and as studious as I'd been in certain respects, unlike my elder brother Nathian or even our middle brother Revic, I'd never been taught to manage even our small family estate, as nobody had ever thought I'd inherit it. To find myself in line for something equivalent to a dukedom was, therefore, entirely beyond my capacity.

An ugly realisation wormed its way through my heart. Cae deserved not only a spouse who returned his love, but also one who could govern alongside him, perhaps even for him at times. Was that me? Could that ever be me? What good would it do to love my husband if I couldn't be what he needed?

I felt abruptly sick. We'd be at court tomorrow, where my presence would be yet another complication in Cae's life: a problem he'd have to answer for, and still without any guarantee that I'd stay, or be worthy of him if I did.

Markel clicked his fingers to get my attention; I glanced over and found his gaze narrowed. "You're overthinking this," he signed.

"Not overthinking," I signed back. "Thinking just enough."

He made a rare, frustrated vocalisation. "You *can* run a yaserate," he signed emphatically. "You and Caethari together would be good at it. I'm not trying to tell you what to do, but just—don't sit here and talk yourself out of it as though it's all impossible. Actually take your time and *think*."

"I'll try," I said, swallowing, though it felt as useless as a vow to fathom the ocean's depths. "I promise I'll try."

Markel considered this, studying my face. "All right," he finally allowed, giving my shoulder a companionable bump with his own. "But I want you to be happy, Velasin. I want you to fight to be happy. Imagine what you'd be saying to me, if our positions were reversed!"

"That's *different*," I mumbled. "You're *you*."

Markel's face softened. "Just think about it," he signed again, "and know that, whatever you decide, you'll have my support."

And with that, he rose and headed off to his own chambers opposite, leaving me to wonder what in the moons I was going to say to my husband.

Half hoping he'd return soon enough that I'd be forced to extemporise, half in dread of yet again putting my foot in my mouth, I petted Spoons absently, kicking my heels against the bedframe for some minutes before finally summoning the strength to strip out of my fine things. I showered and prepared for sleep with little conscious awareness of doing so, my thoughts preoccupied with the implications of Markel's pep talk. I was so distracted that, once I was clean and dry, my ablutions completed, I slipped into one of the hipwraps Ru Merit had provided without quite realising, only to be drawn up short by a glimpse of my own reflection in the mirror. I stared at myself, heart pounding as I traced the slight dip at my waistline. It was my first time wearing a hipwrap, a garment which, to my Ralian sensibilities, appeared ineluctably feminine; I'd coveted them before now, wondering when I might have the courage to attempt one, and had evidently made the decision without consulting myself.

This felt enough like a metaphor for my current situation that I flushed and turned away, hurrying to shrug into a green silk robe. I'd just finished knotting it loosely when I was interrupted by a tentative knock at the door. My heart did something complicated at the sound; it was just like Cae to knock when he didn't need to, worried even now about intruding on my privacy. But I still didn't know what to say to him, and so I took a deep breath before turning the handle, preparing myself to face him.

But when I opened the door, I found myself looking, not at Cae, but at Asrien.

"May I come in?" he asked—a little shyly, and in Ralian. Startled, I found myself looking him up and down. Like me, he'd undressed for the evening, his face washed clean of powder and paint. His blond hair was slightly damp at the ends, worn loose around the collar of an oversized red velvet robe, which he clutched closed over his chest. Rather than a hipwrap, he worse loose silk pants, as a Ralian gentleman might in the privacy of his rooms, and I couldn't help but notice that these fit him perfectly—unlike the robe, which despite his grasp on it was in danger of skewing open over one pale shoulder.

"All right," I said warily, replying in the same language. I stepped back to admit him, and Asrien hurried in past me. As I closed the door, he perched on the end of the bed, worrying the seam of his robe with the hand not holding it shut, and I felt a brief bloom of anxiety at being seen in my hipwrap by someone other than Cae. Not that it was visible beneath my robe, which fell to my knees; it was just that *I* knew I was wearing it, and so I had to fight to suppress an embarrassed flush.

"I'm sorry," Asrien said suddenly, not meeting my gaze. "For being sharp at dinner. I was . . . I didn't mean it."

"All right," I said again, a questioning note in the words. I wasn't sure why he was here or what he wanted, but without his stylish adornments, he looked smaller, younger—not helpless, but lost in a way I knew too well.

Asrien picked angrily at a stray thread, then abruptly stilled, his shoulders slumping. "I thought it would be different here," he said. "And it is. But it's not what I imagined." He laughed bitterly. "I didn't know how to imagine this."

"Imagine what?" I asked, but I had a sinking feeling I already knew.

"What it's like for men like us, who've never had to hide." He darted a glance at me, then looked down again, plucking agitatedly at his robe. "All these ways I am, I thought—I thought I just *was.*

Would always be. That we all were." He looked up, an angry vulnerability in his gaze, mouth twisted. "Sharp. Secretive. Competing for points. With each other. For each other. And Tithena is still like that. There's still *political games*." He pronounced the phrase like a synonym for *garbage*. "So naturally I wind up playing them, because that's what I know. But they're not about *me*. And if I fail, there's no—" he waved a hand, causing his robe to fall open and almost off, though he didn't appear to notice; "—no *risk* of being revealed, and yet there *is* a risk to being Ralian."

I didn't like feeling sympathy with Asrien, but neither did I care to discuss with him the apparent divergence of my feelings from his own on the issue of politics, not least because I was still processing the prospect of one day running a yaserate. Instead I asked, carefully, "What sort of risks?"

Asrien cut me a withering look. "Your own husband has worked to keep you ignorant of what you're walking into. Isn't that a risk?"

"If it is, I hardly need you to tell me about it," I shot back, stung to hear my earlier criticism of Cae in Asrien's mouth. "My marriage is none of your concern."

I'd expected him to argue, but instead he stilled, an odd expression on his face. Then he rose, his robe pooled behind him on the bed, and stepped towards me. Though his arms were folded across his chest, a hint of pale pink nipple still peeked from behind his forearm.

"Isn't it?" he asked, softly.

I swallowed, abruptly discomforted. "Why would it be?"

"Because for all its faults, I love Ralia, and I want to go home someday." He moved closer—slowly, as though I were a horse in danger of spooking, his voice more naked than I'd yet heard it. "And so long as you stay married here, I fear that to be impossible."

It was like being slapped. I jerked backwards, staring at him. "What?"

"Why else do you think I'm here, now?" He flitted his fingers as if to indicate the room, the estate, the whole of Tithena. "Before this, I was in Eliness. Gossip travels fast in port cities; faster than elsewhere. I was already under suspicion, and when news of your marriage reached us, I was the nearest available target. I had to leave." His expression was close to pitying. "Velasin, what did you think would happen? I don't mean in Farathel, between King Markus and his offsiders; I mean everywhere else in Ralia. As word spreads further, who do you think will bear the brunt of it? Who will suffer?" His smile was pained. "I don't say this to blame you; I might not know all the details, but I understand that you never meant to be revealed this way—and even if you had, you couldn't have known how things would end up; and even if you'd suspected it, you still had to get out of Ralia; you still had to *survive.* But now that you're here, it's different."

As a child, there were times when my brothers sought to get me in trouble with Father by reporting something I'd really done, but without the context that made the act comprehensible. *Velasin broke a window!* Revic had gleefully tattled once, leaving me to stammer that a bird had attacked its reflection in the glass so violently and repeatedly that, when it finally fell to the ground and I opened the window to check on it, the pane had shattered the instant I closed it again. Father, though, hadn't liked what he saw as my attempt to evade responsibility for my actions, and as I'd stood before him, a hot, fearful panic had crept through me as I worried that it really was my fault. I felt the same way now: I'd done exactly what Asrien said, and was so horrified by the implications that I didn't know how to argue against my own culpability.

"Different how?" I asked instead, dazed.

"Because," said Asrien, stepping closer again, "you don't have to stay married." Tentatively, he extended a hand to me, curling his slender fingers loosely around my wrist, his brown eyes huge and earnest. "Tithenai law is kind to spouses who want a divorce, and unless I miss my guess, you don't love the yaseran." His thumb moved slowly back and forth, stroking along my veins, and through the all-encompassing fear and shock, I felt a new unease. "You wouldn't even have to divorce, if you didn't want to go through the legal proceedings, and who could blame you for that? You could just leave, and after a time, the yaseran could appeal to have the marriage annulled on the grounds of abandonment."

"Leave?" I croaked. I was breathing too fast, a claustrophobic dizziness ringing through my head, throat, heart. I stared at Asrien's fingers around my wrist and felt a lurch of wrongness in my stomach. He'd taken hold so gently that I hadn't initially registered it as grabbing, but all at once the touch felt wrong, and I jerked my hand back, staring at him.

Undeterred, Asrien stepped closer. "Just leave," he said softly, raising the hand I'd shunned to trail its fingertips along my jaw. "You deserve better than this," he said, and I froze in shock as much as fear as he leaned up to kiss my throat. "We both deserve better, don't we?"

He lifted his mouth to mine, an exploratory press. I couldn't move, and then I felt the soft, wet flick of his tongue against my lips, seeking entrance, and my body finally answered me, both hands rising to shove him away.

"Don't *touch* me!" I snarled, or maybe sobbed; the words came out as raggedy as if I'd torn them from living muscle. Asrien was smaller than me, and I'd shoved him hard enough that he'd stumbled; he looked genuinely shocked for a moment, and then his expression cooled, becoming a mask.

"My apologies," he said, aiming for insouciant but sounding stiff. "I appear to have misread the situation."

"You have," I said, hands clenched by my sides.

A flash of the cutting smile I'd seen at dinner returned. "How silly of me, to think you'd care for the rest of us." His lip curled. "Or yourself."

"Get out," I rasped.

"That's the real tragedy of being Ralian for men like us, you know." He sighed, tossing the words at me as he sashayed over to retrieve his robe. He made a show of shrugging into it, casting me a pitying look as he did so. "We don't know how to be happy, let alone how to do what's best for ourselves." He laughed mirthlessly. "I certainly don't."

"*Out,*" I said again, the single word all I could manage. *We are not tragedies.*

"On the other hand," he went on, continuing as if I hadn't spoken, "it makes us more forgiving than we ought to be." He paused before me, a flicker of something in his face, then raised a hand to smooth the front of my own robe, neatening the closure across my chest with a short, firm tug. "If you change your mind," he said, his tone a hair away from conversational, "you know where to find me."

With that, he left. The door clicked shut, and I stared at it for three full seconds before my legs gave out. I dropped down in an awkward spraddle, wobbly as a newborn foal, and stared dumbly at my hands. I was shaking, I realised distantly, my throat tight. Part of my mind was working furiously, comparing Asrien's botched attempt at seduction to Killic's assault like a tailor holding a fabric swatch to a ruined coat to see if it matched; another part was numb, as empty as the void at the heart of a whirlpool; and yet a third part was reliving the moment I'd learned of Killic's infidelity, wondering if I'd just dealt my husband a similar pain. After all, hadn't I been the one to let Asrien into our rooms? Hadn't I stood there, dumb and yielding, as he made his intentions clear? I'd pushed him away, but not soon enough.

What would I say to Cae? What *could* I say? I'd shamed him at dinner, then proven so contrary in the aftermath that he'd stalked off to get some respite from me. He could be back at any time; my heart jolted at the thought, and my gaze jerked back to the door, certain it would swing open and admit him that very moment.

But nothing happened. The door remained closed and Cae

remained absent, and so I stayed uselessly in place, my thoughts a horrid snarl. The worst of it was that Asrien had a point: I hadn't considered what my marriage would mean for other men like us in Ralia. It wasn't something I could control, and moons knew, I'd seen enough ugliness to know that the kind of person who wished us violence didn't lack for justifying excuses—the mere prospect of our existence was sufficient provocation. None of us could ever shrink ourselves small enough to satisfy such hatred, so what was the point in trying? And yet we *did* try, because there was far too often no other path to comparative safety. We kept ourselves secret, but here I was, flouting that secrecy before two nations for the sake of a marriage I hadn't asked for, but which I found myself wanting to preserve, striving to find balance with a man who loved me, but whom I didn't love, whose needs were incompatible with my expertise, and yet which Markel thought I could attempt—and still, *still,* I'd let Asrien corner and kiss me like some guileless Farathel berry at his first illicit gathering.

And yet, and yet . . . I shut my eyes, my breathing ragged as I struggled and failed to reconcile the evening's events. My legs began to numb from my awkward posture, but I stayed where I was, certain that I didn't deserve the comfort of bed until Cae returned and I'd given him the chance to throw me out.

But Cae didn't return. I don't know how long I sat there, mired by guilt and the pull of unanswerable questions, but as my physical aches became harder to ignore, it finally dawned on me that perhaps I already had my answer.

What if Cae had never planned to come back to me in the first place?

The thought was paralysing, panic-inducing—almost absurdly so, given what had preceded it, and yet I couldn't shake it. A bubble of manic laughter escaped me. *Which is it, Velasin?* snarled an internal voice. *Do you want him to come back or don't you?*

I don't know, a different voice answered wretchedly. *I just want it to not be my fault.*

All at once, I realised I was exhausted. Unless I wanted to hunt through the estate for Cae to have things out with him now—which I viscerally didn't, not least because I still had no idea what to say to him—then sleep was my best option. I considered going across the hall to ask Markel's opinion, but he was likely already abed, and in any case, I could all too clearly imagine the look he'd give me and the words that would likely accompany it: *Go to sleep, Velasin.*

Hissing at the cramp in my legs, I hauled myself upright and hobbled over to bed, where I crawled in facedown and lay, starfishing twitchily, until my limbs no longer hurt. I screwed my eyes shut, certain I wouldn't be able to sleep but determined to make the effort, and promptly blundered into a deep, sticky unconsciousness. The next thing I knew, I was awake again, my limbs as stiff and heavy as if I'd never once moved in my sleep. Morning light streamed in from the window above the bed; I blinked in slow adjustment to it and rolled on my side. Muzzy as I was, I didn't initially process the significance of the undented pillows beside me, the lack of humming from the bathroom, until I smoothed a hand over the cool, unrumpled sheets and realised they hadn't been slept in—and then, all at once, I understood.

I've lost him.

I wanted to deny it, but I could think of no reason for Cae to have kept away except that he was avoiding me; that my feeble attempt at apologising had been too little, too late when weighed against my myriad inadequacies. I clutched the coverlet to my chest like a scandalised maiden from the randier type of Ralian gentlemen's literature and choked back a sudden burst of hysteric laughter at the irony: that I'd gone from fearing the prospect of sharing my husband's bed to grieving his absence from it. And then, almost eerily, I calmed, because whatever else could be said of Cae, I didn't believe he'd put either of us through the ordeal of appearing together at court if he was already planning on leaving me. But even so, how was I to tell him about Asrien?

I was yet to answer this question when the bedroom door swung open, revealing both Cae and Markel. Cae looked exhausted: there were dark circles under his eyes, and he was covered in straw and dirt, as if he'd been rolling around in a hayloft.

"Apologies," Cae rasped. "I was—that is, I didn't mean to stay out all night, but—"

"Your idiot husband fell asleep in the stables," Markel signed tartly, making sure that Cae could see him. "Which means the entire estate is now gossiping about the apparently fragile state of your marriage, which means your guests are surely aware of it, and even were they not, as Ciet Nevan has already sent his servant back to Qi-Xihan to have things readied for his and your arrival, the gossip will spread regardless."

"I only meant to rest my eyes for a minute," Cae mumbled, glancing at me with a hangdog expression. "And then suddenly it was morning. I'm sorry, Vel."

I stared at him, a jumble of words howling behind my teeth. *Asrien kissed me last night. I don't deserve you. If I can't run a yaserate, what use am I? Do you want me still? I don't know what to do.* I wanted to confess, but I've always been cowardly, and in the moment, I realised I was fearful of Markel's disapproval, too; or worse yet, of his forgiveness. The silence stretched awkwardly, Cae looking more remorseful by the moment, and it was this expression which finally jolted me into speech.

"It doesn't matter," I said, biting back a whirling mix of emotions. "We have to get ready." I rose from the bed, then hesitated, a sudden lump in my throat. "Unless you—unless there's anything else you'd like to say?" *Unless this is it,* I'd wanted to ask, but once again, I couldn't get the words out.

Cae winced guiltily, but shook his head. "There's not. I'm sorry. I'll get cleaned up." He hurried to the bathroom.

Markel raised a pointed brow at me, arms crossed. I flushed and strode to the wardrobe, pretending I couldn't see it. If I was to get through the morning with any semblance of dignity, I had to put my stupid, incomprehensible feelings aside and act like a person, and if that meant lying to the people I cared most about in the world, well. I was hardly under any illusions as to my worth as a human being.

"We ought to take most of these new things," I said aloud—firmly, to forestall any attempt at a change in conversation, though my throat was painfully tight. "Regardless of whether we end up staying at court or at the house in Qi-Xihan, they're nicer by far than anything we brought with us."

Markel made a disgruntled noise, but mercifully didn't say anything more, and so I threw myself into our final preparations before the capital, seeking distraction in action. Having agonised over my clothing the night before, I was at least familiar with my options for court, and so was able to make a swift selection for the day's attire. By the time Cae emerged, freshly washed and shaved, Markel had already bustled off with most of my new things, which left me to be the one to say, "Pick what you're wearing; Markel will pack the rest," before taking my own turn in the shower, studiedly refusing to interpret the expression on Cae's face or think about how he stood where Asrien had.

Even so, I couldn't shut off my heart entirely, and halfway through combing my hair, I realised I was angry at my husband. Of all the absurdities! I glared at myself in the mirror, yanking hard on the knots and snarls as a form of self-penance. What right did I have to be angry at Cae? Just because he'd slept in the fuck-ing *stables* in preference to our bed and left me thinking myself abandoned—an abandonment I likely *deserved*, after letting Asrien kiss me—

The urge to rush out, fall to my knees and beg for Cae's for-giveness was as sudden as it was overwhelming. I gripped the edge of the sink with my free hand until the knuckles blanched, scalp stinging from the brush.

Stop it, I told myself firmly. *He's already stressed enough about appearing at court; what good would it do, to give him an extra worry now? You can tell him tonight.*

It felt like cowardice. It *was* cowardice. I bit my lip until I tasted blood.

When I'd finally mastered myself, I emerged to dress alongside Cae, who was taking a conspicuous amount of time over his clothes. He kept glancing at me as if he hoped I'd say something to him, but I, selfish creature, pretended not to notice, because he didn't deserve to be snapped at or importuned with the litany of my failings and I didn't think myself capable of anything else just yet.

Once Markel confirmed we were all packed up, Cae and I were summoned to an unnecessarily lavish breakfast courtesy of Ru Merit and thir staff, where Ciet Nevan proceeded to make innocuous conversation about the weather while Asrien shot me a series of knowing looks over the baked eggs. It would've been unbearable if not for the timely intervention of Spoons, who spent the majority of the meal alternately weaving around my feet, mewing for scraps and trying to get on the table. The eventual compromise involved her sitting on my lap, accepting titbits of meat and cheese—and, to my great surprise, bread—while purring continuously. Her antics did more to clear my mood than I would've thought possible given Markel's enforced absence from the meal, and though my clean, good things ended up lightly rimed with fur as a result, I considered the trade-off more than worth it.

As the meal wrapped up, Cae suddenly excused himself; I didn't think much of it until he returned with his sword at his hip. Or, no—not his sword, but a different one, presumably borrowed from the estate's armory, the hilt and scabbard more ornate than the one he'd carried from Avai, and thus better suited to match his fine attire. A shiver ran through me at the sight: even without the pursuit of my would-be assassin, it made sense for a nobleman of Cae's rank to go armed at court, and yet something about the image of a weapon beautified to pass as fashion unsettled me in the moment.

Cae tracked my gaze to the sword and grimaced apologetically; I shook my head, denying the apology was needful, and he subsided.

With breakfast done, we thanked Ru Merit for the clothes and thir hospitality—which thei, as Yasa Kithadi's agent, waved off as a trifle—and promised to inform thim of whatever accommodations we wound up taking in the city, whether at the yasa's property or elsewhere. Spoons stalked out to blink at us as we mounted up, and I'll admit to having waved farewell to her as much as to Ru Merit before we turned down the drive and departed, Ciet Nevan in the lead.

We were perhaps halfway between the estate and the city when the sense of danger represented by my would-be assassin returned to haunt me. For a moment, I froze atop Gift like a statue; then I breathed again, taking stock of where we were: on an open road, in broad daylight, with no geographical quirks inviting of accident or ambush anywhere nearby, and with Ciet Nevan, who was also armed, as an additional deterrent. Even so, my heart pounded, and I found myself dropping back to ride alongside Markel, who was once more leading our laden packhorses.

Clicking his fingers to catch my attention, Markel signed, "They won't know I can speak Tithenai at the capital. Should I play the listening game?"

Gratitude formed a lump in my throat. Still, I signed back, "What about our companions? Didn't you meet their servant last night?"

"I did," Markel allowed, "but only in passing, and in any case, I didn't get the impression he'll be coming along to court. And your *friends*—" he cocked an amused brow towards Asrien and Ciet Nevan, "—haven't spoken to me at all."

A breath whooshed out of me. "Yes, then," I signed. "Thank you, Markel."

Slyly, Markel signed back, "You should go and tell your husband." And then, with a flash of mercy, added, "He really does feel badly about last night."

I glared at him; Markel only grinned. Even so, I urged Gift on to keep pace alongside Cae, who was staring grimly ahead with his hands clenched on the reins.

Catching his attention, I signed carefully, "Markel will play the listening game for us."

A tiny amount of tension ebbed from Cae's shoulders. "That's a relief," he murmured aloud.

"What's a relief?" asked Asrien, who'd dropped back to join us. He was riding a neat golden mare, her mane and tail braided with pale green ribbons, but her sweet appearance was belied by an aggressive tendency to lay her ears back and snap at Alik and Gift if she felt they were coming too close. *Like horse, like rider,* I thought, and bit my lip against a mean little burst of laughter.

"Oh," said Cae, flustered, "oh, just—riding in greater numbers. It was only the three of us before, and with someone in pursuit—"

Asrien made an understanding noise. "Of course!"

He tried to steer his mare closer, but yelped in annoyance when she snaked out her neck to try and bite Alik, who rolled his eyes and sidestepped to avoid her. Embarrassed, Asrien turned red and began to apologise, but after all his sly looks over breakfast, I couldn't stop myself from quipping sweetly in Ralian, "It's all right; some creatures just don't know how to socialise without showing their teeth."

Asrien glared at me for that, but otherwise behaved himself, for which I was grateful, and in due course, an uphill turn in the road brought Qi-Xihan's enormous, distant wall into proper view. I gaped at it, struggling to comprehend the sheer scale of what I was looking at: I'd glimpsed it the previous day from the rise at Ravethae's boundary, but the distance had been too great to do the sight justice. The structure must have been a hundred and fifty feet tall, absolutely dwarfing anything I'd ever seen in Ralia, encircling the whole front of the city, which was cradled on its other three sides by sheer mountain cliffs.

"Moons," I whispered, "how did they build so big?"

"With magic, purportedly," Cae answered, a touch of pride in his voice. "But also considerable engineering skill. The walls are sixty feet thick in places, cored with solid earth. They've never been breached."

"I can imagine," I said faintly. The walls looked silvery at a distance, but as we came closer, I could see they'd once been painted in places—massive, abstract geometries of black, white and pale blue, squarish circles within circles and chasing, flowing lines whose meaning must've been significant once upon a time, to justify the effort of creating them, but which were now fading into genteel opacity. I was on the brink of asking Cae about it when my attention was caught by something else: a strange, vertical straggle of structures along the adjacent mountainside. The scale was so vast that it took me a moment to process what I was seeing, at which point my mouth fell open.

"They're *building*?" I exclaimed. "Up *there*?"

"Technically, they're building *in* there," said Cae. "What's outside is mostly used to make light and air shafts, or pulleys to bring equipment up and waste rock down. All the real expansion goes on inside the mountain, because it's the only available space." He gestured meaningfully to indicate the whole of Qi-Xihan, snug in its vale between wall and mountains. "There's work on the eastern faces, too, but the western caves are the oldest."

I nodded dumbly, not caring if I looked the gawking yokel, and with a wrench of will turned my attention instead to the city's three main entrances. These were spaced at even intervals along the wall: a trio of massive arched gates, each easily wide enough for twenty mounted soldiers to have ridden through abreast, and all—as far as I could see, though the distance played merry hob with my sense of scale—aswarm with people coming and going. My awe grew in concert with our approach, and when it was finally our turn to pass beneath those massive walls, a shiver passed over me.

Ralia boasts more than one walled city—notably the port city of Aroven and the citadel of Tithe near the border with Khytë, though I've never seen the latter—but the depth of Qi-Xihan's walls was astonishing. The gate through which we entered was more like a tunnel, long enough that the light dimmed in the middle, while the walls on either side, despite the great weight of stone above them, contained rooms populated by the city guards. I half expected us to be stopped and questioned, but though other guards were stationed on either side of the gate, none of them raised so much as an eyebrow at our passing.

When we emerged into the city itself, my breath caught all over again. Whereas Qi-Katai was built on a hill, with the Aida seated at the pinnacle of several tiered districts, Qi-Xihan lay on a gentle upward slope, so that the city, though spread out, gave the impression of a wave, swelling towards the bright crest of the palace. It was impossible to miss, not only due to the size of the structure or even its pinnacle location, but also because, from where we'd halted just beyond the middle gate, a broad, lengthy roadway snaked ever upwards towards it, traversing the entire city. My eyes tracked the lines of it, widening as I reckoned its scope: though various twists and turns were hidden from view by buildings and the steadily rising ground, the road itself was made of distinctive white stone, which stood out against the colourful rooftops and grey paving used elsewhere.

"Properly, it's called the Asa's Ribbon," said Ciet Nevan, moving up alongside me, "built to honour Asa Sinyavi, oh, five hundred years ago?" He grinned, the sunlight glinting off his glasses. "These days, though, it's mostly known as the Stagger, on account of—well." He waved a hand to indicate the loops and turns. "It's like a drunk's progress, ambling downhill."

I snorted despite myself. "And now we get to climb it."

Ciet Nevan raised a brow. "Do you want to stop by the yasa's house first? It should be on our way."

I glanced at Cae and was oddly relieved when he shook his head. "No," he said, with just a hint of sigh. "If we end up there, so be it, but I'd rather just get this over with."

Asrien opened his mouth at that, doubtless to make some tart remark, but kept silent at a pointed glance from Ciet Nevan.

"Come, then," said the ciet. "Asa Ivadi awaits."

And so we began our final ascent along that bright, white road.

15

Up close, the royal palace at Qi-Xihan made for a breath-taking sight: an asymmetrical yet balanced collection of domes and towers, grounds and gardens, grand halls and colonnades. It was not one building, but many, some linked by covered walkways or dedicated paths, others set at a remove, but all sheltered behind a great curving wall, made of the same white stone as the Stagger, which separated the palace grounds from the city. In order to gain us admittance at the main gates, Ciet Nevan produced a palace token—a thumb-sized lozenge of carved ivory inlaid with ebony and etched with distinguishing symbols, strung on a loop of braided white leather—and held it out for inspection. There must have been some charm or cantrip embedded in the piece to verify its provenance, as the lead guard waved a glass wand over it, and the glass lit up blue in response. Once this was done, he handed the token to a colleague, who copied its symbols down in a massive ledger along with all our names. True to the ciet's word, Cae and I were expected, and a runner was sent accordingly to notify the asa of our arrival.

We hadn't even crossed the main forecourt, with its beautifully tiled mosaics around a gleaming central fountain, before we were intercepted by a trio of liveried functionaries. All three bowed deeply. The tallest man, who appeared to be in charge, introduced himself as Ru Pyras and his companions as Ru Roya and Ren Kesu, then proceeded to greet each member of our party by name and title—all, of course, save Markel, whose presence went unac-knowledged. Though we'd both spent years enduring the stratified indignities of the Ralian class system, where my visibility was paramount and his impossible—and for all that a similar thing had happened at Ravethae—it still took me aback, though in the next instant, I felt stupid for having been surprised. I grit my teeth as Ru Pyras continued his needlessly effusive welcome, not wanting to make a bad impression for Cae's sake, yet hating the stark reminder that, though Tithena was a more enlightened place than Ralia in certain respects, it was still hierarchical.

Which was, perhaps, a hypocritical thought to have; moons knew, it wasn't as if I'd ever spent much time in Ralia's radical circles, for all that I'd occasionally brushed up against them. Whatever social bravery I possessed had never extended to railing openly against Ralian norms, and while it would've been easy to blame my silence solely on fear, the truth was that I didn't know what other shapes society could take. I experienced a moment of intense, impotent frustration: all by itself, I wanted my knowledge of Markel's worth and the anger I felt at his slighting to shake the whole world into fairness, but if feeling alone were enough, then the world would've looked very different.

The thought drew me up short, and I recalled again the point Markel had made to me the night before: that I kept on thinking of myself and my authority in Ralian terms, subjected to Ralian consequences. What did radicalism mean in Tithena? The Conclave under Asa Ivadi seemed to me a more practical system than King Markus's council of lords, but did that mean it existed beyond the possibility of improvement?

"Vel?" said Cae, his query interrupting my reverie, and I realised with a start that he'd made several failed attempts to get my attention.

"Yes?" I said, flushing. "Sorry, I was distracted."

"Clearly," sniped Asrien.

"I was just saying, tiern," said Ru Pyras, in a tone that was too polite to be impatient, and yet which managed to convey the bored impatience of underlings for those whose rudeness they cannot openly rebuke, "that the asa has extended an offer of lodgings to you and Yaseran Caethari, should you be gracious enough to accept her hospitality. Should it suit your requirements, I would be pleased to lead you to the Velvet Suite in the Heart Annex, but as the yaseran has deferred to your judgement in this matter—" he smirked ever so slightly, which told me what he thought of *that*; Cae flushed a little at the implied criticism, and I felt a renewed rush of dislike for Ru Pyras, "—the decision rests with you. Do you accept?"

Almost, I accepted automatically, but caught myself as a niggle of uncertainty wormed its way through my consciousness. I glanced at Cae, whose tension told me nothing beyond his general unhappiness with the situation; Asrien, however, was struggling not to look smug, while another of the functionaries—the one who'd been introduced as Ru Roya, a short, neatly shaven man in his thirties with unusually deep-set eyes—wore an expression cousin to one I was used to seeing on Markel's face when some nobleman or other was in the process of making an error to our advantage.

Velvet Suite. Heart Annex. The locations themselves meant nothing to me, but all at once, I realised why they sounded familiar— the Velvet Chair, Ru Kisian Faez, represented foreign affairs on the Conclave, belonging to the cluster of appointed seats known as the Heart, which relationship Asrien had explained to me only last night.

Understanding bloomed in me like a sunflower.

"The *Velvet* Suite?" I asked, daring to raise a querying eyebrow, as if I were in full command of the situation rather than bluffing wildly. "Not the Jade Suite?" Clan Taedu's seat on the Conclave was the Jade Chair, and if the Velvet Suite was related somehow to the Velvet Chair, it was entirely possible that each chair came with designated accommodations within the palace. I was guessing, but when the functionaries' eyes widened in surprise, I knew I'd hit my mark.

"Ah," said Ru Pyras, licking his lips. He exchanged a quick glance with Ru Roya—but not, I noted, with Ren Kesu—then bowed low to Cae and me in turn. "Forgive me, yaseran, tiern—a slip on my part. Yes, of course the Jade Suite is open and ready for use by Clan Taedu's heirs. Ru Roya will see your man there, and if you'd all be so kind as to entrust your mounts to Ren Kesu"—he gestured to his other companion, an angular, broad-shouldered man in subtly different livery, who I realised now was likely a groom—"I will take you to see the asa."

"Our thanks," Cae managed, flashing me a grateful look. I smiled at him, heart pounding just a little when he smiled back, then turned to Markel, checking in with a meaningful glance to ensure he was still amenable to our plan. On receiving a tacit nod in return, I turned to Ru Roya and said, "My servant, Markel, is mute. He came with me from Ralia, but if you show him where to go and what to do, he'll understand."

Ru Roya raised his brows at this, but otherwise didn't comment, which was helpful: strictly speaking, everything I'd said was true, and given that Markel's facility with Tithenai might well be revealed at some point, I preferred not to lie outright, letting the assumptions of others do the work for us.

"Of course, tiern," he said. "I'll bear that in mind." Bowing again, he walked over to Markel, took a presumptuous hold of Grace's bridle, and began to lead him away, our string of laden mounts following in his wake. I watched them go, then followed suit with my companions and dismounted Gift, patting her on the neck before handing her over to Ren Kesu, who accepted both the reins and my murmured thanks with a brusquely deferential nod. I considered asking whether our mounts would end up in the same place as Grace and the packhorses, but decided against it; I'd find out sooner or later, and in the interim I could plead genuine ignorance on the matter if I wanted a pretext for wandering the grounds.

Ru Pyras opened his mouth again, doubtless to make some

pompous announcement about where we were headed next, but was rather amusingly forestalled by an angry squeal from Asrien's mare. I stifled a burst of inappropriate laughter: evidently, my countryman hadn't thought to warn Ren Kesu about her biting tendencies, with the result that he'd tried to lead her from the same hand as Alik, with predictably poor results. Swearing under his breath, Ren Kesu was forced to do an awkward little jig, tugging the mare one way while trying to swap the various reins around, until he finally had the other three horses with long leads on one side and the mare held shortly on the other. It was an imperfect solution, and I did feel for him—it was yet another mark against Asrien, that he'd not warned the poor fellow, and I felt a fresh flash of guilt at not yet having confessed about his kiss to Cae—but as Ren Kesu was clearly competent, I allowed myself to enjoy Ru Pyras's sourness at having his moment stolen.

With the horses finally gone, the functionary sniffed and led us briskly towards the largest of the nearby buildings. A formidable four-storey structure with a vast domed roof, it was linked to the forecourt by a flight of deep stone steps leading up to a columned entrance hall. As we passed into its shade, a shiver of premonition ran up my spine, and I found myself reaching for Cae's hand, squeezing tightly. He gripped back before letting go, and when I looked at him, his expression was too complex for me to fully interpret. Even so, the yearning in it kicked me in the ribs. With no time to process what that meant, I took a deep breath, my bootheels clicking against the tiled floor, and braced myself as Ru Pyras gestured for the ornately carved, wood-and-metal double-doors ahead of us to be opened, which were so large that it took three guards on either side to accomplish that feat.

We entered a vast hall, easily two storeys high, whose gleaming inlaid floors squeaked slightly under our footsteps, and whose walls were lined with portraiture of what I took to be Tithenai rulers past. Another set of doors, less massive but still imposing, awaited us at the far end, and as we approached, I could hear the murmur of voices from the other side.

"Beyond is the throne room," Ciet Nevan murmured—somewhat redundantly, and yet I still nodded appreciation. We were walking in a line behind Ru Pyras by then, with Cae on my right, the ciet on my left and Asrien on his. "The asa's court must already be in session."

"Any advice?" I ventured, as the guards at the end of this hall moved to admit us.

"Be honest," Ciet Nevan replied, and that was all we had time for before the final doors were opened, a ringing voice announcing us as we crossed the threshold.

"Presenting Yaseran Caethari Aeduria and his husband, Tiern Velasin Aeduria, accompanied by Ciet Nevan Ori and Lord Asrien bo Erat!"

I swallowed hard, skin prickling as the court conversation fell first to silence, and then to whispers. The room contained easily two hundred courtiers in addition to a smatter of guards and servants, and yet the space was large enough to feel depopulated. The floor was white marble veined with golden streaks, while the massive dome I'd seen from outside, which soared four storeys overhead, was revealed to be made of pale green glass, so that a corona of jade-gold light encircled the distant dais and the thrones which sat atop it: one for the monarch, one for their consort and a third, presumably, for their heir, though as we came closer, I saw that only the central and largest throne was occupied.

This, then, was Asa Ivadi: a hawk-eyed woman in her middle fifties, her black hair shot with grey and bound in a braid that encircled her head like a coronet, a deliberate effect intensified by the way each strand was interwoven with rose-gold wire studded with gemstone flowers, though aside from two rings, she wore no other jewellery. She had a squarish face, the stubborn set of her jaw softened ever so slightly by the way her skin had started to loosen with age. Laughter lines crinkled the corners of her eyes and mouth, just as frown lines did her brow. She was stout, but not stocky, dressed in a rich purple halik which, somewhat like the lin I'd worn to last night's disastrous dinner, was unsleeved on the left side and covered only her shoulder on the right, showing off the grey silk undershirt worn beneath it, the rounded neck of which was embroidered with silver vines. The halik itself was bedecked with rose-gold wire and diamond flowers to match the ones in her hair, while her grey silk nara—of a slightly darker shade than her undershirt—bloused at the knee where they tucked into tall white boots. Her brown skin was slightly weathered, tanned darker from the sun than I would've expected for a monarch, and as Ru Pyras stepped aside and bowed to her, I felt her gaze on me like a tangible thing.

"You are welcome in my court," she said. She had a low voice, dryly inflected in a way that confirmed little while suggesting much, and at the sound of it, her courtiers instantly fell silent. "Yaseran Caethari." She spoke his name as a pronouncement, not a question; nonetheless, it had the undeniable impact of a summons, prompting Cae to step forwards, drop his right knee to the stone—not the left, I noted, as would have been done in Ralia—and bow his head in obeisance.

"Asa," he said. "I thank you for your courtesy."

"You appear to have made good time from Qi-Katai," said Asa Ivadi. "Or did my courier find you elsewhere?"

"At Avai, asa."

"Ah, yes." Almost imperceptibly, her ringed hands twitched in her lap. "My condolences, yaseran, on the circumstances of your recent elevation—and your sister's, come to that. I cannot say I knew Tieren Halithar well, but he was a good steward of his territory, and Tithena is poorer for his loss." She did not mention Laecia.

Cae twitched and said hoarsely, "My thanks, asa. Our whole family grieves."

"And yet, you wear no mourning."

"I do not believe the wearing of ribbons or the colour of my clothes make my grief more real, asa, nor that their absence makes it less." Cae's voice was raw, and I found myself fighting the urge to step in and haul him away from her, especially when a titter ran through the room. When the asa raised her hand, however, it instantly ceased.

"Grief is a complex thing," she said softly, "and mourning many-hued."

Cae said nothing to that, and nor did anyone else. Silence briefly reigned as a second monarch, and for a moment, the lines on the asa's face looked deeper than before, as if newly carved by a chisel. Then she relaxed—I hadn't known her tense until it ebbed away—and a tiny smile twitched the corner of her mouth.

"And have you any additional report to make?"

Far too late, I recalled that second, doubled missive in the asa's original summons: *I bid you travel discreetly. Observe the state of Tithena and report your findings to me.* I'd meant to discuss it with Cae before our arrival, but in the mess of the last few days, the opportunity had scarcely arisen, and last night—well. Cae, who'd frozen in place, appeared likewise caught off guard—so much so that he raised his head and flashed me a panicked look before recalling himself and turning back to the asa. Nonetheless, the damage had been done; she tracked his gaze to me, raised a perfectly manicured brow, and said, "Perhaps Tiern Velasin would care to answer?"

Stifling a curse, neck hot beneath the eyes of the court, I stepped forwards and took a knee beside Cae, only just stopping myself from kneeling on the Ralian side out of habit. My thoughts whirled—there must be something, anything I could tell her—but as images of our journey from Avai flashed through my head, my overwhelming memory was the fear of pursuit; those long, awful stretches of road with no towns or villages in sight, where a successful ambush could so easily have meant death—

Ah, I thought, and readied myself to gamble once again.

"Asa," I said, inclining my head and hoping my voice sounded less watery aloud than it did in my own ears, "from what we've seen, Tithena prospers. Your people are well-fed, your roads well-maintained, and your towns hospitable." I licked my lips, giving myself a final moment to reconsider, then ploughed on with, "But there are dangers to travel, chiefly the many stretches of road which go unwatched and unguarded. If any sort of accident befalls your people there, no help can be easily found."

A murmur rippled through the room; I did my best to ignore it, focussing instead on trying to read anything from Cae, whose shoulder was close enough to mine that I could almost feel the heat of him through our clothes.

"And do you propose a solution to this problem?" asked the asa, voice deceptively mild.

My heart sped up. "I would not presume to tell the asa anything of governance," I said carefully, "but as you have asked, I have heard it said that a system of watchtowers might be worth considering." I mentally logged a debt of thanks to Qarrah.

The murmuring of the courtiers swelled louder, and this time, the asa did nothing to stop it, presumably because the court was entitled to its outrage at the prospect of a Ralian interloper instructing their monarch.

"Watchtowers," echoed the asa, when the murmuring had ebbed a little. I dared a glance upwards, and though her expression didn't seem much changed, I nonetheless had the impression that her attention had sharpened. "What a novel suggestion. May I ask, does such a system exist in Ralia, tiern?"

I bobbed my head like some idiot heron. "In places, asa—mostly along the coast, near the Rhysic Straits and along the Speckled Sea, where their benefits in the event of storms and piracy are held by the local gentry to outweigh the imposition of oversight and the expense of maintaining them. Inland, though—" I shrugged and dared to venture an almost-smile, hoping to win a tiny bit of favour at the expense of my countrymen, "—well. There are many lords who mislike the idea of expending resources for the primary benefit of commoners and merchants, or who else prefer certain of their territories to remain unobserved."

The murmuring swelled again, louder than before. The asa smiled sharply, revealing that one of her canines had been replaced with a diamond fake. "I imagine," she said, "that the late Lord Ennan vin Mica was among those opposed to their presence?"

"He was," I said, a flicker of memory recalling when I'd last heard the matter debated in Farathel. Somewhat dryly, I added, "He never cared for oversight."

"And what of your father, then?" The asa raised an inquiring brow. "Having inherited vin Mica's lands, does he too wish for such privacy?"

I opened my mouth. Closed it again. I was hit, all at once, with the unhappy realisation that I'd somehow made an error, or at the very least blundered into a patch of Tithenai politics I was ill-equipped to navigate. The asa's questions weren't idle, and the reaction of her courtiers spoke to something more than simple amusement at my presence. With retreat impossible, I could only hope that my answer didn't make things worse.

"He has shared no confidences with me on that point," I said carefully, which was a polite way of saying that he'd functionally disowned me for my interest in men and would sooner have me whipped on sight than discuss security with me, "but in the past, he has been, I would say, neutral on the subject of watchtowers. But as he owes his present elevation to King Markus and has no desire to be branded a second vin Mica, should the throne ask it of him . . ."

"I see," said the asa. She smiled again, neither kindly nor unkindly, but rather in private satisfaction. Her diamond tooth winked like a tiny star. Turning her attention back to Cae, she said, "You appear to have made a more interesting marriage than anticipated, Caethari Aeduria. How fascinating." And with that, she waved us away, our interview done.

I lurched to my feet and realised I was sweating profusely. As the chatter of courtiers resumed around us, Cae grabbed my arm and steered me away from the asa's throne, Asrien and Ciet Nevan following in our wake without ever having been acknowledged. I felt a sudden flare of near-hysteric gratitude that, if nothing else, the asa hadn't raised the subject of my being Cae's heir after all.

We'd no sooner found a bit of space in which to recollect ourselves than a courtier broke off from the surrounding pack and approached us. He was stocky, strong-bellied and of middling height, with a bouncing stride and a neatly manicured goatee, his black hair pulled back from his face in eight flat braids capped with gold beads. There was something vaguely familiar about the cast of his face, but it wasn't until he reached us, bowed and introduced himself that I registered why.

"Ru Kisian Faez, the Velvet Chair, at your service," he said. His tone was jovial, but laced with a clear thread of worry. "Well! That's certainly set the fox among the chickens, hmm?"

"What? Why?" asked Cae, his big, warm hand still curled around my bicep. He looked at me in confusion, hand falling away, and I startled myself with how keenly I mourned its loss. "Vel?"

"I suspect I've blundered," I said, struggling to keep a sudden weariness from my tone. I massaged my temples, as much to block out the sight of Asrien's smug grin as to ease what felt like a sharply incipient headache. "How and why, though, I've no idea."

"The asa has been proposing a watchtower system to the Conclave for some months now," said Ciet Nevan. "It has proven . . . controversial, shall we say, and for much the same reasons Tiern Velasin listed."

I winced. "Ah."

"Quite," said Ru Kisian. "The Will has endorsed it, the Circlet has opposed it, and the Heart—unusually, but crucially—has been split on the matter." He paused, then added tartly, "My colleagues are enjoying an unusual divergence of opinion."

I took a moment to parse this, sifting through the details of Tithenai governance that Asrien had imparted last night, stubbornly shoving aside all memory of what had come after. "The Heart are the asa's appointed chairs, are they not?" I asked. "Shouldn't that mean they—you—take her side?"

"Historically, yes," said Ru Kisian. "However, as Asa Ivadi values competence over sycophancy, we as her appointees are encouraged to speak plainly, and as it stands, the Marble, Horn and Glass Chairs are all opposed, albeit for different reasons."

"The *Marble* Chair is opposed?" asked Cae. As the Marble Chair was responsible for public works, he was understandably baffled—as I was, for that matter—while both Ciet Nevan and Asrien looked quietly thrilled to be hearing insider gossip.

Ru Kisian waved an irritated hand. "Ru Niria Xin is not opposed in *theory,* but there are other projects she deems more urgent than watchtowers—notably repairs to the seawalls in several major ports, all of which sustained damage over the last storm season. The asa's view is that seawall repairs fall under the purview of the individual nobles in whose territory they reside, and are therefore not a matter for public works; however, as multiple walls need repair, and as the nobles in question are notably tight-fisted, Ru Niria proposes that seawalls be redesignated for national, rather than local, upkeep, after the manner of certain main roads. And while the asa technically acts as the treasury's representative on the Conclave, the actual treasury is in favour of Ru Niria's plan, as it justifies the levy of a seawall maintenance tax." He snorted. "Meanwhile, the Horn Chair is opposed because Cietena Atharo Sao, titled noble that she is, has sided with the Circlet, while the Glass Chair thinks the proposal has sanitation issues which, in its current iteration, have yet to be fully addressed, and as such will not endorse it."

I blinked. "Sanitation issues?"

"Drinking and shitting," said Asrien, with just a trace of snicker.

Waspishly, I cut back, "Yes, thank you, I am familiar with the concept of sanitation. But how does it apply to watchtowers?" Ciet Nevan was poised to reply, but the answer hit me before I could give him the chance. "Oh! I suppose if you station folk anywhere for any length of time, they need water and privies; watchtowers would be no exception."

"Just so," said Ru Kisian. "It's never just one expense."

Beside me, Caethari made a pained noise. "I truly *hate* politics," he said plaintively.

Too late—*again;* I was starting to feel decidedly slow, which served to make me cross with myself—I realised what my first question should've been. "And what about Yasa Kithadi?" I asked. "Does she support it?"

"The last time the matter was raised, she abstained," said Ru Kisian delicately. "As did the Brass Chair, Ren Kavaro Yina"—the people's representative, I recalled—"both on the grounds that they needed to give the matter further consideration. In the yasa's case, it's well-known that she's generally abstained from contentious votes while serving in absentia; Ren Kavaro, however, is an elected official whose supporters within the capital are themselves divided on the merits of the plan." He paused, then added, "And of course, the Brass Chair must always work hardest of anyone to secure political alliances; with the vote effectively split but the asa unable as yet to force a tiebreak, I suspect he's waiting for either side to offer him something meaningful in order to sway his choice."

I winced in sympathy. By my count, that was two abstentions, eight opposing and six in favour—a knife-edge of contention.

And I'd just dumped us into the middle of it.

"I'm sorry, Cae," I mumbled, unable to look him in the eye. "I keep getting you in trouble."

"Vel, that's not—"

"Tierns!"

The energetic shout cut Cae off short; indeed, it was loud enough that several other nearby courtiers likewise fell silent. Turning, I found a trio of noble youths approaching us, and realised with a start that they were the three we'd rescued from the Sihae. Frantically, I strove to recall their names in time to match them to faces.

I recognised Tiern Ethin by the blooming, hoof-shaped bruise on his forehead, his curly hair loose and gleaming; to his left was the delicate, dark-skinned Ciet Yarasil, and to his right was Ciet Irias, stocky and bronze. I was ashamed to find that I couldn't remember their clan-names, but any embarrassment on that count was avoided when they reached us, bowed and introduced themselves once more—presumably for the benefit of Asrien and Ciet Nevan, who returned the courtesies with an air of bemusement.

"You left Riverwatch before we could thank you," Tiern Ethin said. There were deep circles under his eyes to match his spectacular bruise, his freckles stark against olive skin still blanched from pain and healing, but the fervour in his voice rang clear. "You saved our lives, tierns—sorry, tiern and yaseran." He dipped his head to Cae, gaze flickering between us. "Regardless of how and why the bridge fell, you risked yourselves for us." He faltered, and all of a sudden, he looked every bit as young as he was—a boy frightened by his first real brush with mortality. "And I—perhaps Yara and Iri would've lived if you hadn't acted, but I—" His hand rose, fingertips brushing the bruise that had seen him knocked unconscious in the water. "I would not. And so I am at your service." And then he bowed, a jerkily heartfelt gesture.

"Us, too," said Ciet Yarasil; Ciet Irias nodded vigorous agreement. "We haven't Ethin's connections, but still—"

"Forgive me," said Ru Kisian, interjecting delicately, gaze flicking to Tiern Ethin, "but did you say you are Tiern Ethin *Talae*?"

"He is," said Ciet Irias, bristling slightly. "What of it?"

"I mean no offence," said Ru Kisian quickly. "It's just that Tiern Velasin is new to court, and so is unfamiliar with the major clans."

"Ah," said Ciet Irias, relaxing slightly. And then, to me, "Ethin's grandmother is Tierena Keris Talae, the Amber Chair."

As I struggled to process this development, Tiern Ethin groaned slightly. "Iri, please!"

"Well, she is!" Ciet Irias crossed his arms stubbornly. "Are we to pretend otherwise?"

"It's not like I have her ear," grumbled Tiern Ethin, half to his friend and half to me, "but—anyway. Yes."

"That is . . . useful to know," I said, faintly. And then, because they were still looking expectantly at us, "We're only glad we were able to help. Right, Cae?"

"Of course," my husband said quickly, clearly relieved to be thrown a conversational line he was capable of catching. He hesitated, then said awkwardly, "Your horses. Were any of them recovered, or—?"

As one, the boys' faces fell.

"My Ember fought free downriver, but her leg was shattered," Ciet Irias said, swallowing hard. "With no healers near, we had to—mercy was the only way. The others haven't been found."

"I'm sorry," Cae and I said as one.

Ciet Yarasil shrugged, the gesture both sad and angry. "You couldn't have saved them," he said, though I felt a pang of kinship at the loss in his expression. He scrubbed his eyes with a wrist, coughed, then straightened and said, with forced cheer, "At any rate, we survived."

"We don't wish to monopolise your time," said Tiern Ethin, "but we are reachable through the palace, and I hope—I hope you will consider us friends."

"Of course," said Cae, and I echoed him, touched.

"Forgive me for eavesdropping," said a new voice, so deep and smooth that I shivered involuntarily, "but am I to understand you *both* effected a river-rescue of these three young worthies?"

There was a note of almost mocking incredulity in the question, and even without having seen the speaker's face, I knew it was me he doubted. Cae and I both turned, my husband already bristling as he said hotly, "In fact, it was Vel who leapt in first—" and then he stopped, presumably as arrested as I by the sight of our new interlocutor.

Though neither of us was exactly short, he was more than a head taller than Cae, and even more powerfully built, his absurdly broad shoulders and muscular arms straining the seams of both lin and undershirt. I gauged him to be in his middle thirties, his dark olive skin tanned darker still by a life clearly spent outdoors, though there were no russety sunstreaks to match the iron threads in his long black hair, which fell around his shoulders in thick, unbraided waves. He was clean-shaven, with strong brows, a prominent nose that must've once been straight, but which now bore a rakish crook suggestive of multiple breaks, and eyes so dark an amber they looked almost black until the light hit them just so. His fitted lin was simple black and belted at the waist, worn over a crisp white undershirt and tight charcoal nara tucked into tall black boots; his only jewellery were the iron rings in his ears—three on one side, two on the other—while the back of his left hand was tattooed with a design I couldn't quite make out. Like Cae, he wore a sword at his hip; unlike Cae's, both hilt and scabbard were plain, hard-worn leather, with no pretensions towards beauty to obscure their function.

Beside me, Ciet Nevan inhaled sharply before bowing to the newcomer. "General," he said respectfully. "You honour us with your attention."

"Do I," said the man flatly, clearly unimpressed with Ciet Nevan's courtesies.

"And that would be my cue to leave," said Ru Kisian, gracing the newcomer with an unimpressed look.

The general snorted. "Ever the coward, Kisian."

"It's hardly cowardice to know when you're not wanted," Ru Kisian countered. "It's a skill you might do well to practice, hm?" And with that, he flashed me a tidy grin, mouthed *Good luck!* and vanished back into the crowd.

The general absorbed this all with an expression of mild contempt at Ru Kisian's abrupt departure. He waited a beat, then turned to me, his full lips quirked with disdainful amusement. "Is it too much to hope that you know who I am?"

I gave a short, sarcastic bow to cover my suddenly racing pulse. *General* was a title I'd heard applied to only one man in Tithena, and as with so much else that had been relevant this morning, I owed the knowledge to Asrien. "General Naza Karai, the Iron Chair," I answered. And then, because I've never had a particularly well-developed survival instinct, I added, "You don't want me here."

The general snorted. "What a childish way of putting it," he said. "*You,* tiern, I couldn't give a shit about; it's your fucking country and what this"—he gestured rudely between Cae and me—"*alliance* represents that I take issue with."

I smiled brightly at him, because it was that or show fear. "I'm inclined to take that as a compliment."

The look I received in answer could've stripped paint. Before he could respond, however, Asrien chose to insert himself in the conversation, head cocked to peek coyly up through his lashes—and given their difference in height, it was quite a way up—at the general.

"And what do you think of Ralian expatriates otherwise, sir?" The *sir* was in Ralian, a deliberate bit of cheek, and I had the sudden thought that Asrien's survival instincts were, if possible, even worse than my own. I also felt an odd swell of relief at seeing him so openly flirt with an ill-advised target—or rather, relief that Cae could see him doing so, as it would make it that much easier to explain how a man apparently bedding his uncle had come to approach me in the first place.

Slowly, General Naza gave Asrien an even more lingering, predatory once-over than he'd given Ciet Nevan. "Little," he said finally, his voice a dark rumble, before turning back to Cae, whom he favoured with a judgementally raised eyebrow. "By all accounts, the Wild Knife was a thorn in Ralia's side these last few years, and yet—*this.*" He flicked the fingers of his tattooed hand to indicate me, head tilted in mock puzzlement. "Does the shape of the saddle they've forced you to not chafe, yaseran?"

For a moment, Cae looked angry; then his expression smoothed into his bland soldier's mask. "Personally," he drawled, "I don't find being ridden a hardship."

The general laughed at that, gaze flicking over me once more, and I flushed to the roots of my hair to realise the innuendo had been both deliberate and received as such. "Well," he said speculatively, sizing me up as he had the others, a hint of tooth bared by his smirk, "if nothing else, I had heard the Ralian tiern was an *excellent* horseman."

Moons, but that flustered me! Cae boasting about our bedplay to the general was one thing; him evidently joining in while still wishing me gone was another. As accustomed as I was to such banter among my litai circle in Farathel, I'd not been prepared to find it here, or at least not so soon or so openly, and as I floundered for how to respond, my cheeks and throat flushed, the general's smirk only deepened.

"Tiern Velasin?"

The querying voice was a godsend. I turned; the speaker was a woman in, I gauged, her late fifties or early sixties, whipcord-lean and sharp-eyed with a long, iron-grey braid, dressed in a pink halik patterned with red and yellow flowers over a paler yellow undershirt and dark red nara. The clothes looked new, but the clashing colours didn't flatter her weathered, sun-browned skin, nor did they pair well with her ostentatious gold torc, which was shaped like outstretched wings encircling her throat, the tips swooping down to meet on either side of a round pink sapphire nestled in the hollow of her throat. Shrugging apologetically, she slipped her right hand into her left sleeve, as if she were scratching an itch.

"Yes?" I said, wondering who she was and how she fit into the day's events.

She pulled out a knife and, smiling, slashed my throat.

I n my experience, when things well and truly go to shit, they
tend to go there fast, and this was no exception.

Several people screamed as Velasin's pretty throat opened
like a second mouth, myself included; sunfucking stars, who could
blame us! Seconds ago we'd been talking, and now we were staring in stunned, useless horror as Velasin clapped his hands to the
wound and staggered to one knee. Bright blood oozed around his
fingers; Caethari hauled him into his lap as he, too, tried to hold
his throat shut, all while shouting desperately for help, and meanwhile that terrible crone just stood there cackling. Nevan and the
general had her on her knees in an instant, the general's sword at
her throat as Nevan used his belt to bind her wrists behind her
back, which struck me as a pointless bit of gallantry: even if she'd
been resisting and half her present age, the asa's guards were already moving towards us.

As were the trio of youths from before, the ones Caethari and Velasin had apparently rescued from the river. All of them looked terrified, but the slim, pretty one, Yarasil, moved with determination,
dropping to his knees by Caethari's side. I saw him speak, though
the actual words were lost in a clatter of arms and armour as the
guards arrived, and then—my stomach lurched—Caethari lifted his
hands from his husband's neck—prised Velasin's up, too, though he
struggled against it—so that Yarasil could shove *his actual sunfucking
fingers* into the hole in Velasin's throat.

"I've got the artery," he said—shakily, but loud enough to be
heard. "I can hold it, but we need a healer—"

"This feels very odd," rasped Velasin, and I near leapt out of my skin; I hadn't thought a man with a slit throat could talk! But then, I supposed, the old woman hardly looked strong; the knife had got his veins open, but mustn't have bitten deep enough to harm his voice.

"The healer's coming," Caethari said, sounding desperate. "Don't talk, just—just lie still, keep your heartbeat slow—"

Velasin made a coughing noise that was not quite laughter. Yarasil swore, wrist jerking as he worked to keep a hold of the artery. "Slow? At a time like this?" He was breathing fast, his bloodied hands gripping Caethari's forearm, eyes rolling wide and terrified. Looking at him made me feel sick, but I couldn't quite look away, either. *Fuck me,* I thought, staring morbidly at the place where Yarasil's fingertips vanished into Velasin's open throat, and then, *sunfucking stars, the Shade'll have my head if he dies.* Which maybe should've made me get down on my knees and do something to help, whatever that might've been, but I'm not a healer, and anyway, I didn't fancy getting his blood on my trousers. There was a lot of blood by then, the scent of it making me queasy. It was a good job Nevan had opted for useless heroics, or he might've noticed; I'm pale enough that any sort of stomach upset makes me look like a waxwork, and I try not to make a habit of looking vulnerable around men I'm fucking for reasons other than pleasure.

"A healer's coming," one of the guards said—to Caethari, not me. "Just hang in there."

"Easy for you to say," Velasin croaked. His face just then looked whiter than mine, and my gut lurched as he raised a red-drenched hand to stroke clumsily at Caethari's jaw. "Shh," he said weakly, "It's fine. It'll all be fine."

"It's not fucking fine!" Caethari said, voice shaking horribly. He grabbed Velasin's hand and squeezed it, which is when a better person would've felt guilty about trying to seduce him the night before, instead of worrying if they were about to throw up. That's the funny thing about blood: I can cope just fine with seeing my own—sun knows, I've had enough practice—but other people's is a different story.

Mercifully, the healer showed up then—a woman, because this was Tithena, her scarred and muscular forearms bared where her undershirt's sleeves were tied up at the elbows. She knelt and set to work quickly, not that I could see much of the details; only the glow of her magic as she, presumably, sutured Velasin's artery back into wholeness, along with whatever else the knife had cut. We'd attracted quite a crowd by then, though the guards were doing a good job keeping the bystanders back—all save one, who was looming over the captured would-be murderer together with Nevan and General Naza, which made for a truly ridiculous sight. Imagine thinking you needed three big men to guard one scrawny old woman you'd already captured!

"Who sent you?" the general demanded of her, tipping the woman's chin up with his swordpoint. A stupid part of me almost laughed—the Shade had done the same thing to me back in Eliness—but I managed to keep my big mouth shut, which was well enough, as the woman's only answer was to start cackling again.

"Take her to the cells," the general said disgustedly, and as the guard obeyed, she kept on laughing—barking and shrill, like a fox that's eaten the fun kind of mushrooms.

"You can let go now," said the healer—to Yarasil, I realised, as he finally withdrew his shaky, bloody fingers. I held my breath—I had a vested interest in Velasin vin Aaro remaining a live embarrassment rather than a dead complication—and then exhaled relief when, three seconds later, the healer rocked back on her heels and said, "I'll need to keep him a day for observation, but barring any unforeseen complications, he ought to live."

As if that was the permission they'd been waiting for, the watching courtiers all began talking at once, a spreading ripple of gossip. Another time, I might've slipped away to eavesdrop, but I needed to keep in the heart of things, and so moved over to Nevan, who was still missing his belt, and made a show of clinging to his arm.

"Are you all right?" he asked, voice low.

My answering shudder was unpleasantly real. "I don't like blood."

"He isn't awake," said Caethari, voice choked with panic. Velasin lay limp in his lap, a shiny pink scar scrawled freshly across the meat of his throat. "Why isn't he awake?"

"Because I've put him into a healing sleep," the healer said gently. And then, to Yarasil, "Who taught you to pinch an artery like that? You likely saved his life."

"Our estate has sheep." The pretty boy's voice was a whisper; he swayed where he knelt, and his two friends, who'd been hovering uselessly nearby, chose this moment to step up behind him, each one setting a steadying hand on his shoulder. "Mother says a responsible steward should know firsthand how all the work is done, so she had me learn, and when we—when we kill a sheep, we make a cut in the chest and, and squeeze the veins, so they die softly, they don't suffer and sour the meat"—he looked sick as he said it, which I hardly begrudged him; the comparison had my own stomach roiling—"so I thought, I thought if I just—if I did that, I could hold it closed, and he wouldn't—"

He broke off midsentence, lunging aside to vomit spectacularly all over the floor. I clung tighter to Nevan and shoved my face in his shoulder, trying to breathe shallowly; I've an unpleasant tendency to vomit when others do, just from the smell, and right then, that was the last thing I wanted to happen. I was concentrating so hard on keeping my gorge down that I missed what happened next: I caught a snatch of what sounded like Caethari thanking the boy, a scuffle of movement, and that was it, until Nevan squeezed my shoulder and murmured, "The guards have mopped it up now."

Mortified, I pulled away, wiping at my face and shoving my hair behind my burning ears, and looked up just in time to see Caethari heft the unconscious Velasin into his arms and stand, a look of tender anguish on his face.

Guilt twisted in me like a swallowed eel. I shoved it ruthlessly down, as I'd done last night with Velasin; as I'd done half a dozen times in the past three days, and would doubtless do a dozen more before this was over. If it was only my own neck at risk, I'd have confessed everything and thrown myself on the mercy of Asa Ivadi my first day in court, but if the Shade thought me a failure, it was my mother who'd suffer for it, and she'd already suffered enough on my account.

Focus, I told myself sharply, ignoring the grief on Caethari's face, the loll of Velasin's head against his chest. I was here to break up their sunfucking marriage, not make friends, and more importantly, Velasin's wounding meant I had to change tack, and fast. Caethari was besotted with his prickly mess of a husband, which was why I'd aimed my initial attentions at Velasin. But even if he hadn't turned me away last night—the memory filled me with hot, sour shame—I couldn't seduce a badly wounded man on his sickbed, to say nothing of the fact that if whoever was trying to kill him made another attempt, I might well get caught in the crossfire. But if they succeeded anyway . . .

I forced myself to consider the prospect, thoughts racing. It was *possible,* of course, that the Shade wouldn't carry out his threats if Velasin died by Tithenai hands before I managed to break the marriage alliance, but I wouldn't gamble on it, partly because such a murder would throw up new complications for the throne, but mostly because the Shade was an utter bastard. The swift, merciless solution would've been to kill Velasin myself—to make up a lie about how stung I was by his rejection, perhaps even claim we'd been lovers once in Ralia, then finish him off before he had a chance to recover—and for my mother's sake, I forced myself to consider it. But even if I'd borne him a personal grudge, I couldn't see how to do it openly—and it had to be done openly, or there was no point—without getting myself either captured or killed in the process, so I firmly set it aside.

And if I couldn't kill Velasin, then I had no choice but to save him; and to save him, I had to find out who was after him. As the old woman with the knife could hardly have been responsible for the assassination attempts he'd faced on the road, I didn't believe for an instant that she was acting alone. No; whoever was after Velasin was organised, and given the mess of Qi-Xihan's politics, it could've been anyone. Working with Caethari to unmask them was my best bet, and if I couldn't use that time to seduce him away from his husband, well . . . perhaps, at the very least, I could wedge them enough apart to achieve the same goal.

As I made my choice, the Shade's words echoed in my head: *Your value, such as it is, lies wholly in your usefulness as an instrument to your betters; beyond that, you bring nothing to anyone.*

Tell me something I don't know, I thought sourly, and forced myself to step forwards.

"Let me help," I said to Caethari, not having to fake the wobble in my voice.

"Me, too," said Nevan quickly, not to be outdone, and I felt a spark of irritation at his insistent heroics. "Let us carry him for you, yaseran."

"No," said Caethari. "Thank you but—no. I can. I can bear him."

"His servant," I blurted suddenly, recalling Velasin's earlier conversation with the functionaries. "The mute. He only knows Ralian, doesn't he? I can fetch him for you; he won't understand anyone else."

Caethari's eyes widened. "Markel," he breathed, a new look of horror on his face. "Oh gods, *Markel*—" He swallowed hard, visibly mastering himself, then squared his shoulders and said, "If you could fetch Markel, that would be . . . I would be grateful. We'll be, uh—" He glanced helplessly at the healer.

"In the Circlet Infirmary," she provided, straightening. Her hands were bloody to the wrist, and my gaze skittered off the sight the same way I'd been conspicuously not looking at the remaining smears of blood and vomit on the floor.

"Of course," I said, and as they headed to the courtyard door,

I followed them—as did Nevan, who I supposed had the familial right to it, but whose presence still itched at me. It wasn't any guilt over betraying him—our arrangement had been a pragmatic and nonexclusive one ever since I'd tracked him down my first week in the capital, though he'd proven to be a surprisingly good fuck—so much as the fact that reading him was harder than I'd have liked. Not that he was a master of subtlety; it was just that I was used to fucking men in secret, so that even the act of being propositioned told you something about the gap between a man's public and private selves. But here, there was no gap; or if there was, it had nothing to do with sex, which meant I had nothing familiar to work with.

We were almost at the door when suddenly, Asa Ivadi's voice cut across the court. "Yaseran Caethari! A moment, if you please!"

Caethari froze in place, which meant the rest of us had to stop, too. The asa inclined in her head in thanks, then called out, "General Naza!"

Surprised, I turned in time to see the big man drop instantly to one knee, head bowed. "Yes, asa?"

As the asa rose, the crowd of courtiers parted like reeds around a riverboat, clearing her a direct path to the general. She crossed it slowly, her measured voice carrying to every corner of the now-silent room.

"I find it . . . unsettling, shall we say, that a guest of this court was nearly killed as the Iron Chair stood next to him. Surely a man of your skill might've intervened?"

The general stiffened. "Forgive me, asa," he said, his voice a thrilling growl. "It should not have happened."

"Quite so," said the asa, halting before him. She stared down at him, letting the silence stretch before finally adding, "Nonetheless, I will give you a chance to redeem yourself." He jerked at that, like a hunting dog catching the scent, but didn't otherwise move. "I am putting you in charge of ascertaining the motive behind this attack. You will begin by questioning everyone present." Pitching her voice louder, she said, "With the exception of Yaseran Caethari and those attending him, no one may leave until they have spoken with either General Naza or one of the guards under his command. Whoever that woman is, however she gained entry here, I want to know."

"Asa," the general acknowledged, bowing his head further. "It will be done."

"Of course," said the asa. She extended a hand and touched him lightly on the head, then stepped away and glided back to her throne, a susurrus of gossip exploding in her wake.

General Naza stayed put for a moment, then straightened slowly, shooting a murderous glare in our direction. Just for a second, his dark eyes caught mine, and I shivered like a rabbit in the shadow of a hawk. Or a bear. Gods, he was big!

Focus, I told myself sternly, and wrenched my gaze away to follow Caethari outside, where the audience chamber opened out into a courtyard.

"Markel should've been sent to the Jade Suite," Caethari said anxiously, not slowing his stride. "If he's not there, perhaps the nearest stables—"

"I'll find him," I promised, and veered off on my self-appointed errand. A part of me wondered at how readily Caethari had accepted my gambit—Markel was only a servant, which made fetching him a courtesy, not a necessity, even if he'd understood Tithenai—but he was clearly in shock; doubtless he'd have said yes to anything if it felt like doing something.

I'd only been at court a few times, but the main buildings were simple enough to navigate once you realised how their names and usage were modelled after the Conclave. The Circlet Infirmary was north-east, at one end of the curving two-storey structure that lay behind the domed audience hall; the Circlet Suites, however— including the Jade Suite—were in the north-west wing. I headed there at a swift walk, not wanting to draw attention to myself by running; I was yet to be so much as questioned by any of the palace guards, who were used to assuming that anyone within the complex had a right to be there, and yet the paranoia wouldn't leave me.

Happily, if perhaps unsurprisingly, I reached the doors unmolested and took a moment to orient myself. There were six Circlet Suites, three on each level: Pearl, Ebony and Opal on the ground floor, with Jade, Amber and Silver above them. I climbed the staircase, located the correct door, and knocked.

And waited.

And waited.

I knocked again.

Nothing.

I stared at the door for another interminable span of silent seconds before finally trying the handle. It was locked, which made sense—as Velasin's servant, Markel would've been given the keys—but that didn't tell me where he'd gone.

Fighting annoyance, I took a deep breath and tried to think. Markel was Ralian. Most Ralian servants wouldn't wait in their master's rooms alone, lest it be taken as presumption; but then, most Ralian servants wouldn't have been given the key in the first place. As he didn't speak Tithenai, Markel might've assumed that Velasin would receive his own key, thereby leaving him free to go—where? The servants' quarters? There would be one in the building for the general staff, but the Circlet Suites all had dedicated servant accommodations, which Markel would've been shown.

My stomach growled, reminding me of how long it had been since breakfast. I was briefly annoyed, then realised I had my answer.

"The kitchens," I muttered, and strode off back the way I'd come. For the sake of expedience, I'd learned, most of the bigger palace buildings had their own dedicated kitchens—in this case, an annex set midway between the suites and the infirmary—and here as in Ralia, they were largely neutral spaces. Provided you didn't get in the way, anyone was free to loiter at the tables, sharing a bite to eat, swapping gossip or enjoying the heat from the ovens. Anyone could be inconspicuous in a kitchen.

The thought brought on an unwelcome pang of homesickness. Growing up, I'd spent a lot of time in the kitchens at what was now my mother's estate, sitting hidden under the big table as the scullery maids gossiped overhead. Cook always knew I was there, but often she was the only one, which meant it was her who answered when Lord bo Erat came storming in, demanding to know where his pathetic excuse for a son was. She hadn't always shielded me—she couldn't have—but she'd played dumb when possible, and I'd loved her for it. She made the best venison pies I've ever had, rich and savoury, with soft, flaky crusts and meat that was always juicy, never dried out by the oven, but all her meals warmed and filled. Now, I was stuck with Tithenai fare, which often left me feeling like I hadn't eaten at all. At least in Eliness, people had known to pair their fish with something more substantial, and there was still beef if you could afford it. But as best I could tell, cows in Tithena were primarily kept for milk, not meat. People still ate them, of course—the Tithenai weren't that stupid—but it was mostly the temples who did so, some quasi-religious tradition whose origins were vastly less important to me than the fact that I hadn't had steak since I'd been here.

I entered the kitchen with my mouth watering, though not for whatever was currently being prepared. Kitchen hands and scullery maids bustled about as a tall kem cook roared orders from thir spot by the stove, so I tried to keep out of everyone's way as I scanned the room for Markel. After a moment, I found him seated at a big table, companionably helping to peel a bowl of sweet jewel onions as the servants on either side of him gossiped over his head in Tithenai.

"Never mind Jade and Amber," one was saying, "I heard we'll have Pearl and Ebony here in a minute, because of the seawall business."

"Pearl and Ebony," the other scoffed, "they won't come themselves; they'll send representatives, same as always."

"Oh? You're certain about that, are you?" The first speaker leaned in closer across the table, a conspiratorial look on her face;

Markel leaned back to give her room without looking up from his onion. "Because Neri says *Silver* is coming."

"Fuck *off*," said the second speaker, awed and a little scandalised. "Neri never said that!"

"She did," said the first speaker, smugly dropping a peeled onion in the basket. "And you know if Silver comes, the others will, too, just to get a look at thim, because—" She noticed me eavesdropping and broke off abruptly, her voice going smooth and polite. "Can we help you, ren?"

"I'm here for this one," I said, gesturing to Markel. And then, switching to Ralian, "You need to come with me. Your master's been attacked."

• • •

Markel jerked his head up, staring at me. Setting down his onions, he was around the table in a flash. His hands started to move in unfamiliar shapes; then he stalled, made a frustrated face and fumbled with the flap of a squarish leather pouch attached to his belt, withdrawing a small slate and a type of chalk pen I hadn't seen before. He scribbled on it hastily, then turned the slate to face me, revealing two queries in rushed, blocky handwriting:

WHAT HAPPENED? IS HE ALL RIGHT?

Nodding thanks at the other two servants, who eyed us with clear curiosity but didn't otherwise intervene, I put a hand on Markel's arm and steered him out of the kitchens, not answering until we were back in the relative privacy of the main hall.

"He'll live," I said, "the healer's with him now, but some crazy old woman came at him with a knife. The yaseran sent me to bring you, so—" I tried to move us both on, but to my shock, Markel dug in his heels and pulled away, wiping his slate clean and dashing out another query:

IS HE AWAKE?

"No," I said slowly. "The healer put him to sleep, but—"

Markel cut me off with a raspy noise I hadn't known he could make. He glared at me, wiped the slate again, and wrote a new question:

WHAT HAPPENED TO THE WOMAN?

I stared at Markel, looking at him properly for perhaps the first time. He was taller than me, which most people were, but excepting the breadth and development of his shoulders, we had similarly narrow builds. His skin was deep tan, his nose aquiline and his mouth stubborn, and despite his shaved head, he was handsome. He wasn't wearing livery, which I suppose made sense, but his clothes were still anonymously plain. His eyes, though, were so sharply intelligent that when he glared, I almost felt cut by it. As I hadn't answered, he tapped the slate with the pen, an annoying little *clack-clack* sound, and raised an irritated brow at me, as if to say, *Well?*

It would've been impudent even if he hadn't been a servant; as it was, I bristled furiously.

"She was captured," I snapped, stalking towards the infirmary so that he was forced to follow. "Taken to the cells by General Naza."

My stride was quick, but Markel's was quicker; he wiped his slate clean, scrawling something out as he bounded half alongside me, half ahead of me, then planted himself in my path and all but shoved the slate in my face. It read:

WE HAVE TO SPEAK TO HER NOW!

Now was underlined several times. I made an outraged noise and crossed my arms.

"*We* don't need to do anything; I'm not your fucking assistant. If you want to go, go—or better yet, get your yaseran to take you!"

I tried to dodge around him, but Markel wasn't having it. Like a child playing keepaway, he repeatedly blocked my path until, exasperated, I stopped again—at which point, he wrote a new message on his slate and held it out once more, the writing cramped to fit into the space:

THINK! HOW DID SHE GET INTO THE PALACE? DID SHE HAVE A TOKEN, LIKE THE ONES WE USED? SOMEONE HERE HELPED HER. IF SHE CAN NAME THEM, SHE'S A THREAT TO THEM, WHICH MEANS SHE'S IN DANGER. WE DON'T HAVE TIME TO WAIT!

Hatefully, this was an excellent point; how maddening, that he'd been the one to make it! Thoughts whirling, I said, "Even if you're right, we're better off getting the yaseran first. Or do you think the guards will let the two of us in?"

Markel stamped his foot at me, wiped his slate and wrote:

CAETHARI WON'T BE ANY USE WHILE VELASIN'S HURT! BUT IF WE GO OURSELVES, HE HAS PLAUSIBLE DENIABILITY, WHICH KEEPS THEM BOTH SAFE.

Maybe it was an odd thing to get hung up on, but the fact that he wrote their names untitled hit me like a shock of cold water. It was more familiarity than I'd expected, and given his total lack of deference towards me, I had the uncomfortably late realisation that Markel might be more than a servant. I shut my eyes, partly to help myself think but mostly because I suspected it would annoy him. What did I have to lose? If we tried and failed, then so be it; if we tried and succeeded, I was one step closer to keeping myself safe. And it would give Caethari a reason to trust me.

I opened my eyes and promptly rolled them at Markel's incredulous look.

"Fine," I said, "we'll go to the cells, but don't blame me if it doesn't work." I smirked at him. "Just let me do the talking, okay?"

Markel shot me a glare that would've skewered a lesser man. In response, I smiled and started walking. Probably I shouldn't have known where the cells were, but as I had a vested interest in staying out of them, the first time Nevan had brought me to court, I'd made it a point to find out, so that I'd know if I was ever being taken there under false pretenses. The dungeons, such as they were, lay at the westernmost end of the palace complex, accessible through a plain, squarish façade that backed right up against the sheltering mountain wall, so that the actual cells, like the expanded sections of Qi-Xihan we'd seen at the city's entrance, were buried inside the rock. As the entrance was guarded, I hadn't been inside before, and as we approached, I'm not ashamed to say that my heart beat faster.

We'd just come in sight of the guards when, from the corner of my eye, I became aware of a change in Markel's demeanour. Up until then, he'd stridden along so fast that the only reason he hadn't taken the lead was because he didn't know where we were going. Truth be told, my calves were aching from keeping his pace, but all of a sudden he dropped back—not so sharply as to be conspicuous, but enough to put him a deferential step behind and to the side of me. I almost laughed: it was a perfect Ralian manservant's positioning, close without being unobtrusive. The laugh died, however, when I saw how he'd changed his posture, shoulders curling in slightly with his head down, the better to look inoffensive. Even his slate was gone, tucked back in the pouch at his belt. If I hadn't seen him before this, I wouldn't have looked at him twice.

Well, that's him playing his part, I told myself. *Better make sure I play mine.*

So I did the opposite: lengthened my stride while slowing my pace, the better to look unconcerned; set my shoulders back; fixed a blankly imperious expression on my face, for which I channelled my last memory of the Shade. I didn't know if the guards would stop us, but important men always assumed they had the right to be wherever they were, and so I didn't check my stride as we reached the doors.

To my shock, we were allowed in without question. *Sunfucking stars,* I thought, and was briefly prepared to chalk it up to a miracle, until we were through and I saw what lay before us: a tall stone desk, flanked on either side by guarded doors leading back into the prison, manned by a uniformed guard. A logbook sat before him, and as we approached, he straightened slightly, frowning.

"How may I help you, ren?" he asked, a slight dubiousness in his gaze as he took in me and Markel. I tried to project confidence. General Naza had ordered the woman brought here, but I was gambling on him still being stuck in the audience hall, interviewing witnesses; if he'd already come himself and ordered her to be kept in isolation, we were fucked. "I'm Lord Asrien bo Erat, here on behalf of Yaseran Caethari Aeduria to question the woman who tried to kill his husband, Tiern Velasin Aeduria," I said, pitching my voice to sound both bored and impatient.

The guard frowned at me. "The yaseran hasn't come himself?"

"The tiern nearly *died,*" I said, not having to feign my disbelief. "The yaseran can't leave his side, but of course he still wants justice! We need to question her!"

The guard looked slightly chastened at that. "Well, naturally," he said. "My apologies, ren—" I suppressed my annoyance at that; was my Ralian title really so difficult? "—I just need your palace token to record in the book—not yours personally, of course, but the tiern's or the yaseran's, whoever deputized you."

Well, fuck. I swallowed, working to keep my face blank. There was no point in trying to bully him into accepting my token instead, as I didn't have one—I was here as Nevan's guest, not in my own right. I had no idea what to do or say next, and so was utterly unprepared for Markel to step meekly forwards, bow and present a palace token to the guard on his outstretched palms.

I froze, watching with disbelief as the guard produced the same kind of wand as they had at the gates, the glass lighting up blue as he scanned the token. Nodding to himself, he set the wand aside and proceeded to write us down in his log, pen scratching against the paper, before finally handing the token back to Markel, who bowed again and restored it to his pocket.

"Take the right-hand door—your right, not mine," said the guard, gesturing vaguely towards his colleague. Then, more loudly and over his shoulder, "Palar! Take these two to cell fourteen."

"This way," said Palar, turning to unlock the door to the cells. I shot Markel a viperous glance as we moved, but of course he couldn't answer it.

Through we went, the broad-shouldered Palar leading the way

into the tunnel beyond, which had been carved straight into the mountain who knew how many years ago. The setup was chillingly simple: a passage for the guards ran down the middle, with cells hewn from the living rock on either side, their presumable occupants hidden behind heavy wooden doors. Magelights lined the tunnel roof, which was low enough to make even me feel cramped.

"Here she is," said Palar, as we reached the seventh door on the left. Withdrawing a ring of keys, he carefully unlocked it. "She's chained up, so don't worry about that. Standard procedure is fifteen minutes by the timer—" he indicated a small wooden hourglass hung on his belt, currently positioned so that all the sand was in the bottom half, "—but if you need longer, let me know. I'll be waiting out here." He pulled the door open and stepped back, expectant.

The thing about stepping into a prison cell for any reason—even if I'm innocent, or innocent as far as the guard unlocking it knows—is that I'm always afraid I might not be let out again. Showing it, though, would make it a self-fulfilling prophecy, so I nodded coolly, thanked Palar, and swept into the cell as if it could never swallow me, refusing to shudder as the door thunked shut (but hopefully not locked) behind us.

Mercifully, the cell had a magelight of its own, illuminating the spare, stone room as brightly as if we stood outside. The old woman—just as hideously dressed as before, though notably minus the garish torc; most likely the guards had swiped it—was seated primly on a stone bench, wrists manacled before her and one ankle shackled to the right-hand wall by a sturdy length of chain. (Nevan's pointlessly sacrificed belt was nowhere to be seen; probably one of the guards had taken that, too.) She smiled grimly at the sight of us but didn't otherwise move—understandably, as her halik and nara were both torn in ways that spoke of rough treatment, while new bruises bloomed on her wrists and forehead. The whole thing made my stomach twist; say what you would of Ralia, but we don't make a habit of abusing old women, even if they are prisoners.

I waited until I heard Palar step away down the hall to give the illusion of privacy (though I'd have been shocked if he wasn't still in earshot) before turning to Markel and saying acidly, "Were you going to tell me you understood Tithenai, or did you plan on making me feel stupid?"

Markel fished his slate from his bag and wrote out an answer:

WHO SAID I KNOW TITHENAI? I RECOGNISED THE WORD FOR PALACE TOKEN, AND I KNEW YOU DIDN'T HAVE ONE.

"Hah!" I scoffed. I wasn't sure I believed him, but that was hardly the most important thing right now, and I was on the brink of saying so when, from across the room, the old woman chuckled.

"Now, that's unexpected," she said—in Ralian, not Tithenai. I whirled and stared at her, too taken aback to feel gratified that Markel was equally startled. She had a north country peasant's accent, as poorly matched to the situation as her nara was to her halik, and all at once, I realised that I'd never actually heard her speak Tithenai back in the audience hall; that she'd only said Velasin's name.

"Oh, you don't need to look so shocked," she said, smiling broadly. "I speak Tithenai, too. But if it's all the same with you, I'd rather stick to Ralian. *They* don't speak it, after all." She tipped her chin smugly in the direction of the guards.

I stepped closer without conscious volition. "Who sent you here?" I asked. "How did they get you into the palace?"

She cackled. "You nobles, you're all the same. Even when you're using us, you don't care who we are, 'less it benefits you."

I raised a brow. "Can I take that to mean that you're not expecting a rescue?"

"You can," she said, matter-of-factly. "I rather expect I'll die here."

The idea that she'd wind up double-crossed and dead didn't shock me; it was why I'd agreed to come here in the first place, so we could get her testimony before it happened. But her easy acceptance of it rocked me back on my feet. "What?" I said, stupidly.

She sighed as if I were slow. "Poor little lordling. Let me give you some advice: when those with power make pawns of lesser folk, whatever assurances they make, whatever vows they whisper, whatever riches they offer, they *lie*." Her gaze was piercing, and in that moment, it felt as if she could see right through me, *into* me, to where the Shade's claws were sunk. "The only way through is to get what you can while they're giving it, then run if you can or make peace with the worst if you can't. And as for me, well. I was done for anyway." A touch of bitterness tinged the words as she tapped her manacled hands to her chest. "I've a canker of the breast, too deep now for anything to be done. My own mother died the same way—died slowly and in horrible pain, for want of a healer's mercy. I've not long left, whatever happens here. But this way, my grandchildren have money enough for a better life than mine, and as the gods witness me now, you can bet I told them to run with it." Sharp satisfaction lit her eyes.

I didn't know what to say to that. Trying to sound as if I knew what I was doing, I said coolly, "You don't deny, then, that someone hired you?"

She snorted. "What would be the use in that? My accent's no better in Tithenai, and a body like me doesn't wind up in a place like this without the aid of someone higher up the chain. But rich folk are stupid, aren't they, lordling? Or rather, they think other people are, which amounts to the same thing. Which is why I was told to lie to you—oh, not you *specifically*, just lie to whoever asked, assuming I lived long enough for questioning." She grinned. "I've a whole sob story I'm meant to spin about how I came to be here, and why, and most of it's even true, if you bothered to check. But, well." A feral aspect crept into her smile. "I've never been much good at doing what I'm told."

I stared at her. "If you've no loyalty to whoever hired you, why not just give us their name?"

"Because fuck you too, that's why! Fuck all of you!" She spat the words, her sudden vehemence catching me off guard. "Lords and ladies, tierns and tierenas and tierenai, rich folk of any stripe—you're all the same in the end. You never think about the rest of us until you have to, and by then it's too late. *Why not just give us their name?*" She threw my own words back at me in a mocking tone. "None of you has ever helped me, so why should I help you? There's nothing you have I want, and unless I miss my guess, you haven't the stomach for torture."

"Don't help us, then," I said, feeling slightly nauseated at the prospect of doing her violence. I felt jittery, on edge, and not just because none of this was going the way I'd expected it to. I didn't want any kinship with her, but I was too aware of the hold the Shade had over me not to feel like I was looking into a bleak, warped version of where I might end up. "Why not tell us your sob story? The true parts, anyway. Let's start with this: I'm Lord Asrien bo Erat, and this is Markel—" I floundered, realising far too late that I didn't know Markel's family name, or even if he had one.

To my annoyed mortification, Markel stepped forwards, bowed, and wrote the answer on his slate for both of us to see:

JUST MARKEL.

The old woman's brows rose subtly. "Huh," she said—to Markel, not me. She squinted at him, head cocked as her sharp eyes looked up him and down. "You're not moneyborn, are you." She cocked a thumb at me. "You serve this one?"

I'd half expected Markel to take the chance to mock me, but instead his expression turned grave. He cleared his slate and wrote:

NOT HIM. VELASIN, THE MAN YOU TRIED TO KILL. I OWE HIM MY LIFE.

"*Tried* to kill, is it? I guess that means he lived. Ah, well." She sighed, raising manacled hands to scratch her jaw, and looked sidelong at Markel. "A word of advice to you, too. In the end, whatever you owe a man like that will always be less than what they take."

Markel's expression sharpened. Eyes hard, he wrote:

I WASN'T BORN WITH A SLATE AND PEN. I NEED NO LESSONS IN HOW MEN TAKE, OR FROM WHO, OR WHY.

"I suppose you don't, at that," she said, slowly, and leaned back against the prison wall, contemplating us anew. Her lip twisted wryly. "Huh. All right, then, Just Markel. For the sake of your slate and pen, you can have the short version." She glanced briefly at me, as if to see if I'd offer any objections, but it was Markel she spoke to. "I grew up in Vaiko—Vaiko as it used to be, before vin Mica's greed ruined it. My mother was Ralian, my father Tithenai. That was more common then, though mostly when Ralians married across, they married like to like, as your master did. Does that shock you, lordling?" Her gaze flicked unerringly back to me, and I'll admit it did; stars know what my face was doing. "We called it coming over the mountain, and no small number of townsfolk met their spouses that way. Happened often enough that, for a time, the border-Ralians became more accepting of it, including vin Mica's mother, who held the seat before him. But her son . . . well. King Markus saw to him in the end, when it was his own fucking house in danger, but before that—before it mattered worth a damn to anyone not living through it—there were years of polite pretence in Farathel and Qi-Xihan, because who wants to make a fuss over just a few bandits? Just a few farmers? Just a few lives ruined?"

Her voice turned hard. "My father was one of the first who died, when vin Mica's banditry started. He was a trader. A good, harmless man, robbed and left to freeze to death in the Taelic Pass, and did anyone care? They did not. It went on and on, until finally the Wild Knife showed up, that Tiern Caethari, but my husband was already dead by then, too, and without him, we had no choice but to sell our land for what little it was worth and move away. No other provision was made for us by those in charge, but why would they bother? Too little, too late; that's what nobles give you. So." Her narrowed gaze swung back to me. "When all these years later, along comes someone offering coin to be their cat's-paw, of course I say yes. My grandchildren deserve a piece of the prosperity that was taken from me, and they'll have it now. If that means I die here fast, instead of slowly a month or a year from now, then so be it."

I swallowed, distressed without wanting to be and angry at it.

"Revenge?" I asked. "What sort of revenge pins the blame on the blameless? Caethari and Velasin didn't kill your father or your husband, and if Vaiko is to flourish again, their marriage needs to work." I flinched internally as I said this; I was, after all, trying to end that marriage. "I could understand being angry at Caethari, but why Velasin? He's done nothing but—but come over the mountain!"

"I suppose that's true," she said, almost meditatively. And then she grinned. "But like I said, lordling—I've never been very good at doing what I'm told."

I had no idea what that meant, but before I could ask, someone rapped on the cell door—Palar, I realised with a start, come to tell us our time was up.

"Please," I said quickly, willing the angry old bat to stop being so *stubborn*. "Just tell us who paid you. What does it matter now?"

"It matters, lordling," she said, smiling beatifically, "because I get to tell you *no,* and that's sweeter to me than any fruit."

"Your name, then," I said desperately, wanting to salvage some lead for us to go on. "Not your family name, just your name. What harm can that do?"

"Rens?" called Palar. "Are you done in there?"

The woman pursed her lips, and for a moment, I thought she'd tell us nothing. Then:

"Syana," she said at last, proudly. "And don't you forget it."

"I won't," I said, and meant it.

◆ ◆ ◆

We were almost back to the prison entrance when Markel tugged on my sleeve, forcing me to halt and look at his slate. It read:

ASK THE GUARD IF SHE HAD A PALACE TOKEN ON HER.

Mentally cursing, I swallowed my pride and did as he suggested. Palar paused with his keys halfway to the door, considering, then shook his head.

"No, ren," he said, "though we did search thoroughly." I told myself that I was imagining the hint of leer in his voice, because the alternative was too sickening to contemplate.

"Thank you," I forced myself to say instead.

Markel bent straight back to his slate, writing on it as we went through the door and out into the main atrium, where the guard who'd written our names in the logbook nodded to acknowledge our departure. My skin crawled, but I nodded back, and managed to leave at a walk, not a run.

"Well," I said, once we were safely out of earshot of the external guards and I felt free to start walking quickly. Markel's deferential posture had likewise vanished, and he was once more keeping pace beside me. "That was pointless. What have we learned? Nothing."

Markel popped in front of me with a shake of his head and once more held up his slate. A vicious part of me wanted to grab the damn thing and smash it to pieces on the stone, just to see how he'd react. Instead, I set my jaw and read:

WE NEED TO TAKE HER DESCRIPTION TO THE GATE GUARDS. EVEN IF SHE THREW HER PALACE TOKEN AWAY, THERE SHOULD BE A RECORD OF IT.

I glared at him. "Are you always like this?" I asked irritably, quickstepping in the direction of the main palace gates. "Buzzing around like a horsefly trying to drive a herd over a cliff?"

Markel's chalk pen squeaked against the slate, which he shoved in front of me without breaking his stride:

BUZZ BUZZ, LORDLING.

"You little shit," I said, torn between annoyance, amusement and reluctant admiration. "Where in blazes did Velasin find you?"

The chalk squeaked again. This time, I turned to look at the slate before he could hold it out for me. It read:

IN A BROTHEL.

I hauled up short, staring at him. "Fuck off. Really?"

Markel grinned at me, brows waggling as he nodded.

I huffed and started walking again. "Liar," I muttered. "I bet you're his bastard half-brother or something, aren't you?"

Markel made a rasping noise that I took for laughter, eyes crinkling at the edges. I felt briefly pleased with myself, then recalled in a lurch that I was trying to bring his beloved master grief, which instantly soured my mood. I bit the inside of my cheek to keep from saying something either cutting or inane, and walked faster despite my aching calves, the better to get our frustrating association over with.

"Fucking Shade," I muttered aloud in Tithenai. I darted a glance at Markel as I said it, but if he understood, his face betrayed nothing; he only looked at me quizzically, a hint of humour in his mouth as if he suspected me of cursing about him.

Soon enough, we'd trekked our way down to the main palace gates, where Markel immediately fell back into his deferential servant act. The guards on duty were the same ones who'd let us in earlier, and I felt a jolt to realise how little time had passed between then and now.

"How can I help you, ren?" the elder guard asked respectfully. She was tall and heavyset, looking quite at home in her armour—so much so that, if I'd only seen her in passing and not actually stopped to speak with her, I might've assumed her a man. The thought was disquieting for several reasons, none of which were helpful; I shoved them aside and adopted a grave expression.

"There's been an incident in the main audience hall," I said. Having switched back to Tithenai, I found myself fighting the urge to glance at Markel, whose face was just out of view. "Tiern Velasin was attacked. The culprit is in custody, but we need to know how she entered the palace. We're not faulting you," I added quickly, as defensiveness flashed in the guard's eyes. "We believe she had a palace token, but as it's no longer in her possession—"

"Of course," said the guard, relaxing slightly. "What did she look like?"

"An older woman with hideous taste," I said tartly. "Red nara, a pink halik with red and yellow flowers, a golden torc in the shape of wings—"

"I remember her!" said the second guard, excited to be useful. He looked closer to my age, with large front teeth and a prominent throatstone. "She came through in a lull, about an hour after the open court started." So saying, he stepped over to the logbook, which sat on a handy stone lectern, and began to run his finger down the columns, scanning for a familiar name. His companion moved to look over his shoulder, and when his finger paused on a particular entry, she nodded firmly and said, "Yes. Her."

I moved beside them, coming to see for myself. "Cietena Alu Nyas," I read aloud. "You're certain?"

"Absolutely," the first guard said with conviction. "Even if she hadn't been dressed so oddly, I'd have remembered her, because she came alone in between two groups of nobles I recognised, but hers was a new face. But," she added hurriedly, as if worried I'd rebuke her for a lack of caution, "that wasn't so unusual, as open court is often when newcomers show up. We aren't in charge of issuing palace tokens, and of course the gate guards rotate, so it's not as if we should have seen her before."

"Of course not," I said. "My thanks, rens; you've been most helpful."

They bowed to me as I stepped away, already heading back up towards the palace proper. Markel waited until we were out of earshot, then tugged on my sleeve and tilted his head, silently asking for a translation. *If he really does know Tithenai, he's an excellent actor,* I thought grudgingly, and gave him a quick rundown of what the guards had said in Ralian. Markel nodded as I spoke, but insisted on stopping every few feet, peering about the ground if in search of something. I didn't know what he was doing at first, then made an exasperated noise when it clicked.

"She won't have just thrown her token on the *ground!*" I protested. "What would be the point in that?"

Markel looked at me and raised a single, pointed eyebrow.

"You're insufferable," I muttered, and started scanning the path as we moved slowly back towards the audience hall. It was pointless, surely, but no more pointless than anything else I'd done so far, which almost made it soothing.

We'd just reached the courtyard where Ru Pyras had met us when the sound of approaching footsteps jerked my attention up from the ground and towards the rapidly approaching figure of General Naza.

"Fuck," I muttered, straightening. "That didn't take long."

"Asrien bo Erat," the general rumbled, coming to loom over me. "I've been looking for you."

"General Naza," I replied, shivering deliciously as his gaze pinned me through like a butterfly specimen. "I was just on my way to present myself to be interviewed."

"Were you," he said coldly.

"Of course!" I said, batting my lashes at him. "Why would I lie to you?"

"If you are not a liar," said the general, "explain why, when I went to the cells just now, I learned that you'd questioned my prisoner." He glanced abruptly sideways, as if he were noticing Markel for the first time. "And who is this?"

"A servant," I said. "He belongs to Tiern Velasin. He's mute."

The general's gaze slid off him so fast, you'd have thought that Markel was made of glass. Unobserved, Markel smirked at me, waggling his fingers in mock farewell. *You little* shit, I thought fiercely.

"And why shouldn't I have questioned the prisoner?" I asked, turning back to General Naza with a hand on my hip. "You'd clearly left no instructions to prevent it." I smirked up—and up, and *up*—at him. "That smacks of oversight on your part."

"You questioned my prisoner *in Ralian*," he growled again. "After she'd attacked *another* Ralian. That smacks," he said, leaning down—and down, and *down*—to set his mouth to my ear, "of *conspiracy*."

I swallowed hard. Sunfucking *stars*, he was big! How was anyone meant to concentrate on anything else?

"A coincidence, I assure you," I said, dry-mouthed.

The general straightened, smiling without any humour. "A co-incidence you will now do me the courtesy of explaining." He cut a glance at Markel, yet barely seemed to take him in. "You. Dismissed," he said, and whether because he understood the words or because the tone itself was enough, Markel bowed and left. I saw him flash me a backwards glance, which was strangely heartening, and then—

General Naza's large, callused hand closed firmly around the back of my neck and *squeezed.*

"Hngl," I said, or something else equally eloquent.

"Come with me," he growled, and *kept his fucking hand there* as he proceeded to haul me away for questioning.

And the thing is—

The thing is, I've a weakness for being manhandled. More than a weakness: it does something to me, like having all my thoughts shaken loose and replaced with warm, soft sand. Combined with fucking, it's the best thing in the world, and though Nevan had many fine qualities both in and out of the bedroom, tossing me around until my brain disengaged wasn't one of them. Factor in my enforced dry spell in Eliness and the trouble that had sent me there in the first place, and it had been nigh on a year since I'd last had the chance to indulge, which had left me starving for it. I just hadn't known how badly until that moment, when my thoughts began to dissolve like spun sugar dropped in wine.

Even so, and despite my unravelling brain, I knew I had a decision to make: to pull away and, if not fight, then at least attempt some sort of self-preservation, or to let whatever was happening keep happening, regardless of where it led. The first option was the smart one, but even if I'd been in the habit of making clever choices, the idea that I could overcome the general in whatever way was ludicrous. At best, I could make him let go of me, but even if I managed that much, there'd still be no escape from him. I had no idea what type of questioning he had in mind for me, only the paranoid certainty that I was bound to be discovered or hurt at some point during my stay in Qi-Xihan, so why not now? Despite my provocation and his disdain, I knew enough to know when a man found me fuckable, and for my sins, it was a very mutual sentiment.

Of course, I had no way of knowing what the general meant by grabbing me like that; the fact that I associated such roughness with a very specific type of bedplay didn't mean the same was true of him. But whether I was wrong or right, with Syana's bruises fresh in mind, Velasin a failed seduction and the general's hand on my neck, I found I didn't care whether I ended up fucked literally or in the metaphoric sense, or even both at once; what mattered was that I didn't have to be responsible for it. Ever since the Shade had made his threats in Eliness—or perhaps long before that, if I was honest—I'd lived with an anxiety so constant and all-consuming that I often forgot I was capable of existing without it. But when someone else took charge of me, it melted away, and in that moment, it didn't matter that General Naza didn't like or trust me, or that I shouldn't trust him; I just wanted not to have to *think*.

Perhaps I should've been scared, but I wasn't; the hand on my neck was steadying, and if the general had thought to release me, I'd doubtless have dropped to the ground in mortifying fashion, but he didn't, and I didn't, and so I chose to let myself go, thoughts shifting further into that pleasant, warm-sand state with every step we took. I drifted, and when I came back to myself somewhat, I found he'd brought me into some room or other—a study? an office? sunfucking stars, we could've been in the Iron Suite for all I knew—and shut the door, his fingers still digging into me.

"Now," he said, finally deigning to speak. He gave my neck another squeeze, and I was aware in a distant way that he likely meant it to be menacing, but my body only read it as *more, yes, good*. "Let's have the tru—"

He broke off abruptly, and at first I didn't know why, until I realised I'd let out a faint, embarrassing moan.

All the way from the courtyard—up until that moment, in fact—the general had been beside me, his face out of view. Now he moved to stand before me, and as his hand was still warmly curled around my neck, this put us quite close together.

"Look at me," he said, in that deep, rich voice.

Shuddering, I obeyed. His eyes were black amber, fixed on mine. He frowned slightly, something that wasn't quite a smile quirking the corner of his mouth.

"Huh," he said, and gave me a small, experimental shake, as if I were a ragdoll whose stuffing was all at one end. I moaned again, louder than before, my mouth hanging stupidly open, and the expression became a mocking, wicked smile.

"Well, will you look at that," he murmured, sliding his hand upwards to grip my hair, palm cradling my skull. He left it there a moment, fingers spreading carefully, then gripped and tugged my head back in a way that made me whimper. "Aren't you sweet."

I hung in his grasp, dazed and needy, uncaring of how I'd come to be where I was or what I'd been doing beforehand. Everything had been emptied out, replaced by the wants of the moment, and what I wanted above all else was for whatever was happening to *keep* happening.

Carefully, almost consideringly, the general ran his free hand over my chest, stroking proprietarily up and down, before letting it rest around my throat. His thumb pressed against my pulse-point, and just for a second, his grip tightened, letting me feel a fraction of his strength. I felt a brief spike of fear, but no true panic; my whole body thrummed like thunder had been poured through it, and then he relaxed again. As his hand withdrew, I wheezed out a breath, trembling for more.

"Sweet," he said again, sounding almost surprised. His fingertips skated along my jaw, thumb stroking my bottom lip. "Are you always this easy?"

I made a noise that might've meant *yes* and might've meant *no*, but which first and foremost meant *please*. The general chuckled, pressing down on the centre of my lip; my mouth opened for him, head still tilted back as he slid two fingers onto my tongue. He tasted of salt and skin with a tang of something metallic, and as the fingers pushed deeper, I realised I was hard, though there was no urgency to it. Slowly, the general pushed into me, almost to the back of my throat; he held his fingers there until I swallowed around them, then withdrew and fucked them lazily in again, in and out, until I was panting harshly and my chin was wet with spit.

"Huh," he said again, and let his fingers rest on my tongue, pressing down just enough that I couldn't relax my jaw. His eyes glittered, tracking the bob of my throat as I swallowed around nothing. "If this is an act, kiensa, it's a very odd *choice* of act."

At the word *kiensa,* I moaned around his fingers. Like many Tithenai words, it had no clear Ralian counterpart; it was a diminutive endearment used primarily for pets and children, though between adults and especially among litai in Qi-Xihan, Nevan had said, the connotations were . . . particular.

The general's gaze darkened. Slowly, he withdrew his fingers from my mouth and wiped them on my cheek, a spitcool line of skin. When I didn't protest this, he hit my cheek with his palm, the contact too light to be a true slap, but still echoing one in form. He waited a moment, then did it again, harder. Then again, and the sting of it had me whimpering, his fingers still buried in my hair, my body thrumming with pain-pleasure-want and the seeping thrill of not being in charge of myself.

"Are all Ralians like this, or just you?" the general mused. I didn't know if he was speaking to me or to himself until a beat had passed and he added, twisting his hand just a little bit tighter, "Well? Are you?"

Words were very hard to reach; my answer came out slurred. "Just me."

"That's good, kiensa." The general's voice was a dark purr, like sun-warmed velvet brushing against my skin. "As it's just you, we're going to play a little game. For every truth you tell me, you get a reward. For every lie, you get punished. Nod if you understand."

I bobbed my head, whimpering slightly.

"Good," said the general. He let go of my hair, and I mourned the loss of contact for the half-second it took to realise that he was untying my lin, which was fastened closed at my hip. My breathing was loud in my ears as his big, dexterous hands undid the toggles one by one; the lin fell open, and he eased it off my shoulders with surprising gentleness, letting the stiff, patterned silk drop to the floor. He studied me a moment, then grasped the hem of my undershirt.

"Lift your arms," he said, and I obeyed. The world went briefly dark as the pale, soft linen covered my eyes. I blinked, and there was the general, smiling that sharp, dangerous smile. I shivered, nipples pebbling under his scrutiny as much as from the cool air—and then he knelt, hands skating down both my legs, before reaching my right ankle.

"Lift," he said, and I obeyed like a horse being shod, though as he was removing my shoes instead of fitting them, it ended up a slightly backwards metaphor. When I was completely barefoot, he looked up at me, one brow raised in pointed, smirking acknowledgement of the bulge in my nara. *Should I run?* a part of me wondered, but the question went unanswered as he gripped my thighs. I flushed hot, swaying as he slid his hands back up me and stood, a giant once more. He glanced around the room until his gaze lit on something I couldn't see; then, with no warning, he gripped my hair again—from the front, this time—and hauled me over to whatever it was. As we moved, my brain became an overtipped hourglass, full of nothing but falling sand. Lightning ran from my stinging scalp through my heavy limbs; I went almost deadweight, but before I could fall, the general caught and rearranged me. I wasn't sure how at first, and then I dimly processed that I was sitting on his lap, which meant the object he'd walked us to was a chair. He took a moment to settle himself, then pulled me back, my head lolling against his collarbone, and spread his thick thighs to splay my smaller ones open athwart them, propped in place by his knees. I felt deliciously obscene: my bare feet dangled above the floor, my muscles so lax that, had he not been keeping me upright, I would've easily keeled over.

Slowly, General Naza skated his free hand up my naked chest, paused, and pinched my right nipple. I made an undignified noise and bucked against him, squirming as he did the same to the left, then the right again, over and over, until my whole chest was aching in the very best way.

"Responsive," he murmured. I read it as praise and moaned, earning myself a chuckle. "Now then, kiensa." His right hand moved higher, fingers curling around my throat like the wings on Syana's torc, while his left slid beneath the waistbands of my nara and smallclothes, not so much gripping my cock as enclosing it completely. I shivered; I wasn't small in terms of my proportions, but I was compared to most men, and especially to him. I fit in his hand like a toy. "Here's how this will work. Tell the truth, and be treated sweetly." He squeezed my throat to compress the big veins, not my windpipe, all while giving my cock a long, slow stroke; I bucked against him, crying out with pleasure. "Lie, and be treated . . . less sweetly." The grip on my throat changed to a chokehold; he twisted my cock like a farmhand trying to pull a reluctant apple from the branch. I made a garbled, airless noise and writhed on his lap, but didn't grab at his arms or scream or try to rise, because he'd given me rules, and in my soft-sand state, the rules were what mattered.

His demonstration complete, the general relaxed his grip and I flopped back against him, panting and shivering, my cock still desperately hard.

"Do you understand, kiensa?"

"Yes," I croaked.

"Yes what?"

I fumbled with the question through the haze of my thoughts, groping uncertainly towards an answer. "Yes . . . General?"

"Not General. Not for this." There was a note in his voice I was too far gone to interpret, though part of me still noticed it. "Think. If I call you kiensa, what do you call me?"

The answer rose through my mind and popped like a bubble reaching the ocean's surface. There was another word Nevan had mentioned when he'd explained the other meaning of kiensa; an archaic honorific used towards those of higher rank which now persisted only in its borrowed bedroom context.

"Yaren," I whispered.

"Good," crooned the general, and gave my cock a long, torturously slow stroke in reward. "Now. First question." His voice was so deep, I felt the rumble of it in my chest as much as with my ears. "What is your full, true name?"

I swallowed. "Lord Asrien bo Erat."

"Good." A squeeze to my throat; a stroke to my cock. Soft, warm sand instead of thoughts.

"Where and when did you first meet Velasin vin Aaro?"

"Yesterday, at Yasa Kithadi's estate." My voice sounded distant in my own ears, almost dreamlike. The general made a frustrated noise, but still rewarded me: a squeeze, a stroke. Each time he stopped the flow of blood to my head, my whole body sang.

"Were you behind today's attempt on his life?"

"No."

"Do you know who was?"

"No."

He made a frustrated noise, displeased with my answers, but no punishment came; only what I'd been promised. I was desperately hard, trembling beneath his hands.

"The old woman. Is she Ralian?"

"No."

His hands tightened, harder than before, but not to the level of a punishment. His next question came out a growl.

"Then *why does she speak it*?"

"She said . . . she said she was from Vaiko," I gasped. "Her mother was Ralian."

"Did you know that before you spoke to her?"

"No!"

"Then what made you try it?"

"I didn't," I panted, overwhelmed.

"You didn't?" The general's voice turned dangerous, thumb pressing hard against my throat. His hand tightened around my cock, not twisting—not yet—but the promise of it spiked my pulse.

"I didn't, I mean—I didn't try, I wasn't—I wasn't trying to talk to her, I was talking to Markel—"

"Markel?"

"The servant, the mute. Ah!" I jolted as he pinched the crease of my thigh. "He—he only knows Ralian, so I spoke to him, and she heard me and spoke back!"

This time, the reward was gentle. Sweating now, I shut my eyes and tipped my head back, trembling as he petted me.

"She told you her mother was Ralian, but not who sent her?"

"Yes!"

"What did she say, exactly? Take your time."

Somehow, I stammered out an account of what Syana had told us, and for every piece of information, the general's hands rewarded me. My cock was leaking so freely that his grip had turned slick without yet going tacky, while spots were starting to dance before my eyes. I felt like I was floating above myself despite still being anchored in my body, as if my consciousness had somehow doubled. Two Asriens, overlapping each other.

"That's good, kiensa," the general murmured, hands stilling as I finished. Either deliberately or by accident, he rocked against me, his erection a thick, hot line against the crease of my arse. "Just a few more questions, and then we're done."

"Yes, yaren."

"Why did you come to Tithena?"

Unease twisted through me. "Because I had to."

"Why did you have to?"

Don't answer that! a buried part of me thought, and so I whimpered instead, shaking my head from side to side.

The general made a disappointed noise. "No answer is the same as a wrong answer, kiensa. One more chance: why did you have to come?"

"I can't—" I began, then choked off as his hand tightened on my throat with killing pressure, fingers cruelly twisting my cock. My vision greyed; I struggled against him, thrashing and failing to gasp around the pain, but the panic I felt had nothing to do with his hands and everything to do with my inability to please him.

After several torturous seconds, he relaxed his grip. I sucked in air and sobbed on the exhale, tears leaking out of my eyes.

"Shhh," he said, thumb stroking along the line of my throat. "Take your time, kiensa."

"I can't," I whimpered. I turned my head as if to bury it in his shoulder, but all I managed was rubbing my cheek against his chest. "Yaren, please, I can't—"

"You can," he said, almost soothingly. "You will."

I shook my head, but to no avail. He waited a moment, then asked again, voice softer than before: "Why did you have to come to Tithena?"

"Please," I croaked out, "please, he'll kill m—"

I choked into silence, writhing as he twisted one way, crushed another. My vision went completely black; I was briefly terrified, but as the general relaxed his grip, a strange kind of peace came over me. Air flooded into my lungs, and I sobbed again, my throat as wrecked and raw as my heart. I was already under a death sentence, but if I died here, at least my mother would be safe; there'd be no point in harming her if I wasn't alive to take a lesson from it.

Between the Shade and General Naza, I chose the general.

"One more try," he murmured, dipping his head to speak the words against my ear. There was something almost tender about it. "Why did you have to come to Tithena?"

"Because the Shade made me," I whispered.

The general kissed my cheek, hand gentle on my throat as he stroked my cock. I sobbed again, this time in gratitude, hips bucking into the touch.

"Who is the Shade?"

"A spymaster. He's—his name is Lord Cato."

"What's his clan-name?"

"I don't know, I swear, I don't know—"

"Shh. I believe you, kiensa. What does the Shade want from you?"

"He wants—he wants me to break up the marriage. Ah!" He was stroking me steadily now, not pausing between questions; my whole body was arching up, electric with the need to come.

"How are you to manage that?"

"Seduce them. Either of them. Or if, if I can't"—I was panting now, the hand around my throat little more than a warm caress—"kill Velasin. Make it look like he spurned me. Like I was jealous."

"What happens if you fail?"

I choked back a sob. "He'll kill my mother."

Just for an instant, his grip on me stilled. "Was that all he black-mailed you with?"

"No."

"What else?"

"I like men. Only men. And I had debts."

"That's all?"

"That's all."

"Poor kiensa. How cruelly you've been treated." He tipped my head back, choking me gently, just the way I liked. "Shh, it's all right now, we're done. You can come."

I hadn't known I was waiting for permission until he granted it, and suddenly I was shuddering through the most powerful climax of my life. White spattered up my bare chest, but yaren kept his hand where it was, wringing the aftershocks out of me until I was shuddering with overstimulation.

By the time he finally released me, I was a sobbing, shaking mess, my whole face wet with tears. I felt him shift behind me as if in preparation to stand, and all at once, the soft sand of my thoughts froze into ice, because this was when it ended; when it *always* ended. I'd be once more set in charge of myself, left to stumble through the aftermath of my own poor choices, which tended to be as ugly an experience as the one that came before had been exhilarating.

Except that the general didn't stand. Instead, he rearranged me until I was sitting sideways across his lap, my back propped up by his arm. I blinked at him, dazed and trembling and unable to read his expression. Slowly, he put a hand to my jaw, thumb stroking across my cheek, a slight furrow between his dark brows.

"Shh," he said, and leaned down to kiss me, deep and slow, tongue fucking my mouth in an echo of his fingers. I moaned into the contact, grabbing his lin for purchase, and when we broke apart, I was panting all over again.

"Please, yaren," I babbled, suddenly terrified of leaving; or worse, of being left. "Please, let me stay, I'll be good, I promise I'll be good—"

"You want more?" he asked, one brow rising.

I nodded frantically.

He considered a moment, then smiled wickedly. Spreading his legs, he eased me down to kneel between them, once more threading his hand through my hair. Unlike me, he was still hard, and I watched, greedy and riveted, as he pulled his thick cock out of his nara, giving it a slow, meaningful stroke.

"Open," he ordered, and so I did, eyes falling blissfully closed as he pushed himself into my mouth.

◆   ◆   ◆

Later, I made my way back to Nevan's rooms. He startled as I came in, then relaxed enough to just look faintly disapproving.

"There you are," he said, rising to greet me. He squeezed my shoulder, brow furrowed, glasses slipping down his nose as he looked me over. "I was beginning to worry. Markel said you'd been taken for questioning, but—"

"I'm fine," I said, and approximated a smile. "The general is more bark than bite."

"Well, that's a relief." He hesitated. "Have you eaten? I was thinking I'd ring for some food."

I flushed, recalling the gentle press of the general's fingers against my lips as he hand-fed me titbits from his own plate. "I'm fine," I said again. "Just tired." I probably ought to have flirted with him, or kissed him, or done something else normal, but I didn't have the energy. The best I could manage was to ask, after an awkward pause, "How's Velasin? Any change?"

"He's stable," said Nevan. "Not yet awake, but that's not surprising."

Another pause. Nevan looked close to saying something serious, but changed his mind at the last second, like a horse refusing a fence. "All right," he said instead. "Rest, then."

I nodded and went through to the bedroom, shutting the door behind me. Goosebumps prickled my arms as I stripped, remembering the general's hands. *What am I to do with you?* he'd asked at one point, and I, returned to my soft-sand state, had murmured back, *Whatever yaren wants.* And so he had, at length and with skill, which would've been enough on its own, except that he'd also done the unthinkable and treated me so kindly before sending me off again that, even now, I couldn't decide which part of our encounter I'd imagined, the impossible gentleness of the after, or all the delicious cruelty of the before.

Naked, I walked to the glass and stared at my reflection. He'd left marks on my hips, my inner thighs, to say nothing of how thoroughly he'd used me elsewhere. I traced them over, pressing lightly against each bruise, then turned and climbed into bed, the cool sheets a balm to my sensitized skin. I closed my eyes and slipped into an easier sleep than any I'd known in months, my last thoughts of our parting conversation.

You'll be of use to me, then? the general had asked, thumb grazing across my mouth.

Of course, I'd said.

Part Four

CAETHARI

16

Caethari knelt by Velasin's bedside, gripping his limp, cool hand between his own. They'd moved him from the infirmary to the Jade Suite an hour ago on the say-so of Ru Saeri, who'd been the one to knit his throat back together in those horrible, bloody minutes when Cae felt as if the walls of his world had fallen. She'd stayed with them at first, working on Vel and making sure his arteries were fully repaired, until the threat of magical overextension had forced her to delegate. After that, six different healers had taken turns throughout the day, each sitting a silent vigil as their magic worked to keep Vel alive. Cae had watched them anxiously, not knowing what they were doing but unwilling to distract them by asking questions. It was only when Ru Saeri returned that he ventured to beg an explanation.

"It's the blood loss," she'd said softly, watching as one of her junior healers worked. "Blood is what fuels us; when we lose too much, it stops the body from functioning as it should. Ideally, we'd be able to transfuse blood straight from one person to another, but right now, that's a triage option, because it doesn't always work and we don't know why. There are academic theories that try to explain it, some of which have shown promise when applied in the field, but in the meantime"—she gestured towards Vel—"it's safer to coax the body to produce more on its own." She sighed. "The problem with that is not overtaxing the patient. Blood is made up of multiple parts, most of which replenish fairly quickly; the most important one, however . . . well, under normal circumstances, it takes weeks—months, even—to recoup what was lost, and without it . . ." She shook her head. "Anyway. That's why it takes so many of us: we're trying to strike the right balance, helping your husband's body to replenish the simpler blood-parts using his own energy, but donating ours to fuel the more complex component."

Cae swallowed. Without meaning to, he thought again of Mauri, the soldier his younger self had let die in pain, too green and proud and cowardly to offer her battlefield mercy. "And he, if you . . . if you weren't here—if this had happened somewhere else, and he lost that much blood, even with his throat sewn up, could he still—?"

"He would have a chance," said Ru Saeri, in the gentle tones of a healer used to negotiating with distressed kin. "Not a good chance, perhaps—certainly not as good a chance as we're giving him now—but a chance nonetheless." And then, more gently still, "In my experience, yaseran, upsetting hypotheticals aren't helpful things to dwell on."

He'd nodded at that, resuming his seat in the infirmary. Nevan kept him company for a time, during which he kindly pointed out, as the healers hadn't, that Cae still had Vel's blood on his face and hands, providing a wetted handkerchief to help clear it off. Cae thanked him, but couldn't muster the energy for further conversation, and eventually the ciet was called away, presumably to help with General Naza's investigation. At some indeterminate point after his departure, Markel arrived, took one look at Velasin, and blanched as pale as Cae had ever seen him, almost staggering in his shock. Cae rose, a lump in his throat, and set a tentative arm to Markel's shoulder.

"It's all right," he said, as much to convince himself as for Markel's sake. "The healers have—they fixed his throat, and they've been giving him—not giving him, I mean—they've been helping him grow more blood—not *grow*," he said, agitated, running his hands through his hair, "I don't mean grow, there's another word for it—Ru Saeri explained it all, I just can't remember—"

Markel made a rare, rough noise and embraced him, squeezing

hard. Cae froze up for all of a second, then collapsed against him, clinging on and shaking as he hadn't since the last time he'd been forced to sit at Vel's sickbed, uncertain of if and when he'd wake up, and in what condition.

When Markel finally pulled away, his eyes were wet.

"I'm so sorry," Markel signed desperately. "Asrien told me he'd been hurt, that he'd live, but I didn't realise it was this serious, or I'd have come straight back."

Cae blinked at him, a strange ache in his chest. "You didn't come straight back?"

Which was how he learned about the gossip Markel had over-heard in the kitchens, his decision to bully Asrien into taking him to the prison, their interview with Syana, the subsequent conversation with the gate guards, the missing palace token registered to Cietena Alu Nyas, and Asrien being hauled away by a suspicious General Naza. By the time they were done, Cae was buzzing with the need to act, though in what way, he wasn't quite sure, beyond sending Markel to let Nevan know what had happened to Asrien. It felt . . . wrong, somehow, to make no bid to see the other Ralian released, when General Naza was clearly so hostile to them—or at the very least, to make sure of his fair treatment—but Cae didn't know what strings to pull to effect either outcome, and even if he had, he couldn't have left Velasin. He waited for Markel to return with Nevan's thanks, hoping distantly that his uncle by marriage would know what, if anything, to do about Asrien, and resumed his vigil in a state of exhausted agony.

Compounding this was the nagging sense that the name Cietena Alu Nyas was somehow familiar; Cae tried his best, but he wasn't good at keeping track of people with whom he didn't routinely as-sociate, and so he remained stumped. When Ru Saeri finally re-turned again, examined Vel and pronounced him able to be moved, Caethari had almost wept. As before, he carried Vel to the Jade Suite, laying him gently down on the bed they were yet to share.

266 · Foz Meadows

"He should wake sometime in the next few hours," Ru Saeri said. "I and my staff will be on call if you need us, but until then, I think it's better for all of you that he rest somewhere private."

"Thank you," Cae had croaked, and so here he was, still clutching Vel's hand, unable to look away from the scar on his throat. Though no longer quite so puckered and livid as it had been that morning, it was still painful to witness: a raised, rosy seam slashed diagonally across the left side of Velasin's neck, as long as Cae's littlest finger and nearly half as thick. There was bruising around it, too, and with an ugly pang, Cae realised that Syana had cut directly through the fading lovebite he'd given Vel on the bank of the Sihae. *There's a metaphor in that,* Cae thought a little hysterically, and bit back a burst of inappropriate laughter. Vel himself was pale, though thanks to the healers working to replenish his blood, he was nowhere near as ashen as he'd been earlier. Even so, his cheeks were sunken, giving him a hollowed-out look. To Cae, he looked thinner all over—felt lighter, too—but he didn't know whether that was just his perception, or if the repeated healings really had left him diminished.

"He was just starting to look healthy again," he croaked to Markel, who was seated in a chair on the opposite side of the bed. He hadn't spoken in some time, but Markel nodded wearily, as if they'd been in the middle of a conversation that had only briefly paused.

"He's never been good at taking care of himself," Markel signed, though his eyes stayed fixed on Velasin. "Being in Farathel, knowing other men like him, that helped. But when we were younger . . ."

He let his hands drop, a sad, fond look on his face.

"What about when he was younger?" Cae asked after a moment. His stomach gave an odd lurch. "We've talked about a lot of things, but not . . . there's a lot he hasn't told me."

Markel's mouth quirked. "A lot of it isn't for me to say," he signed. "But some parts . . ." He hesitated, then ventured, "He's told you how we met?"

"He has," said Cae, feeling oddly guilty at the admission. Markel had been eleven when Vel, aged not quite fourteen, had found him beaten, bloodied and left for dead outside one of Farathel's riverside brothels. Vel had carried Markel into the night, begging help from strangers and eventually finding it in the form of Aline, a metem healer in one of the poor districts, after which he'd brought Markel home and convinced his father to let him train as his valet and bodyguard. It wasn't the kind of story you forgot in a hurry.

"You don't need to look so worried," signed Markel, a flicker of smile on his lips. "I don't mind you knowing." Then the smile died, his gaze turning back to Velasin. "What he won't have told you is that he spent the next two years afraid I'd find out he liked men."

Cae froze. "What? I thought—" He broke off, trying to recall exactly what Vel had said, but the precise wording eluded him. "You didn't know?"

"He told Aline while I was passed out," signed Markel. "And when I woke up, I realised she was metem." His eyes took on a strange, sharp light that Cae had never seen before. "Children in brothels learn early. I knew what it was to be metem, for women to want women, for men to want men, all kinds of desires. I also knew . . . other things. Things I never told Velasin." A shadow passed over his features, the implications enough to make Cae's stomach roil. A part of him wanted to ask, but even if it had been his right to know, he wasn't sure he wanted to. Markel watched him, and then, just like that, his expression cleared, face soft as he looked at Vel. "He knew I'd met Aline. That whatever I had in the world, I owed to him. And still, he was afraid to tell me. For a long time, I didn't know why, not really. It wasn't until he made his Farathel friends that I understood."

"What was it?" Cae asked, but in a strange way, it felt like he already knew.

"He was lonely," Markel signed simply. "He didn't get along with his brothers. He knew boys his own age, but none he was close to. There was only me, and that was . . ." His expression changed again, flickering as he stared past Cae, hands slowing as he signed. "He wanted us to be friends, and we were, but publicly, I could only be his servant. It made me so angry sometimes, because I had no control, no—" he flicked his wrists irritably, struggling to find the right word, "—no *say* in things. Because I couldn't leave; I couldn't choose; I couldn't change how any of it was. Or at least, that's how it felt. Except that I really did like him. I liked him so much! He found out about sign-speech for me! So it should've been fine, shouldn't it? That's what I kept wrestling with. If it's fine, I should be happy to stay, no matter what. Servants aren't allowed to be angry at their masters, especially not masters who act like friends."

His hands stilled for a long moment. Cae watched him, riveted, subconsciously holding his breath.

"So," Markel finally continued. "One day, I snapped. We'd argued over something, I can't remember what—it was a petty, stupid thing—but it was the last straw. I started breaking things, screaming as much as I'm able. I told him I didn't want to be his pet servant anymore, and the look on his face . . . I don't think he'd realised until then that I didn't think I could leave. That, in my mind, he might not let me." His face did something compli- cated, and it took Cae a moment to realise that Markel was strug- gling with deep emotion, mouth twisted with the effort of keeping it off his face. "Before we could talk, his father came up and found the room half-destroyed. Velasin said he'd done it. His father had him caned." He swallowed, looking away, hands shaking slightly as he signed. "When he came back, he told me he was sorry. He said that I should know he liked men, because if he was exposed one day, I might suffer for it, too, and he didn't want that, so if I wanted to leave, for that or any other reason, he'd understand. And he tried—" Markel faltered then, briefly resting his face in his hands before continuing, "—he tried to give me money—money *he'd saved* from the little he was permitted of his own—so that I wouldn't have to make my choice based on need. So I could stay or go, and know I had coin either way, in case I changed my mind in the future. As if he hadn't been the one to insist I was paid a fair wage in the first place! As if I hadn't been saving it since the very first week!" He scrubbed his hands across his eyes and let out a shuddering breath. "He was lonely," Markel signed again, "but he would've rather been lonely forever than have me stay out of obligation. Even at fifteen."

Cae swallowed hard, staring down at Vel's sleeping figure as if he'd never seen him before. His heart ached.

"What's his brother like?" he asked, grasping desperately for a safer yet related topic and somehow finding one. He signed as he spoke, as much to have something to do with his hands as to try and practice. "His living brother, I mean, Nathian. He's told me a little about Revic, but—well."

Markel's expression turned wry, though with a hint of relief that suggested he, too, was glad for a change of conversation.

"Lord Nathian is . . . very like his father," he signed, rolling his eyes. "He values appearances highly, dislikes being challenged and hates even more when he's wrong. He's unimaginative and overly formal, but to his credit, he does care deeply for his wife and children." He grinned. "Just about the only thing he and Velasin have in common is stubbornness. It's a family trait."

Cae snorted at that, and was on the brink of replying when a knock sounded at the suite's main door, which was in the next room over. Cae moved to answer it, but Markel shot him an exasperated look and rose instead, leaving the bedroom door open as he moved into the suite's main room.

"Sorry to intrude," said Nevan, faintly audible from the doorway. "I was just in the infirmary, but Ru Saeri said Velasin had been moved here. May I come in?"

"You may," called Cae, pitching his voice to carry.

The door clicked, followed by the soft sound of footsteps on carpet. His uncle and Markel appeared in the room, the ciet's expression softening when he saw Velasin.

"Has he woken yet?" he asked.

"Not truly," Cae said, rubbing his face. "I thought he had a while ago, but he was just sleeptalking."

"Sleeptalking? You're sure?"

"He mumbled *What about the reseko?* and then rolled over," Cae replied wryly. "Not exactly the height of consciousness."

"But he's . . . well?"

"As well as we could hope for, under the circumstances." Cae swallowed against the sudden tightness in his throat. Vel could've died so easily—would've died, perhaps, if Ciet Yarasil hadn't known that saints-blessed trick to keep him from bleeding out. "We . . . he's going to be fine." He said it firmly, the better to believe it.

Nevan set a hand on his shoulder, giving a comforting squeeze. "I'm glad to hear it," he said. He hesitated, letting out an awkward little cough as he pulled away, then added in a rush, "All that being so, I've been asked to extend you an invitation to a gathering tonight."

Cae blinked, thinking for a moment that he must've misheard. "I'm sorry?"

Nevan had the good grace to look slightly embarrassed, glancing aside as he pushed his glasses up his nose. "A gathering," he said. "A party in the Mazepool Gardens. To introduce you to court."

Cae stared up at him. "Velasin nearly *died*," he said, feeling slightly insane. "That woman cut his *throat,* he hasn't even woken up yet, and you want me to just *leave* him here? Alone? To go to a *party?*"

"Strictly speaking, it's not my party," he said, as if that made it better. "The Amber Chair, Tierena Keris Talae, has arranged it, and she asked me to pass on her message."

"The Amber Suite is literally *next door,*" Cae said, disbelieving. "Why wouldn't she come herself?"

"Because she's the Amber Chair," the ciet replied dryly, "and busy seeing to party preparations."

"No," said Cae, fighting down a burst of misdirected anger. "Thank you, but no. I'm not leaving him."

Carefully, Nevan said, "It's not that I'm not sympathetic, or that I don't understand your feelings, but—"

"But what?" Cae snapped.

His uncle sighed. "Caethari, you deferred to your husband before the whole court this morning, when the asa had asked a question of *you*. Whether you meant to or not—accurately or not, even—you've given the court the impression that Velasin speaks for your marriage on political matters, and as he's Ralian, that's . . . well. You need to show that you can participate without him, at the very least."

"I don't want to," Cae insisted, aware that he sounded petulant but unable, quite, to shake it. "Saints, I hate this! He was nearly killed—shouldn't that be an extenuating circumstance for anyone?"

Nevan opened his mouth to reply, but before he could, a tired voice croaked from the bed, "What's extenuating who?"

"Vel!"

Cae scrambled out of his chair, kneeling to grasp his husband's hand. Vel smiled weakly at him, fingers exerting the lightest possible pressure on Cae's own as he tried his best to squeeze back.

"Did we wake you? Are you all right? Saints, of course you're not, what a stupid question—medicine!" Cae knew he was babbling, but couldn't stop himself. "Ru Saeri said to call her when you woke, that you might need medicine, something to stop the pain—"

"Soon, maybe." Vel blinked languidly, head tipping to take in Markel and Nevan before finally resettling on Cae. His gaze was unfocussed, hooded lids struggling to stay open. "Am I awake?"

"Awake as you've been all day," said Cae, trying and failing not to sound too desperate about it.

Vel considered this. "I'll take your word for it," he said. "It's just that it's hard to tell. I keep dreaming about you." And then, plaintively, "I'm thirsty."

"Markel, would you—" Cae said, only to find that Markel had preempted him, a glass of water already in his outstretched hand. Cae took it gratefully, supporting Vel's head as he leaned upright to drink. A tiny trickle of water curved away from his mouth and ran down his throat, beading on his scar, but Vel ignored it, finishing the whole glass and asking raspily for another. He received it, and another after that before finally lying down again with a satisfied sigh. Only then did he turn back to Cae and ask, "What's this about a party? I think I heard you before, but I thought I'd made it up."

"The Amber Chair is hosting a gathering," Cae said, refusing to feel anything about his presence in Vel's dreams. "Nevan thinks I should attend, even with you here; I disagree."

Vel sighed, smiling tiredly. "The ciet is right," he said. "You should go."

Cae fought a wholly useless urge to pull his own hair out. "Someone tried to murder you, and you want me to act like nothing happened?"

"Not that." Vel made an effort at shaking his head, though all he really succeeded in doing was smearing his hair back and forth across the pillow. "Not to pretend this away. To show strength despite it. To show you're not afraid." And then, in Ralian, "Please, Cae? They'll think you're hiding behind my skirts."

Cae blinked at him, confused. "But you don't wear skirts."

Markel clicked his fingers to get their attention. Rolling his eyes, he signed, "It's a Ralian expression; it implies a man is cowardly or childish for requiring a woman's protection, or for otherwise citing a woman's views as an excuse for inaction." He shot Velasin a look that was equal parts fond and frustrated, signing his next remark with pointed exaggeration. "As Velasin is *not* your wife, it doesn't apply here, and shouldn't apply in any case, as it's based on the idea that women are lesser beings. Which we're well aware *isn't true.*"

Cae's lip curled with involuntary disgust. "Quite."

Velasin winced. "Apologies," he mumbled, still in Ralian. "That's not—I didn't mean it like that." He lolled his head beseechingly towards Cae again, fingers twitching across the blankets as he found and reclaimed Cae's hand. "I just . . . don't want them to think less of you because of me. You need and deserve the respect of the court. I've cost you too much already. I don't want to cost you this, too."

Cae inhaled sharply, the reminder of his loss a knife in the ribs. "Don't," he said roughly, squeezing Vel's fingers as hard as he dared. "That's got nothing to do with this."

Vel looked away. "Doesn't it?"

There was an awkward pause, which broke when Nevan coughed and said, "Well. All that aside, Tiern Velasin is right about one thing: you need the court's respect. We all pray that Yasa Kithadi lives many years yet, but sooner or later, you'll inherit the yaserate, and be it a year from now or ten, those people"—he gestured to indicate the palace, its inhabitants—"will remember what happened here, as will their heirs."

Cae shut his eyes and imagined Nairi ordering him to go. This shouldn't have worked, and yet somehow it made things easier. "All right," he said heavily, looking once more at Vel, the tangle of their fingers. "I'll go. I can't promise I won't make a hash of it, but I'll go."

Vel exhaled with relief, a tired smile etching the corners of his mouth. "Good. That's good. Thank you. Markel will help, he can listen, stand guard—"

"No," said Cae firmly. "He stays with you." Locking eyes with Markel over Vel's head, he said, "There's no one else I trust to keep you safe."

"But—" Vel tried weakly.

"No," signed Markel, holding his hands where Vel could see them. "He's right. Someone has to stay with you, and if it can't be him, it's me."

"All right," Vel sighed, subsiding against the pillows. He looked heartbreakingly tired, and yet there was something fierce in the gaze he fixed on Cae. "Just, please be careful. I don't want you to get hurt, too."

"I won't," Cae promised, and kissed him, a brush of mouths he'd meant to be chaste, but which deepened of its own accord, Vel gasping into it, tugging on his hand to pull him closer. For several seconds, Cae's brain whited out; he cradled Vel's face with his free hand, swallowing every desperate, cherished noise that meant his husband was alive, and might well have climbed in next to him, had Nevan not reminded him of their audience with a short, polite cough.

Embarrassed but not the least repentant, Cae straightened up again. The flush in Vel's cheeks was all the more vibrant against his recuperative pallor, and Cae felt a brief flash of smugness at having put it there before the reality of what he'd agreed to sank in. *I don't want to leave you like this. How am I meant to leave you?* But he couldn't say it aloud, and so he forced himself to straighten and turn back to Nevan.

"When should I be ready?"

"I'll come for you in an hour," the ciet replied, sounding relieved. "And now, if you'll excuse me, I have to go and get Asrien ready; he fell asleep earlier and I hadn't the heart to wake him, but he'll be furious if I give him any less time than this to dress." He glanced awkwardly at Markel, as if struggling over whether or not to address him directly, then turned back to Cae instead. "Thank you for letting me know what became of him earlier."

"Of course," said Cae. "He took no harm, I take it?"

"None," said Nevan, "though of course it wore him out. Dealing with General Naza could weary even the saints, but tired or not, I've never known him to miss a party."

From the corner of his eye, Cae saw Markel, who'd tensed at the first mention of Asrien, relax incrementally, as if in relief. "I look forward to seeing him, then," Cae said, and hoped it was true.

He saw Nevan out with a minimum of fuss, then returned to Vel's bedside, perching on the edge of the mattress to once more take his hand.

"You truly think I should go?" he asked, hoping selfishly that the answer would be *no*.

Vel smiled tiredly up at him. "I don't *want* you to go," he said, "but we need you to."

"I know," Cae said, though he didn't, not truly. He suppressed the urge to reiterate his dislike of politics; they both knew perfectly well he hadn't chosen this, and complaining further would've been childish. "I promise I'll try my best."

Vel nodded slowly. A strange expression crept onto his face, a mix of hesitance and something else Cae didn't know how to interpret. "Cae," he said, "you should know . . . Asrien, he—I, I mean—"

"What?" Cae asked, when Vel floundered into silence.

Vel shut his eyes. "Just . . . be careful around him," he mumbled. "He has his own agenda."

Bending down, Cae kissed Vel's forehead. "I will," he promised. And then, as much to reassure himself as his husband, "After all, it's only a party. I'll be fine."

17

I hate this," Cae muttered, fidgeting restlessly with the ring-hilt of his jade-handled knife as they neared the entrance to the Mazepool Gardens. Technically, he didn't need to come armed, and it would've been an insult to bring his sword, but after weeks of being hunted, he felt naked without any armaments at all; without Vel or Markel or any other friends nearby; without the presence of guards he knew and trusted. He glanced at Nevan, dressed in a dark blue lin adorned with knots of seed pearls, and then past him to Asrien, brightly pleased with himself in a fitted white halik embroidered with red and gold koi, and tried not to feel unutterably ridiculous by comparison. It wasn't that he looked bad, per se—Markel and Vel had both helped with his choice of clothes, a square-collared lin in forest green patterned with lighter green and gold beadwork over tight, gold-brown nara, a leather belt and a soft cream undershirt—but more that he felt conspicuously out of his element. Everyone here would know what had happened to Vel, to say nothing of the loss of Cae's sister and father: all his vulnerabilities were on display, and Cae would doubtless be forced to discuss them.

"You'll be fine," said Nevan absently. He'd switched out his tortoiseshell glasses for a slimmer, round-lensed pair set with thin, silver metal frames, which made him look sharper, somehow.

"That's easy for you to say," Cae muttered. "It's not you they'll be eating alive."

Nevan blinked, casting Cae a look that managed to be both surprised and judgemental. "Come now, yaseran; you must've done this sort of thing before."

"Obviously, yes; I'm just no good at it." He gestured ahead of them to the towering hedge-wall guarding the Mazepool Gardens, the dense green foliage interrupted by a single stone archway hung with glowing paper lanterns in honour of the party, the braided metal gates left invitingly open. "For starters, I don't know who anyone is."

"Oh, I'd be happy to help you with that!" said Asrien, sidling up beside him with an easy smile. "I know I'm a newcomer, but I've still been at court longer than you."

"Thank you," said Cae, after a beat in which he weighed Vel's earlier warning against his very real need to get people's names right. "I'd appreciate it."

"It's my pleasure," said Asrien, cheeks dimpling. He was a pretty little thing, Cae had to admit, but not quite to his taste, though he couldn't have said why and was, in fact, slightly surprised by his own judgement. He kept an eye on Asrien as they approached the archway, noting the favourable way in which his halik showed his nipped-in waist; how the upcoiled braids of his fine blond hair displayed his slim neck to best effect, set off by the dangling sway of a pair of tasselled gold earrings; how his eyelids were winged with gold paint, emphasising the honeyed flecks in his bright brown eyes—all details of pleasing artistry, and yet none of it moved him. *But if Vel were to dress like that . . .* The resulting image was enough to leave him dry-mouthed.

Oh, he thought, trying very hard not to trip over his own feet at the realisation. *Oh, I really do love him.* Which wasn't news at this point, truly; it was just that, even during the height of his infatuation with Liran, he'd still been susceptible to the charms of others—never sufficiently to want to act on them, never that, but the awareness, at least, had been there. Yet here he was, so completely unmoved by Asrien that he suddenly wanted nothing more than to rush back to the Jade Suite, rip off his finery and climb into bed beside Vel. Though, to be fair, he'd wanted to do that all along.

There were no guards standing before the archway and its open gates, but once they passed through the tunnel beyond, where blossom-laden branches from the hedge-wall had been trained to grow overhead in a pretty, enclosing bower, one of a pair of smartly dressed palace functionaries politely checked their names against a guest list. Cae did a double take at the sight of them: it was Ru Pyras and Ru Roya, the men who'd tried to wrongfoot him about their accommodations only that morning. Cae tensed, bracing for some new mischief, but though both men clearly recognised him, neither said anything more than a respectful, "Welcome, yaseran," before waving them through to the gardens, which were already populated by Qi-Xihan's rich and powerful.

"I've not been to this part of the palace before," Cae confessed, trying very hard not to sound nervous.

"Nor I," said Nevan, nudging his glasses farther up his nose. "Generally speaking, access is restricted, though more on account of the hot spring itself than the gardens. But the hedge-maze is reputed to be a wonder of its kind."

Cae nodded; he knew that much, at least. The hot spring for which the Mazepool Gardens was partially named lay at the heart of a towering hedge-maze, built hundreds of years ago to protect the waters, which were said to have healing properties. The gardens themselves acted like a decorative forecourt between the hedge-wall and the maze, with raised flowerbeds and sculpted fountains set between sweeping paths of black or white pebbles raked into curling patterns. Paper lanterns, colourful and fey, were strung overhead from a series of cleverly inconspicuous poles and wires, while a quartet of musicians played a lilting, friendly tune on a combination of flute, pipes and strings. In defence to the changing season, braziers were set up at strategic points around the space, and with the hedge-wall serving as a windbreak, the atmosphere in the gardens was noticeably warmer than the outside air had been.

Liveried servants walked among the guests, proffering cups of wine and platters of small, exquisite foods, and it was only when Cae caught the scent of the latter that he realised, with a sudden cramp in his stomach, that he hadn't eaten since breakfast. Which was all his own fault: Markel had prodded him to call for a meal more than once, but Cae had declined, insisting he'd eat when Vel woke up and not before, anxiety having chased away his appetite. Now he was still unsettled, albeit for a different reason, but suddenly and powerfully hungry. His gaze tracked the nearest servant, a short woman carrying a tray of savoury pastries, and before he could second-guess himself about whether it was gauche to beeline for the food, he approached and took three, scarfing them down with a soldier's brisk practicality.

Beside him, Asrien laughed. "I take it the food meets with your approval, yaseran?"

Cae swallowed his final mouthful and nodded; the pastries turned out to be full of warm, spiced meat and a gravy-like sauce, filling without being heavy. "Very much so," he said, feeling slightly forlorn at the realisation that the servant had moved on.

"If you'll excuse me," said Nevan, "I see someone I need to talk to," and slipped away towards a nearby cluster of people, leaving Cae and Asrien behind. Cae felt vaguely unsettled about this for all of two seconds, at which point another servant approached with a tray of drinks, disrupting his nerves.

"Here," said Asrien, taking two cups and handing one to Cae.

"My thanks," said Cae, accepting the drink as much to have something to do with his hands as for any other reason, and took a tentative sip, surprised and pleased to find it was hot, spiced cider. He made a note to be careful how much he drank on an empty stomach, but his tolerance had always been high and the cider sat well with the pastries, which went some way towards settling his nerves.

"Yaseran!" cried a warm, musical voice. Cae tensed for a moment, frowning slightly as a well-dressed figure approached them. It was Ru Kisian, the gold beads at the ends of his braids chiming slightly as he walked. He wore a stiff, sleeveless yellow halik closed across his stomach with a single corded toggle, displaying a slice of the lustrous pink silk undershirt beneath, paired with belted umber nara that bloused where they tucked into tall, buckled boots.

"I'm glad to see you in attendance," said Ru Kisian. "What with the morning's, ah, unpleasantness, we didn't have time to speak properly."

"You're Liran's cousin," Cae blurted. "Sorry, that's—obviously that's not important, I just—"

"Liran!" exclaimed Ru Kisian. "Of course, I'd forgotten you two know each other—how is he these days?

"He's well," said Cae, feeling thick-tongued and stupid. "And—oh!" He flushed, belatedly remembering his manners. "This is Asrien— Lord Asrien bo Erat," he amended hastily. "He's a guest of my uncle's."

"The other Ralian, yes," said Ru Kisian, flicking a quick smile at Asrien that was charming without being warm. "Lovely to make your acquaintance."

"Likewise," said Asrien prettily.

"Yaseran," said Ru Kisian, slipping his arm through Cae's and guiding him away from Asrien even as he asked, "Might we speak privately for a moment?"

"Uh—"

"Wonderful," said Ru Kisian, propelling Cae to a sheltered space between a fountain and the hedge-wall. Glancing around them, he dropped Cae's arm and said, still smiling, "Yaseran. Excuse my bluntness, but are you a fucking imbecile?"

"What?" said Cae.

Ru Kisian's smile tightened around the edges. "Saints preserve me. Yaseran, you are married to a Ralian man. I approve of this. I was instrumental, in fact, in making it happen, though obviously the original plan has been somewhat, shall we say, *corrupted* by now. However, this morning you made the, ah, *questionable* decision to imply, before the entire court, that said husband speaks *for you*—and by extension your marriage, and thus your future yaserate—on all political matters. Said husband was then tragically attacked—and I do wish him a swift recovery, along with my condolences for the shock you must be feeling—which is why, of course, he isn't here this evening. What this does *not* explain is why, in his absence, you felt it advisable to enter this gathering with, and I cannot emphasise this enough, *another* Ralian man on your arm. Do you understand me?"

"Ah," said Cae. He took a long swallow of cider to quell the unsettling roil of embarrassment in his stomach. "Ah, that's—I take your point. Thank you. But, really," he said, affronted on one particular point, "I didn't come in with Asrien on my *arm*. I didn't even touch him! He's my uncle Nevan's guest, not mine."

"A distinction I'm sure will matter greatly to your husband," Ru Kisian said wryly, "but not, as it happens, to those who already think you overly swayed by foreign interests."

Cae blinked at Ru Kisian, nonplussed. "You are quite literally in charge of foreign affairs," he said. "Am I not supposed to be building ties with Ralia?"

"Ye-es," said Ru Kisian, in the tones of a teacher trying to impart a very simple lesson to a particularly dim student, "but not in such a way as to make it seem like the Ralian government is getting a toehold in *ours*."

"Well, it's not," said Cae, more snappish than he meant to be, embarrassed at needing something so obvious explained to him. Far too late, it occurred to him that the day's events had perhaps impacted his judgement; he was mentally exhausted from his vigil at Vel's bedside and hungry besides, struggling to parse the sort of basic implications that even he, with his lack of affinity for politics, would normally have understood. *Focus,* he told himself sternly, and after taking a moment to gather his thoughts, he drew a breath and said, "Vel's family have practically disowned him, and we've no idea what the Ralian crown even thinks of our marriage. Unless you've heard something to that effect?"

"Not officially, no," Ru Kisian admitted. "We know King Markus is aware of the match, but he's made no formal response to it yet—not to his own court, and not to us. Our intelligence suggests there's a lot being said behind closed doors, but what the end result will be is, as yet, opaque." He made an odd little humming sound, then added delicately, "And of course, there's the matter of whoever tried to kill Tiern Velasin this morning. And why." He raised a pointed eyebrow.

Having had Markel's account of Asrien's conversation with Syana—a luxury of information which Ru Kisian presumably lacked—it took Cae an awkward moment to parse his inference. "You think the Ralians are behind it?"

"That's one possibility, certainly," said Ru Kisian, "though it would be unusually tactless even for them to try something so overt as a public assassination, regardless of how they feel about, ah, relationships such as yours. Even an accidental death would be sure to draw suspicion."

At the words *accidental death,* something clicked in Cae's brain. A horrible rush of cold anxiety swamped him, and he could do nothing to keep it off his face, as Ru Kisian looked instantly concerned.

"Yaseran? What is it?"

"All the way to Qi-Xihan," said Cae, voice numb, "someone's been trying to kill us. To kill Vel, rather, but only in ways that could pass for an accident." He felt sick, sick and stupid for not having considered Vel's countrymen as possible culprits before now, too mired in guilt about the issue of his inheritance and the deaths it had already caused to widen his suspicions, but now—

Ru Kisian's mouth formed an O of shock. "Tell me everything," he said firmly, and because he was Liran's cousin and an ostensible ally both to Ralia and his marriage, Cae did so, beginning with the fire at Etho and ending with the rescue at the Sihae River. Ru Kisian listened sharply throughout, and when Cae was done, he rocked back on his heels and made a frustrated noise.

"What a mess!" he hissed. "A saints-cursed mess, and no mistake! As you say, it could be down to inheritance politics, but your wedding has certainly kicked the metaphorical beehive! And as whoever it is took care to try and arrange an accident, it would seem odd to attribute this morning's clumsiness to them, too—unless, of course, they've grown tired of their failures, and are trying to hurry things up? But, hmm, no, that doesn't quite fit, either," he went on before Cae could venture a response, "as by all accounts sneaking an assailant into the court would've required preparation, or at the very least inside knowledge—and yet we can't rule it out, either."

Swallowing, Cae made a desperate bid for levity and said, "Does that mean I'm forgiven for my idiocy? You could put it about that I'm trying to, ah . . . keep my enemies close? Or at least feign ignorance."

Ru Kisian favoured him with a sympathetic look. "Well, at the very least, I can see you've had bigger things to worry about than who accompanies you to a party. I apologise for my sharpness, yaseran; it's just that it's so damnably difficult to make progress around here!"

"Of course," said Cae, relieved, and was on the brink of saying more when Ru Kisian was hailed by an extremely short, round woman in equally round glasses, approaching at a speed that had her glossy black braid, which fell almost to the backs of her knees, swishing madly behind her like the tail of an agitated cat.

"Sikana!" Ru Kisian exclaimed, looking genuinely surprised to see her. "I didn't think you could make it—"

"Never mind that," said Sikana, sparing an apologetic glance for Cae before switching her full attention to Ru Kisian. She was out of breath, and panted a little as she said, "I've just had word that Silver's on thir way."

Ru Kisian looked nonplussed. "My dear, we already knew that—"

"Not to Qi-Xihan," she said, interrupting. "*Here.* To the palace. To this party, even! Thei're already in the city!"

"Oh sweet saints," breathed Ru Kisian, eyes going wide. "Of all the times—!"

"Silver," echoed Cae, the word not quite a question. There was a tickle of recognition in his mind, something he should know—and then he recalled Markel's full report to him earlier, including the kitchen gossip he'd overheard, which he'd relayed as close to verbatim as possible without knowing what it meant. Cae hadn't paid it much mind at the time, being far more concerned with anything pertaining to Vel and his assailant; now, though, it clicked. "You mean the Silver Chair?"

"Yasai Qiqa Ykran," Ru Kisian confirmed. "Saints know how long thei must've been travelling to have arrived now, but it'll certainly make things interesting!"

"Interesting, he says!" exclaimed Sikana, thwapping Ru Kisian gently about the ribs. "More like a fucking disaster! We haven't planned for this!"

"Sikana works with me," Ru Kisian said to Cae, somehow maintaining eye contact while gently grabbing her wrist and holding it still until she stopped hitting him. "And can be something of an *alarmist*."

"Yes, well," grumbled Sikana, snatching her hand back. "One of us has to be, especially when someone keeps gambling with our plans—"

"I beg to differ," Ru Kisian interrupted. Rolling his eyes, he flagged down a passing servant, took two cups of cider from the proffered tray, pushed one into Sikana's hands and promptly downed the other. Cae watched, morbidly fascinated, as Sikana scowled and did likewise, grimacing slightly at the effort of drinking the whole thing at once.

"There," she said, making a face. "I have *partaken of the festivities*." Her scowling inflection suggested this was by way of reference to some earlier conversation. "Will you come with me now, please?"

Ru Kisian heaved a put-upon sigh. "The things I do for friendship," he said. "All right, very well." And then, to Cae, with a touch more gravity, "I appreciate your predicament, yaseran, and will do what I can to find out who's been targeting you. But until then, please try to be a little more circumspect, hm?"

"I promise nothing," said Cae, and won himself a startled bark of laughter as Sikana grabbed her employer by the arm and hauled him off, hissing fiercely up at him.

"That looked complicated," said Asrien, materialising at Cae's elbow as if from thin air. Cae startled, prompting a sweet smile from Asrien. "Sorry, sorry; I promise I wasn't eavesdropping. I just have very good timing." He pouted. "Also, you abandoned me."

"Sorry," said Cae, though leaving Asrien hadn't been his choice.

"Luckily for you, I used my time wisely," Asrien said, tipping his head to indicate a knot of people some small distance away. "Let me introduce you, yaseran—it is, after all, what I'm here for."

Cae considered objecting, but as he couldn't think of a polite re-phrasing of Ru Kisian's concerns, Asrien took his silence for assent, linked their arms together and towed him over to make some new acquaintances. It was more than a little overwhelming; no sooner had Cae been introduced than their various names, relationships and titles swam out of his head like so many fish through a gaping net, too many to retain. He did manage to disentangle his arm from Asrien's without mishap, which was a small mercy, but the only one on offer, as a young cietena whose name he'd already forgotten promptly expressed her shock and sympathy at the attack on Vel. Cae froze up, not knowing how to discuss the matter with strangers nor wanting to try; everyone was looking at him, the cietena with a horrible embarrassed pity, and only when Cae stammered out a halting thanks for her concern did Asrien step in to steer the conversation towards safer waters.

As their chatter flowed around and over him, Cae found himself taking frequent refuge in his cider, which was easier than speaking. Better yet, when his cup ran dry, he used it as an excuse to slip away in ostensible search of another, and had just claimed a fresh cup for verisimilitude's sake when he was hailed by a deep, familiar voice.

"Yaseran," said General Naza. He tipped his head to indicate Asrien and his cluster of associates. "I see you've been making friends."

"That's one word for it, yes," said Cae. He straightened, knowing it was a poor move to goad the Iron Chair but unable, quite, to help his sharpness. "Tell me, has your investigation made any progress since this morning? Or is the attempted murder of my husband such a small thing that you feel content to postpone it for an evening?"

The general smiled sharkishly. "You're here, too, are you not?"

Cae flushed, refusing to be baited. "That doesn't answer my question."

"You'll be apprised in due course." The general's eyes glittered. "Discretion is paramount, naturally."

"Naturally," Cae spat back, and might well have said something he later had cause to regret, had the conversation not been interrupted by the arrival of a stately matron in, Cae guessed, her late fifties. Her flawless golden skin was classically Tithenai, but her silver-streaked hair was dark brown rather than black, her nose was distinctively tip-tilted, and her eyes were such a starling shade of amber as to look almost orange—an impression she clearly sought to cultivate, as the lids were lined with umber paint rather than kohl. She was dressed lavishly if you knew what to look for, understatedly if you didn't; Cae by rights should've fallen into the latter category, but after years spent around Liran and Riya (and Laecia, though he shied away from naming her in his thoughts) he'd absorbed enough secondhand information about cloth and couture to be reasonably well-informed. In presumable deference to the time of year, her halik was high-collared and long-sleeved, an iridescent wool-silk blend in sky blue trimmed with small pink pearls whose uniformity of size and colour spoke to their breathtaking expense. Her nara were loose, a paler pink even than the pearls, tucked into heeled blue boots with shining silver buckles. Aside from a pair of rose gold and sapphire hairpins adoring her upcoiled braids and the matching earrings in her ears, her only jewellery was a silver chain, worn over her halik, bearing a circular disc etched with gold and enamel, which Cae, far too late, recognised as cousin to his grandmother's seal.

"Yaseran Caethari Aeduria," she said, in a warm, low voice, inclining her head respectfully. "I'm honoured by your attendance."

"Tierena Keris Talae," Cae replied, struggling to keep his composure. He felt oddly small before her, though even in her boots she stood easily a head shorter than him. "I . . . I thank you for your courtesy."

The tierena accepted this with a downward sweep of her lashes before flicking her gaze to the general and saying coolly, "Commander— sorry, *General* Naza. I thought the morning's misadventures might've kept you busy tonight, but evidently not."

The general bared his teeth in what was very nearly a smile. "What can I say? I'm a social animal."

Tierena Keris sniffed. "Even scavengers are, I suppose."

"Better a scavenger than a parasite."

"Oh! You *wound* me!" She smirked, clutching a theatrical hand to her chest. "I am *wounded,* General. Sharpen your tongue any further, and your sword will fall blunt."

General Naza pulled a face that resembled nothing so much as the chattering disgust of a house cat for an out-of-reach bird. "You'll excuse me, tierena, but I've better ways to spend my time." Nodding curtly to both of them, he scowled and strode off into the party.

"My apologies for the Iron Chair's poor manners," said the tierena, turning back to Cae. She smiled gently. "And for the lack of welcome your husband received this morning. How is he faring?"

"Much better," Cae rasped. The question knocked about in his chest like a swallowed chestnut, threatening to dislodge what little calm he'd mustered since leaving the apartments. His knuckles creaking around his cup, and he took a sip to steady himself against a sudden, manic urge to go haring back to Vel's bedside, just to make sure that nothing had happened to him or Markel in his absence.

"I'm glad to hear it," said Tierena Keris. Something trembled in her face, there and gone like the flash of a fish's tail beneath the water, and her voice shook only slightly as she said, "I want you to know, I'm indebted to you both for the service you did my grandson. If he had drowned—" She choked herself silent, an awkward pause hanging between them in which Cae, whose thoughts felt laboriously slow, belatedly recalled her kinship with the young Tiern Ethin, before she continued, "Well! Suffice to say, I am extremely grateful." And she bowed to him—a half-bow, certainly, and performed with the unaccustomed stiffness of a woman who seldom had cause to bow to anyone, but all the more deeply felt for this, such that Cae, who hadn't expected it, felt briefly and intensely mortified.

"It's Vel you should be thanking, not me," he said, trying very hard to sound steady and grateful instead of panicked. "I went in for his sake, but he dove for the boys without hesitation. I . . . I would like to believe I'd have acted as selflessly as he did in his absence, but as I cannot say so for certain—"

"Nonsense," said the tierena, her gentle scoff cutting through his self-deprecation like a cheesewire. "You give yourself too little credit, yaseran. All I've ever heard of you attests to your bravery in the field; your revetha sings your praises, and clearly your grandmother agrees, or else you would not bear your current honour."

Cae stiffened, thrown once again into perilous conversational waters. "It's not as if she had much of a choice," he said—lightly, he hoped, though grief clawed at his tightened throat. He drank again in a poor attempt at soothing it. "Riya could hardly have claimed both titles."

"True," conceded the tierena, a knowing light in her eyes, "but she might yet have passed you over by other means—none common or recently precedented, it's true, but when have such paltry concerns ever stopped Kithadi Taedu from working her will on the world?" She smiled as she said this—sharply, but with an unmistakeable, albeit wholly unexpected, fondness.

"Do you know her well?" Cae asked.

"In a manner of speaking. We inherited within months of each other—her first, which was surprising for both of us." To Cae's querying look, she explained, "Kithadi's father died of a fall from his horse, but my kigé had been sick for years. Nobody thought thei'd outlive Ekkana Taedu, least of all me. It was a strange time for both of us. We'd known each other before then, of course, but afterwards . . . well. It's hard not to bond over something like that."

"Of course," Cae echoed.

Sympathy flashed on the tierena's face. "It's a shame she's not here," she said, "though for your sake more than mine. I don't like to criticise Kithadi, but so much pain could've been avoided if she'd only named Inavi her heir when she first came of age."

At the mention of his mother's name, Cae's stomach gave an ugly jolt. "It wouldn't have been fair," he said, pricklingly aware that he was repeating a story he'd been told multiple times, but which, until now, he'd never really questioned. "My father was already tieren of Qi-Katai when they married, and they knew they wanted children."

"Inavi always did," said the tierena. She sighed, looking oddly wistful. "Do you know, before she met Halithar, she might have married one of my sons?"

Cae's mouth fell open in shock. "I didn't," he stammered, having been wholly unprepared to receive this information. "I—"

"No need to look like that." The tierena's tone was amused. "There was no romance involved, I assure you; Kithadi and I considered the alliance, that's all."

"Oh," said Cae. And then, floundering back towards the original point, "Naming my mother her official heir would've pulled her between duties; made her feel as if her life with us was always going to be temporary." *And then she left anyway,* he thought bitterly.

"Perhaps," said Tierena Keris, in the careful tone of someone who disagreed but was trying to be diplomatic about it. "Either way, it hardly seems fair that you've been thrown in the deep end like this, let alone under such exhausting circumstances." She watched him a moment, then stepped close enough to set a gentle hand on his shoulder. "For what it's worth," she said quietly, "I'm sorry for your loss."

As small a kindness as this was, it was too much to bear. "Thank you," Cae choked out, and then, "Excuse me," managing the barest courtesy of a half-bow before striding off into the gardens. He wanted a sword and the space to swing it; he wanted to be back with Vel; he wanted Laecia to still be alive and innocent of her wrongdoings, his father still tieren, Riya still happy in Kir-Halae. He wanted not to feel so bruised and adrift, as though he were a boulder careening haplessly down a hillside; and he wanted, more than anything, to be given a task he was good at—something clean and simple, whose rules and execution he understood. *I shouldn't be here,* he thought wildly, gaze darting around the gardens. Some partygoers were looking at him, but most were immersed in their own affairs, laughing and drinking and chatting among themselves. Out of nowhere, Cae recalled the story Vel had told him about his grandfather and the drunken bear, and suppressed a burst of inappropriate laughter. He wasn't anywhere close to drunk, but he felt like that bear regardless, big and lumbering and out of place, and apt to break whatever he set his hands to.

He downed the last of his cider, which had cooled since he last took a sip, and cast about with shaking hands for somewhere to set the cup. He was just about to abandon it on the edge of a planter when a servant appeared and took it from him; Cae mumbled thanks and pressed himself back against the hedge-wall, which couldn't support his weight—or not comfortably, anyway—but which at least helped him to feel less conspicuous.

This time, he noticed Asrien's approach and felt almost grateful for it. "Here," said Asrien, handing him a fresh drink—not cider this time, but brandy mixed with spiced milk and cream. "You look like you need it."

"I should eat something," Cae said, but took a sip anyway, a bloom of warmth spreading all the way down his throat.

"There's food over here," said Asrien, nodding his head to indicate a distant cluster of people.

Cae hesitated. "I'm not reall—"

"You don't have to be good company," Asrien promised, a hint of amusement in his voice. "Just stand there, look pretty, and eat what you like."

"That's the best offer I've had all evening," Cae muttered, and let himself be coaxed to where some cunning person had requisitioned one of the trays of titbits. To his startlement, this new group of people included Ciet Irias, Ciet Yarasil and Tiern Ethin, though once he'd recovered from their enthusiastic greeting, he realised his surprise was foolish. *Of course they're here,* Cae chided himself, *Ethin is Keris's grandson, and the others are his friends.* He should've known he'd see them and braced accordingly; as it was, he found himself gripping Ciet Yarasil's hand and thanking him profusely for saving Vel's life.

"It was—truly, it was the least I could do, I—I'm only glad I could help," the ciet stuttered bashfully. He swallowed, slender throat bobbing, and managed, "How is the tiern faring now, if I might ask?"

"He's . . . he's recovering well," Cae said roughly. And then, in a fit of madness, because it was that or pitch the conversation into a desperately awkward silence, "You should come and visit him tomorrow, when you've a moment. All three of you," he added, and was rewarded with a chorus of enthusiastic promises to do just that.

"Have you met my grandmother, yaseran?" Tiern Ethin ventured.

"I have," said Cae.

"Oh," said the tiern, sounding almost disappointed. "That's— I'm glad you have, I just—I would've introduced you, if you hadn't."

"I appreciate it," said Cae, and then found himself at a loss for what to say next. Before the conversation could falter, however, Ciet Irias took the initiative of introducing Cae to the rest of those present, prompting a rush of new faces, names and titles.

Cae tried his best, but as before, he found it hard to focus on who was who or what was being said. He felt shocky and strange, off-kilter in a way he didn't know how to reconcile with the gathering's cheerful atmosphere. Even so, as he ate and drank, he became aware of himself as a subject of interest, not just from those around, but from strangers on the periphery of the group, or others stood at a distance. He would catch people looking at him speculatively, with amusement or pity or judgement, some tittering or whispering among themselves, and as much as he'd have hated for any of them to ask him openly about Velasin's near-murder, his status as heir to the yaserate or the deaths of his father and sister, there was something almost worse in being left to wonder which of these things most made him a subject of pity.

Probably all of it, he thought with a flash of anger, and then, chest aching, *Saints, Vel, I wish you were here.*

A burst of laughter went up from the group in apparent reaction to a joke Cae had missed, and for the first time, it occurred to him to wonder where Nevan had got to. He looked around the gardens, trying to pick him out, and spotted what looked like a familiar figure over near the entrance to the hedge-maze. Draining the last of his drink, the final third of which he'd been nursing for some time, he set the cup down, excused himself (though nobody was really listening) and headed towards the ciet.

"Nevan?" he called, and was relieved to be proven right. His uncle turned, posture tense, but relaxed when he saw it was Cae.

"How are you faring?" Nevan asked. "Has Asri been taking

good care of you? Inasmuch as that's helpful," he amended wryly, looking Cae over. "Sorry. I know you'd rather have stayed with Velasin, but—"

"It's all right," Cae made himself say, as much because Nevan looked preoccupied as because his own pulse suddenly ticked up. A prickle of sweat broke out on the nape of his neck; he pushed his braid aside and rubbed at it. "It's not your fault."

Nevan nodded absently, peering past Cae as if he were looking for someone. Cae half turned, trying to track the line of his gaze, but his head swam a little at the motion. He shook it and looked away again, aware that Nevan's affairs weren't his business and, more importantly, that he didn't want them to be.

"Have you seen the hot spring yet?" Nevan asked suddenly.

"What?" said Cae, a beat too late. He tugged at his collar, which was starting to feel tight. "Oh. No. I haven't."

"You should," said Nevan. "It's beautiful."

Though phrased as a suggestion, this had the feel of an instruction, though Cae couldn't have said why. He swallowed, abruptly conscious of his tongue—did it always take up so much space in his mouth?—and was searching vainly for a reply when Asrien once more appeared by his side, glancing curiously between them.

"Cae hasn't seen the hot spring yet," Nevan said, as if in answer to an unasked question, and Asrien's eyes lit up.

"Me neither!" he said. "I've been meaning to go all night, come on—" He took Cae's arm and began to tug him excitedly towards the maze entrance. Cae stumbled slightly, struggling to right himself; he felt off-balance, blurry and overheated.

"It's hot," he mumbled. "Asrien, isn't it hot?"

"What?" laughed Asrien, grinning up at him. "Yes, the hot spring is hot. It's in the name."

"Not the spring," said Cae, listing slightly into the hedge-wall. "I mean now, the air. It's hot. Isn't it?"

Asrien blinked at him. "I suppose," he said, sounding puzzled by the question. He took a step back, one hand loosely clutching Cae's wrist as he looked him up and down. "Maybe the alcohol warmed you up."

"Maybe," Cae agreed dizzily.

Asrien smiled up at him through his lashes. "You'll be fine," he said, and led Cae into the maze.

18

The night air was cooler away from the braziers and lanterns; Cae should've been cooler, too. The maze was lit with strings of tiny magelights wound through the hedge-walls, like stars trapped in crystal; they gave off no heat, but Cae still felt hotter and hotter, sweating into his undershirt as profusely as if he'd been sparring under a summer sun. He kept tugging at his lin, wanting to pull it off but knowing, in some dim and distant way, that he wasn't allowed to, though it was harder and harder to remember why. All he could do was follow Asrien as he led them deeper into the maze, unerringly knowing which paths to take. Part of Cae felt amazed by this, as though Asrien were performing a magic trick of instinctive navigation, though an inner voice suggested that this was something Cae ought to be good at, too; that there was an obvious trick he was missing. It made him feel anxious from time to time, but the thought was a slippery one, easily subsumed beneath his awe at the beautiful magelights, the guiding press of Asrien's fingers against his own, the twisting fascination of the maze itself and—above all—the cresting heat in his body.

He was hot and light and oversensitized, only distantly aware that he'd been worried and upset before, because it felt nonsensical in the moment. What was there to be worried about here, with Asrien's bright laughter chiming sweetly against the magelights?

"Nearly there, I think," said Asrien, and when he laughed, Cae laughed, too, happy because his friend was happy. He stumbled as they rounded a corner, suppressing a hiss as his undershirt, now tacky with sweat, chafed against his nipples. His fingers felt electric against Asrien's, as though his skin were throwing off tiny sparks; a small part of him found this confusing, but mostly he was delighted by the novelty of it. *Vel should feel this good,* he thought, and only realised he'd spoken out loud when Asrien turned, brow furrowed, and asked, "Vel should feel what?"

"The sparks," Cae said, struggling to speak consciously, as though speech were a sword-trick he hadn't tried in years. He held up their joined hands to demonstrate, waggling them back and forth at the wrist. "This. The sparks. Vel would like it."

Asrien pouted, but the expression seemed more for show than due to any genuine hurt. "What does it matter what Vel would like?" he asked, stepping closer. "He's not here."

"But Vel always matters," Cae said, confused. "He matters most of all. I love him," he added, in case that wasn't clear. "He's so sharp, and his eyes are like, like—" He tipped his head back, seeking inspiration in the sky, and found it in the form of Ruya's Eye, the smallest moon, which was currently a waning crescent, tip-tilted in the firmament like a perfect golden sickle. "—like that," Cae said, pointing. "His eyes smile like that when he's happy." He sighed, a pleasant ache in his groin that went well with the heat of his body. "I want him so much to be happy. I want him so *much*—"

"We're here," interrupted Asrien, and it was only then that Cae realised they'd been walking and talking at the same time, and now they were through. Ahead of them, the maze opened into a roughly circular clearing, unmanicured grass flowing up to the muddy clay edge of the hot spring, the waters wreathed in steam. It was bigger than Cae had expected, broad and deep enough for swimming laps, the way his revetha had learned to swim in the barracks. A single tree, trunk slender and branches twisting, leaned gracefully over the pool, growing from a humped, natural rise in the ground. Boulders and a scatter of smaller rocks broke through the grass at its base, and though its leaves were mostly gone or turned reddish-gold, a number of round, golden magelights hung from its boughs like fruit. They swayed in the breeze, trailing streaky arcs of light in

Cae's dizzied vision; somewhere in the back of his mind, this registered as worrying, but in the moment, all he saw was their beauty.

Still clutching Asrien's hand, he let himself be led to the poolside, and when Asrien knelt, Cae copied him, folding awkwardly downwards with a heavy thump, half on the clay and half on the grass. Distantly, he worried about staining his fine clothes, but shrugged it off, captivated by the mineral tang of the water. He trailed his free hand into the spring, which was hot rather than merely warm. Given the heat in his body, this ought to have been uncomfortable, and yet there was something soothing about it. He withdrew his hand, gaze snagging on the water droplets pearling on his fingers before trickling down his wrist, there to be soaked up by the cuffs of his undershirt.

"Hot," he said again, meaning both his body and the water. He looked beseechingly at Asrien. "Why am I still hot?"

"You're wearing too much," said Asrien. His smile in the moonlight shivered like a breaking wave, his eyes curiously bright. "You should try to cool down." When Cae's response was to paw with frustrated clumsiness at his lin, not remembering right away how it fastened, Asrien moved in closer and murmured, "Here, let me."

Nodding, Cae sat back on his heels, swaying slightly as Asrien undid the side buttons of his lin, helping him to remove it. He felt briefly improved, but he was still unpleasantly conscious of all the places his undershirt was stuck to him with sweat. He plucked at the dampened fabric, dissatisfied, and exhaled with relief when Asrien leaned in and gently untucked the shirt from his nara, knuckles and fingertips grazing Cae's sides as he lifted it over his head.

Cae gasped at the brush of the cool night air against his oversensitized skin. He tipped his head back, the stars swimming in and out of focus like a shoal of minnows. Belatedly, he realised that he was hard; that he had been for some time, the one type of heat blending seamlessly into the other. He ran a wondering hand over his chest, inhaling sharply as he brushed his nipples.

"Vel?" he asked—of the night, of Asrien. His whole body sang with promise. He shut his eyes, the better to cope with his dizziness. "Where's Vel?"

"Vel's not here," murmured Asrien, "but I am."

Dazed as he was, Cae didn't immediately process the slim, cool hands unbuckling and removing his belt as belonging to someone other than his husband; he had asked for Vel, and so it made sense that Vel would answer. When the owner of the hands straddled him, he frowned: the weight was wrong, too light and oddly positioned to be Vel, but when he opened his mouth to ask what was happening, he found himself being kissed. Cae kissed back for a moment out of reflex before stopping, confused. Having shut his eyes, it was surprisingly hard to open them again, but when he did, he found Asrien in his lap.

"You're not Vel," he said, dumbly. A strange anxiety bloomed in him, strong enough to penetrate the heat and confusion and dizziness; strong enough to make him realise, far too late, that he wasn't thinking properly; that something was amiss.

"It's all right," soothed Asrien, leaning in to kiss him again. He'd twined his arms around Cae's neck, which made it hard to dodge; nonetheless, he willed some control into his arms, which felt strangely detached from his body, and pushed Asrien back at the hips.

"I'm not for you," said Cae, which both was and wasn't what he'd meant to say; it was hard to think, harder still to form sentences. "This isn't—no. I don't feel right."

"You don't have to feel *right*," said Asrien, swaying close again. His voice was gentle, almost hypnotic, as his hands slid over and up Cae's thighs. "You just have to *feel*."

Cae shook his head stubbornly, grabbing Asrien's wrists and pushing them out, so that he was held at something approximating arm's length. His thoughts stumbled and galloped into each other with the unhelpful chaos of puppies even as his body thrummed with arousal, but on this one point if nothing else, he was clear: Asrien wasn't Vel, and Cae didn't want him.

"No," he said again. "I'm sorry. Not with you."

An ugly sort of hurt flashed on Asrien's face. "Why not?" he demanded. He tried to wriggle his way out of Cae's grip, but Cae put a stop to that by taking both of his wrists in one hand and squeezing them together. Asrien huffed and glared at him. "You're *drunk,* it doesn't even count!"

"I'm not drunk," Cae said automatically, and realised in the same instant that it was true: drunk didn't feel like this. *What's wrong with me, then?* he wondered, but before he could parse the answer, his attention snagged on Asrien's words, and he blinked back to the present moment, confused anew. "Why wouldn't it count?"

Asrien's expression turned coy, as if he'd sensed an opening. "Because every man is two men," he said, leaning his body forwards to try and overcome the obstacle of his trapped wrists. "The one he is sober, and the one he is drunk." He arched against Cae's hold, neck tilted prettily to one side. "Why deny one just to spite the other?"

This made no sense to Cae, and not just because he was struggling to think at all. A fresh wave of heat rippled through him, pulsing in his cock, his core; he inhaled sharply, eyes falling shut as he braced against it, hand cinching tighter around Asrien's wrists in a way that drew a gasp from the other man. He let go reflexively, shuddering as Asrien fell against him. His senses were muddled, everything simultaneously too much and not enough, and he groaned when Asrien climbed back onto him, grinding pointedly against his cock.

"You see?" Asrien panted, kissing up Cae's neck. "You're not him. You're the other you. Just enjoy it."

Cae made a frustrated noise, head swimming. He set his hands on Asrien's hips and squeezed, resulting in a pleasured exhale and a nip to his neck. For a perilous moment, he wavered between selves: not drunken and sober, as Asrien had suggested, but between the Cae who accepted the burden of his thoughts and the one who craved their absence. As aroused as he was, it wasn't that any part of him wanted Asrien; the greater temptation lay in letting someone else think for him, *decide* for him, absolving him of the need to be aware, to choose, to act; to instead be inchoate, chosen, acted upon. He was just so fucking *tired*. The past few weeks had been exhausting enough, and after the morning's events, he hadn't wanted to come out at all; had wanted only to stay with Vel—

And there it was, the choice above and beneath all other choices. "Vel," Cae murmured—half-sad, half-dazed, all yearning. He pushed himself back and Asrien forwards, so that Asrien slid off Cae's lap with dull, stunned *thump*. He blinked his eyes into functioning for long enough to take in Asrien's startled face, wet mouth hanging open with shock, and said firmly, "I just want Vel." And then, because Asrien seemed upset by this, "You deserve someone who wants you, too."

Asrien flushed first pink with embarrassment, then red with hurt. He slapped Cae across the cheek, the smack of the impact more shocking than the strength of the blow, then slapped him again, but more weakly than before, a stunted sort of reflex. It looked like there were tears in Asrien's eyes, but for all Cae knew, that could've been a trick of his ringing head.

"*Fuck you!*" snarled Asrien, clutching his arm to his chest. "You're not—this isn't—what the fuck is the point of you?"

Cheek smarting, Cae ventured bewilderedly, "Do people need points?"

Asrien laughed and swore viciously in Ralian; or at least, it sounded like swearing, but in his current state, Cae couldn't parse it properly. "What is it about me," Asrien said, high and sharp, "that always makes men the opposite of what I need them to be?"

"Not everything is about you," Cae said helpfully. He didn't really understand why Asrien was so upset; he was still so hot, and the world kept swimming in and out of focus, making it hard to hold the thread of the conversation.

Asrien shot him a look of pure disgust. "You think I don't know that? Nothing is about me, until it is; then everything is about me, until it isn't." He struggled to his feet, swiping at his eyes with the back of his hand. There were grass and mud stains on his fine white halik, and when Cae swayed forwards to poke at them, Asrien made an angry sound and kicked his arm away, though as with the slap, there was no real strength to it. Even so, the contact knocked Cae off-balance, and he fell back down at an odd angle, hands slipping on the damp clay.

"What's wrong with me?" he mumbled. Sweat prickled down his spine; his arousal had ebbed briefly, but in exchange he felt dizzier than ever.

"Your taste in men," said Asrien nastily. He kicked Cae's shin, watched him for a moment, rubbed his eyes a final time and then declared, "You're pathetic, you know that? Both of you. You deserve each other." And then, before Cae could respond to this, he turned and stalked off into the maze.

Cae flopped back on his elbows, panting faintly. Absurdly, he was still hard, his skin still burning. He starred at the blurry stars, trying to will some focus into himself, and finally, the thought came to him: *I've been drugged.* It was the only thing that made sense, but it wasn't a helpful thought. Knowing didn't bring him clarity or do anything to restore control over his limbs; all it did was make his stomach twist with a distant anxiety, as though he were in the process of running up a debt he knew he'd be forced to pay later.

He stared at the hot spring, mesmerised by the curls of steam rising from the surface of the water. Beyond and around him, the hedge-wall gleamed and rustled, darkly verdant despite the time of year, the greenery periodically silvered by proximity to those winking crystal magelights. He lay back, heart too fast and breath too quick, the whole world swimming around him. He lolled his head to the side, trying to anchor himself in the sharp tang of the water—at which point, as if from a great distance, he recalled that the spring was supposed to have healing properties. *Water sobers you up*, Cae thought, and with a panting effort, he rolled himself over and into the spring with a muffled splash.

The hot water came as a shock, somehow. For a horrible moment, he almost blacked out from the heat alone; he flailed in place, and realised too late that, in his addled state, he'd neglected to take his boots off first. This wouldn't have been a problem if the spring were shallow, as he'd vaguely assumed it must be, but as he stretched his feet down to try and find the bottom of the pool, he kicked only water. *Oh no,* Cae thought distantly. Bubbles streamed past his face. He sank farther and farther, and was seconds away from panic when, finally, his feet hit the ground.

Fumbling forwards to find the edge of the pool, Cae braced himself, bent his legs and shoved upwards with all the strength he could muster. It was too dark and his vision to fogged to see, but even with his boots on, his nostrils stinging with the metallic tang of the water, he didn't have far to go. He hadn't taken a proper deep breath before rolling into the spring, but his lungs were strong—

His scalp prickled with cold as his head broke the surface of the spring. But before he could draw breath—before his eyes had even cleared the waterline—a tight hand fisted in his hair and shoved him under again.

For a terrible moment, Cae froze. All his upward momentum vanished, and in the next second, the weight of his boots began to drag him down again. He kicked furiously, but to little effect, the heat as much of a problem as the lack of air; he was dizzy and weak, lungs burning. Desperately, he clawed at whoever was holding him, struggling to prise their hand from his hair, but he couldn't see what he was doing. By sheer blind luck, he caught their wrist and dug his thumb into the tendons, forcing the fingers to spasm open, but even as the first hand let go, a second gripped him by the braid, and he realised with a terrible bolt of clarity that if he didn't do something quickly, he'd drown.

Kicking out sideways instead of down, Cae hit the spring wall and grimaced. Eyes stinging, he reached again for the hand in his hair, prised it off, and—in the second before his assailant could grab him again—used his remaining strength to kick off the wall with both feet, hard, propelling himself towards the spring's centre. He thrashed blindly forwards, determined to put himself beyond reach. Fingers grabbed at his nara, his heel, but Cae fought them off—and in his elation, he opened his mouth.

Air rushed out of him in huge, bright bubbles. He flailed again, kicking desperately for the surface—he was close, so close!—but he'd put his body sideways to push off from the wall, resubmerging his head, while his booted feet were still too heavy, dragging him down. He began to sink again, body blaring alarms at the lack of air, but he willed himself to hang on, to stay conscious. *Kick off from the bottom,* he thought wildly, but he sank and sank and his boots touched nothing but water. Far too late, he realised the spring was deeper in the centre; that he didn't know how far down he'd have to go for leverage. He twisted in the water, trying belatedly to grab for his boots, to pull them off, but his lungs were empty and his vision dark—

A body pressed against him, arms encircling his chest from behind. Cae thrashed weakly, but could manage no further resistance; was forced to hang in limbo as whoever-it-was hauled him—up? Cae had the brief thought that he must've twisted himself upside down, that he was being dragged towards the bottom of the spring, and then his head broke free—his whole head this time, not just the crown—and he gasped in a lungful of air, coughing and spluttering around the unpleasant taste of the water.

"Fuck me, you're heavy," panted an unfamiliar voice. The arms around him tightened briefly, and he realised this was his rescuer. "Help me out a bit."

With Cae kicking in feeble assistance, whoever-it-was dragged him bodily to the pool's edge and out like a half-landed fish. Chest heaving, Cae lay stunned for some moments. He ached from throat to core, lungs burning more than they had from the smoke at Etho. His stomach convulsed, and he had a half-second's grace in which to mumble a warning before he retched painfully onto the grass, bringing up what little he'd eaten at the party in a squalid, watery mess.

"Good," murmured the stranger, their voice languid now that they weren't hauling Cae out of the water, the vowels stretched around a lazy northern accent. A firm hand rubbed his back, then patted between his shoulders before withdrawing. "Got any more in you?"

Cae shook his head, or tried no. "Not water," he gasped. "Drugged."

"Ah." He heard a rustling sound, as of sodden fabric being rearranged. "Well, that explains it. Did you fall in?"

Cae nodded weakly, then shook his head. He was shivering violently, his skin no longer hot. "Rolled in. Someone held me under," he said urgently, though the words were broken up by coughing. "Tried to drown me. Did you see them?"

"Sorry," said the stranger. "I caught a glimpse of someone running off, but then I saw you going under and figured you needed help more than whoever it was needed chasing."

"Thank you," Cae rasped, and only then did he lift his head sufficiently to get a look at his rescuer.

The stranger wore a kem's green braid at thir collar and looked to be somewhere in thir late thirties or early forties, with golden brown skin, high cheekbones and a long, angular jaw. Thir face was framed by unbound hair that would've been reddish when dry, but which was now dark brown; thir eyes were sharp and black under neat brows, complemented by a strong nose and a mobile mouth, its expressive lips quirked somewhere between humour and judgement. It wasn't the face of anyone he recognised, but as a veritable ladder of gold rings and emerald studs adorned the cartilage of thir right ear, thei clearly weren't at the party by accident. "Who—?"

"Call me Qiqa," thei said. This rang a bell in Cae's addled senses, but before he could figure out why, Qiqa returned the question. "You?"

"Caethari," said Cae.

"Huh," said Qiqa. Thei were silent for a moment. "Can you sit up?"

"Let's see," said Cae. He braced himself and swayed upright. His vision was still hazy, but not as badly as before, for all that the water had left his eyes smarting. With the bulk of the drug, whatever it was, expelled from his stomach, his senses were starting to clear, and as he rubbed his head, he realised why his rescuer's name was familiar. "Yasai Qiqa Ykran," he said, though it came out more like a question. "You're the Silver Chair."

"Amber, Jade, Silver, what does it matter? We're all insufferable."

Thei said this so tartly that Cae was startled into laughter, though the sound quickly devolved into coughing. Qiqa patted his back again before thrusting a bundle of fabric into Cae's arms. "These are yours, I take it?"

It was his lin and undershirt. Cae nodded, shrugging into the undershirt for propriety's sake, though it felt as unpleasantly sticky against his damp skin as it had when he'd stripped it off. Now that the heat was leaving him, he'd begun to feel chill and queasy, a nascent headache throbbing at his temples and the base of his skull. Horribly, he wanted to cry, though whether from nearly drowning, the drug leaving his system or simple fatigue, he didn't know.

"You don't look well," said Qiqa, reaching out to tip Cae's chin up with a fingertip. Thei peered at his face and whatever thei saw there evidently didn't impress. "We should get you back to your quarters."

"Do I have to go through the party?" Cae asked, voice small. It wasn't that he didn't want to be seen in his present state, although that was also true, but rather the fear that someone would try and talk to him.

Qiqa snorted. "Fuck the party," thei said. "We can go out the way I came in, through the second path. There's more than one way through the maze," thei added, at Cae's look of surprise. "If there wasn't, whoever tried to drown you would've passed me going the other way. Do you think you can stand?"

Cae nodded grimly, draped his lin over his forearm, and forced his legs to take his weight. He wobbled precariously halfway up, but Qiqa caught him with an arm around his waist, and after a moment, he was able to stand, though the yasai still supported him. Cae's boots squelched unpleasantly as they began to move, Qiqa steering him towards the hedge-wall. Squint though he might, Cae couldn't make out the entrance to the maze until Qiqa was physically leading him into it. The path was hidden behind a corner section of hedge cut to form a baffle; unless you knew what to look for, it was practically invisible.

Through they went, the way still dimly lit by those same small, starry magelights. Cae stumbled more than once, and every time, his heart gave an odd, shaky lurch. The hedge-walls seemed to loom over him: they were almost twice his height, and in the darkness, the strange shadows cast by their leaves and branches, coupled with the silvery sheen of the magelights, made the place feel haunted and otherworldly, like a test to be set before saints. Qiqa clearly knew the way by heart, unerringly choosing this right or that left, never once leading them into a dead end, and yet Cae couldn't shake the gnawing fear that he'd be trapped in the maze forever.

"Where does this path let out?" he asked, as they traversed yet another junction.

"Into the asa's private gardens," said Qiqa.

"Oh," said Cae. "That's . . . I'm surprised it's open?"

"It's not," said Qiqa. "There's a locked gate between the two." Thei flashed Cae a conspiratorial grin. "Fortunately for us, I have a key, though I'd be obliged if you kept it to yourself."

"Of course," said Cae, who was in no position to bargain.

"Excellent," purred Qiqa. "I'll consider that your payment for the rescue."

Cae opened his mouth. Closed it again. *Vel would know what to say here,* he thought, and in the next step he nearly went to his knees, because oh gods, *Vel.* How was he to explain any of this to Vel?

"You going to be sick again?" Qiqa asked, not ungently.

Cae shook his head and, with immense effort, straightened. His stomach lurched like a storm-racked ship. "Keep going," he said, and Qiqa was kind enough to oblige him.

For the first time since his rescue, Cae recalled the events preceding his time in the water. He remembered Asrien on his lap and clenched his fists in belated frustration. *Saints, what was he thinking? He's involved with Nevan, and he already knows I'm married!* He was hardly unaware of infidelity as a concept, but the idea that anyone could think Cae would be a willing party to it made him want to stalk back into the party, grab Asrien by the collar and ask what in Zo's sainted name he thought he was playing at. And while Vel was on his sickbed, too? It was the deepest sort of insult, though as he compared the so-called logic behind Asrien's proposition—*every man is two men, the one he is sober and the one he is drunk*—with his upset at Cae's suggestion that he find someone who wanted him, he grudgingly supposed that it hadn't been personal. Saints knew, Ralia was a hard enough place for men of their inclination, but that didn't lessen the sting of being lumped in with the kind of man he was evidently used to.

Which raised another ugly question: how would Vel react when Cae told him what had happened? Vel, after all, had warned Cae not to trust Asrien, and in his panic about the party, he'd done exactly that, letting himself be led away into the maze, there to be propositioned and kissed by a man he didn't want. Cae's stomach churned: even after their argument of—saints, was it only the night before?—he didn't *think* Vel would blame him or suspect him of real infidelity, but that didn't mean he wouldn't still be hurt by Cae's foolishness.

Lost in these thoughts, he only belatedly noticed that Qiqa had brought him to the door of the Jade Suite and was now, presumably, waiting for Cae to admit them. Mumbling embarrassed thanks, Cae knocked softly—he'd not brought the key with him, which felt like a mercy in hindsight, as he'd doubtless have lost the

308 · *Foz Meadows*

damn thing in the water—and had to wait only seconds for the door to open, an attentive Markel on the other side.

"I'm back," Cae croaked feebly. His throat really did feel awful. "This is Yasai Qiqa Ykran, the Silver Chair. Thei saved my life."

Eyes widening, Markel stepped back and admitted them both, hovering tensely as Cae and Qiqa disentangled themselves. Cae, to his deep embarrassment, nearly fell down again and had to be helped to a settee; apparently Qiqa had been taking more of his weight than he'd realised.

"I won't intrude," said Qiqa, flicking thir gaze to Markel but speaking to Cae. "But if you want to speak further, Jade, you know where to find me. As will anyone you might send my way in reporting this, for that matter." Thei paused, cocking thir head. "*Do* you wish to report this? Now, I mean. I could be persuaded to drop by the relevant offices before turning in for the night."

Cae shook his head. "My thanks, but it can wait until morning. I'd rather have the chance to speak to my husband first, but right now—" He cast a longing glance at the bedroom.

"Of course," said Qiqa. And then, with a conspiratorial glint to thir eye, "Just remember our agreement, yes?"

"Of course," Cae echoed weakly. The promise nagged at him, but he was too tired to fathom why; like so much else, it would have to be a problem for later.

With a satisfied nod and a farewell flick of thir fingers, Qiqa saw thimself out. Cae waited as Markel relocked the suite behind thim, then slumped back against the settee, utterly spent.

"Is Vel awake?" Cae asked, not daring to look at the bedroom.

"He's not," signed Markel, coming to stand before him. "He tried to wait up for you, but he fell asleep an hour ago." His gaze roved worriedly over Cae. "You're soaked to the skin. What happened?"

"I was an idiot," Cae said, swallowing hard. "Markel, I—something happened."

"You can tell me when you're dry," signed Markel, and before Cae could complain, he knelt and, with his usual efficient care, gently removed Cae's sodden boots. With this done, he hauled Cae bodily upright and into the suite's bathroom, helped him to pull off his nara—though not, for the sake of mutual modesty, his smallclothes—and all but poured him into the bath, running a cascade of blissfully warm water over his head from the wall-mounted spigot. Cae hissed at the temperature: he hadn't realised how cold he'd become on the long, stumbling walk back from the maze, nor truly registered that he was still intermittently shivering. His stomach churned unpleasantly; he felt queasily unmoored, the brighter lights of the suite intensifying his headache, but at least his vision was no longer blurring and skewing the way it had before. He had a sudden premonition that he was going to feel very hungover come morning without having earned it through anything enjoyable, and took a moment to be thoroughly annoyed about how unfair this was.

As his chilly fingers were somewhat lacking in dexterity, it took him several fumbling attempts to unbraid the mess of his hair, struggling to pick the tangled ribbon out of the snarls in order to finger-comb them into something manageable. Still, he managed it, and sighed with relief as he rinsed the mineral scent away under the tap. He'd just looped it behind his ears and sat back when he felt Markel's fingers against his scalp, tugging gently. His first thought was that he'd missed a snarl or some errant bit of debris, but when the pressure continued, he realised with a lurch that Markel was sectioning out his hair to redo the braid.

Shocked, Cae lurched away from him so violently that he sent a wave of water sloshing over the edge of the tub. He spun around and stared, as betrayed as if Markel had groped him; Markel, for his part, was wide-eyed with startlement, hands held up to show he meant no harm.

"Did I hurt you?" Markel signed.

"You were *braiding* my *hair*," Cae exclaimed, unable to keep the affront from his voice.

"Yes?" signed Markel, his expression baffled. "It'll tangle again if you sleep with it wet and loose."

Belatedly, Cae recalled the difference between Ralian and Tith-enai customs. Markel was a trained valet; doubtless he'd helped with Vel's hair on hundreds of occasions, though contemplating this now made Cae feel vaguely unsettled. Forcing his racing heart to calm, he said, flustered and off-balance, "That's *personal*."

Markel blinked, a look of dawning comprehension on his face. "Personal to you?" he asked. "Or personal to Tithenai in general?"

"Both," said Cae. "It's—even Liran never did my braids, do you understand? I'd let my sisters do them in a pinch, perhaps my grandmother, but otherwise it's just for Vel." He paused, and was then compelled to mumble, "If he wanted to, that is."

Markel looked slightly poleaxed by this, and was still for several moments before finally signing, "I'm sorry. I didn't know."

"I know," said Cae, and turned back to finish washing. Not that he took long; the heat from the bath was starting to make him feel drowsy, and he desperately wanted to tell Markel what had happened before he fell asleep, if only to get an idea of how Vel was likely to react in the morning. Unbidden, Markel went back into the bedroom and returned with a robe and a hipwrap, leaving Cae alone to dry off and change. He hesitated over whether to rebraid his wet hair before deciding against it; he was too tired to bother, and if he had to wash it again in the morning, then so be it.

As he left the bathroom, he looked in on Velasin, still fast asleep in their bedroom. It was hard to tell in the low, warm glow of the single illuminated magelight, but Cae fancied his colour looked slightly better than it had done earlier. He swallowed, resisting the urge to wake his husband for further reassurance, and returned instead to the suite's main room.

Cae sat heavily on the same settee he'd occupied earlier, noticing distantly that his wet boots had already been removed elsewhere. Markel pulled up a chair to sit opposite, and only then, leaned forwards with his elbows braced on his knees, did he look intently at Cae and sign, "Tell me."

In fumbling bursts, Cae confessed the whole sorry story: the drugging, the maze, his near-drowning, Qiqa's rescue. Markel's face hardened as Cae described Asrien's attempt at seduction, but he didn't interrupt, watching blankly as Cae drew the narrative to a close.

"I didn't—Markel, I need you to know—I need *Vel* to know—I didn't mean to make Asrien think that I, that he, that there was any chance—I didn't encourage him at all, he left when I made it plain, but—"

"Stop," signed Markel. He looked upset, and for a horrible moment Cae thought he was about to be lectured, until Markel leaned in and signed, "Caethari, you were *drugged*—if not by Asrien himself, then certainly to his advantage. He knew you weren't well and tried to use that against you. Stop apologising for what he did and answer me this: are *you* all right?"

Cae opened his mouth. Closed it again. Saw the anger in Markel's eyes, and realised it wasn't directed at him, but was rather on his behalf. Realised, for the first time, that he perhaps had cause to feel a different kind of upset, and took a moment to consider whether or not he did.

Slowly, he said, "I'm all right. I'm not . . . hurt, in that way." And then, because Markel—understandably, given Velasin's history, and perhaps also given the braiding incident in the bath—still looked worried, he added, "I'm insulted that Asrien thought I'd betray my husband, and I'm annoyed he was so handsy in trying to convince me, but no, I don't feel—" he gestured helplessly, trying to conjure an appropriate word, "—importuned?"

Markel eyed him critically, then nodded, his shoulders relaxing slightly.

Hesitantly, because this hadn't occurred to him before Markel brought it up and he felt foolish for not having considered it earlier, Cae asked, "Do you really think Asrien was the one who drugged me?"

"It's possible," Markel signed. He looked abruptly exhausted.

"When I was with him earlier, it didn't seem like he bore you a grudge, but that's hardly conclusive. We don't know enough about him. What's more important right now is that somebody tried to kill *you* when Velasin wasn't present. Which begs the question: is this the same person who was targeting Vel on the way here, or the person behind Syana, or someone new?"

"Fuck." Cae groaned, rubbing a hand over his face. "I'm too tired for this." He tried for a smile but managed something closer to a wince. "Can't the powers that be leave off from trying to kill us for a single godsdamned day?"

Markel's expression was grim. "Apparently not."

Sighing and with only the slightest wobble, Cae levered himself to his feet. "I need sleep," he murmured. Then he paused, uncertain, and glanced back at Markel. "Unless you think I should wake him and tell him now?"

Markel considered this, then shook his head. "It'll keep until morning."

Cae nodded, the gesture both thanks and acceptance, and made his way to the bedroom. Vel was still fast asleep, and for a moment, Cae could barely breathe for the sight of him. His hair on the pillow was tangled, and Cae had a sudden, intense urge to fetch a comb from the bathroom and brush it clean; to wind in a single, small braid against those rich, soft waves. But Velasin hadn't permitted him that intimacy, and so he exhaled, discarded his robe and climbed carefully in beside him, hypnotised by the gentle rise and fall of his chest. As exhausted as he was, he wasn't sure he'd be able to sleep, but between one blink and the next, he must've crashed into oblivion, because the next thing he knew, he was being frantically shaken awake by Markel.

"Whazzit?" Cae slurred, scrubbing reflexively at his gummed-up eyes. His whole body felt stiff, as if he'd spent all of yesterday sparring. "What's happened?"

"Syana's dead," Markel signed frantically. "I went to the kitchens and the whole place was buzzing with it—she was found dead in her cell this morning. Murdered overnight—poisoned, it looks like."

Cae sat bolt upright. "What? By who?"

"Nobody knows yet," signed Markel, "but if the servants know, then everyone knows, and that means—"

A sonorous booming cut him off, as of an angry fist banging on the suite's main door.

"—the general will want answers."

19

F uck," Cae said. He sat up, realising only as he did so that Velasin had curled against him during the night, his forehead pressed to Cae's shoulder, and experienced an angry pang of loss at not having time to savour it. Unlike last night, his thoughts were mercifully clear, and he winced as the implications of Syana's murder hit him like a thrown brick. General Naza had little love for Ralians even before Markel and Asrien had snuck in to interview his prisoner—and depending on the general's movements yesterday, they were possibly the only ones who'd done so, which was something to keep in mind—but, maddeningly, Caethari made for a good suspect regardless. Syana, after all, had tried to murder his husband; it was only natural to think he might've sought revenge. *Would that I had,* a part of him thought bitterly. *It would've been a better use of my time than that fucking party.*

Taking a deep breath, he looked down and cupped Vel's cheek in his hand, indulging in running a thumb across the bone. Vel made a soft, sleepy noise and burrowed incrementally closer, the moment ruined only by the increased banging on the suite door.

"Cae?" Vel mumbled, brow furrowing at the noise. "What is it?"

"Shh," said Cae, heart twisting like wet clothes in a laundryman's hands. "It's nothing. Go back to sleep."

But Vel, stubborn creature that he was, did the opposite, forcibly blinking himself awake. "What is it?" he asked again. "What's wrong?"

More banging. Swallowing a curse, Cae leaned down and pressed a kiss to Vel's forehead. "Markel can tell you," he said. "I need to get the door."

With that, he slipped out of bed, shrugged on the robe he'd discarded the night before, smoothed out his hipwrap and strode into the suite's main room, remembering only as he stood before the door that he'd forgone braiding his hair and slept with it wet. Hoping the effect wasn't too horrific but unwilling to check in a mirror, he finger-combed it into some semblance of neatness, smoothed it back behind his ears and, finally, answered the door.

True to Markel's prediction, he was met with the scowling face of General Naza, who pushed straight past Cae into the suite.

"Yaseran," he said, with the barest hint of politeness. "I have some questions for you and your husband." He craned his head towards the bedroom, but stopped short of actually entering.

"You may recall that Velasin is unwell," Cae said curtly. "Whatever you wish to ask can be asked of me."

"Possibly," the general conceded, smiling with an abundance of teeth and a dearth of humour, "but as what I have to say concerns him, I would prefer to see you both."

Cae opened his mouth to protest this, but was forestalled by a croaked, "It's all right," from the bedroom doorway. He whirled, appalled and anxious to see Vel standing there, leaning heavily on Markel. He wore a half-open robe and loose white nara, and grimaced an unfriendly acknowledgement at the general as he eased his way to the settee. The general watched him with catlike intensity, waiting until he was seated before saying, "Your would-be murderer was poisoned last night. I wonder if you know anything about it."

Vel tensed up, but kept his expression bland as he blinked and replied, "Only what you've just told me. I've been rather indisposed since the event itself." He raised a hand, fingers flicking with languid sarcasm to indicate his scar.

"You have," allowed the general, cutting his gaze to Markel, "but your servant has not." And then, to Cae, "As I understand it, he and Asrien questioned the prisoner on your authority."

"Asrien certainly did," said Cae, "but Markel, as you may know, is mute. He was present, yes, but not the inquisitor. And if you've spoken to Asrien, then you already know that the prisoner didn't reveal her employer."

"So he claims," said the general, stalking incrementally forwards. "Either way, it's clear you had motive for killing her."

"What motive?" Cae said. "Without her, I've got no leads to find out who wants Vel dead."

"But you do have revenge," countered General Naza. "And you certainly had opportunity. As best we can tell, her food was tampered with last night—"

"Like you, I was at the tierena's party—"

"—during the period," the general forged on, overriding Cae, "when you suddenly and notably vanished from the proceedings." He cocked his head. "Can you account for your whereabouts, yaseran?"

An unpleasant sense of foreboding crawled its way up Cae's spine. He didn't know how much of the truth to tell, if any; whether it would be safer to dissemble. It was the kind of calculation Vel excelled at making, but as his husband was yet to be apprised of the night's events, he could hardly look to him for guidance.

Which meant the choice was his: to trust the general, or to lie.

"I was indisposed," Cae said after a beat. "After what happened to Vel . . . I didn't remember to eat all day, and then I went straight to drinking. I don't usually lose my head like that, but I must've had more than I realised." He swallowed, cheeks unaccountably hot. "I went into the maze with Lord Asrien. We talked, he left, and then—and I'm not proud of this—I ended up in the hot spring. Boots and all." He met the general's gaze. "And while I was in there, someone tried to drown me."

From the corner of his eye, Cae saw Vel flinch, but didn't dare acknowledge it.

"Another murder attempt?" asked General Naza. He raised a

sceptical brow. "And you didn't report it to anyone, even after what had happened to your husband?"

"I was more concerned with surviving it," Cae snapped. "Which I only did with the help of Yasai Qiqa Ykran. Thei saw me going under and saved me."

"Going under? I thought you said someone was drowning you."

"They were."

"So the yasai saw them? Passed them on thir way in?"

"No, thei—" Cae started, and then broke off, remembering far too late his promise not to reveal Qiqa's possession of the key to the asa's gardens, without which he could neither explain how Qiqa had entered the maze-heart from a different direction to Cae's assailant nor, crucially, how Cae had left the maze without being seen again at the party. He didn't know the yasai, and beyond the fact that thei'd saved Cae's life—which was, admittedly, significant—he didn't owe thim anything. The general was already sceptical of Cae's account; if he redacted those details, he'd appear even more of an unreliable narrator. If pressed by Qiqa later, he could always claim that he'd forgotten the conversation, or else that the promise wasn't binding by virtue of having been made while he was drugged. But—

Every man is two men: the one he is sober and the one he is drunk.

Cae was not two men.

"Yes?" prompted General Naza.

"It's a maze," said Cae. "Whoever attacked me could've hidden in a side path while the yasai went past."

The sceptical eyebrow arched even higher. "Implying they gave up on drowning you *before* the appearance of a witness?"

"They had me by the hair at the edge of the pool," said Cae, working to keep his voice even. He was practiced in making dispassionate recounts of violent, unsettling events in which he'd played no small role; he was not, however, accustomed to doing so to an audience predisposed to view him as liar. "I broke free and pushed myself to deeper water, at which point they gave up and fled before I could see them." He suppressed a shudder at the memory. "But I was, as I mentioned, drunk, and still wearing my boots. I couldn't surface. That's when the yasai found me and brought me back here."

"I don't recall seeing either of you leave the party."

"We were discreet," said Cae. "Or at least, I assume we were. I wasn't really paying attention."

"And then?"

"And then we came back here."

"Can your husband vouch for this?"

Cae swallowed a curse. "Markel—"

"Of course I can," said Vel. He leaned back against the settee as he said it, the posture baring his throat in a way that emphasised both his scar and his unconcern for the general's glower. His voice was slightly raspy, but his diction was perfectly clear. "Markel let him in, I woke up to say hello, and we went to sleep. He stayed here the whole night afterwards."

"Hm," said Naza. A slow smirk spread across his face. "I wonder, will that story change once you hear an alternate version of events?"

Vel smiled sharply. "I can't see why I would."

"Because," said the general, coming to perch on the settee's arm, "I've already spoken to Asrien this morning, and his account of events is . . . quite different, shall we say." The smirk deepened. "By his account, the yaseran was indeed drunk, but they didn't *talk* in the maze. They—"

"You're implying they fucked?" Vel interrupted, to General Naza's clear annoyance. Cae's stomach churned; outwardly, Vel looked unconcerned, but Cae knew him well enough by now to see the tension in his hands and throat, the particular armoured fakeness of his smile. "I'm sorry, General—were you hoping to shock me? I know I'm Ralian, but that hardly makes me sheltered."

"One might think," said the general, eyes glittering dangerously, "that you'd be more concerned by the prospect of infidelity."

"And so I might be," Vel said lazily, "were the messenger other than yourself." He quirked his mouth, subjecting General Naza to a saucily disparaging once-over. "You've hardly made your dislike of our marriage a secret, General, and even if you hadn't, you're plainly here to accuse and unsettle. Given that, why in the world would I trust your account of things over Caethari's?"

"It's not my account, but your countryman's."

Vel snorted laughter, his gaze as mocking as his voice. "And Ralians *never* lie, least of all to other Ralians—or to Tithenai, for that matter. Which makes your valuing of Asrien's account over Caethari's somewhat . . . incongruous, let's say." He tipped his chin, assessing the general with his hooded gaze. "Is Asrien also a suspect, General? Or your agent?"

For a moment, the general looked positively furious; then a mask smoothed over his face—*a soldier's mask,* Cae thought, akin to the one he used himself—and he sat back, for all the world unbothered.

"Of course Asrien is a suspect," the general said. "Why else would I have questioned him? This whole business stinks of Ralian interference in my court; I don't trust any of you as far as I could throw you."

"Oh, I don't know," drawled Vel. "You look like you could throw us pretty far."

The general's jaw worked silently for a moment. "Noble of you, to trust in your husband so," he said. "Whether the court gossip will be so lenient is another matter entirely. And speaking of lenience," he went on, rising once more, "I may yet want to speak to this one." He indicated Markel with a flick of his finger. "After all, who's to say you didn't send him out last night to do your bidding? It's easy enough for a servant to infiltrate the barracks kitchens."

At that, Vel really did tense up. "Markel was with me all night," he said harshly. "After that woman slit my throat in open court, do you really think I'd send him away and leave myself unprotected?"

"Stranger things have happened," said the general. "And he wouldn't have needed to be gone for long."

"Markel is mute," Cae interjected. "Even if you took him, how do you plan to question him?"

The general's expression sharpened. "Oh, I'm sure I'll find a way." He paused. "Unless, of course, I was to encounter new information that would render such questioning moot."

"We'll bear that in mind," Vel said coldly.

The general bowed, the gesture all mockery. "Be sure you do," he said, and left without another word.

In his wake fell silence, deep as snowfall.

Cae was the first to break it, inhaling raggedly as he turned to his husband. "Velasin, I—"

"Tell me everything," Vel said, voice brittle. Whatever strength he'd mustered in the general's presence had evaporated in an instant; he was slumped back against the settee looking painfully fatigued. "Not just whatever happened with Asrien. The whole night."

Swallowing against a sudden lump in his throat, Cae did so, faltering his painful way through memories of his conversations with the Iron, Amber and Velvet Chairs, as well as the trio of young noblemen, Asrien and Nevan before reaching the story of the maze. He'd felt, if not calm, then detached when relating those events to Markel, but in the cold light of day, with Vel's expression unreadable as he listened, Cae's heart began to pound painfully in his chest.

"I should've understood what was happening sooner," Cae said, wretched with embarrassment. "I was just—I felt so hot, and everything kept spinning—"

"It's all right," said Vel, voice strained. It was the first interjection he'd made since Cae began talking. With visibly difficulty, he said, "What happened next?"

Strangely, it was easier to describe being almost drowned, despite the inherent foolishness of having been the one to put himself in the water. When he admitted to the full truth of Qiqa's rescue—his willingness to conceal the yasai's secret key from General Naza did not extend to his husband—Vel's gaze sharpened in a way that made the hairs on his nape stand up.

"And then thei brought me home, and I told Markel what had happened," Cae finished.

"That's true," Markel signed, when Vel glanced at him for confirmation. "He wondered if we should wake you, but I said no, though in hindsight, that might've been sensible."

Vel gave a strange, distracted nod. He stared vacantly at the far wall for a moment, seemingly lost in thought—and then, out of nowhere, he rose, stood unsteadily before Caethari, took his hands, and folded himself to his knees, head bowed.

"Vel?" asked Cae, alarmed. "What is—what are you—?"

"I'm sorry," Vel whispered, pressing his forehead to Cae's knuckles. "This is my fault." Shaking, he looked up at Cae through his lashes. "Asrien propositioned me in our rooms at Ravethae. Kissed me, as he kissed you. He said—" He faltered, throat working soundlessly for a moment. "—it doesn't matter what he said. I just. I should've known then that he wasn't—that it wasn't really about me, that he had his own agenda; I should've found you and told you, but I was—I was ashamed, I didn't—I'd already been so angry at you, I didn't want you to hate me—"

"Vel," Cae begged, going to his knees in turn. "This isn't your fault—"

"He *hurt* you," Vel croaked, and Cae went still, a horrible coldness washing over his skin. Vel was breathing too hard, too fast, alarming splotches of colour forming on his still-too-pale cheeks. "If I'd told you—if you'd known, if—"

Cae made a pained noise and folded Vel into his arms, cradling the back of his head. "It's all right," he murmured roughly, stroking Vel's hair. Distantly, he was aware of his anger at Asrien, the sort of cold, seething fury that was sure to come out at some point, but in the moment, feeling it was less important than Vel. "Shh, you're all right, I'm all right—"

"But if I—"

"Shh," Cae said again. He shut his eyes, rocking Vel slightly from side to side without meaning to, alive to the scent and feel of him. "You didn't do anything wrong." He pulled back slightly, cupping Vel's face in his hands, thumbs smoothing across his cheeks as he met his trembling gaze. "I promise you, I'm all right." And then, more softly, "Are *you* all right?"

Vel made a sound that was not quite laughter and nodded. "I wasn't," he said, "not—not at the time, but now . . ." He hesitated, then blurted, "It wasn't like with Killic."

Something in Cae unknotted that he hadn't known was fouled. "Good," he breathed, and rested their foreheads together. "For me, either."

Velasin grabbed the front of Cae's robe and clung on tight, and for a moment the two of them hung together, as if suspended in time.

Then Markel, whose presence Cae was ashamed to admit he'd forgotten about, made a pointed, throat-clearing sort of noise and startled them both into pulling apart like youths caught fumbling in the stables, although Vel retained his grip on Cae's clothing.

"As pleased as I am to see you talking," Markel signed, "we have other things to worry about. Who drugged you? Who tried to kill you? Who poisoned Syana, and who sent her in the first place? And are any of them connected to whoever was trying to kill Velasin en route to Qi-Xihan?" He looked genuinely frustrated, and small wonder; the past day had somehow managed to triple their problems alarmingly.

"You're right," said Cae, though it pained him to have to focus on anything other than Velasin. He nodded thanks to Markel, then looked to his husband, gently stroking along his arm. "What do you think?"

Vel frowned, glancing at Markel. "The general said you and Asrien questioned—Syana, was it? The woman who attacked me?"

Amidst everything else, Cae had somehow forgotten that Vel was yet to hear that particular story, and sat back on his heels, watching with only partial comprehension as Markel, reverting to his standard signs, gave a swift, concise summary of the previous day's events, including Asa Ivadi assigning General Naza to investigate Syana's attack. Vel absorbed all this with a look of concentration, hands slacking their grip on Cae's robe. As distraught as he'd been moments earlier, having information to work with and a problem to solve seemed to steady him, and when Markel was done, Vel made a thoughtful noise.

"That's . . . not what I'd expected," he said at last. He paused, then added ruefully, "Inasmuch as I've had time to expect anything, that is. Coming over the mountain." He murmured this detail almost to himself—a little wistfully, Cae thought—then shook his head, refocussing. "All right. All right. Is there any point investigating exactly how Syana was poisoned? She expected to die, and I don't imagine that whoever she dealt with bothered to interfere with her food themselves."

Cae shook his head. "The kitchens aren't exactly restricted; anyone could've slipped in, and that's assuming nobody had access to her meal once it was en route. We'd have to question the entire kitchen staff, get a list of whoever was in and out, and it still might not be accurate. If we were in Qi-Katai and I had access to people I trusted, that would be one thing, but here . . ." He shrugged.

Vel nodded reluctant agreement. "Then can we assume, do you think, that the general wasn't able to question Syana before she died?"

"I think so," Cae said, considering. "If she'd told him something she didn't tell Markel, he'd have held it over us, but if she'd said the same to him as to us, or told him nothing, he'd have accused us of collusion."

"That makes sense," said Vel. "If he's in charge of the whole investigation, he wouldn't have had time, especially not with the party in the evening. He might've delegated it, of course, but if that were the case, he'd—wait." He blinked, looking back at Cae. "*Does* he have subordinates? In the palace, I mean, not in the army."

"He's been put in charge of some of the asa's guards," Cae said slowly, "but they're not his own people. Which is likely deliberate on the asa's part: he's a general, not an investigator, and she knows he's hostile to Ralia. If she hadn't put him in charge of this, he'd still be looking into it on his own, but this way, he's surrounded by her people. She has oversight. Which is likely why he's doing everything himself: to maintain as much control over what he learns as possible."

"You're right," said Velasin, sounding gratifyingly impressed. "But if he's doing everything himself, and finding out who killed Syana takes priority today—"

"—then we have a window of opportunity to go after whoever employed her before the general gets to it," Cae finished.

Vel grabbed him again, his slim fingers cool around Cae's wrist. "Cietena Alu Nyas," he said urgently. "Wherever she is in the capital, you need to find her; to see how Syana ended up with her palace token. I'd come with you, but"—he gestured wryly at himself, neck to knees—"I'm hardly in the best condition right now."

A pang went through Cae at the reminder. Saints, Vel hadn't even eaten yet, or seen a healer; it was a wonder he was even lucid. But then, that was Velasin all over: as lovely as a sunset and as stubborn as a stone.

"I'll go," Cae said, "so long as Markel stays with you."

"Agreed," Markel signed emphatically, getting in ahead of Vel's objection.

"Absolutely not," said Velasin, crossing his arms and pouting like a thwarted child. "No! *One night* I let you out by yourself, and what happened? You were drugged, imposed upon and nearly murdered. Markel is going with you."

"Markel is staying *here*," said Cae, squeezing Vel's leg for emphasis. At the flash of pique in his husband's eyes, Cae's throat tightened, and he promptly switched tactics. "Vel, be reasonable. We're both in danger right now, but I've got the better chance of defending myself alone if someone tries again. I'll be careful, I promise—believe me, I've no wish to undergo a repeat of last night's adventures—but if I'm constantly worrying about you here alone, I'll be useless. I'll probably fall and break my neck at the first busy crossing I come to." He tried to make his eyes as big and pleading as his sisters and Liran had always insisted they could be. "Please?"

Vel made an aggrieved noise and tugged on Cae's wrist in mock anger. "That *face*," he muttered, though just fondly enough that Cae's heart gave a hopeful lurch. Vel glared at him for a moment, then rolled his eyes and sighed. "Fine," he said. "Just don't—don't get hurt again, all right? Or I won't be held responsible for my actions."

"Agreed," said Cae, and dared to lean in and kiss his cheek. Vel inhaled at the contact, the sound so small and sweet that Cae was instantly suffused with heat. In the same instant, he was stricken to realise that he didn't know where he stood with Vel: so much had happened in so little time, the both of them caught up in the aftermath of the previous day's events, that they'd had no space in which to speak about anything else. Nor was there any time now: whatever else could be said of General Naza, he bore an open grudge against both their marriage and them as individuals. Cae needed to get out ahead of him before someone did manage to kill him or Vel, which meant he couldn't afford so much as a spare half-hour in which to linger over breakfast with his husband, let alone sit down for a meaningful conversation about their feelings.

This was maddening for all of a moment; then Cae flipped it about in his head, shoulders firming to the task. In order to win the space necessary to speak and be with Vel, he simply had to uncover and capture whoever was trying to kill them, and the first step to doing *that* was finding who'd sent Syana.

Wordless, they rose together, Vel swaying as they did so. Markel rushed to help him, but Vel made an affronted noise.

"I want a wash before I'm forced to lie down again," he grumbled. "I can do that much without help, surely."

Behind Vel's back, Markel caught Cae's eye and signed, "I'll call the healer once you're gone."

"Please do," Cae signed back, "and make sure he eats breakfast. Whatever he wants, so long as he gets something in his body, and plenty of water."

"Of course."

"I can feel the pair of you mother-henning me from here," Vel called from the bathroom door. "It smacks of conspiracy."

"You'll be cared about and you'll like it!" Cae called back.

Velasin let out a startled bark of laughter. Buoyed by the smugness this engendered in him, Cae clapped Markel on the shoulder and went to get dressed. At some point—probably last night, during the terrible party—Markel had taken the time to unpack their things, so that Cae's clothes were neatly arrayed at one end of the wardrobe, Vel's at the other, including the road-stained clothes they'd had laundered at Ravethae. He considered the lot of them, working to pick out something practical.

The sense of purpose focussed him: after so long spent on the back foot, waiting for their mystery assailant to strike without being able to pursue or prepare for them beyond keeping alert, it was a relief to finally be *doing* something. Under the circumstances, he would've liked a cuirass or a breastplate, but even if he'd wanted to spare the time to try and requisition one from the palace armoury, it would've been a conspicuous thing to wear alone, and so he opted to work with that he had. This turned out to be a long-sleeved, high-collared halik made of strong yet supple green leather bossed with curling vine patterns, buttoned snugly from throat to groin but slit at the hips and belted so he had somewhere to hang his scabbard; thick hemp nara tucked into his sturdiest boots; and a silk undershirt lined with linen. Leather would work to turn away a slashing blade, but silk would deter a piercing one: in combination, it was as close to armour as Cae could come without actually wearing any, and with winter settling in, it had the added benefit of being warm.

Next came his hair, which, when he looked at himself in the glass, he was dismayed to realise was not only bent out of shape from having been slept in wet, but *fluffy*. Muttering curses under his breath—for all that he didn't care for General Naza's opinion of him, it was nonetheless embarrassing to have been interviewed in such a state—he dragged a brush through it, fished around for some ribbons and a wooden hairpin on the dresser, and pinned it away in an upcoiled braid.

Only then did Cae consider the issue of arming himself. He had two swords to choose from, the one he'd liberated from his grandmother's estate and the blade he'd brought from Avai, and after everything, the prospect of either at his hip was a comforting one. But while anyone might go armed through Qi-Xihan, swords were not a customary adornment for social calls, and as the point of this outing was information-gathering, he begrudgingly conceded it was probably better to go without. This left his jade-handled knife, which was both small enough to be unobtrusive and comforting in a different way, by virtue of having been a marriage-gift from Velasin. He'd worn it to the party last night and so assumed both it and his belt must be wadded with the lin and undershirt he'd removed at the pool, but when he looked for his discarded things, he couldn't find them.

"Markel," he called, poking his head back out to the main room. "My clothes from last night—where are they?"

"I set them aside for laundering," Markel signed. "Why do you ask?"

"It's just, I can't find my knife, the lovely one Vel gave me—was it with them?"

Markel blinked. "No," he signed. "It wasn't."

"Are you sure? It would've been attached to the belt."

"I'm sure," Markel signed firmly. "There was no belt, no dagger—only your clothes."

A twisting, guilty lurch swooped through Cae's stomach. He had a vague idea that Asrien had removed his belt before climbing on him, and it was Qiqa who'd handed him his bundled clothes as they left the maze. Had the dagger been among them? Cae couldn't remember, which meant one of two things: either it was still near the hot spring, or else he'd dropped it on the way back.

"Fuck," he muttered. At Markel's raised eyebrow, he explained his realisation; Markel winced in sympathy. "There's no time to look for it now," Cae said, "but—keep an eye out, will you? It has to turn up somewhere." And then, slightly pleading, "Please don't tell Vel I lost it."

"I won't," signed Markel. "Not yet, anyway."

Cae exhaled his thanks. The loss of the knife was small in the scheme of things, and yet he felt it as a personal failing. It was the first—and, thus far, only—gift that Velasin had given him, and Cae had lost it, and as he'd already ruled out taking a sword with him, its absence meant he'd be forced to go about his day unarmed. Not that he was incapable barehanded; even so, the lack of a blade made his fingers itch unpleasantly.

"You look worried," said Vel.

Cae jumped. There was Vel emerging from the bathroom, his wavy hair damp against the vivid, water-warmed pink of his scar, his lithe form clad in nothing more than his poorly knotted robe. Cae swallowed hard. *You have work to do,* he reminded himself sternly, refusing to be hypnotised by the droplets of water beading on Vel's freshly shaven jaw. *Clues to follow. Assassins to find.* And *you lost his knife.*

"You look good," said Cae's mouth.

"I look like a fish who got caught on the hook," Vel countered, fingers rising to touch his scar.

"A beautiful fish, if so."

Vel flushed. "Aren't you meant to be off investigating?" he asked, two spots of colour high on his cheeks. He flicked his hands imperiously at Cae, for the all the world like a farmwife scaring chickens away from her flowerpots. "Go on, shoo!"

Cae grinned at him. "Your wish is my command," he said, and with a theatrical half-bow, he turned and left.

20

In deference to his empty stomach, Cae stopped by the nearest kitchens and, with the cook's blessing, helped himself to two fresh jidha and a half-cup of khai. He also took the opportunity to ask where he might find Ru Kisian Faez at this time of morning, and after some consultation among the servants, he was told that the Velvet Chair kept an office two wings over. Armed with directions, Cae thanked them all and set off. It was some time since he'd been to the palace, but the directions proved clear, and soon he was knocking on Ru Kisian's lavishly carved door.

After a moment, he was admitted by Sikana, the young woman he'd met the night before. Combined with her circular glasses, her height and roundness lent her a distinctly owlish look, and when she cocked her head and blinked at him in surprise, Cae was forced to stifle an inappropriate chuckle.

"Yaseran?" said Sikana. "We weren't expecting you, were we?" And then, turning to call back over her shoulder, "Were we expecting Yaseran Caethari?"

"We were not," came Ru Kisian's voice, "but by all means, let's see him!"

Sikana waved Cae in to a richly appointed office. The floor was carpeted with colourful rugs in the bold geometric patterns common to Nivonai textiles, while the walls were covered in curio-laden shelves. The room was dominated by a large mahogany desk, behind which stood Ru Kisian—and against which, to Cae's surprise, Qiqa was leaning, one hip cocked as casually as if thei were at a tavern bar.

"Am I interrupting?" Cae asked.

"No, no!" Ru Kisian waved him over. "The yasai merely stopped in to update me on thir plans for this visit." He shot Qiqa a mildly exasperated look. "Which is very much appreciated, assuming thei actually stick to them this time."

"Life is a river of chaos we all must cross, my friend," drawled Qiqa. "It's not my fault you're afraid to get your feet wet."

"My feet are perfectly wet," retorted Ru Kisian. "*You,* however, are frequently bent on submerging yourself, to say nothing of anyone caught in your immediate vicinity."

"I believe this particular metaphor has run its course," Sikana interjected, getting in ahead of Qiqa, who shut thir mouth with a look of amused respect. "Yaseran, was there something particular you wanted to discuss?"

"Yes, actually," said Cae. "Ru Kisian, are you familiar at all with Cietena Alu Nyas?"

Ru Kisian looked momentarily wrongfooted. "Cietena Alu—oh! Now, there's a name I haven't heard in a while. I don't know her personally, but I certainly know of her. Why do you ask?"

Truthfully, Cae said, "I heard someone mention her recently; the name rang a bell, but I can't for the life of me think why, and it's starting to bother me."

"*Ahhh,*" said Ru Kisian, his expression thoughtful. "Yes, assuming you ever met her, it would've been years ago—she's an absentee landholder for a small patch of territory outside of Qi-Katai."

"Qi-Katai?" Cae echoed, shocked. Syana had come from Vaiko; if the cietena held territory nearby, that could potentially explain the link between them. "She—what?"

Ru Kisian nodded. "She's lived in the capital for over a decade now, I believe. I'm sure I don't need to tell you of all people how villages across that whole region withered and died as a result of Ennan vin Mica's predations. The cietena's properties were among the worst affected. When the local economies began to falter, she tried to shore things up and stick it out, but eventually, those communities failed, and she opted to liquidate her other assets and relocate here rather than stay. I believe she still owns the land and collects such rents as exist to be collected—she periodically shows up at court and demands that the areas be rehabilitated, although she's never had a practical case for doing so—I think she originally made the same requests of your father, but of course, at the time, he was in even less of a position to grant them, hence her escalating to beg the asa directly—but otherwise, she's very much a recluse."

"You seem to know a lot about her," Qiqa observed.

Ru Kisian snorted. "One, I know everyone, and two, she was on my longlist of people I considered asking to support the Ralian alliance." He gestured at Cae by way of illustration.

"Why didn't you, then?" Cae asked.

"Because frankly—and I don't mean this as a slight, just an observation—I judged that approaching her would've done more harm than good. She's never at court and holds no political sway, and the few times she has shown up, she's generally been looked on as a bore and a nuisance. Which isn't to say I *agree*," he added, glaring meaningfully at Sikana, who'd stifled a snort, "but one has to be pragmatic about these things, hm?"

"I didn't know," Cae said. The admission brought on a pang of guilt: it was always Riya and Laecia who'd kept abreast of Qi-Katai's politics, the status and position of the local nobility, guilds and other landholders, while Cae had been preoccupied with his revetha. Though he'd worked in his own way to save lands like the cietena's, fighting back both bandits and vin Mica's men, he hadn't given much thought to the specific nobles whose territory he was dealing with except when they were in front of him asking for help, and that hadn't been often. Usually, he'd dealt up front with villagers, farmers, traders and other such folk directly affected by the violence, whether that meant stolen livestock, burned buildings or worse. It was his father to whom the landholders had complained during those years, and his sisters who'd been in attendance to learn the political ins and outs of dealing with them. And yet Cae was the one who'd been marked to inherit a yaserate: an even larger territory than the demesne that was now Riya's, and rife with far weightier responsibilities.

You can wallow about it later, he told himself sternly. *Focus!* What mattered here was Cietena Alu Nyas, and whether she was responsible for the attack on Vel.

Out loud, Cae said, "I don't suppose you have her address, do you?"

Qiqa looked amused. "You planning to pay her a visit, Jade?"

"Why not?" Cae countered, thinking fast. "After all, the whole point of marrying Vel was to fix what vin Mica broke. Riya wants to start routing trade through the Taelic Pass again as soon as possible, and that's got to be good for the cietena." Both Qiqa and Ru Kisian were still giving him strange looks, and so he let a little of his worry over Vel bleed into his voice as he added, "And I need a distraction. After yesterday . . ." He trailed off, and sure enough, the confused looks became sympathetic.

"Of course," said Ru Kisian. "I must have it written down somewhere—a moment, a moment!" He began to rummage through his desk drawers, rattling the contents and muttering under his breath, until Sikana made an exasperated noise and said, "Oh, *do* give over," hip-checked him out of the way—a surprisingly effective manoeuvre, given her diminutive stature—and retrieved a leather-bound volume from the bottommost right-hand drawer.

"Ah, yes, thank you," said Ru Kisian, as Sikana proffered the book with a roll of her eyes. He opened it, leafed through the contents for several seconds and then finally uttered a triumphant little *ah!* noise. "Here we are," he said, tapping the relevant line. "She's in a townhouse on the second row off Nem Street, which is a few blocks back from the Stagger."

Cae consulted his limited mental map of Qi-Xihan. "That's not too far," he said. "But if her finances are as diminished as you said, I'm surprised she can afford it."

"The area wasn't as fashionable when she first bought in," said

Ru Kisian. "And I don't believe she's been able to do much by way of upkeep. The garden is quite overgrown." Ru Kisian hesitated, his gaze narrowing. "Yaseran, you're not about to do something *political,* are you?"

"Me?" Cae said, all innocence. "I haven't a political bone in my body."

Ru Kisian made a face. "I suppose not," he conceded. "Nonetheless, I find myself concerned."

"Your concerns are noted," Cae said. "My thanks for the address."

"Let me walk you out," said Qiqa. "Assuming our dear Velvet has no further use for me, that is?" Thei raised a questioning brow at Ru Kisian.

"Not at all," he replied.

Bowing, Cae and Qiqa made their way to the door. It was only once they were outside and walking together that Qiqa turned to him and murmured, "You seem less worse for wear this morning than I feared you'd be."

"Don't be fooled," Cae said dryly. "Everything aches, and my head feels like a horse kicked it. But it's comparable to a bad hangover after a full day's training, and I've practice enough at coping with that, so."

Qiqa laughed. "That's a relief, then."

"To that point, though, you should expect a visit from General Naza sometime today."

"Ah," said Qiqa. "I assume he's in a foul mood, what with his prisoner being poisoned."

"You've heard about all that?"

"My dear Jade, the attempt on your husband's life was all anyone was talking about yesterday. Even if Iron had tried to keep his prisoner's death a secret, gossip that sweet would've surely slipped out regardless."

"I suppose so," said Cae. And then, hopefully, "You didn't happen to pick up a jade-handled dagger last night, did you?"

Qiqa blinked in surprise. "No. Why, have you lost one?"

Cae's shoulder's slumped. "Yes," he admitted. "It was on my belt at the start of the night, but I must've lost it in the maze. It was a gift from Vel, and I very much want it back."

"I'll keep an eye out," Qiqa said, then cut him a sly look. "I don't suppose your little errand has anything to do with any of this? The poisoning, that is, not your missing dagger."

"Not at all," Cae lied, but something in Qiqa's expression suggested thei didn't believe him. He was contemplating whether to admit the truth when, suddenly, an urgent voice hailed him from across the courtyard. Cae stopped and turned, surprised to see Nevan hurrying over to him.

"Caethari!" he panted. He was slightly short of breath, his undershirt visibly stained with sweat at the arms and throat. "Have you seen Asrien this morning?"

"I haven't," Cae said coolly.

"Fuck," muttered Nevan, oblivious to Cae's tone. He pushed his glasses up his nose and ran a hand over his hair, then did a slight double take as he properly registered Qiqa. "Apologies," he said. "I don't mean to interrupt, I just—he didn't come back to our rooms last night or show up this morning for breakfast, and with that prisoner turning up dead, I—"

"You think he might've killed her?" Qiqa asked.

Nevan looked appalled. "What? No! Though I worry he might be blamed."

"Is it possible," Cae asked, trying very hard to sound helpful rather than deeply scathing, "that Asrien shared someone else's bed last night?"

"Of course!" said Nevan. When Cae blinked at this, he explained, "We've made no promises to each other. It's only, if that happens, he usually comes back for breakfast."

Fighting back a wholly unhelpful urge to lambaste Nevan for Asrien's choices, Cae said instead, "Perhaps he's still in General Naza's custody. He's already questioned him about my movements last night, and he's not above keeping a Ralian locked up out of spite."

Nevan swore again. "The thought had occurred to me," he admitted, "but I'd hoped I was wrong. Thank you, Cae." And with a harried bow, he hastened off again.

"What an odd man," remarked Qiqa, after a moment.

"Odd how?"

"If you don't see it yourself, I'd prefer not to explain it."

"Fair enough," said Cae.

They resumed walking, a companiable yet strangely anticipatory silence growing between them. When Cae hesitated at a turning of paths, silently mulling whether to ride or walk to the cietena's residence—on foot won out, as the address wasn't too far from the palace and Alik deserved a rest after weeks of travel—Qiqa waited beside him without asking why they'd stopped, then continued on with him again. It was pleasant, but also perplexing, and as they neared the palace gates, Cae found himself wondering if the yasai intended to tail him the whole way to Nem Street.

He was on the verge of asking this when Qiqa said, "I have my own business in town, but I wish you well of your errand."

"Oh," said Cae. He felt oddly disappointed, though he couldn't have said why. "You, too."

They exited the gates together, Cae reflexively thumbing the palace token in his pocket as they passed the duty guards, and emerged into the wintry morning light of Qi-Xihan.

"Good hunting, Jade," said Qiqa. Thei flashed him a broad grin, and for the first time, Cae realised that thir incisors were set with gemstones: little chips of diamond that winked in the sun.

"You, too," Cae echoed, and watched with fond bemusement as Qiqa strode off into the city, thir flamboyant red halik flapping in the breeze.

Thus abandoned, he squared himself to the task and set off down the Stagger, eyes peeled for the eventual turning that would, he hoped, lead him to Nem Street. It was some time since he'd last been to Qi-Xihan, but what Cae's recall lacked on the subject of names and politics it more than made up for in matters geographic, and he found his way with little difficulty. This close to the palace, the buildings were mostly residential: a mix of large, luxurious manor blocks, complete with walled gardens, and less ostentatious rows of townhomes such as the one he was searching for. Even so, a number of street-vendors were still gamely plying their trades to various passersby: toymakers aiming their wares at excitable noble children, various food-sellers offering an aromatic mix of drinks and comestibles, criers hawking the latest scandal-sheets. Thinking Velasin might find it amusing, Cae bought one of the latter and folded it away in his pocket, though as he did so, he felt yet another pang over the missing dagger.

I'll find it later, he promised himself, and carried on his way.

Eventually, he reached the turning he wanted, and proceeded into the arterial side streets deviating from the main promenade. Almost instantly, things became quieter, the foot traffic less. Cae made good time in his navigations, only once taking a wrong turn, before finally fetching up at the front gate of Cietena Alu Nyas's townhouse.

At first glance, there was nothing special to distinguish it from its neighbours: a high stone wall ran the length of the street, interspersed with wood or metal gates to the various two- and three-storey properties, all of which were set behind courtyards or gardens to give the residents greater privacy. But as Cae looked closer, he could see, not the disrepair he'd expected, but signs of recent prosperity. The wrought-iron gates were newly painted, while the garden beyond showed signs of reordering, with freshly dug soil showing places where new plants were yet to go, or where old ones had been ripped out. Shiny new paving stones lined the path from the gate to the door, which bore a glossy coat of brilliant red paint, and when Cae rang the gate-bell for admittance, it too appeared to be new, the bright brass untouched by so much as a speck of tarnish, while the pull-rope was sparkling white.

After less than a minute, a servant emerged from a side door and bustled down the path towards Cae. It was a young girl, her livery crisp and new beneath an equally unblemished apron, and her eyes widened at the sight of Cae, who guessed her to be no more than sixteen.

"May I help you, ren?" she asked, a little breathlessly.

Cae smiled at her. "My name is Yaseran Caethari Aeduria. I know I'm not expected, but I was hoping I might speak to Cietena Alu Nyas? I'll happily wait."

"Oh!" The maid's hands flew to her mouth, then dropped again, twisting in the apron fabric. "Oh, yaseran, I'm—I'm so sorry, but my mistress hasn't risen yet, and I'm—we are, I mean, the new staff—we're under strict instructions not to wake her for anything, as she doesn't sleep well most nights, and—is there any chance you could leave a card and call again later?"

"I'm afraid not," said Cae, injecting as much regretful apology into the words as possible. He considered leading with the missing palace token, but as he didn't have the item itself to prove that it had gone missing from the house—and as he didn't want to be viewed as hostile by the staff—he opted to take a different tack.

Coaxingly, he said, "The cietena's lands adjourn the city of Qi-Katai, which is my family's territory, and I have news of recent political developments that should be to her financial advantage. I understand you shouldn't wake her normally, but under the circumstances, might you make an exception?"

The maid looked so anxious at this, Cae worried he'd pushed too hard, too soon and would be turned away—saints, he wasn't good at this sort of thing! But after a moment, she gave a tremulous nod and unlocked the gate, admitting him.

"You can wait in the foyer," she said, "if—if that's all right, yaseran? She might yet wake soon, and if not, I'll ask the housekeeper what to do. She's been here longest," she added, at Cae's look of incomprehension, "and, well, it's not that she's in charge of visitors, but she is in charge of us, and she knows the mistress best!"

"How long have you worked for the cietena?" Cae asked.

The maid lit up at the question. "Oh, only a few weeks!" she gushed, opening the main door. "It's such a good opportunity, and seeing all the work done on the house has been so exciting, tradesfolk coming in and out, and so much food! It used to be only the housekeeper on staff, but now there's me and the gardener and the errand-boy, too, so I haven't felt even a bit lonely!" She kept up this patter as she led Cae through the foyer and into a receiving room which, like the house's exterior, showed clear signs of recent renovation. These changes, however, were still incomplete, betraying the poor state in which things had previously been kept. Brighter patches on the otherwise faded walls betrayed the removal of artworks that were yet to be replaced, the paint visibly peeling in places. The couch on which Cae sat boasted several new cushions, but the fabric of the seat itself was threadbare, in dire need of reupholstering. Everywhere he looked, the signs of longstanding genteel poverty were being progressively overwritten by new prosperity, and after everything Ru Kisian had said, he wondered at its source.

With Caethari seated, the maid asked if she could bring him anything to eat or drink—he declined for the moment, uncertain of how long he might be kept waiting—reiterated her need to seek the housekeeper's council and then hurried off to do just that. Barely two minutes later, she returned in the tow of the housekeeper, a stern, compact woman who was seventy if she was a day, her white hair primly braided in a low knot.

"Yaseran," she said, her deep voice scratchy with age. "Your visit is unexpected, but I do not think it will be unwelcome, once my mistress has risen for the day."

"I'm glad to hear it," said Cae.

"Have you been offered refreshments?"

"I have."

The housekeeper cast an approving look at the maid. "Very good. In that case, if you are content to wait, I hope you won't think us poor hosts if we attend to our chores?"

"Not at all," said Cae.

Thus assuaged, the housekeeper bowed and led the maid out again, leaving Cae to settle in on the couch. He could hear the servants bustling to and fro in the kitchen, or occasionally catch a glimpse of them as they went past the doorway that led to the downstairs hall, but otherwise, he was left to his own devices. At one point, a child Cae assumed was the errand-boy poked his head around the corner and goggled quietly at him before a sturdy, middle-aged man who must've been the gardener grabbed him by the ear, shot Cae an apologetic glance and dragged the boy away.

This was more amusing than upsetting, though as with everything else, it made Cae wonder at the cietena's apparent change in finances, that she could afford to hire three new servants. He was trying hard not to leap to conclusions about her role in the attack on Vel—with the household in a state of flux, it was entirely possible that some visitor had stolen her palace token, its absence as yet unnoticed given her infrequent appearances at court—but the longer he was left waiting, the more on edge he felt. His gaze kept straying to the main staircase, which led to the second floor from the opposite side of the foyer. The cietena's rooms would be upstairs, along with the cietena herself, and the more time passed, the more tempted Cae was to simply disregard propriety, head up and knock.

He'd been waiting for the better part of twenty minutes when there came a sudden commotion from the hallway.

"It's back!" the errand-boy shouted. "I heard it just now, I swear it's back!"

Whatever *it* referred to was evidently important enough to bring all four servants hurrying out of the kitchen.

"Are you sure?" asked the housekeeper, the maid hovering anxiously at her elbow.

"Yes!" the boy cried. "Yes, I swear, I *swear*—"

"Show us, then," said the gardener. "Whatever it is, it's not having any more of my leeks!" And with that, all four headed off in the same direction, towards the kitchens and, to judge from the distant sound of a door banging open and the remark about leeks, the rear garden.

Cae sat a moment, ears straining, but could hear nothing further. He was, he realised, completely alone; if he wanted to see the cietena before General Naza swooped in to question her, then this was his chance. If anyone caught him wandering around, he could always claim he'd been looking for a bathroom, which was slightly gauche but theoretically plausible, and so, before he could second-guess himself, he rose from the couch and padded up the stairs, which creaked underfoot despite their carpeting.

The second floor was shabbier than anything he'd seen in the foyer; evidently, the cietena's refurbishments were yet to reach this far. The first two rooms he tried were both unlocked, full of furniture covered in dust sheets and boxes of who knows what, while the third was indeed a bathroom. This left the fourth door at the end of the hall, and as he approached it, Cae felt an odd lurch of anxiety. He was, after all, violating several firmly established social conventions about how to behave as a guest, and he had no proof that the cietena was actually involved. If it hadn't been a matter of his husband's safety, he would've turned around and gone straight back downstairs, but as it was, he forced himself to keep going.

He knocked on the door before trying the handle. "Cietena?" he called. "It's Yaseran Caethari Aeduria. I need to speak with you."

No answer.

Swallowing hard, Cae knocked again, and after several more seconds of silence, he gave in and twisted the handle.

The scent of fresh death hit him before he even saw the body, waved towards him by the breeze coming in through the wide-open bedroom window, beside which stood a dresser whose various drawers were all half-open, the contents either spilling out or already on the floor. And in the centre of the room, a shrunken elderly woman in an outdated, Ralian-style nightgown lay sprawled in bed, a spreading pool of blood soaking the mattress and blankets. Her sightless eyes were open, and embedded in her chest—

Cae froze, his body going numb.

Embedded in the cietena's chest was his missing jade-handled dagger.

White noise rushed through Cae's ears. He knew he ought to leave, to get back downstairs at the least and out of the house at best, but even if he escaped before the body was found—and even if his conscience would allow him to leave the dead woman for her servants to find—the dagger implicated him in a way he was yet too stunned to process. Nobody here would know it was his, but that didn't matter: if the murderer had gone to the trouble of using it, then they meant for it to be found by someone who could link it to Cae—and he, all unknowing, had managed to show up and implicate himself anyway. He took an involuntary step closer, half because of the dagger and half to get a better look at the body. With how thirstily the bedding had sopped up the blood, it was hard to tell how recently she'd been killed; what was clear, however, was that she had to have been struck at least twice to have bled out so much, or else the unwithdrawn blade would've served as a makeshift stopper.

Go, Cae urged himself, *leave, go now,* but he'd already visited the house, the staff would know he'd been out of sight for long enough to have slain a sleeping woman, and the dagger was *his,* which meant that, even if he did the sensible thing and called out for help, he'd still be suspected later. If he ran, he had to run with the dagger, but running, too, would make him look guilty. *Fuck.*

Feet moving of their own accord, he found himself at the cietena's bedside. He stared at the dagger's handle, hating himself for having lost it in the first place. When had it been taken from him, and by whom? Had he dropped it on the way back from the party, or left it in the grass by the maze's hot spring? Or had it been lifted from his belt by some light-fingered soul even earlier than that, and he hadn't noticed?

His fingers flexed, wanting to reach for it, but before he could decide whether to reclaim it or not, a piercing scream broke the oppressive silence of the dead woman's room. Cae turned, silently cursing the trap in which he'd found himself. In the doorway stood the wide-eyed maid, her slim hands clapped to her mouth in shock—and beside her stood General Naza, a sword at his hip and a darkly triumphant smile on his face.

"Yaseran Caethari Aeduria," he intoned, "by the investigative authority placed in me by Her Majesty Asa Ivadi Ruqai, I'm arresting you on suspicion of murder."

For a fleeting instant, Cae considered resisting. He could grab his dagger and jump from the open window, or else take his chances with the general one-on-one and hope in either instance that there weren't more guards waiting outside. But even if he'd succeeded, that would've made him a fugitive from the palace, and as a fugitive, he'd have no chance at all to see Vel.

"I cooperate," Cae said, as calmly as could. He proffered his hands as the general approached and pitched his voice to carry. "But I didn't do this."

"I'll be the judge of that," said General Naza, and under the terrified gaze of the weeping maid, he cuffed Cae's wrists.

Part Five

VELASIN

21

Historically, I have never been a good patient. It's not that anyone truly enjoys recovering from illness or injury, but some are better able to tolerate it than others, and I'm atrocious at sitting idle. Kept confined without occupation, I grow fractious, and while I'm rationally aware that medical advice exists for a reason, once I'm through the worst of whatever's ailing me at a given moment, I can never quite remember what it is. As such, once Ru Saeri had stopped by, worked her restorative magic on my person and then left again, despite her insistence that I spend the day abed, I immediately made a nuisance of myself to Markel by insisting on getting dressed.

"You don't need clothes," he signed at me emphatically. "You need to *lie down*."

"I can be dressed for that, surely," I retorted. "What if we have visitors?"

"Then you can either greet them from under the blankets, or I can chase them off."

"What if I want to sit instead?"

"You're too tired for sitting."

"I'm not tired," I said, which was only half a lie. My body was tired, yes, but my mind was desperately awake, and with Cae dispatched to investigate the potential link between Cietena Alu Nyas and Syana, I was filled with a strange, buzzing need to contribute.

In the end, we compromised: Markel allowed me the dignity of smallclothes and a clean, soft pair of nara, but otherwise, I was to stay in my robe. With this done, I submitted to being herded back to bed, lying down atop the covers as if in parody of noble decadence. I didn't stay there for long, however: the instant my stomach rumbled, and despite Markel's offer to bring me a tray, I rose and went to the table in our living space, helping myself to the frankly obscene amount of food my friend had snuck out to acquire during Ru Saeri's visit. I'd eaten some earlier, too, but with the amount of healing I'd so recently undergone, the ru had advised me to eat frequent small meals to replenish my energy, and I found this to be no hardship. Even so, the act of chewing and swallowing pulled slightly at the still-tender scar on my throat—not painfully so, but enough that I noticed—and I felt a pang of pointless vanity over it. More practically, I wasn't looking forward to having to shave around the scar, but that, at least, was a problem I could postpone for a day or so more, and so I forced myself to focus on the positive, like the fact that I was alive at all.

I'd just set aside my plate when there was a knock at the apartment door. Markel shot me a look which very clearly expressed his preference for a lack of socialisation, and which I returned with a stubborn look of my own. Sighing, Markel conceded defeat and went to answer the door, which turned out to have Tiern Ethin and Ciet Yarasil on the other side of it. Rather than receive them at the table, I stood to welcome them in and then ensconced myself on the settee, gesturing for my young visitors to avail themselves of the chairs. As they did so with puppyish eagerness, Markel shot me a pointed look before melting into the background, taking up an unobtrusive servant's posture off to the side.

"We're so glad to see you well!" said Ethin, once I'd thanked them for visiting and they'd both vehemently insisted I be informal with them, prompting me to extend the same offer in return. "Irias is coming, too, he just had to see to some family business first, but we didn't feel we could wait." He then proffered me a bouquet of crocuses and snapdragons, beautifully wrapped with a blue silk ribbon. "These are from all of us," he said. "To cheer you as you recover."

"Oh!" I said, surprised. Of course I'd noticed the flowers, but had assumed in an offhand way that they must've been given to him by an admirer. More flustered than I'd have liked to be in response to such a kind and simple gesture, I inhaled their scent, then passed them to Markel with instructions to find them a vase of water, which he promptly set about doing, before offering thanks to my guests.

"It was the least we could do," said Yarasil, pleased. "Really, though, it was all Ethin."

"It was not!" Ethin said, smacking his friend on the shoulder, though his cheeks had visibly warmed. And then, to me, "Truly, it was a group effort."

"I believe you," I said, and offered what I hoped was a welcoming smile. I had precious few allies at court, and I wasn't about to turn down potential friendships on the basis of youth, least of all when Yarasil's steady hands had helped to save my life. I looked at him, assessing: he was exquisitely favoured, his dark eyes huge in his delicate face, but though he was trying hard to present himself as an eager, attentive guest, there was something faintly haunted in his expression.

"And how are you, Yarasil?" I asked, as gently as I could.

"I'm well," he said—too quickly, the words coming out in a gulp. "Very well, very glad to have helped—"

"I don't doubt your word," I said, "but if you didn't feel well at any point, that would be deeply understandable. I don't remember much of what happened, but had our positions been reversed, I doubt I'd have been sober for the next week. Not that *you* ought to be drunk," I added hastily, when Yarasil jerked in his seat. "I just mean, I tend to be stupid about these things, and too much wine is an excellent way to be stupid. Probably it would be more sensible to go for a walk, or talk to someone, or—" Moons, what would Cae do? "—swing a sword around until you feel better. I just." I came to a rambling halt and offered what I hoped was an encouraging smile. "I am grateful to you, and as such, I would hate to see you suffer for your kindness."

"I—thank you," Yarasil stammered.

"Velasin is right," said Ethin, setting a hand on his friend's shoulder. "You can always talk to me or Irias."

He was trying to look serious and dependable, but radiated so much earnestness that I almost laughed, not because I thought any less of him, but in fond amusement of youth's perpetual inability to perceive itself as such. Biting my lip against the impulse, I steered the conversation towards gentler waters, offering them such food as was available and asking after their families. This carried us through several minutes of pleasantries, until Ethin coughed and ventured, "You were sorely missed at the party last night."

I smiled wryly. "Believe me, I'd have preferred to be there, too."

"It's just—" Ethin hesitated, glancing at Yarasil and then back to me. "—well. I don't want to gossip, but the yaseran . . ." He lowered his voice and his lashes both. "He, well. He vanished into the maze with Asrien, and we never saw him afterwards, and—truly, I don't mean to make you worry, especially not with everything else going on, but if it were *my* husband who'd done such a thing, I'd want to know about it."

His tone held no malice, his face full of the same earnest concern he'd deployed against Yarasil. Even so, I felt a slight pang at the slander to Cae, but took care not to show it.

"It's all right," I said instead, smiling. "My thanks for your concern, but truly, I've no cause to doubt him."

"Are you sure of that?" Ethin pressed—reflexively, it seemed, for in the next instant he flustered badly, cheeks burning as he raised a mortified hand to his mouth. "I'm sorry!" he said, and then flushed all the harder as his voice cracked on the words, prompting Yarasil to stifle a snort of laughter. "I'm sorry, truly, I just—you've been wed so little time, and under such strange circumstances, and—and someone keeps trying to kill you! And here you were, lying sick abed, and he was out at a *party,* and—and you deserve better treatment than that." He bit his lip, then added, a little shakily, "I'd certainly never treat my husband that way."

For a moment, I was dumbfounded, wondering whether I could afford to show offence, or if this meant Ethin was part of one of the factions opposed to the Ralian alliance—but then his throat bobbed, and he looked at me through his lashes again, and I realised, with a belated and embarrassed burst of clarity, that the answer was much simpler than that: the young tiern was enamoured of me.

Oh no, I thought faintly, distantly aware that my own cheeks, too, had warmed. It was very much a new experience for me: always in the past, I'd been the pretty young thing making eyes at the worldly older man, and yet now, somehow, I'd wound up on the opposite side of that equation without noticing. A sudden flipbook of my limited interactions with Ethin played through my head: we'd spoken at the riverbank, and when the bridge broke, in a fit of idiot heroism, I'd leapt in to save him. Cae and I had then vanished before he could thank us, and when he'd next seen us again, I'd ended up with my throat cut, Ethin standing by as Yarasil saved me, and then Cae's attendance at the party had made him think that, on top of everything else, I was being undervalued by the husband I'd married for duty.

Put like that, it was all very dramatic: exactly the sort of thing to stir the heart of a young romantic—which, judging by the flowers that I now realised he'd absolutely chosen for me, Ethin clearly was.

"Oh," I said aloud—stammered, really. Moons, this was mortifying! If it had been political, I might've known how to react, but as it was, in addition to being just a tiny bit flattered, I was embarrassed for the both of us. "Oh, that's—I mean, ah—"

Mercifully, whatever I'd been failing to say was interrupted by a knock at the door, which Yarasil, quietly dying at our mutual awkwardness, positively leapt to answer. "That'll be Irias!" he exclaimed, and was proven correct in short order. Irias, for his part, looked wild-eyed and out of breath as he entered, and all at once, a tingle of foreboding prickled the nape of my neck.

"Oh gods, Tiern Velasin!" he cried. "I'm sorry, I came as fast as

I could—I was on my way here when I saw, I heard—that is, your yaseran's been arrested for murder!"

Time froze around me, thick and viscous as winter honey. "I'm sorry," I said faintly, heartbeat loud in my ears. "Can you repeat that?"

"General Naza just marched him in himself, in handcuffs! The gate guards asked why he was bound, and he told them, *for the murder of Cietena Alu Nyas,* and I didn't stay long enough to hear anything else, I just ran right here!"

I wasn't conscious of standing, but I must've done, because suddenly I was surrounded by people, Markel and the lordling trio blocking my path to the door. I felt as if I were somehow outside my body, fear and anger building in me like stormclouds. Cae was a soldier, perfectly capable of killing in self-defence or on a battlefield, but murder? That, I knew for a lie—which meant that Caethari was once more in danger on my account.

"Tiern Velasin!" said Ethin, in a tone that suggested he'd spoken several times already. He took hold of my forearm, gentle but insistent, and in a distant part of my mind, I noticed how much it spoke to the situation, that Markel didn't stop him. My body thrummed like a bowstring aching for release as he said, "Please, let us be your agents in this. Tell us what we can do for you—" Yarasil and Irias nodded furiously, overlapping each other with urgently voiced agreement. "—and we'll do it."

Focus, I tried to tell myself. *Be sensible. Use the tools at your disposal.*

Aloud, I rasped, "Where can I find the asa?"

The lordlings exchanged nervous glances.

"*Where?*"

"This time of day, I'd imagine she's in her receiving rooms in the Little Palace," Ethin ventured nervously. "But—"

"Could your grandmother help me?"

He hesitated. "Are you—that is, I don't mean, but—are you absolutely sure of the yaseran's innocence?"

Rather than answer such an absurd and insulting question, I simply stared at him. His throat bobbed as he swallowed, and he hurried on with, "That is, I can't promise anything, but I can certainly ask her!"

"Please do," I said. It came out almost like an order, and Ethin nodded quickly.

"What about us?" asked Yarasil, standing shoulder-to-shoulder with Irias. "We want to help, too."

For a moment, the scar on my throat seemed to pulse. *Syana,* I thought, heart racing. *This all comes back to Syana.* If the cietena had truly paid Syana to kill me, then the trail was cold—but if nobody else was involved, then who had killed her in turn, and why? Had they framed Cae on purpose, or was it just a question of bad timing? Either way, with Alu Nyas dead, I was grudgingly forced to admit that, were I in General Naza's shoes, I wouldn't be rushing to look for additional culprits, either. He'd already suspected Cae of Syana's death, and with Cae now implicated in the murder of her putative employer, from an outside perspective, it all looked neatly wrapped up.

But I knew beyond proof that Cae, my Cae, would not have poisoned Syana or murdered Alu Nyas, which meant that whoever had murdered them was still at large; which meant, in turn, that I badly needed to know where Syana had come from. If she'd truly been employed by Alu Nyas, then their murderer might be an additional accomplice; but if she'd been sent by someone else entirely, the choice of palace token either incidental or meant to throw off the scent—

"All right," I said slowly, thoughts whirling. "All right. The woman who attacked me yesterday, Syana—do you remember what she looked like?"

"Yes," said Irias, and promptly rattled off a surprisingly detailed description of both her and the clothes she'd worn, which had been mercifully distinctive. I nodded at him.

"I need you to find where she came from," I said. "Never mind who got her into the palace—where was she before then? Looking like that, someone must've seen her, remembered her."

"Where do we start?" asked Yarasil.

"The Stagger," I replied. "Ask at inns, at food stalls—anywhere she might've been seen or stayed before she came here." I paused, remembering something, and glanced at Markel for confirmation. "You said Syana arrived at the palace about an hour after the asa announced an open court?"

Markel nodded. "That's what the gate guards said."

"And I'm assuming the whole city isn't notified when there's an open court?"

"Yes and no," said Ethin quickly, visibly burning to be of use. "It's announced throughout the palace, but there's a green banner flown over the main gates to let outsiders know, and there's runners who keep watch to report to certain families or figures in case they want to attend. So it's always possible to find out—"

"—but the further you are from the palace, the longer it takes," I finished. "So she must've been close, or else she wouldn't have arrived so soon. It's a long shot, I know, but we need to start somewhere, and right now, I don't know anything."

"Leave it to us," said Irias, clapping Yarasil on the shoulder. "We'll find out, tiern, I promise!"

"And I'll talk to my grandmother," Ethin added.

"My thanks," I said, and moved with them towards the door.

"Wait," said Ethin, surprised. "You're not staying here?"

"Of course not," I said, a renewed urgency burning through me. I'd done the responsible thing by pausing to assign tasks and confer with my allies, and that meant I was now free to do what I wanted. "I'm going to get my husband back."

"Please," signed Markel, hands high as he once more blocked my path. "Velasin, be reasonable. You're nowhere near fully recovered, and Caethari won't be in any immediate danger. He's a yaseran, they won't dare harm him, not while he's in custody—"

"*Won't dare harm him?*" I hissed, incredulous. It was as sharply as I'd spoken to Markel in I didn't know how long, and the shock of it showed on his face. "Someone tried to *drown* him last night, and he already stands suspected of killing Syana. No, no; whoever this is, they very much dare, and I will not have it. I will *not*!"

"All right, all right," Markel signed frantically, back-stepping as I moved forwards. "That was a stupid thing to say, he's clearly in danger. But so are *you*! You need to stay here and heal—Velasin, you're not even dressed!"

"And whose fault is that?" I demanded.

"At least put some shoes on," Markel signed frantically. "You can't see the asa barefoot!"

Wretchedly, this was a decent point—though not, I realised, as vital a one as if we'd still been in Ralia. Were a courtier of my standing to appear half-dressed and dishevelled before King Markus, regardless of the context, their grandchildren would still be answering for the scandal; but this was Tithena, which had wholly different notions of modesty and deportment. Back in Qi-Katai, I'd once seen Cae stroll through the Aida wearing nothing but a towel, and while the standards in Qi-Xihan were surely a *little* more stringent, I had a sense—potentially guided by my own impatience, but a sense nonetheless—that I'd win myself more sympathy by reminding the court of my recent near-death than by attempting to look presentable.

All this passed through my head in a flash. I nodded jerkily. "Slippers, then," I said, not having the patience necessary to endure the lacing of boots, and waited fractiously in place as Markel scrambled to find them. They were soft, exquisite things, lined on the inside with rabbit fur, but still sufficiently soled to survive a jaunt outside. I slipped them on with a muttered curse as one caught on my heel, balanced precariously on one foot to tug it straight, then lurched upright again.

Stomach roiling, I stormed out into the hallway, only vaguely aware of Markel and the trio of lordlings scrambling in my wake. My slippers slapped softly against the marble floor, and I'd made

considerable forward progress before realising that, having been
unconscious yesterday, I had no idea how to get to where I wanted.
I came to a halt, heart pounding in my chest, and found myself
surrounded by a cluster of anxious faces.

"Well?" I snapped, rather churlishly. "Are you helping or not?"

"We are!" insisted Ethin, and quickly dragged his friends away,
the three of them hurrying off in the opposite direction.

Markel watched them go, then signed, "I don't suppose you'll
reconsider this?"

"No," I said firmly. And then, because he still looked worried
and my heart had lodged itself somewhere high in my throat,
"Markel, I can't let something else happen to him on my account.
I *can't.*"

Sighing, Markel nodded. "Where do you want to go, then?"

I set my jaw. Possibly there were subtler options, but I didn't
know enough of Qi-Xihan's politics to be sure of what they were,
and in the moment, I could think of only one person with the authority to overrule General Naza.

"Take me to the asa," I said. "To her receiving rooms in the
Little Palace, wherever that is." I hesitated. "Do you know where
that is?"

"I can find out," signed Markel. "Why don't you go back to the
suite, and—"

I started walking again, and he broke off, walking quickly to
keep pace with me. He shot me an exasperated look, but didn't
argue, concentrating instead on navigating through the palace.
Though he was ostensibly in the lead, it was I who set the pace, and
a faster one than was strictly advisable under the circumstances.
I knew in a distant way that I was being absurd—that there was
wisdom in having Markel go and assess the lay of the land before
leaping in myself—and yet it changed nothing. The whole time I'd
been talking to Ethin, Yarasil and Irias, I'd felt like my heart would
beat out of my chest, I was so worried for Cae. Now as in Qi-Katai,
he was being targeted because of his marriage to me, and I couldn't

bear it. The image of him hurt or restrained kept playing through my mind, urging me on despite the increasing protests of my body, and the farther Markel led me, the more urgent it felt.

By the time we arrived at the Little Palace, I was lathered in sweat, my skin cold and clammy to the touch. My ears rang faintly, my pulse erratic, and as it fell to me, wide-eyed and frantic, to explain our business with the asa to the duty guards, I'm sure I must've looked an utter spectacle.

"I am Tiern Velasin Aeduria, husband to Yaseran Caethari Aeduria," I said, my voice pitched somewhere between angry and hysterical, "and I need to see the asa *now*."

The guards exchanged looks which communicated more clearly than words their belief that I was a madman. Nobility and madness, however, are far from being mutually exclusive states, and as I was already within the palace grounds—albeit dishabille, panting and half-crazed—and as, more to the point, Markel had had the presence of mind to bring along my palace token, which they were able to scan with a wand like the one I'd first seen at the palace gates— they didn't turn us away.

Instead, the taller guard looked at me and said, "You're expected. This way, please."

I was too grateful at being let in to think much about how and why a spontaneous visit should've been anticipated; too grateful, and too tired. My legs were wobbly as we proceeded into the Little Palace; I swayed on my feet, and Markel grabbed my arm to keep me upright, flashing me a look of worried reproach I pretended not to see.

"I'm fine," I muttered, though I had enough sense to keep leaning on him.

After passing through a hallway and several doors, we arrived in a circular room. The gently curved walls were painted with detailed murals of what I took to be scenes from Tithenai history, while the centre of the room was dominated by a suite of green velvet couches arranged in a semicircle beneath the glass dome of the roof. A single chair, slightly larger than the others, was set in the middle, in which sat Asa Ivadi, looking every bit as regal as she had the day before. On her right was Ru Kisian Faez, the Velvet Chair, his brow furrowed with worry; Ciet Nevan, equally distressed; and a handsome, sharp-jawed kem with russet hair, a sly quirk to thir mouth and dark, clever eyes. Seeing me glance at thim, Markel tugged my arm to get my attention and released me just long enough to sign discreetly, "Yasai Qiqa Ykran."

I nodded thanks, but absently so, as my attention had already swung to the singular figure at the asa's right: General Naza, his hulking physique almost comically oversized compared to the delicate couch on which he sat.

My vision briefly whited out, though whether from rage or exhaustion I couldn't have said; only that, when I came back to myself, I'd reached the centre of the room and was staring down General Naza.

"Give him back," I said, shaking. "Caethari has done nothing."

The general looked me up and down, as if I were a particularly fascinating insect he'd found in his bedroll. "Whatever he has or hasn't done, you've hardly been in a fit state to have witnessed it. And," he growled, interrupting my nascent protest, "invalid or not, you'd do well to remember your manners before the asa."

My open mouth snapped shut. Stifling a curse, I turned to face Asa Ivadi, whose shrewd gaze regarded me with neither pleasure nor hostility. Gracelessly, I fumbled myself to one knee—very nearly falling over in the process, as I recalled at the last possible second that Tithenai knelt opposite to Ralians, and my strength was quite depleted—and bowed low with a hand to my heart, blood rushing to my head.

"Asa Ivadi," I rasped. "I beg you, please. My husband is being framed. He would not do this. He did not do this." And then, the imploring words wrenched from me as I looked up once more, "Please, release him."

The asa's hands shifted minutely where they were folded in her lap. A slice of sunlight fell on her from the overhead dome, limning her in a glow that picked up the subtle golds in her brocade silk halik. In that dry, unreadable voice, she said, "Having delegated the investigation of these attacks to General Naza, and having no reason to doubt his competence, I would be a poor monarch to overrule him on a whim."

"I thank the asa for her trust," rumbled General Naza, glowering in my direction. "Tiern Velasin, you have no *proof.* As touching as your faith in your husband is, that faith is not a defence that any reasonable soul would accept, least of all in light of the evidence against him." He began to tick his words off on his fingers. "Last night, he vanished from Tierena Keris's gathering during the period of time in which the prisoner Syana was poisoned, his whereabouts unaccounted for. This morning, he was found standing over the body of Cietena Alu Nyas, whose palace token was used to admit Syana—again within the window in which her murder took place—with his knife in the victim's chest. He had means, motive and opportunity: namely, seeking revenge for the attempt on your life. I'd be a fool not to suspect him."

My head swam. Markel, having followed my lead, was now kneeling behind and to the side of me—on both knees, as a Ralian servant would, but close enough that, when I began to waver, his hand shot out to support my elbow. Thus steadied, I grasped angrily for my words and said, "You say that he was unaccounted for last night, but as we both told you this morning, someone drugged and tried to kill him at the tierena's party! What of that?" I swung my gaze to Yasai Qiqa Ykran and said, "Is that not so, yasai?"

"It is," said the yasai, inclining thir head. All eyes swung to thim, but if thei were perturbed the sudden attention, thei didn't show it. Glancing at the asa, thei said, "The yaseran was drowning in the hot spring when I found him. I brought him out and helped him home."

General Naza scoffed. "All that proves is that Caethari was drunk and foolish. Unless you've some proof of his drugging or a description of his supposed assailant to offer, we've only his word that anything untoward happened."

"And is a yaseran's word worth nothing, then?" I snapped. "Or mine? Do you doubt the attempts on our lives that have followed us the whole way to Qi-Xihan? Your prejudice against Ralia is one thing, General, but it ill serves this investigation if you prejudge the matter a simple one on the basis of which outcome best suits your politics."

General Naza tensed. "And what right have you, to accuse me of malfeasance?" he snarled.

"I have every right, as your incompetence is imperilling my husband!" I shot back. "The asa charged you with this task, but you've made no use of her resources. Had you bothered to interview Syana when she was still alive, you might've learned for yourself who her master was—but you didn't, did you?" I swung my free arm to indicate the palace at large and only just managed to keep from toppling over at the gesture. "No! You've insisted on moving at snail's pace, doing everything yourself instead of delegating so much as a single interview to anyone in the asa's employ, swinging your cock about rather than getting things done!" I was shouting now, trembling with the effort of it as the general's expression turned ever more outraged. "If you truly believed Cae guilty of Syana's murder, why waste your precious time threatening us this morning? Why, if you believed he posed a real danger, would you have let him leave the palace grounds in the first place? It would've been a simple thing, to restrict his movements; simpler still to have sought out Cietena Alu Nyas before Cae had time to find her house—but you didn't know to look for her then, did you?" I laughed harshly. "How long did it take you to interview the gate guards and see whose palace token Syana used to gain entry in the first place? Either you knew yesterday and were lax about following up the lead, or else you didn't get to it until today—but either way, General, the choice reflects poorly on you. Because I promise you, I swear by the moons and your wretched saints, Caethari has killed nobody, and had you acted sooner to protect the cietena from the real threat—had you taken better care of your prisoner, too, come to that—we would not now be arguing the cost of your inadequacies!"

The general shot to his feet, stung, and for a dizzying moment where my ears rang and my vision whited, I thought he must've struck me, only to realise in the next instant that I was simply feeling the effects of how badly I'd overexerted myself.

"Sit *down,* General," ordered Asa Ivadi. "The tiern might be overwrought, but he's not wholly wrong. I put my resources at your disposal in this matter, and your failure to utilise them is both conspicuous and embarrassing."

General Naza looked furious, but inclined his head in acceptance of the chastisement and sat again, hands fisted on his knees. "My apologies, asa. I take full responsibility."

"As well you should," she replied, and flicked her gaze to me. "That being said, Tiern Velasin, the general's errors are not the chief factor in play here. The cietena was killed with your husband's knife, and he was found standing over her body. Such a matter must be thoroughly investigated—as must the apparent involvement of Cietena Alu Nyas in the attempt on your life. That her palace token was evidently used to admit the murderer doesn't prove she was a willing co-conspirator, and as the issue of her guilt has bearing on the distribution of her estate, I would not see her condemned without fair cause."

Behind me, I heard the doors open, and a carrying female voice said, "I believe I may shed some light on this matter, asa."

I turned my head and watched the approach of an authoritative-looking woman in a gold and burgundy halik, her brown and silver hair coiled around her head in a braided crown. As Ethin hurried in at her heels, I realised this was Tierena Keris Talae. Her amber eyes widened slightly as she took me in, prompting me to retie my gaping robe—moons, I really had made a spectacle of myself!— but didn't linger on me, gaze snapping instead to Asa Ivadi.

"Keris," the asa said, acknowledging the tierena's bow. "I will be glad of whatever context you can offer. However—" and here she looked at me, "—perhaps someone might first find Tiern Velasin a chair?"

"I'll help!" said Ethin, hurrying forwards. He fumbled out a bow to the asa, then took my free arm and, with Markel's help on the other side, levered me upright. I'm ashamed to say I swayed between them, leaning heavily on Markel as Ethin led me over to an unoccupied couch to the asa's left, adjacent to the one occupied by Ciet Nevan, Ru Kisian and Yasai Qiqa. Markel, of course, would hardly be permitted to sit beside me, and yet I suppressed a wince as he knelt by the armrest, supporting me there as Ethin claimed the space to my right.

"Thank you," I murmured to him, reclaiming my arm to sign the same to Markel.

"I came as fast as I could," whispered Ethin, and then fell silent as his grandmother began to speak.

"As I believe Ru Kisian can affirm," said the tierena, "Cietena Alu Nyas was the mistress of various lands and properties within the jurisdiction of Qi-Katai; lands which have been greatly diminished in both upkeep and value since Ralian aggression killed trade through the Taelic Pass." She paused, shooting me an oddly sympathetic look, before continuing. "As such, and assuming Ralia chooses to honor their alliance, the cietena would have stood to benefit directly from Yaseran Caethari's marriage to Tiern Velasin."

"That seems a bold assumption to make," interjected General Naza, "given Ralian pigheadedness around unions between men."

The tierena made a long-suffering noise and shot him a look of profound disappointment. "I say *would have,* not because the cietena is dead, but because she sold those lands not long before the alliance was formalised."

A murmur of surprise ran through the room, led chiefly, to my surprise, by Ru Kisian, who'd been silent until that point. "Are you sure?" he exclaimed, looking shocked. "What—that is, I don't mean to doubt you, but I've heard nothing, seen nothing to this effect—" He broke off, swallowed, and then said, "Is the identity of the buyer known?"

"That is yet to be determined," replied the tierena. "Indeed, I only became aware of the sale quite recently, and secondhand— evidently, she was using the money to finance a grand refurbishment of her home." She sighed. "I didn't know her well, but from what I gather, Alu Nyas was a proud woman. She didn't like to be perceived as living in reduced circumstances, and so she'd grown distant from her former social circles—meaning, she was unlikely to have known about the alliance before it happened. But when the sale restored her finances, she began to venture out again, at which point—"

Yasai Qiqa finished the thought with a click of thir teeth. "— she would've learned about the marriage, and the value she'd just lost."

"A cruel twist," murmured Ciet Nevan. I was hardly one to talk, but he looked drawn, pinched and unhappy around the mouth.

"None of this proves her guilty of the attempt on Tiern Velasin's life, of course," said Tierena Keris. "But were she involved, it might explain her motive."

"But if she felt sufficiently hard-pressed to have sold her ancestral holdings," Ru Kisian countered, "who's to say she didn't sell other things, first? Say, her palace token, hm? Such sales are forbidden, of course, but that's never stopped anyone sufficiently desperate."

I smiled sharply at General Naza. "Tell me, General—have you interviewed the cietena's household staff yet? Or is that yet another task you felt unable to delegate?"

The general met my look with a boiling glare. "Under the circumstances, tiern, it felt more important to arrest the man standing over the body than to hang around chatting."

"That's a no, then."

"Enough!" Asa Ivadi flung up a hand, forestalling General Naza's reply, and glanced between us with all the exasperation of a teacher confronted with two quarrelling students. "Tiern Velasin,

362 · *Foz Meadows*

your point is well-made, but on my authority, until he is either cleared of blame or another suspect presents themselves, your husband must remain in custody; that is how the law works. And you, General Naza, *will* make use of my people and report their findings and yours with all due haste, or else I will rescind your authority in this matter. Am I understood?"

"Yes, asa," I said, bowing from the waist, as the general muttered the same. I hesitated a moment, then said, unable to keep the pleading tone from my voice, "May I at least see him?"

Something in the asa's expression softened. "You may," she said, "but briefly, and under supervision."

I exhaled hard and bowed forwards again, as much in thanks as because I was in danger of fainting. I felt wobbly and unmoored, a keelless boat set loose upon a choppy sea, and in that moment, I was achingly conscious, not only of my physical vulnerability, but of the pitying looks of everyone around me. Had I more strength, the pity would've angered me, but as it was, I felt only relief at the prospect of seeing Cae. Inhaling deep, I lifted my head with tremulous effort and met the asa's gaze.

"Thank you," I whispered.

22

Exhausted though I was, I insisted on seeing Cae straight-away, refusing all suggestions—and there were several—that I rest and recompose myself first, unable to trust that something wouldn't happen to him in the interim. Markel clearly wanted to join in on the scolding, but aside from any concerns about betraying our relationship to be more familial than that of servant and master, his hands were firmly preoccupied with the difficult task of keeping me upright, in which effort he was assisted, much to Ethin's annoyance, by Yasai Qiqa. Ethin himself was remanded to his grandmother's side as our conference broke up, though he cast a longing glance in my direction before being led away. Ru Kisian and Ciet Nevan exchanged some murmured words before parting in opposite directions; the asa, naturally, remained where she was, but not before instructing General Naza—now pointedly flanked by two of her personal guards—to see me to my husband.

I don't remember the journey from the Little Palace to the prison where Cae was held, except as a series of fleeting impressions: Markel's and Yasai Qiqa's hands supporting me, the bright flash of daylight overhead, the shushing sound of my slippers against the stone. My heart juddered in my chest with all the irregularity of a spinning top kicked down a flight of stairs, and while my overexertion was certainly the root cause, there was something else there, too. I felt clammy and queasy, a little as if I were seasick and a lot as if I were drunk, but on being led into the prison's stony interior—on seeing Cae before me—I sobered as instantly as if I'd been doused in cold water.

The cell in which Cae resided was, as such things go, a middlingly hospitable one, albeit lacking in privacy. The room was recessed in the natural rock on three sides, with the fourth consisting of floor-to-ceiling iron bars, some hinged into a padlocked gate. Light and fresh air circulated from a handspan aperture set high in the ceiling, though there were also a pair of magelights. There was a stone platform bed with a blanket, a wooden table and chair, and a tiny modesty alcove behind which, I assumed, lay whatever passed for a toilet, which was some small mercy, but not my primary focus—because there, standing in the middle of the room at a soldier's ease, was Cae. He looked exactly as he had that morning—braids still coiled around his head, still dressed in silk and leather—and if he'd been manhandled or otherwise disarrayed by General Naza's zeal, I could see no sign of it. But at the sight of me, his eyes went wide, and my heart clenched fiercely as he rushed to the bars and gripped them.

"Vel?" he croaked.

As if in a dream, I pushed away from my helpers and went to him. We reached for each other in the same moment, hands sliding from wrists to forearms, Cae reaching within the voluminous sleeves of my robe to grasp my bare skin. He looked me over frantically, thumbs stroking the sensitive skin in the crooks of my elbows, and choked out, "Saints, Vel, are you all right? You ought to be resting!"

Everything around me slowed and blurred, as if I were an insect encased in tree-sap. My heart wrenched erratically against my ribs, for all the world like a leashed dog straining to greet a friend, and I realised, in a bright and sudden unfurling of truth, that I loved him. *Oh,* I thought stupidly. The realisation washed through me with all the sweet shivering shock of brandy drunk on an empty stomach. I stared at my husband, at the desperate worry in his face, and felt my blood beating within me like wings. I'd thought myself in love before, but in that moment, the strength of my feelings for Cae cast every prior romance in the retroactive light of infatuation. I had yearned for love, had hoped for, cherished and feared it in nearly equal measure, but all of that paled before my sudden certainty that, if my heart was a ship, Caethari had become its harbour.

"You idiot," I breathed, and kissed him—or tried to, at least. The iron bars pressed against our faces, shallowing what should've been deep, and I whined in giddy frustration at the circumstances. I sucked on Cae's lip and pulled back again, my fingers clutching desperately at his arms. "I'm going to get you out of here," I whispered fiercely. "I swear it."

Cae looked as dazed as I felt. "Vel," he said urgently, "you have to know, I didn't—"

"I know."

"The knife—saints, it's the one you gave me, I'm so sorry—I wore it last night, but I must've lost it somewhere—"

"I know."

"No, *listen.* Ru Kisian said she was low in income, but the house was full of new staff, new paint, new furnishings—she'd come into money somehow—"

"She'd sold her land, according to Tierena Keris," I said. I leaned in closer again, feeling half-insane from the contrast between my feelings and what I could safely say. "If she was behind Syana, it would explain her motive—but then, who killed her, and who bought the land?"

"Her room looked like it'd been searched," Cae said urgently, voice pitched for me alone. "I don't know if they found what they were looking for, but it's a start." And then, sliding his big hand farther up my arm, warm fingers curling possessively around my bicep, "You should be in *bed,* Vel. I'm fine in here, but if anything happens to you—"

"You won't be fine in here unless I get you out," I countered. "Cae, I"—*love you, I love you*—"can't just sit back and hope for the best. I know I'm hardly in the best condition for any of this—" I leaned in, pressing our foreheads together as much as the bars allowed. "—but

I have to try, do you understand?" I wanted to confess my realisation, but couldn't bring myself to do so: not when it was still so new, and least of all when he was locked up, the two of us being scrutinized by the guards and General Naza.

And Yasai Qiqa, I recalled belatedly—the same kem who'd rescued Cae from drowning. Why had thei been at the asa's meeting? Why had Ciet Nevan and Ru Kisian, for that matter? Had they been summoned, or had the news of Cae's arrest drawn them in, as it had me? Yet more questions to which I badly needed answers, but in the moment, I could do nothing but set them aside for later.

"I understand," Cae said roughly, "but that doesn't mean I have to like it."

Nodding, I focussed on the tangible reality of my husband, for now unharmed and whole, if not yet free. Releasing his arm, I reached up to trace his cheek with a fingertip, alive to the way his breath caught at the contact; at the way my own stuttered in sympathy. I met his gaze and tried to will him the knowledge of everything I didn't dare to say aloud, but all I succeeded in doing was raising my already elevated pulse. Had Cae's eyes always been so dark?

"That's enough," called General Naza, his tone surprisingly civil. Despite this, my hackles rose; I trembled against the bars, as if I could melt through them by sheer stubborn desire alone.

"I'll be all right," Cae murmured, smiling crookedly. He raised a hand to my throat, thumb brushing tenderly against my scar. "Just stay alive, Vel. That's all I ask."

"You, too," I whispered, and despite the general's palpable impatience, I grasped his chin and drew him in for a parting kiss. I released him only reluctantly, but tired as I was, when I looked at General Naza, a spark of something dangerous kindled in my chest. With a final, lingering glance at Cae, I stalked over to the general and into his personal space, aware that I looked ridiculous against him, but not caring.

"I know you think little of me," I said, voice tight, "but understand this. If anything happens to Caethari while he's in your charge—if he ends up harmed in any way—I will eat your heart."

Luckily for my personal safety, but less so for my pride, General Naza was more amused by this than anything, as if I were a puppy yapping at a mastiff.

"Your loyalty is touching," he drawled. "As you've pointed out, however, I have more and better tasks to oversee than chaperoning you, so." He beckoned imperiously to Markel and Yasai Qiqa—the latter of whom he acknowledged with a dip of his head—and waited as they stepped up to support me once more. I was mildly outraged by this, until I felt Markel's steadying grip on my elbow and realised I'd been swaying on the spot.

"Come on, now," murmured Yasai Qiqa, and with that I was ushered out—away from Cae, but not from the revelation that I loved him.

As the anger which had sustained me through my interview with the asa and my trip to the prison ebbed, I became belatedly aware of my laboured breathing, to say nothing of the sheen of slick, cold sweat on my limbs. The chill air stung my exposed skin, and more than once, I stumbled over nothing, my stomach yammering.

"I'm not feeling well," I mumbled sheepishly—for Markel's benefit, though with his hands occupied, he couldn't answer.

"I'm astonished," Yasai Qiqa said dryly. "You really are a fascinating specimen, aren't you?"

"So I've been told," I managed, and then fell silent again, my attention wholly dedicated to the task of not passing out.

As we entered the Circlet Annex, I found myself struggling to keep upright. Embarrassed, I stuttered out an apology as we drew in sight of the suite, and was on the brink of asking if Markel would be kind enough to draw me a bath when I registered two familiar figures waiting before our doors: Ciet Nevan and—my pulse spiked with fury—Asrien.

"Ah," murmured Yasai Qiqa. "Now, *that's* interesting."

Markel made a rare vocalisation, a sound pitched somewhere

between complaint and warning as his grip on my forearm tightened, but despite my exhaustion, I felt a reviving flush of anger. With clumsy strength, I shoved free of my caregivers, stalked up to Asrien—who looked first surprised, then openly alarmed—and slapped him with all the force I could muster. He let out a cry and staggered back, clutching his cheek; I grabbed his lin and shook him like a hunting dog with a duck.

"You poisonous little berry," I snarled in Ralian. "*What did you do to Caethari?*" And then, as several pairs of hands moved to haul me back, "Get *off*!"

A scuffle ensued, or something like one; my pulse was thundering in my ears, my limbs abruptly as weak and unresponsive as overcooked noodles. I felt strong arms around my waist, bucked once against their hold, and then—

"Oh gods, is he well?"

"Get him inside, quick!"

The world dissolved in a blur of light and colour. I juddered weakly, though not by choice, my body spasming with all the helplessness of a landed fish. I blacked out for a time—it felt like several minutes at least, though I have no idea how long it truly was—and came to in a state of groggy disorientation. After some sticky blinking, I found I'd been divested of my slippers and robe—though not, mercifully, my nara—and laid out on the bed, a compress on my forehead and a sternly unimpressed Ru Saeri seated at the bedside, holding my wrist as she healed me.

I made a slurred, incomprehensible attempt at speech, alerting her to my return to consciousness. Her eyes widened slightly as if in relief, then narrowed again in unequivocal judgement.

"All hail the idiot patient," she said, the sarcasm undercut with a note of guilt-inducing professional worry. "Master of poor decisions and unnecessary risks. You nearly put your heart in failure, do you understand that?"

I winced. "I'm sorry," I rasped, my throat unpleasantly dry. "I didn't mean to."

"Idiot patients never do." She glared at me a moment longer, then softened her expression. "I understand the morning's circumstances have been . . . taxing, let's say. But having expended considerable effort in keeping you alive, tiern, I'd appreciate it if you took better care to remain that way."

"I will," I said meekly, which seemed to appease her. I tipped my head slightly, glancing around the room until I found Markel, standing at the foot of the bed with his arms crossed and a tense look on his face, Ciet Nevan hovering at his shoulder. "Sorry, Markel. I do make your life hard, don't I?"

"You're an abominable fool," signed Markel roughly, "and if you ever do anything like that again, I'll sew you into your clothes and sew your clothes to the mattress."

"That's fair," I signed back, my fingers shaky, and shut my eyes again, receding into a not-quite-drowse as Ru Saeri finished her work.

Some minutes passed, until, with a grumbled noise, she released me and stood, smoothing her hands down her nara. "Now," she said sternly, addressing Ciet Nevan but glaring at me. "He's to rest for the rest of today at *least*—no exertion, but as much food and water as he'll take, though it's best if he eats a series of smaller meals than too much at once. If he looks at all faint again, call me right away, and I'll have someone see to him."

"Of course," said the ciet, and I wondered at his participation in the process before recalling that, as far as anyone in the palace knew, Markel had no understanding of Tithenai. The reminder of why we'd undertaken that particular ruse had a sharpening effect on my senses, and in a rush, I recalled my attack on Asrien. A part of me felt ashamed for it—in my Farathel circles, such a fight between men of our shared inclination would've been gossip fodder for weeks, if not months—but the rest of me felt toothily unrepentant. And, more to the point, Asrien was far from exonerated when it came to the attack on Cae. Despite my throbbing head, my thoughts were clear: whatever Asrien's agenda—*assuming he has one beyond playing fox in the henhouse,* I thought cattily—he'd clearly intended a seduction of Cae, and might very well have drugged him to that purpose. But the attempted drowning . . . while it was certainly possible Asrien was responsible, it felt less likely, though I struggled to pinpoint why.

For the first time since arriving in the capital, I let myself recall Asrien's attempted seduction of me. At the time, it had hurt, not only because he'd blamed me for the likelihood of my marriage causing more and worse mistreatment of our fellow litai in Ralia, even claiming to have been cast out himself on my account, but because receiving an unwelcome advance, however clumsy and abortive, had pricked my memories of Killic. As such, and considering the rather dramatic events of the previous day, I'd had precious little time in which to ponder Asrien himself, and as I finally did so, I found myself frowning.

"Are you all right?" asked Ciet Nevan, and I jolted at the reminder that both he and Markel were still in attendance, my thoughts having wandered so swiftly that I'd forgotten my surroundings.

"I'm well, or as well as can be. Just a little thirsty." I forced a smile for his sake, then turned to Markel. Raising my still-shaky hands, I signed, "I do need a drink, but I also want to ask Nevan about Asrien. Is he still here?"

"The yasai's keeping him company in the lounge," Markel signed back. "He clearly wants to talk to you, but he won't say what about. I'll get you some juice, if the kitchens have any."

"Juice would be wonderful," I said aloud in Ralian. "Thank you, Markel."

"Don't do anything foolish while I'm gone," he signed, then bowed and left, the picture of a dutiful servant.

Ciet Nevan watched him go, frowning slightly as he pushed his glasses farther up his nose, and I took the opportunity to study him in turn. We'd barely spoken since the party at Ravethae, and both his presence and his proximity to Asrien—or rather, Asrien's proximity to him—intrigued me. Nevan was handsome, certainly, his reddish hair striking against the brown of his skin, and I was yet to see or hear of anything to his direct discredit, but that meant little in the scheme of things. I didn't want to consider the possibility that he was a party to Asrien's actions, and yet the still-painful example of Laecia forced me to do so. What might Ciet Nevan gain, I wondered, if my marriage was disrupted?

Wait.

The thought drew me up short: *was* Asrien trying to disrupt my marriage? I'd hit on the notion in a backwards way, but now the idea had occurred to me, I found that it fit. Why else attempt seductions of both Cae and me? Why else seek us out in the first place by attaching himself to the ciet? I drew a deep breath, the realisation filling my mouth with bitterness. If Asrien was trying to break up my marriage, it was *possible* he was acting out of jealousy, but as he was already living in Tithena and, by his own account, unable to go home—and as he'd already talked his way into Ciet Nevan's bed, for that matter—this made little sense as a motive. But if he was acting on someone else's behalf . . .

I stifled a curse. I might be wrong, but of all the factions who wanted the alliance to fail, I could think of only one who'd attempt this particular tactic.

"You gave us all a fright, seizing like that," said Ciet Nevan, once more breaking my chain of thought. He rolled his shoulders, huffing a laugh. "I'm glad you woke up. I'm not sure what Caethari would've done if I'd had to tell him otherwise."

Guilt twisted through my stomach, intertwined with a pang of love so sharp, it felt like I'd swallowed a needle. "I'm glad it didn't come to that," I said, truthfully. "I've already put Cae through so much."

The ciet smiled crookedly. "Perhaps," he conceded. "But he appears to think it a worthwhile trade."

"And do you?" I asked boldly.

He seemed surprised by the question. "I certainly hope so," he said, removing his glasses and cleaning the lenses with a small cloth pulled from his pocket. "I'd wish the same for any new marriage, but that's not why you're asking." He returned the cloth to its keeping place and set the glasses back on his nose. An odd look stole over his face. "Do you suspect me of something, Velasin?"

My lips quirked of their own accord, gaze flicking to indicate the bedroom door and the people who lay beyond it. "Should I?"

He sighed. "This is about Asrien, then."

"It might be," I conceded. I studied Ciet Nevan, struggling for a way to hint at my suspicions without completely betraying them, and settled on, "It doesn't strike you as convenient, the way he found us through you?"

The ciet snorted. "I'm not an idiot," he said. "Out of everyone in Qi-Xihan, I know he sought me out for a reason, but I'm no more in his confidence than he's in mine. We're of mutual use to each other, that's all."

"I can see how you're of use to him," I said, "but what does he bring to you?"

Ciet Nevan smiled, the expression somewhere between self-deprecation and sadness. "Company," he said, "and the knowledge that he has no expectations of me beyond what the moment entails. I have . . . blundered, previously, in the latter regard. Not all marriages are as blessed as yours." And then, before I could fully process this, he excused himself, bowed, and exited the room.

Whatever I'd been expecting, that wasn't it. Lost in thought, I stared at the window until Markel returned with my juice—as well as, because he was Markel, a tray of assorted foods. Thanking him, I allowed myself to be levered somewhat upright and extra cushions placed behind my back, and was annoyed to find that even so small an exertion left me briefly light-headed.

Markel shot me a knowing look and passed me the juice. I sipped it gratefully, sweet and cool against my dry throat.

"I'm sorry," I murmured. "I didn't mean to worry you."

"You never do," Markel signed. "And yet."

"And yet," I echoed. "I know I don't say this often enough, but thank you, Markel."

He rolled his eyes, lips twitching. "I wiped you down, you know."

"You what?"

"While you were unconscious just now, when Ru Saeri was here. I wiped you down. You were sticky with sweat, and I didn't want to have to change the linens."

I groaned. "I'm sorry. Remind me to pay you a bonus for it."

"A bonus? More like hazard pay."

"My sweat isn't that bad!"

"Oh?" Markel raised an eyebrow. "So you're volunteering to wash me, then?"

"Hazard pay it is," I said, and let him feed me a small, miscellaneous pastry. My stomach rumbled gratefully, and for the next few minutes, we ate in silence, picking through the contents of the tray.

Finally, Markel sighed and signed, "Asrien's still waiting to speak to you. Should I send him away?"

"I'll see him," I said, "but you can sit in."

Markel shot me a withering look. "As if you could keep me out, in your condition."

I cracked a smile at that, and as he cleared the tray, I settled myself back against the pillows, bracing myself for my visitor.

When Asrien entered, I winced to see a faint bruise on his cheek. Evidently, I'd hit him harder than I realised, but as before, what guilt I felt was balanced by my anger at his actions. And yet, as I recalled my recent epiphany, a note of begrudging sympathy curled through my gut. Asrien may have been catty, sly and two-faced, but he was also young and far from home—and, unless I missed my guess, at the mercy of forces far greater than himself. As he approached my bedside, he looked simultaneously hunted and uncowed, and when he sat in the chair that Markel had laid out for him, it was with a slow, animal wariness.

"I'm sorry for that," I said in Ralian, nodding to indicate the bruise.

Asrien snorted. "Don't be," he said, replying in the same language. "I deserved it."

"For trying to fuck my husband, or for trying to drown him?"

"Which do you think?" he snapped, but deflated in the next breath. "For trying to fuck him. Whatever happened afterwards, I didn't see and played no part in." But he wouldn't meet my gaze.

"You drugged him," I said flatly.

Asrien jolted in place. "I didn't!" he said, but it came out shakily. "I didn't—*fuck*." He twisted his hands in his lap, then bit out, "I didn't know, all right?"

My heart sped up. "Know what?"

"That he'd been drugged. I thought he was just drunk and strange, not—*that*."

"Who drugged him, then, if not you?"

"I—"

Asrien faltered. He looked thoroughly unhappy about the conversation, which was hardly surprising, and yet that discomfort was at odds with the fact that he'd been the one to initiate it.

"You came here for a reason," I said, not ungently. "If not to talk about this, then why?"

"Because whatever else might be true of me, I don't want you or Caethari to end up dead," he snapped. "All right? Stars know, I can't exactly afford a conscience, but I can want you to live, at least."

He looked miserable as he said it, though he was trying hard to disguise that fact. Belatedly, it occurred to me that I was seeing him for the first time without makeup; there was a faint scatter of freckles across the bridge of his nose that must've hitherto been hidden with powder, and something about their visibility made him look more vulnerable than before, somehow younger and less polished. He fidgeted his hands in his lap, staring fixedly past me at the wall, and I had the strange realisation that, while I neither liked nor trusted Asrien, I was no longer angry at him.

"King Markus sent you, didn't he," I said, softly. "Or someone working for him."

Asrien jerked as if stabbed. "How did you—" he blurted, and then broke off, cheeks burning with mortification at the slip.

I sighed. "A Ralian litai seeking me out in Qi-Xihan is one thing, but to nock your bow at both me *and* Cae? I'm not stupid, Asrien."

"That makes one of us, then," he said bitterly.

"I'm assuming they blackmailed you?"

"No," he snipped, "I volunteered. Of course I was fucking black-mailed! That's how the Shades operate."

I inhaled sharply. The Shades were spymasters to the Ralian throne, its hands and eyes and ears beyond the palace. While it was technically possible for one to be acting under his own recognizance, the far more likely alternative was that the king himself disapproved of my marriage to Caethari and had taken steps to end it that couldn't be overtly traced back to him. It was a chilling confirmation to receive: the personal enmity of a monarch was no small thing, and for several seconds, I found it hard to focus.

Eventually, I managed, "So, what was the plan—seduce us into infidelity, so the marriage would end and Ralia could blame it on our deviant natures?"

"What else," said Asrien.

I shut my eyes, head pounding. "That being so, I ask again: if you didn't drug Caethari, then who did?"

Silence.

I waited a moment, then looked at him. Asrien was rigidly tense, his posture twisted as if he were trying to lean simultaneously towards and away from me, or from what I represented.

"If I tell you," he said at last, fast and intent, "I need you to promise to help me."

"I can promise to try," I said carefully.

"*That's not good enough!*"

He came to his feet, breathing hard. From his space at the far wall, Markel started forwards, but subsided when I shook my head. For all that I'd struck him, I didn't think Asrien was minded to return the favour, and so I waited, watching as he mastered himself.

"Fuck," he said wearily. He shot me a glare and sank back down, head in his hands. "They threatened my mother," he said to the floor. "I need—if I'm going to help you, I need you to keep her safe. And me, I suppose. But mostly her."

I stared at Asrien, throat tight as my entire conception of him rearranged itself. "Your mother's in Ralia?" I said, working to keep my voice even.

He nodded, still not looking at me. "Lady Jisa bo Erat. She lives at our family's estate outside of Tambry, but she has no love for the place. Neither of us do. I've told her to leave before, but she won't—" He broke off, jaw clenching. "Anyway. If it's a choice between dying in Tambry and living elsewhere, she'll chose living. But I need to get her out."

"I'll try," I said, willing him to believe me. "I don't—look. It should be fairly obvious that I'm not in the strongest position at present, politically or physically." I gestured at myself, and was rewarded with the flickering ghost of a smile. "But I will try, Asrien. I can promise you that much."

"You shouldn't," he said, with a stab of self-loathing. "With what I've done. What I was willing to do."

"Maybe," I said, refusing to acknowledge the ugly satisfaction I felt at his flinch. "For all I know, you might still bite me for this. But still, I'd rather help you if I can."

"Why?"

Because if I don't, I leave you as an enemy at my back. Because Ralia is cruel enough to men like us without being cruel to each other. Because you did not ask for the Shade to use you any more than I asked for Killic to follow me into my father's garden. Because you are young. Because I am young, and have seen enough hurt already. Because I'm sick of having enemies. Because I see myself in you, and wish I didn't.

"Because," I deadpanned, "my life isn't exciting enough."

Asrien snorted. "You're an idiot," he said, but sounded almost impressed about it.

"So I've been told," I said, and waited him out, watching the play of emotions across his face.

At last, he let out a shuddering exhale. "Naza," he whispered. "I think it was Naza."

My chest tightened. "You think, or you know?"

"I think," he said, "but nobody else makes sense. He . . . when he interviewed me the other day, he . . . realised, as you did, that I'd been sent here by Ralia, and you already know he doesn't want the alliance. He was . . . the idea that I could end your marriage, he was in favour of that. He told me he'd make sure that I was welcome at the party, and that I should take advantage of your absence to try my luck with Caethari—with the yaseran," he amended hastily, in response to whatever my face had done on hearing him use my husband's name. "And. Well." He swallowed. "He was the one who suggested I make use of the maze."

I twisted my fists in the blankets, trying to keep my anger in check. If the general had drugged and tried to drown Cae, only to stand before me and declare the whole thing a fiction, to say nothing of casting Asrien's forced seduction as a mutual tryst . . . "I see," I grit out, refraining from swearing or shouting only because I didn't want to risk another seizure.

"It makes sense, doesn't it?" Asrien asked, intent and anxious. "I keep thinking, when that woman attacked you, he was standing right there! A sunfucking general close enough to touch, and somehow he didn't stop her? And then she died before he even spoke to her, but why would he need to, if he's the one who sent her? But. But." He faltered, his expression abruptly lost. "But he's also . . . I mean. Generals, soldiers, men who fight for a living, I've only ever known them to sneer at people who kill underhanded. They think poison is for women, and I know we're in Tithena now, but it's not—some of that still applies, right? Poison's what you use if you're not strong enough for a sword. I could be wrong about all of this. I don't . . . *fuck.* I just don't know."

He looked so genuinely wretched that, for a moment, I found myself at a loss for words. He was miserable, but incomprehensibly so—as though, despite having suggested General Naza's guilt, he was also struggling to conceive of it. I didn't know why that might be or what to say to it, and so remained silent.

Then Asrien said, with sudden determination, "I'll spy on him for you. I'll find out the truth."

I blinked, startled. "Truly? How?"

"I have my ways," he said, grimly. And then, with a trace of his usual acidity, "I'm not *completely* useless."

"All right, then," I said—or tried to, at least. My jaw cracked open on an unexpected yawn, and as if that were a signal on which the rest of my body had been waiting, I suddenly found I was struggling to stay awake.

"You rest," said Asrien, sounding amused. "I'll come and see you again when I know something."

I nodded gratefully at him, and with a parting glance at Markel, he let himself out.

Markel watched him go, then hurried to my side and started fussing with the blankets, tucking me in.

"I shouldn't sleep," I mumbled. "I need—need to get Cae out of prison—" I was silenced by another yawn.

"Ru Saeri said to rest," signed Markel, leaning up to remove my excess pillows. I flopped back down against the bed and felt instantly heavier, sleepier. "If anything else needs doing, I'll see it done. Do you trust me?"

"Of course," I said, surprised by the question.

Markel smiled at me. "Then sleep," he signed, and as though his command were a cantrip, I shut my eyes and drifted off almost instantly.

23

Despite waking periodically to eat, drink and stumble my way to the bathroom, I slept the rest of the day and the whole night, too. If anyone tried to visit me during that time, or if any new crises arose, Markel expertly kept them at bay, until I finally woke the next morning more refreshed than I'd felt in weeks. Markel, of course, was up already, and after giving me a critical once-over and asking a few probing questions about how I felt, he consented to let me shower unassisted, though not before ascertaining that I could stand without wobbling.

I was midway through washing my hair, mentally reviewing the previous day's events, when I was hit all over again by that terrible, wonderful realisation: *I love Cae.* I grabbed the tiled wall for support, near felled by the enormity of it, yet simultaneously wincing with the anxiety it induced. What if I confessed my feelings only for Cae's to have changed? Or, more bitterly ironic still, what if Qi-Xihan's politics claimed my husband before we even had a chance to speak? This fear was such that I rushed through the rest of my ablutions to ask Markel what I'd missed; my pleading, however, was met with refusal.

"No politics until after breakfast," Markel signed sternly, ushering me out to the lounge and the food which awaited me there.

"But Cae—"

"He's fine," signed Markel, and I slumped with relief. "Now. Eat!"

"Yes, mother," I snipped at him, earning myself an eyeroll, but did as I was told. Unsurprisingly, I was ravenous, and set to with a will, devouring several baked eggs with field rice, two jidha, a cup

380 · Foz Meadows

of khai and several portions of fruit in close to record time. Markel watched me like a hawk, and when I was done, he tidied away the tray, brought me a glass of water—I hadn't asked for one, but was grateful of it regardless—and took his own seat opposite.

"Now," he signed. "Before you ask: yes, Caethari really is fine. We've had no official updates from General Naza, but by all accounts, after Caethari's arrest, he spent yesterday with the asa's guards, interviewing the dead cietena's staff, tracking down her acquaintants and going through her belongings. If he's had any startling revelations as a result of that, he's hardly keeping me in the loop—" I snorted at that, and he quirked his lips, pleased at having elicited the reaction. "—but Asrien stopped by again last night to say that, from what he's been able to gather, the general has confirmed the tierena's claim that the lands near Qi-Katai were recently sold. However, it also seems that, for some time prior to the sale, she'd been selling off her jewellery and other personal effects to supplement her income, and while those sales had mostly been delegated to her housekeeper, apparently there were some she made on her own, so—"

"So," I said, frustrated, "she might just as easily have sold her palace token as given it willingly or had it stolen." I chewed on that for a moment, annoyed, then cut Markel a measured look. "Do you think Asrien was telling the truth? Would he lie about that, do you think?"

Markel sat back, considering, a wrinkle between his brows. "No," he signed at last. "I don't think he was lying. The housekeeper might've been, with that story about her mistress making some sales on her own, but whatever Asrien found out, I think he repeated it faithfully."

There was a particular look on Markel's face, one I knew well but hadn't seen for a while. "You like him," I said, surprised.

Markel jumped, as indignant as if I'd flicked wine on a freshly laundered shirt. "I do not *like* him," he signed. "He's a devious little trollop who's caused you no end of trouble, to say nothing of what he did to Caethari—and don't think we're sliding right by the fact that he evidently propositioned you back at Ravethae and you didn't tell me about it." He raised a meaningful eyebrow. "Or did you think I missed that part of your little heart-to-heart yesterday?"

I winced. "I'm sorry," I signed. "I hadn't meant to keep it a secret, truly, I just—didn't know how to process it. Not after everything else. And then we were on the road again, and—well, it's not like I've had an abundance of opportunities, these last few days."

He conceded this point with a wince of his own. "Still," he signed after a moment, his expression oddly hesitant. "You're not . . . upset?"

Now there was a euphemism if ever I'd heard one. For a moment, I recalled my collapse on the cobbles at Etho, the trembling shame that had made me fear my husband's hands, and swallowed down an unpleasant rush of bile. "No," I said—aloud, this time. "No, I'm not upset. I was . . . unhappy, let's say, at the time, but nothing that's lingered."

"Good. I'd hate to have to teach him a lesson about it."

Slyly, I said, "So you do like him."

Markel's expression was pained. "He's a familiar sort of stupid, that's all," he signed. "Like you at eighteen, but with better hair."

"You—!"

"And besides," Markel continued, "he's not exactly having a great time of things, either." He hesitated, then signed in a rush, "I'm sorry, Velasin. The other day, when he and I went to interview Syana, he muttered something about shade or shades, but I didn't place what he meant by it until yesterday; I thought he might've been praying. If I'd been just a little sharper—"

"You're plenty sharp, Markel," I said, smiling at him. "Like an oddly maternal knife."

He pulled a face at that, and we both fell to quiet laughter. It was a blessed relief to be able to laugh, like unsticking a frozen joint. Humour felt like a different kind of healing, and I was on the verge of saying so when an enthusiastic knocking sounded on the door to the suite.

I shot Markel a questioning look, and for the first time since I'd woken, he looked slightly abashed.

"That would be the other thing," he signed, coming to his feet. "Those ciets you sent to investigate Syana came rushing in here late last night determined to make their report, but I told them you were in no fit state to go haring off into the darkness, and to come back again at a civilized hour. That's likely them now, unless something else has happened."

"Markel!" I stared at him, betrayed. "You said there was nothing urgent!"

"It was for your own good," he signed firmly, and went to answer the door—which, sure enough, had Irias and Yarasil on the other side of it. I forced myself to be patient and polite as we got through the inevitable pleasantries, which really meant reassuring them that yes, I was healing well.

With that done, they sat down opposite me and began to narrate the fruits of their labours, voices overlapping in a constant back and forth.

"It took *hours*," said Irias, sounding more thrilled than aggrieved. "The whole day, really!"

"It's why we didn't get back until dark," put in Yarasil.

"It was like playing goose-hunt at midwinter—oh. Do you have goose-hunt in Ralia? It's that festival game with the clues, you know, and the feathers, and there's a story that goes with it, though that's really only for children—"

"It's a shame Ethin wasn't there," interrupted Yarasil, before I could answer. "He loves goose-hunt."

"*Anyway*," said Irias, "we did as you said, and asked practically everyone we met along the whole Stagger if they'd seen an older woman in pink and yellow with a pink sapphire torc, and could they recall where she'd come from and at what time, and most people of course said no, but some did!"

Yarasil giggled behind his hand. "Half an hour in, we found a dapper old cieten who walks part of the Stagger each day, he says, for his health, and it was like he'd been waiting for someone to ask about her so he could complain—he thought her clothes and the clashing colours were *appalling,* which was why he'd remembered."

"But he recalled which side of the street she'd been on, so we stuck to that half, and the further we went, the more people we found—still not many, of course, but enough that we knew we were in the right place—"

"And then we just kept asking and asking, and eventually it got to a point where people were telling us, *oh, I don't know, but perhaps such-and-such does,* and then we'd have to ask where *they* might be, only they never ended up being quite where we'd been told to look—"

"But *eventually,*" said Irias, "we wound up at a tavern called the Stone Hare, about three streets back of the Stagger proper, because someone thought they might've seen her at breakfast there, so we went in and spoke to the landlady, and—"

"And it turns out we'd found the right spot!" said Yarasil, triumphant. "She said Syana had rented an upstairs room from her days ago and paid in advance for a week's lodgings, and nobody's come by to clear it out or take her things, so as far as she knows, it's just as she left it. The thing is, though—"

"The thing is, we weren't sure what we ought to look for if we went in, and we didn't—well. We thought you'd want to see it yourself. So we asked the landlady, could she be sure to leave the room as it was for another day or two, and she told us that as long as it's paid for, it'll stay as it is, but we paid her to let us know if anyone else came looking to see it. So—"

"So all you have to do is go there!" Yarasil finished. "We can even take you—or, I mean, one of us can, but we're meant to see Ethin today, and if one of us goes with you, then the other needs to go to him to let him know why we'll be late."

I took a moment to digest all this, thoughts racing. If Syana had had the key to her room at the Stone Hare on her when she died, then either General Naza was yet to determine where it came from, or else had written it off as irrelevant, though as she'd evidently discarded her palace token prior to her attack on me, I wondered if she'd done the same with her key. Either way, the idea that we might yet steal a march on the general was a compelling one, and while my nape still prickled with caution—rushing to beat him to evidence was, after all, how Cae had ended up framed for murder—I wasn't the least deterred.

"Thank you," I said sincerely. "Thank you both so much, that's more than I could've asked for."

This elicited a veritable chorus of *not at all!* and *it was our pleasure!*, during which I fixed Markel with my best *mother, may I?* expression.

Markel pursed his lips. "I suppose we must," he signed grudgingly.

With that agreed between us, organisation took over. While I fled to the bedroom to dress under Markel's supervision, Irias and Yarasil argued quietly between them as to who would escort us to the Stone Hare, which decision appeared to involve a lot of fervent whispering. Recalling the caution with which Cae had dressed yesterday (while stubbornly refusing to indulge the sharp, sudden bloom of love-longing-worry that accompanied thinking of him), and to Markel's clear approval, I dressed in a leather riding coat over a linen undershirt, blended hemp nara and a pure silk lin, plus my favourite riding boots, all coloured in varying shades of brown and russet. With my damp hair waving around my face and I too vain to stuff it under a hat, I must've looked like a peculiarly energetic autumn leaf, though if Markel shared the sentiment, he was too polite to say so. Or too distracted: while I'd dressed myself, he'd taken the opportunity to duck into his private room, which adjoined the main bedroom, and don both a stout leather vest and a matching pair of vambraces I wasn't aware he'd had with him.

"Is that really necessary?" I asked, though my voice wavered slightly with the question.

Markel shot me what I was prepared to categorise as a Look. "Naivety isn't one of your charms," he signed tartly, and pulled back the edge of his coat to show me the pair of blades sheathed at his hip.

I stared at him. "Where the fuck did those come from?"

In reply, I received another Look. Markel went to move past me, but I grabbed his shoulder, scanning him up and down as if he might've sprouted more hidden weaponry in the intervening seconds.

"No, seriously, Markel—where the *fuck* did those come from? And *when*?"

Markel sighed. "It doesn't matter where they came from," he signed, more brusquely than usual. "The point is that your father, despite his myriad other failings, had me trained for the express purpose of protecting you, and for the last few weeks, I've done a pretty piss-poor job of it. So." He shrugged and looked away, abashed. "Knives."

A swell of emotion rose in my throat and lodged there like a chunk of unswallowed apple. Releasing him, I tipped my head to catch his gaze and signed, "You've always been far better a friend than I deserve. None of this is on you, Markel." And then, because I'd renewed my taste for levity, I added aloud, "Besides, you hardly need them. Your scolding looks are sharper than any blade."

"Ass," signed Markel, thumping me lightly in the ribs. He meant to seem stern, but I caught the flicker of grin as he walked past me to the door, and counted myself one of the luckiest men on either side of the border.

Out in the lounge, it emerged that Yarasil had won whatever back-and-forth he and Irias had engaged in as to who'd play guide. Irias appeared only mildly put out by this, but wished us good luck as he headed off to rendezvous with Ethin. We, meanwhile, locked up the suite and headed for the stables, with Yarasil dashing off to acquire his own mount.

It was the first time I'd been in the stables at Qi-Xihan, and as I caught sight of Gift's soft nose poking over the edge of the stable door, her soft ears pricked with interest, I found myself perilously close to tears.

"Hey there, sweet girl," I murmured to her, while Markel let a nearby groom know, through practiced gesticulation, that we wanted two horses saddled. I pressed my face to her warm, soft neck—her coat was already thickening with the onset of winter— and silently promised us both that, once I had a spare moment, I'd find the time to groom her properly. Until then, however, and with Markel still determined to subject my healing body to as little extraneous exertion as possible, I was forced to stand back and let the grooms saddle her in my stead.

After an interlude which felt far too long but was really no time at all, we finally emerged from both stable and palace: me on Gift, Markel on his sorrel Grace and Yarasil on an exquisite black mare with two white socks and a neat white blaze named Dancer. When I praised her lines, he dipped his head in a mix of guilt and embarrassment and said softly, "She's my favourite. I almost had her with me at the river, but my littlest sister begged to ride her ahead to Qi-Xihan, and I said yes. If I hadn't . . ." His voice trailed off, and we shared a moment of mourning for the horses his friends had lost. Almost, I considered telling him about Quip, but that was an unpleasant story and not something I wished to dwell on, and so, instead, I asked him about his sister.

This turned out to be the right decision. Yarasil's mood lifted instantly, and as we turned onto the Stagger, he explained that he was both the middle child of five and the only boy.

"I can't imagine what that's like!" I exclaimed. "I've only ever had brothers, and in Ralia, past a certain age, it's not encouraged for unrelated girls and boys to play."

Yarasil laughed. "Well, I suppose you could say that Irias and Ethin are like my brothers—we've known each other long enough—but the girls are different."

The resulting conversation saw us all the way down the Stagger, Markel listening in quiet amusement as Yarasil traded me stories about his sisters for my tales of Revic and Nathian. I didn't mention Revic's death, not wanting to sour the mood, but recalling him put a pang in my chest at the realisation that I might never see Nathian again, either. Not that we'd been close at the best of times, but it was a melancholic thing, to realise that breaking with my father and being at apparent odds with the Ralian throne had severed me from my remaining brother by proxy.

With the part of my thoughts not listening to Yarasil, I wondered if I should write to him, and whether I'd receive a reply if I did. Would Nathian disown me as our father had? I assumed so, and yet a foolish part of me persisted in hoping otherwise. I'd spent barely any time with my young niece and nephew, assuming I'd be better placed to play the roguish unmarried uncle when they and I were both a little older, but now—

"Oh!" said Yarasil, the sudden exclamation cutting through my thoughts. "Oh, it must be Saint Yren's!"

"Saint Yren's what?" I asked stupidly, before looking around and realising belatedly that the Stagger had grown progressively more and more lively the farther down we came. Stalls and carts of all kinds now lined the main thoroughfare, many selling brightly coloured streamers and ribbons on sticks, while the air was heavy with the sweet, enticing scent of something fried and sugary.

"Saint Yren's Day!" said Yarasil, gesturing around. "It's easy to lose track of if you're not paying attention, because it's held on the day of the first full moon of winter—which must be Zo, this year," he added thoughtfully, glancing at the sky. I followed his gaze and, sure enough, the largest moon was faintly visible in the sky, whole and round where his sisters, both lower and in different parts of the sky, were sickle and waxing.

"And who's Saint Yren?" I asked, half in genuine curiosity and half to distract myself.

"Oh!" said Yarasil, eyes growing wide. "Oh, well, thei were a mage in service to Ruya's Order some, I think, six hundred years ago? And—"

I let the story wash over me as I took in the assembling festival atmosphere. The human Yren had earned thir sainthood through a life spent healing children of various ailments, many of which, prior to thir advances in medical magic, had been thought incurable, and as thei'd died beneath the first full moon of winter (or so it was claimed), that was when thei were celebrated. There was more to it than that, of course—reports of healings beyond what even a magically talented mortal could've managed without divine aid, the involvement of temple politics—but though Yarasil was an enthusiastic narrator, I was more arrested by the families coming to celebrate. Music skirled through the air; to one side, a trio of singers was setting up, while farther ahead, a small troupe of acrobats had attracted a crowd of onlookers, many of them children.

By this point in my time in Tithena, it shouldn't have surprised me to see two women with their arms around the same apple-cheeked toddler, or two men laughing as one lifted a giggling girl to the other's shoulders, but though I'd encountered other couples like Cae and me, I'd yet to see any as parents, and the ease with which it was treated as normal took my breath away. And yet, to my deep shame, alongside my awe and delight, I felt an unexpected rush of fear, that the scene before me might be somehow imperilled by the beliefs of strangers hundreds of miles away; as though I had become a conduit for prejudices I did not share, but which, as a result of forced and sometimes brutal exposure, I nonetheless carried with me. I could all too readily imagine what certain Ralians would say of the sight, and flinched from the thought as sharply as if I'd heard it spoken beside me.

"Are you all right?" asked Yarasil, and I realised I'd completely lost the thread of whatever he'd been saying.

"I'm fine," I lied. "Just wondering how much busier it's likely to get."

"A lot more, I'm afraid," said Yarasil. "Though really, it's all good fun! But—well. It might be hard to ride the whole way back, with the crowds the way they are, which isn't ideal for you."

"I'm sure I'll manage," I said, and pointedly avoided Markel's glare.

By the time we wound our way through various side streets to reach the Stone Hare, the sun was high and the crowds were such that, despite Markel's clear misgivings, we dismounted and went the last little way on foot. I'd been briefly worried that Gift might spook due to all the new sights and sounds, but though her ears swivelled this way and that, she remained perfectly well-behaved as I hitched her to a post before the inn.

"I'll see you in," said Yarasil, "so I can introduce you to the landlady, but then I really ought to get back, or I'll get caught in the crush and it'll take *forever*."

"Of course," I said, already touched that he'd done this much for us, and after paying a grizzled old ostler to keep an eye on the horses, we headed inside.

The Stone Hare was a roomy, three-storey building which, despite its namesake, was primarily built of brick. Inside, the ground-floor common room was as bustling as you might expect of an inn on a festival day, with a long bar to one side, a kitchen to the other and a slew of tables occupying the middle. I peered about, trying to get a sense of the place, and so was taken off guard when a skinny, weathered woman with a jutting chin and very thick eyebrows approached us and said, somewhat nervously, "You're back, ciet?"

As Yarasil broke into a smile, I realised this must be the landlady. "I am! Ren Masin, this is Tiern Velasin; Tiern Velasin, this is Ren Masin, the proprietor. He's come about Syana, the woman I mentioned yesterday?"

Ren Masin looked at me. "She arrived on the seventh, and I never saw her with anyone," she said. "No guests, no friends, though of course my eyes aren't everywhere. I said as much yesterday."

"That's helpful to know." I inclined my head to her. "Ren, I hate to put you to any trouble, but might we see inside her room?"

Ren Masin swallowed nervously. "Respectfully, tiern, it's not—I don't mean to be obstructive, but when a client pays for a room, it's theirs till the rent runs out. Unless you've the key or the lady's blessing—and she'd have to be here in person for that—I can't just let you in, even if you are nobility."

Making an effort to gentle my tone, I said, "Ren, I hate to bring this news, but the woman, Syana, died yesterday in the custody of the palace guard, after—" I hesitated, uncertain whether to bring myself into the story, "—an attack she made on a courtier's life." At Ren Masin's horrified gasp, I rushed on with, "None of this is to your discredit, of course; I don't mean to make you fearful on that count. But it's fallen to me to find out where she came from"— not strictly a lie, but very much not the full truth—"and for that, I need to inspect her room." I fished in my pocket for my palace token and held it out to her, as it was the closest thing I had to a symbol of authority. "Do you know what this is?"

She nodded tightly, eyes wide and fearful. "Yes, tiern! Yes, of course, if you've come from the palace—" She bit off the rest of the sentence and gestured fervently towards the stairs. "This way, please!"

"I'll leave you to it, then," Yarasil said, and inclined his head at the three of us before heading out, leaving Ren Masin to usher Markel and me to the stairs.

"Will the guards come here?" she asked anxiously as we climbed, already fiddling with the chatelaine at her belt. "Guards coming in is never good for business."

"With any luck, it shouldn't be necessary," I said—another half-truth, but it appeared to soothe her, and we climbed the rest of the way in silence.

Syana's room turned out to be on the third floor. At any other time, the stairs wouldn't have troubled me, but I was discomfited to find myself panting once we reached the top, my skin prickling with sweat. Markel, who had a damnable sixth sense for such things, raised his hands as if to speak, but I shook my head against it.

"I'm fine," I signed to him—low, where Ren Masin couldn't see. "I promise. Just a little out of breath."

"Be honest with me if that changes," Markel signed back, and then we were at the door, Ren Masin flicking expertly through her chatelaine in search of the correct key.

"Here you are," she said, and hovered in the doorway as Markel and I entered.

I didn't exactly want her standing by, but nor did I feel justified in sending her away, and so proceeded as if she were gone, assessing what I saw. The room was small, but not cramped, the furnishings simple and clean. A battered travelling bag sat at the foot of the bed, and as Markel moved to flick through it, I looked at what other effects Syana had left behind. It felt morbidly voyeuristic, and yet sickly fascinating at the same time. *She tried to kill me, and now she's dead, and this is what's left of her.* There was a hairbrush on the room's one shelf, its bristles still laced with brown and silver threads, alongside a leather bracelet set with amber and tiny pieces of haematite. I picked it up without conscious volition, thumb smoothing over the edges. The leather was worn soft from use, the amber scratched in places, as if it had been worn every day—a piece of the real Syana abandoned in favour of her torc and mismatched finery. Something about the contrast struck me powerfully, and without quite meaning to, I found myself pocketing the bracelet, though if someone had asked me in that moment what I planned to do with it, I couldn't have answered them.

Behind me, Markel clicked his fingers to catch my attention. I looked around and found he'd finished going through the travelling sack.

"Anything?" I asked.

He shook his head.

We both considered a moment, and then, with unintentional unison, our gazes drifted towards the bed. There weren't many hiding places in a room like this, and while a more resourceful person might've gone to the effort of prising up a floorboard, something told me Syana had been more simplistic in her actions.

Without speaking, Markel and I both moved to the bed and

raised the mattress. It was difficult to grasp, the ticking lumpen and sagging, and I had no wish to add to Ren Masin's worries by ripping it, but once it was levered upright, we found what we were looking for: a slim leather folio, cracking and worn, tied closed with a bit of twine. I fished it out while Markel kept the mattress at bay, and then we both sat to examine it.

Inside were several sheafs of paper, though not in any apparent order. There were some letters which seemed to be from Syana's daughter, though the handwriting was messy and hard to decipher, along with a few ink drawings on darker scrap paper that looked to be the work of a child. But at the back, on a far better stock than anything else in the folio, was a single, neatly worded document, the mere sight of which raised the hairs on the back of my neck.

It read:

This deed certifies that, by the authority of the landholder, on completion of duties agreed to elsewhere, the property known as the Corner House on Winding Edge in the town of Vaiko under the jurisdiction of Qi-Katai will be restored to its former state and full ownership granted to Ren Syana Nisit, to be inherited by her chosen heirs. This deed becomes legally binding once signed by both parties.

And beneath this paragraph, two signatures: one clearly Syana's, and the other—

I stared at the page, heart pounding. The second signature was as elegantly indecipherable as any I'd seen, but beside it was a seal stamped in bold red ink, and though this had bled slightly, I could still make out the name beneath the unfamiliar crest: Ru Kisian Faez, the Velvet Chair.

24

I emerged from the inn in a daze, unable to comprehend our
discovery. It made no sense for Ru Kisian to have sent Syana:
out of everyone, he most wanted my marriage to Cae to be accepted. Unless he'd lied—but to what end, and why? It had certainly
won him few friends in the divided court, but perhaps that was the
point: having proposed the alliance, it must've come as a shock when
I ended up wedding Caethari rather than Laecia. The dilemma had
fixed him between a rock and a hard place: disavow his own scheme
in deference to Ralian sensibilities and be thought a coward, or continue to promote a match he knew stood little chance of achieving the
desired end? And if nothing else, he would've been one of a handful of
people to know that the late cietena's lands were about to increase in
value, making it a smart decision to snap them up—but no, no, that
didn't make sense. If the alliance failed, then the purchase became
worthless, didn't it?

Unless Ru Kisian had determined that the alliance was incapable of succeeding with me at the core of it, and had taken steps to
protect his investment accordingly, all while holding to his princi-
ples in public.

I'd only met the man briefly, but still, the betrayal stung. And
yet I found myself wondering: why, if the price of Syana's services
had apparently been her family home, had she brought the deed
with her, instead of passing it off to the family members of whose
protection she'd boasted to Markel? Even if she'd thought herself
able to escape the guards, she'd already been dying from a canker of
the breast. If it was real, the deed should've been long since passed

off to her family for safekeeping. Unless she only received it when she arrived in Qi-Xihan—but if so, why hadn't she mailed it away before embarking on her mission? It was possible she'd run out of time—I recalled the point about how quickly she would've had to respond to word of the open court in order to reach the palace ahead of us—but why risk everything for a prize she'd effectively abandoned? Even if, as Markel's account suggested, she'd also been paid in coin already passed to her family, the deed still should've counted for something. The only reason to leave it behind was if she'd arranged for someone to collect it later—

My skin prickled. The missing palace token was yet to be found, nor was there any sign of her room key. She might easily have met her master at the palace and handed them over, especially if she'd run out of time to post the deed and needed someone to do it for her after the fact.

But if so, why had the deed still been left for us to find?

Markel tapped me on the shoulder, jolting me from my stupor. Slipping Grace's reins over his arm—we were leading the horses again, as the crowds had only increased in the time we'd spent indoors—he signed, "Think later. For now, keep your wits about you."

I nodded dully, though it was hard to focus on anything but our discovery. Was the deed a trap? Had someone left it deliberately to cast suspicion on Ru Kisian, the same way Cae's jade-handled dagger had been used to implicate him in Alu Nyas's death? Or was I just grasping at straws, desperate for any excuse not to suspect one of the few people who'd professed themselves our ally?

Beside me, Gift whickered nervously, bumping her head against my shoulder, and as I worked to keep my balance, I cursed under my breath. Away from the Stagger, the streets were narrower, but as the Stone Hare was evidently one of many inns in this quarter, a significant number of festival-goers were pushing towards us, eagerly going in search of wine and merriment. Even with the horses to help make space in the crowd, we were pushing against the current, and in the time that she'd been hitched outside, subjected to noise and strangeness, Gift's earlier equanimity had started to turn to nervousness.

"We need to get out of this crowd," I murmured to Markel. "Find another route back to the Stagger, or—"

A tremendous *bang!* went up in front of us, and I had just enough time to register that the shower of sparks was a firework before Gift reared, screamed and sprang away, yanking the reins from my hand as she knocked me over. I fell, the cobbles stingingly cold against my palms and knees, and coughed as bluish smoke from the firework wreathed the air. People were yelling, frightened and startled by the horse, the noise, the sparks; I had a dim notion that Markel was battling hard to keep hold of Grace, who'd like-wise spooked, but all I could think of were Gift's shod hooves and the throngs of little children I'd seen earlier.

"Markel!" I coughed out. "Markel, get Gift, don't let her hurt anyone!"

I don't know if he heard me, but the next thing I heard was a high-pitched scream as Grace went bulling past me, doing her level best to bolt despite Markel still clinging grimly to the reins. I levered myself to my knees, swaying dangerously as the crowd, no longer blockaded by the threat of flailing hooves, rushed past me; I was clipped by knees and hips, but somehow managed to keep upright. I coughed again, throat stinging at the abuse, and as I doubled over, I felt something push against my shoulder—a sharp, longish nudge, as if I'd stumbled against the edge of a shelf or table.

But there was no shelf or table, and as my pulse spiked, I realised before I even saw my attacker—before I'd even consciously pro-cessed that the nudge I'd felt was a blade skidding off the leather of my coat—that I was in danger. I threw myself sideways, and this time I heard the whistling sound as the knife went by, a hairs-breadth from my left ear.

"Markel!" I yelled again, terrified, but my voice was lost in the noisy panic of the crowd: the nearest people had noticed the knife and were once more pushing and shoving to get out of danger. Sprawled on my back, hands braced on the stone, I finally caught a glimpse of my attacker as he lunged towards me—a tall man, unshaven, his black hair loose to his jaw, olive-skinned and scarred across one cheek—but as I went to scrabble away, a passing foot stomped on my hand. Pain snapped through me; I yanked my hand free, shoving my body backwards, but could do nothing but throw up my good arm to try and intercept the knife—

Something crashed into my assailant from the side—no, some-*one.* For a split second, I thought it was Markel, but this person was bigger, bearing my attacker down to the ground, taking hold of their wrist and smashing it against the stone until, with a spasming curse, they released the knife. A brief scuffle ensued, most of it lost to me as I took advantage of the moment to heave myself upright, and when I looked again, the scarred man was on his knees, struggling futilely as my saviour bound his arms behind his back. With this done, they frisked him expertly, clicking their tongue like a schoolmaster as they fished several small knives and other weapons from various places on my assailant's person, pocketing each one in turn.

For a moment, I could only stare in bewilderment. The newcomer was dressed in an oilskin coat with a matching, broad-brimmed hat, which combination made it difficult to make out anything about them beyond the brown skin of their hands—but then they looked up again, and my heart jolted painfully in my chest.

"*Qarrah?*"

The woman in question grinned at me, giving a sharp tug on the rope that bound her captive. "The one and only."

"But I can't—I don't—what are you *doing* here?"

"Saving your hide," she said simply.

There were many things I could've said in response to that, but I set them aside as, beyond her, I caught sight of Markel, both horses in hand as he jogged towards us as fast as the crowds allowed. The earlier press of bodies had thinned, and I became belatedly conscious of the fact that we were starting to attract onlookers. Before I could voice a concern about this, however, Qarrah hauled her captive to his feet and shoved him forwards by the back of the head, saying, "Follow me."

I glanced at Markel, who looked just as startled as I felt at Qarrah's sudden reappearance, but with little other choice, we did as she said and followed her. I hadn't thought there were any nearby side streets, but Qarrah quickly turned us down an alley so narrow, the horses barely fit: I had to take Gift from Markel in order to lead them single file, and still the saddle leather rasped audibly against the bricks on either side, until we emerged into a tiny open space where the corners of three buildings didn't quite meet. It was barely big enough for all of us, and I had a moment's logistical worry about how we'd get the horses turned around again before realising that the alley kept going, presumably opening out into the next street up, and with that, my focus sharpened once more to the situation at hand.

Markel stared hard at Qarrah's captive, then looked at me with naked worry on his face, only belatedly realising that I'd once again been in danger.

"It's fine," I said quickly, as he raised his hands to speak. "I'm not hurt. But," I added, shooting Qarrah a meaningful look, "I'd very much like some answers."

"Then answers you shall have," she said, and none too gently kicked her captive's legs out from under him, so that he crashed to his knees with a grunt. From somewhere at her hip, she produced a wickedly curved blade and, standing behind him, set it to his throat, forcing him to look up at us.

"Speak," she growled. "Who are you, and who sent you?"

Her captive made a frustrated noise but didn't answer. Qarrah kissed the blade more firmly to his neck and, to my utter shock, repeated her query in perfectly fluent Ralian.

"Fuck you, bitch," the man spat, responding in the same language. "What does it matter now? Just kill me and be done with it."

Qarrah smiled sharply, though positioned as he was, the man couldn't see it. "If it doesn't matter, then answer the question."

He swore again, as vicious a string of profanity as any I'd ever heard, but Qarrah's hand remained firm on the rope, her blade steady and sure at his throat, and eventually, his rage petered out into a sort of disgusted respect.

"You've been the one on my heels?" he said, and laughed, a hoarse, braying sound. "*You?* Fuck me."

"Thanks, but I prefer women," said Qarrah coolly.

"Heh. I 'spose that figures." He sighed, tipping his head sideways, and fixed me with a smile that was three parts malice to one part pity. "You're hard to kill, vin Aaro, I'll give you that much. Stubborn little bastard."

"Who are you," Qarrah growled again, knife pressing just that little bit harder against his throat, "and *who sent you?*"

He snorted. "What the fuck good does my name do you?" And then, before she could answer that, "I go by Rade. That good enough, or do you want my family tree, too?"

"It's enough," said Qarrah. "Keep talking."

Rade looked at me, a smirk on his lips. "Been trying to kill you since Etho," he said, as casually as if we were talking over dinner. "Not that you've made it easy."

"You," I said. Stopped. The words were cottony in my mouth. "The fire. That was you?"

"It was."

I felt as if I was underwater. "And the archer, at the ferry—"

"Me," he said. "And the girth, and the bridge." He made a disgusted noise. "If your friend here hadn't been tracking me, I'd have managed more than that, but. Well. Such is life."

"The firework just now," I said. "That was—"

"Me, again. Yes. Almost had you, too." He rolled his eyes, half turning his head in an effort to stare up at Qarrah. "Though I'd lost you at the gates, but apparently not."

"Apparently not," she echoed grimly. And then, to me, her tone apologetic, "Though I did lose him for a bit, or it wouldn't have come to this."

"How did you find him, then?" I asked faintly.

"The same way he found you just now," she replied. "By watching the palace and waiting to see when you came back out. Which is also why I didn't make myself known to you before this; if I'd done that, he might've melted away again."

Nodding dumbly, I stared at Rade. There was one more question left to ask, and now that we'd come to it, I found that I both did and didn't want to know the answer.

"Before now, you were trying to make it look like an accident," I said, voice flat.

"I was," he agreed. "I don't get paid in full, otherwise. But I figured—hey, knifed in an alley during a festival brawl, that's good enough, right?"

"So, who—" I swallowed, fighting to get the question out. On some level, I already felt certain of the answer, but still, I had to hear it. "Who sent you?"

He laughed, and I braced for him to name Asrien, or else some faction within the Ralian court; or even the king himself, if Asrien's Shade was acting as a rogue agent.

"Your brother did," said Rade. "Lord Nathian."

Beside me, Markel inhaled sharply. I simply froze, unable to process the wrenching dislocation between the blow I'd braced for and the one that had landed.

"What?" I whispered.

It's a terrible thing, to be pitied by a man who's been hired to kill you, and yet there was pity in Rade's eyes, which cut deeper than any blow he'd managed to land. Somewhat hysterically, I began to laugh, because what else was there to do? Not even an hour past, I'd mourned the idea that Nathian might be lost to me forever, only to learn that he'd sent a man to kill me. It was too absurd; I pictured the teenaged Nathian, gangly and self-important, and tried to imagine him hiring an assassin, and the image was so ridiculous that I laughed even harder. Even Rade looked slightly alarmed by my response, Gift whickering worriedly at my shoulder.

"Why?" I choked out, in between gales of horrible laughter. "Did someone put him up to it, or was he just embarrassed?"

"It was all him, far as I know," said Rade. "Said something about a disgrace to the family and not wanting to hurt his children's prospects, which seems stupid to me, but. Well. Nobles tend towards stupidity. That's how I get paid." He shrugged, apparently turned philosopher by his captivity.

"And you didn't—" I battled down my laughter, wishing I could suppress the sickness in my stomach anywhere near as easily. "—just to be clear, you never broke into the palace? Never killed anyone there?"

Rade looked at me as if I were stupid. "If I could've done that," he said, "you'd already be dead. *And* I'd have charged your brother triple for the risk."

"What about a woman named Syana, do you know her? Or Cietena Alu Nyas? Or Ru Kisian Faez? Lord Asrien bo Erat? General Naza?"

With each name listed, Rade's expression only grew more bewildered. "What do I look like, a fucking social butterfly? I only met your brother the once, and since then, I've been working. Not exactly a lot of spare time for attending *soirees*."

As abruptly as my laughter had come, it drained away, replaced by a profound and draining sense of grief. "Oh," I said softly, an awful lump in my throat. Not even King Markus had wanted me dead, though that was hardly due to any kindness on his part. He'd sent Asrien to seduce me away from Cae, not because he valued my life, but because my death was too politically messy to be his first resort. But Nathian—Nathian, who'd cleaned my scraped knees and dutifully helped me to learn my letters in childhood; Nathian, with whom I'd grieved Revic; Nathian, who was a pompous, unimaginative, moralistic ass, but still my older brother—*Nathian* had tried to have me killed, not because he'd been blackmailed or as part of some greater political scheme, but because he thought I was shameful. An embarrassment to the family. Wrong.

It shouldn't have hurt so much. I'd always known what he thought of men like me. I'd braced for it earlier, hadn't I—for the prospect that I might write to him, and never hear anything back? Why did it hurt so much?

"Tiern—" ventured Qarrah, and my gaze snapped towards her. I needed—wanted—a target for what I was feeling, and she was the only one available.

"You lied to us," I said coldly. "Back in Etho, you knew exactly who we were."

"I did," said Qarrah, unflinching. She lifted her chin. "I'm sorry to have caused you any distress, but—"

"But what?" I spat. "Who the fuck are you, really? Is Orin here, too? Why did you get involved in any of this?"

"Orin's not here," said Qarrah. "He escorted your pretty friend back to Qi-Katai as planned, and should still be there, making sure she and your kin are safe. I rode with them briefly, then made my excuses and doubled back to follow you—too late to stop this one from shooting you at the ferry," she said, tapping Rade's throat with the flat of her blade, "but soon enough to start tracking him afterwards."

"But *why?*" I rasped.

"Because the asa willed it," Qarrah said softly—and before I could protest, she sheathed her blade, reached into an inside pocket of her coat and withdrew something, holding it out on the flat of her palm.

It took me a moment to register what I was seeing, but when I did, I almost laughed again, tears of helpless frustration pricking the corners of my eyes.

It was a small carnelian reseko, twin to the one I'd been given by Yasa Kithadi.

Seeing my comprehension of it, Qarrah returned the reseko to her pocket and said, "I'd be happy to continue this conversation, but I think we'd be better off having it somewhere more comfortable, don't you?"

I glanced at Markel, who for once looked as lost for words as I felt. "Do you think we can trust her?" I signed.

"She saved your life," he replied. "That's all that matters to me."

"All right, then," I said aloud. "Where do you want to go?"

"The palace," she said. "Aside from anything else, I need to bring this one in." She gave a meaningful tug on Rade's bindings.

Rade made a face. "Don't suppose there's any chance of you letting me go?"

"Sorry," said Qarrah, not sounding sorry at all, and hauled him to his feet, steering him out the other end of the alley with all the calm expertise of a farmer taking a truculent steer to slaughter. I followed a moment later, Markel bringing up the rear, and after another, even tighter squeeze through the narrow alley, we emerged onto an unfamiliar side street. Here as before, the festival crowds were plentiful, and though my legs were starting to ache, we were forced to walk the horses through the crowds in order to rejoin the Stagger, which was even more heavily populated than before. I braced myself for a long, draining walk back to the palace, but Markel, eternally sharp-eyed, saw that I was tiring and bullied me into riding.

"I'll lead you," he signed, taking Gift's reins and nudging me to mount up. His eyes were worried, and between my heartsickness over Nathian's actions and my growing exhaustion, I lacked the strength to argue. I hauled myself into the saddle without looking at Qarrah or Rade, patted Gift's neck and twined my fingers through her mane for purchase like a toddler on his first pony.

"Remember," Qarrah growled to Rade, who was looking around the crowds with the air of a man desperate for escape. "I'd prefer to bring you in for added testimony, but the asa trusts my word. Play the fool, and I'll leave your corpse in an alley."

"Such fine choices you offer me," Rade snarked, but remained compliant as we began to move, Qarrah urging him forwards with Markel close behind.

Unbidden, I recalled a similarly unpleasant ride in the company of a bound prisoner taken not long ago, back in Qi-Katai, when Cae and I had captured Ren Adan, Laecia's co-conspirator. I'd not expected to mirror that journey anytime soon, least of all with Cae in prison, but here I was, shepherding yet another man who'd tried to kill me. *At least I did without the magical overextension this time,* I thought bitterly, and suppressed another ugly bout of laughter.

The trip back to the palace felt like a fever dream. I slumped in the saddle, too drained by Nathian's betrayal to spare any higher brainpower for the prospect of Ru Kisian's, and all the while, the crowds around us laughed and sang, the crisp air warmed with the mouthwatering scents of festival food and the gaiety of music. From time to time, Markel cast concerned glances my way, but with his hands on two sets of reins and the crush of bodies difficult to navigate, even with Qarrah and Rade forging a path for us, he had little attention to spare.

After what felt like an eternity, we arrived back at the palace gates. Qarrah, it seemed, had her own palace token, and an uncommon one at that: the guards took one look at it and instantly straightened, eager to do her bidding.

"I've a prisoner here," she said. "Remanded on the asa's authority. If someone could transport him to the prison, I'd be obliged. And of course," she added, "I need to be announced to the asa."

"Of course!" said the senior guard, looking flustered, and promptly delegated her two offsiders to fulfil each task, one leading a scowling, swearing Rade to the cells while the other dashed off to inform the asa of Qarrah's arrival.

"Who *are* you?" I muttered, as we started moving again. I hadn't thought Qarrah could hear me, but she turned, flashing me a look that was almost apologetic, though still paired with a semi-mischievous smile.

"I am what I'm required to be," she said, and led us on towards the Little Palace.

25

Arriving at the Little Palace, we found that, in addition to our being expected, there were grooms on hand, ready to take Gift and Grace to the Circlet Annex stable. I dismounted reluctantly, struggling to focus on the moment at hand, and so almost missed the whispered aside between Qarrah and one of the guards.

"How's the mood?" she asked him.

"Tense," he murmured back.

They exchanged a meaningful look, but said no more. Taking advantage of their distraction, and lest anyone try to part me from Markel, I slung an arm around his shoulders and made a show of leaning on him. He looked briefly alarmed by this, but calmed when I murmured, "So they don't send you away," and with Qarrah still in the lead, we proceeded into the asa's territory.

Whether by design or coincidence, we were brought to the same room as yesterday, Asa Ivadi once more presiding regally from her central chair. This time, however, we found her in conference with Tierena Keris and General Naza, one on either side of her, both of whom looked up as we made our entrance.

"Your Majesty," said Qarrah, approaching and going to one knee. "I've come to make my report."

"Speak," said the asa. It was hard to tell, but I thought her tone was warm. "What have you discovered?"

"I've arrested a Ralian assassin named Rade, Your Majesty, who has been in pursuit of Tiern Velasin since he departed for Qi-Xihan."

General Naza straightened in his seat at that, but didn't interrupt, listening with tense fascination as Qarrah continued.

"In the town of Etho, he was responsible for the deaths of nine innocents when he set the inn ablaze. At the Nihri River, he wounded a ferryman as well as Yaseran Caethari, and at the Sihae River, he was responsible for the broken bridge which nearly cost the lives of Tiern Ethin, Ciet Yarasil and Ciet Irias."

Now it was the tierena's turn to stiffen, her mouth a hard, angry line at the reminder that her grandson had nearly been killed.

"And today," Qarrah went on, "he created panic in the festival crowds to make another attempt on Tiern Velasin's life, in the course of which I was able to apprehend him."

General Naza raised an eyebrow. "And was this man also responsible for the actions of the prisoner Syana?"

Qarrah shook her head. "He was not," she said.

"Huh." The general seemed almost disappointed by this, and my hackles rose as I recalled Asrien's accusations. General Naza might not have sent Syana himself, but staring at him now, it was easy to believe that he'd chosen to let her attack me.

"Who sent him, then?" demanded Tierena Keris. "Who is responsible for harming my Ethin?"

Qarrah exhaled. "It was Lord Nathian vin Aaro," she said. "Tiern Velasin's brother."

I'd known the admission was coming, and yet it still thumped me about the heart, to hear it said so baldly. Everyone looked at me, and as the asa's piercing gaze snagged mine, clearly signalling inquiry, I hauled myself forwards, disentangled my arm from Markel's shoulders, knelt beside Qarrah—on the wrong knee again, moons!—cursed under my breath, somehow changed knees without toppling over and said, "It's true, Your Majesty. He confessed it."

"And do you believe him?"

I startled. "Asa?"

"Do you believe him," she said again. "He might well have lied, passing blame to a probable individual in order to mask the involvement of higher powers—the Ralian throne, for instance."

I froze in place, staring aghast at the asa, who watched me in turn with indecipherable calm. I swallowed. Did she know about Asrien? Did she know that *I* knew about Asrien? Or did she merely suspect him, and hope that my reaction would betray the truth? Or did she truly think Nathian a puppet of King Markus? I didn't believe he was, but if the asa didn't take my word for it, the only way to prove otherwise would be to give her Asrien, whom I'd promised to help. *So what if you lied instead?* a little voice whispered. What if I claimed that Nathian wouldn't have done such a thing without external pressure? Would Tithena move against Ralia in retribution? Or might that happen anyway if I told the truth, the damage limited instead to my brother and his family?

For a silk-spun moment, I contemplated hedging my bets and saying Nathian might have been the pawn of higher powers, partly because it was indeed possible, but mostly because, in my heart of hearts, I didn't want to believe he'd tried to have me killed. But I didn't want to lie, and I found that, for all the ill-will I bore my home nation—for all its faults; for all that it had hurt me—I didn't want to hand either General Naza's faction or the asa herself a pretext for hostilities, either.

"I believe him," I said, my voice cracking on the words. "If the throne wanted me dead, they'd have agents both more subtle and more capable to go through than Nathian, to say nothing of a better choice of assassin, and he—Rade, I mean—I don't . . . he gains nothing from lying now."

"You truly mean to tell me," said General Naza, incredulous, "that your brother thinks your marriage sufficient grounds for assassination?"

"Evidently so," I said, unable to keep the bitterness from my tone. My eyes stung, and I blinked away the salt in them.

"Barbaric," he muttered.

"I will, of course, have the assassin questioned further," said the asa, "but I value your assessment of the matter." She paused, looking me critically up and down. "I'll admit to some surprise, however, that you chose to leave the palace today, especially after yesterday's excitement."

I swallowed. For a brief, beautiful moment, I'd been able to forget about the matter of Ru Kisian, but no longer. "I . . . Understand, asa, I mean this as no slight to the general's investigative abilities—" I cut him as polite a nod as I could manage, and received a scowl for my troubles. "—but as I know for certain that Caethari is innocent of Cietena Alu's murder, it occurred to me to wonder: who would go to the trouble of framing him, and why? And as it seemed unlikely that the general would prioritize finding such a person, given his belief in Caethari's guilt, I decided to, ah . . . make my own arrangements."

"Indeed," said Asa Ivadi, in a tone that meant *go on,* while General Naza skewered me with his glare.

And so I told her everything: my reasons for wanting to know where Syana had come from, the logic with which I'd had Irias and Yarasil search for her, and how they'd found success, culminating in my trip to the Stone Hare. As I spoke, I was acutely aware of Qarrah beside me, listening, and realised I had no idea where Markel was. Most likely, he'd either knelt behind me or gone to stand by the wall—certainly, I hadn't heard him leave, nor had his presence been remarked upon—and yet I found myself fighting the urge to turn my head and look for him. I couldn't argue with the evidence of what we'd found, and yet I badly wanted to; wanted a moment alone with Markel to weigh the wisdom of disclosure, if nothing else. But that was a luxury I didn't have, and so I ignored the dull ache in my knee and finished my recitation.

"And did you find anything?" Tierena Keris asked intently.

I nodded, throat dry. "I did," I said, and withdrew the deed from the inside pocket of my coat, extending it towards the asa. I'd half expected either the general or the tierena to take it in her stead, but to my surprise, Asa Ivadi reached out and claimed it herself. Even more surprisingly, she proceeded to read it aloud in her crisp, dry voice: "'This deed certifies that, by the authority of the landholder . . .'"

Her expression was unchanging until the end, when it abruptly became a mask. She stared woodenly at the page, then said, "This bears Ru Kisian's seal."

Beside me, Qarrah swore under her breath; Tierena Keris let out a shocked gasp, while General Naza half leapt out of his seat in his enthusiasm to see the page, which the asa duly thrust in his direction. The general scanned it greedily, then let out a small, self-satisfied *hah!*

"This would make sense, Your Majesty," he said, with mounting excitement. "The man's not a complete fool—he must've realised the Ralians would never accept the current alliance, but didn't want to look two-faced by abandoning it outright. And if he'd bought the land from the cietena hoping to turn a profit, only for the circumstances to sour—"

"Enough," the asa said, her tone just shy of snapping. I winced, and not just because the general's conclusions so closely mirrored my own: I'd once more upset the political balance in the asa's court without fully comprehending the consequences, and that was a dangerous habit to make.

Something about the thought niggled at me, as if I was missing something important. Unable to think what that might be in the moment, I set it aside for later, focussing on the present as Tierena Keris said, "We should, at the least, invite the Velvet Chair to explain himself."

"Yes," said the asa, cutting in ahead of General Naza. "Let's have Ru Kisian brought here immediately." As the guards moved to comply, she looked askance at Qarrah and me and added, "You two might as well sit; it's ridiculous to keep kneeling."

Wincing slightly, I mumbled thanks and hauled myself onto the nearest couch, though making sure to keep a respectable distance between myself and Tierena Keris. Qarrah opted for the space next to General Naza, who seemed less put out by this than I might've expected, quietly cracking her knuckles as we waited. From my new vantage point, I could see that Markel had posted himself to the side of the door, though even at a distance, he looked nervous about being there. I caught his eye, but didn't dare risk signing to him; the tension in the room was palpable, and the longer it went on, the more my nape prickled with sweat.

When the guards finally announced Ru Kisian's arrival, I let out a relieved breath, only to hold it again as he entered. He had a hunted look to him, and as he came to kneel before the asa, it suddenly struck me powerfully that he was Liran's cousin, which perhaps accounted for why, despite my barely knowing him, finding Syana's deed had felt so much like a betrayal.

"You summoned me, asa?" he said.

Asa Ivadi thrust the document at him. "Explain this."

Ru Kisian looked confused as he accepted it. "What—" he began, but the words trailed off as he read the contents. All at once, his skin went ashen; he swallowed hard, hand trembling slightly where it gripped the page. He lowered the document, looking up at the asa with wide eyes. "I—asa, I—"

"Is it true?" the asa demanded, hands gripping the arms of her chair. "Kisian. Did you purchase land from Cietena Alu Nyas?"

Ru Kisian's gaze darted helplessly around the room as if in search of rescue. Then, shoulders slumping, he whispered, "I did."

"Including that property?"

"Yes, asa."

"That's your official seal and signature on the document, correct?"

"Yes, but—"

Asa Ivadi silenced him with a wave of her hand. "Did you employ the woman Syana to murder Tiern Velasin?"

"No!" said Ru Kisian frantically, "No, I would never—"

"Did you murder Cietena Alu Nyas?"

"*No!*" he said again, sounding almost hysterical. "Asa, please, I did not do this—"

"Then explain yourself!" Asa Ivadi cried. "Explain what else I am to think of all this, Kisian!"

"I cannot," he croaked, and fell to both knees in supplication. He looked at all of us in turn, and when his gaze lingered on me, my skin pebbled as if from the cold. "Please, I would not—I bought the land, but nothing more! I know nothing about this deed, I swear by the saints, I'm being framed!"

"As Yaseran Caethari, too, claimed to have been framed?" asked General Naza. "Perhaps the two of you were working together."

"Oh, don't be absurd," I snapped, glaring at him. "What, you think my husband fought tooth and nail to save me in Qi-Katai, waited a few weeks, saw I was being targeted again, hauled me out of a burning building, took an arrow protecting me and dove into a *freezing river* to fish me out, only to turn around and collude with a different set of assassins to cut my throat, and then, when that didn't work, got himself drugged and nearly murdered before sneaking off to kill one of his co-conspirators in revenge for working with him to fail to kill me, only to then languish in prison rather than give up his *other* co-conspirator?" I let out a manic laugh, too angry and tired to find the general fearsome. "If this is your idea of coherent logic, General, then I *weep* for your soldiers."

General Naza made an outraged noise and came half to his feet, only settling when the asa barked his name and gestured him down again. He looked absolutely furious, which I felt pettily pleased about, his neck and ears burning as Tierena Keris said, with excoriating dryness, "Tiern Velasin makes a compelling point."

"Perhaps," said the general, through gritted teeth. "Nonetheless, the fact that the yaseran was found standing over the body, with his personal knife as the murder weapon, possessed of ample motive—"

"Do *you* know anything about this?" Qarrah cut in, directing the question to the still-terrified Ru Kisian.

"No!" he babbled. "No, no, I'm not—I am not working with anyone, this isn't—I've done nothing but buy some land, I hadn't even met the yaseran until he arrived here—"

"Will you please," I snarled at the general, goaded beyond all patience, "for one moment, look at this rationally? You can pretend all you like that Cae wasn't drugged at that party, that nobody tried to drown him, but don't sit there and pretend that you didn't—" I bit off what I'd been going to say: *that you didn't set up Asrien to seduce him,* partly because that was a card I couldn't play without potentially reantagonising Asrien, but mostly because I couldn't prove it offhand. "—that you aren't cutting out any evidence that doesn't fit your theory. You want Cae to be guilty, and so you're not looking for anything else. He was only at the cietena's house because *you* hadn't made time to see her, just like I only found that letter"—I waved a hand at Ru Kisian—"because *you* hadn't bothered to check. And what sense in the world would it make for Cae to commit a murder using, very specifically, the *one* knife that's identifiably his? Why would he let the entire staff see him enter the house, then stand waiting over the body instead of doing literally anything else—wait." I stared at General Naza, a simple and yet damnably belated realisation hitting me all at once. "You interviewed the cietena's staff yesterday. Did you ask them if they'd seen the jade knife on Cae? Because he didn't have it with him. He lost it at the party, or had it stolen there. Ask anyone who saw him leave the palace that morning—*he didn't have the knife.*"

A muscle twitched in the general's face, and that must've meant something to the asa, as she instantly straightened in her chair and said sharply, "Naza. Did you ask?"

Reluctantly, as if he were having a tooth pulled, the general said, "We asked."

"And?"

"And the staff had no memory of it. But that doesn't prove—"

"*Enough!*" snapped the asa, more forcefully than I'd yet heard her speak. She stood at once, and the rest of us stood with her—all except Ru Kisian, who remained kneeling in terrified penance like a rabbit caught in a field between farmer and hound. "I gave you your second chance, Naza," said Asa Ivadi, soft and furious. Standing close as we were, it struck me for the first time that she barely came up to his chest, and yet the general visibly tensed beneath the force of her displeasure. "This has gone too far. I cannot strip you of the Iron Chair, but with Ruya as my witness, I can and will strip you of any authority in this investigation."

The general stiffened. "Asa, please—"

"You will take Ru Kisian into custody at *once*," she continued over the top of him, "and release Yaseran Caethari to the palace at large." Ru Kisian, hearing this, let out a low moan of anguish; selfishly, I could only be glad of my husband's impending freedom. "That will be your last official act in this matter, with control remanded thereafter to my personal guard. You will be questioned as to your previous methods and actions, and you *will* cooperate. Do you understand me?"

General Naza went to one knee, shoulders rigid. "I understand, asa."

"Good," said the asa curtly. "Now see it done."

He obeyed, taut fury in every line of his body as he grabbed Ru Kisian by the back of his lin and hauled him upright as if he were scruffing a puppy, Ru Kisian protesting and pleading all the while. He dropped the deed, which fluttered to the floor, and Tierena Keris swiftly bent down to retrieve it, passing it off to the asa. I felt a pang of unease as Ru Kisian was led away: he'd admitted to the land purchase and hadn't denied the signature was his, but his terror and his lack of an explanation made me more anxious, not less. *He didn't expect the deed to be found,* I told myself. *You caught him off guard; he didn't have time to come up with a plausible excuse, and was so overconfident that he didn't think he'd need one before now. You only feel bad because he's Liran's cousin.* But still, as the doors opened and one of the asa's guards joined General Naza in hauling Ru Kisian away, I locked eyes again with Markel, who looked just as perturbed as I did, and felt my stomach lurch with uncertainty.

"Well!" said Tierena Keris, sounding somewhere between

shocked and breathless. "That was rather more excitement than I was expecting to have."

"That makes two of us," the asa said grimly.

The tierena winced. "Forgive me, Ivi," she said, and it took all my self-possession not to startle at hearing a monarch addressed in public by such an intimate name. "I know you've favoured him."

"I can't believe it of him," the asa said roughly. She rubbed her temples and sat again, necessitating that the rest of us do likewise. "Kisian is many things, but a murderer?"

"Perhaps he was manipulated into it," said Tierena Keris. "He offered no defence, it's true, but that doesn't mean there isn't one; only that he didn't feel free to speak it."

"I hope you're right," said the asa, sounding deeply wearied. "Aside from anything else, appointing new chairs is an utter aggravation, never mind getting them broken in afterwards."

"You could always move the Velvet Chair to the Circlet," said the tierena. When Asa Ivadi snorted, she added slyly, "Or perhaps to the Will? Make it an electable position?"

"Electable by whom, our ambassadors?"

"Why not?" countered Tierena Keris.

Asa Ivadi favoured her with a flat look. "Have you ever tried to get a group of ambassadors to agree on anything?"

"I would've thought the profession implied cooperation."

"Oh, it does," said the asa darkly. "It's getting them to talk to each other that's the problem. They're like snowcats that way: too many too close together, and the claws come out."

"Well, in that case," said the tierena, "you could always appoint Tiern Velasin."

I stared at her. "What?"

She raised a brow at me. "You don't think you're up to the challenge?" And then, to Asa Ivadi, "You must admit, the uproar would be *delightful*."

"Said the spectator to the referee," the asa quipped dryly. But she had a thoughtful look on her face as she said it, and I experienced an unwelcome chill of premonition. As if sensing this, she cut me a sharp-eyed look. "You continue to be an unexpected presence in my court, Tiern Velasin."

"I am . . . not trying to be?" I said, uncertain of whether she meant it as a rebuke or a compliment. Qarrah made a noise at that, as of stifled laughter, but when I shot her an irritated look, her face was serene.

"And yet," said the asa. She let me stew in the implications of that for a moment, then sighed and waved her hand. "You're dismissed, Tiern Velasin," she said. "Go and see your husband. And please, for my sake—try to stay out of trouble."

"I'll try," I said.

"See that you do," she said.

I rose, bowed, collected Markel and made my exit, only belatedly aware of the fact that I was trembling. Too much had happened in too little time; I couldn't hope to process it all, and so clung instead to the one development that made sense: Caethari's impending release.

Catching my eye, Markel signed idly, "I bet there'll be a lot of palace gossip today, once word starts to spread."

My neck heated up. "Is that your way of offering to give me some privacy?"

"It's my way of saying I'd prefer not to hear you two fucking," Markel signed bluntly.

"Markel!" I hissed, then signed frantically, "You don't—you don't know that's what we'll be doing!"

Markel favoured me with a supremely unimpressed look.

I swallowed hard, abruptly conscious of all my failings where it came to Caethari; of all the times I'd pushed him away since that terrible night in Etho. "It's not . . . he might not even want to," I said softly. "I've only brought him pain."

Markel stopped dead and grabbed my arm, pulling me to a halt. I looked at him, surprised, and felt my cheeks burn as he signed to me, strong and certain, "Velasin, that man is besotted with you. If you asked him to lie naked in the road to prove he loved you, he'd start stripping before you'd even finished the sentence." His gaze softened. "All the way here, I know you've had no real privacy with him, even when you've needed it, and maybe all you'll do is talk. But I don't think that's what's going to happen, and I don't think you do, either."

"I love him," I choked out, cheeks burning with the admission. "I don't know when it started, but I—I love him, Markel." I laughed. "It's terrifying."

Markel raised an eyebrow. "More terrifying than half a dozen people trying to kill you?"

"Perhaps not," I conceded, and started walking again, more quickly than before. Rade's attack on the heels of my seizure had hardly done wonders for my condition, to say nothing of all the less fraught exertion surrounding them, but in the moment, I felt possessed by a sort of manic energy, as if I'd been awake for three days obsessing over a puzzle and had suddenly found the answer. My strength was bound to run out at some point, but until then, I was too preoccupied to think of conserving it, and so I pushed ahead, my skin veritably buzzing.

All the way to the Jade Suite, I tried to plan what to say to Cae—how to explain the day's events and in what order; how to broach the subject of my change in feelings; how to apologise for everything I'd put him through—but when Markel unlocked the door and I found Cae on the other side of it, standing bereft in the middle of the room, I lost all my words in three languages. He was barefoot, his leather coat laid over one of the nearby chairs, his boots lined up neatly nearby, and something about the domesticity of the image made my throat tighten. He turned at the sound of our entry, eyes widening as he turned towards me.

"*Vel*," he croaked, and even as he moved for me, I shrugged my coat to the ground and strode to him, so that we met in the middle. He gripped my arms as I gripped his, each of us frantically scanning the other for signs of harm.

"Are you all right?" I blurted—then froze, my gaze flying to his, for he'd asked the exact same thing of me in the very same breath.

"I'm fine," he whispered, and with that reassurance, something in me snapped. "Are you—"

I curled my hands around his neck and kissed him fiercely, cutting off the question. He made a wounded noise into my mouth and kissed back, his big hands fitting themselves to my hips, and I had just enough presence of mind to register Markel shutting the door as he hurried off before I completely lost myself, aware of nothing but Cae's mouth, his scent, his touch. He kissed me and kissed me, and I kissed him, pulling him with me as I walked us backwards toward the bedroom.

"Vel," he panted against my neck, teeth grazing the skin as he kissed towards my scar, "Vel, Vel—" He gasped as I took his earlobe between my teeth and bit it, drawing his head down as we stumbled towards the bed. The backs of my legs hit the edge of the mattress; I sat with a rush of breath, releasing Cae to brace myself on my palms.

"Undress me," I said, uncertain whether I was begging or commanding him, and my breathing hitched as he promptly dropped to his knees between my legs. He looked at me with hungry, fervent reverence as he removed my boots and socks, kissing my bare ankle before leaning up to pull my lin over my head. I shifted my hips and leaned forwards to help him, and the instant the fabric passed over my head, he kissed me again, deep and greedy. I felt light-headed, pulse racing as his hands slid gently up my sides, and when we pulled away again, he slipped my undershirt off me, too, the fabric shivering against my sensitized skin. He kissed up my stomach, biting not-quite-gently at my nipple; I gasped and arched against him, gripping blindly at his lin trying to haul it over his head. He laughed, half-trapped by the fabric, and moved to unbutton the closures, fingers fumbling frantically until they came undone. He shrugged out of the silk and grinned at me, braids disarraying from their crown, and rocked back on his heels to pull off his undershirt, too.

I looked at him, and looked, and looked. He was golden and warm and glorious, and when he surged up to kiss my throat again, I reached greedily for his hair, tugging this and unpinning that, throwing pins and ribbons aside without any care as to where they landed, gasping beneath his mouth, until I was able to card my fingers through the silver-threaded silk of his hair.

"Mine," I whispered, and steered his head up to kiss my mouth, wriggling backwards onto the bed and somehow bringing him with me, until his weight was fully on mine, my legs splayed to make room for him.

I'd been hard since the moment he touched me, and he was, too, the pair of us grinding against each other through the inconvenient layers of nara and smallclothes. I grabbed at his shoulders, his back, his waist, everything a glory of firm muscle and supple skin, except where I caught his scarring, half out of my mind with need and desperation. *I love you,* I thought, but the words wouldn't come; the truth felt too big, too clumsy compared to the urgency of his body on mine after so much fraught and awful distance. The scent of him was overwhelming, sweat-salt-musk that coated my throat and tongue and left me dizzier than if I'd been drunk. I rocked against him, clawing mindlessly at his back whenever he pulled too far away, panting and whining under the joint ministrations of his hands and mouth, the friction of his cock on mine.

"What do you want?" he panted into my collarbone. "Vel, what do you want?"

"You," I gasped back, too broken open to lie. "You, I want you—"

Cae made a feral noise and fitted his mouth to the hinge of my jaw, above my new scar, and sucked a mark there. I bucked up against him, my fingers digging into his arms for blissful purchase, and when he released me, I almost peaked from that alone.

"Can I fuck you?" he asked, and I nodded blindly, a garbled *yes yes yes* flowing from my mouth. In the back of my mind, I heard Ru Saeri admonishing me against undertaking any strenuous activity, but whatever caution she might've imparted vanished when Cae slid down my body, yanked my nara and smallclothes down and swallowed my cock in a single movement, sucking me as desperately as if he were starved.

"*Cae,*" I breathed, writhing under him, embarrassment and need an itch in my blood. I'd already been close to the brink, and part of me knew he meant for me to come more than once, but still, I wanted to last, I wanted—"Cae, oh fuck, moons—*ah!*"

My climax hit so powerfully, it was like falling downhill drunk, if such a state could ever result in pleasure rather than bruising. I lost all sense of where I was—of the room, the bed, the ceiling and floor—and came to gasping, vision starbursting as he swallowed my spend. And yet, perhaps because of all the healing I'd so recently undergone, or because of the weeks we'd spent not touching each other, or some other combination of things—or maybe just because this was Cae—I barely softened in his mouth, my senses still heightened with desperation even as my body sagged with the laxness of a ragdoll. He knelt up between my legs and looked at me with tender awe, leaning down to kiss a smile into my mouth.

"Are you—" he began, just as I begged, "*More,*" and whatever he'd been going to say was swallowed in a groan.

As I lolled in a yearning daze, Cae stripped us both naked, fished the oil from wherever he'd been keeping it, and grabbed a pillow, fitting it under my hips in a way that left me splayed wantonly open for him.

"*Fuck,*" he breathed, and sucked a mark onto my inner thigh, so that I was already trembling when he slipped his slick fingers into me. Fingers, plural: he started with two, and the stinging, sucking ache of it was perfect, as though my body were gasping for the chance to welcome him in. Yet still, he added more oil than usual, until my thighs were wet with it, and when he finally conceded to my increasingly fevered begging, withdrew his fingers and lined up his cock, he slipped and slid the crown of it against me in a deliberate tease, smirking all the while.

"Please," I gasped, "Cae, please, *please—*"

He fit himself to where I was stretched and knocked into me with the delicious, juddering efficiency of a bolt loaded into a crossbow, his forearms bracing under my thighs as he bent me almost in half.

And then he began to fuck me: deep and wild, sweat beading on his forehead. I twined my arms around his neck and bore him down, whimpering at the change in angle, helpless to do anything but lie there and take it, my whole body zinging with pleasure. Distantly, I was aware that I was making a truly ridiculous amount of noise, but it was like my ears were blocked. My cock was fully hard again, smearing itself against my belly as Cae fucked into me, over and over; we couldn't quite kiss, but I caught his bottom lip between my teeth and sucked on it until he growled. I gripped his shoulder with one hand, the other buried in his hair; I wanted to come a second time but didn't know if I could so close to the first.

And then Cae fitted his mouth to my ear and panted raggedly, "I love you, I love you," and it was like being struck by lightning: I lit up, if possible, even more powerfully than before, body going rigid as he spilled in me, warm and wet to match the streaking white on my stomach. I said something then, or thought I did; I half blacked out as the words wrenched out of me, some animal noise I could neither recall nor comprehend beyond the urgency of saying it, and then I collapsed, sweat-drenched and shivering, as Cae lay over me like a blanket, panting into the hollow of my throat.

I don't know how long we stayed like that; only that, at some point, Cae slid carefully out of me, rolled us over and spooned up behind me, tucking his head against my back, his arms around my waist. I must've fallen asleep for a time, or else passed out—either was possible, given my still technically recuperative state—but when I came to, it was to find Cae wiping me clean of our collective mess, a warm cloth working between my legs as he tenderly kissed my hip.

I love you, I wanted to say again, but didn't; or couldn't, rather, my throat stoppered by the strength of what I meant to express, as if something so vast were incapable of fitting through such a small and human aperture. "Cae," I murmured instead, and he looked at me with a softness that stilled my breath. "Cae, come here."

For an answer, he set his cloth aside and pulled me into his arms, rearranging us so that we both fit under the covers. We needed to talk, I knew that; not just about my feelings, but about what had happened elsewhere, and what it meant, and how in the moons we were meant to proceed from here. But in that moment, I didn't care about any of it; only wanted, fiercely and righteously, for everything else to go away and leave us alone. And perhaps Cae wanted the same as me, for he didn't talk: just kissed my forehead where I lay pillowed against his chest, and breathed, and stroked my naked hip, content to let the world do without us, if just for a little while.

I was making nice with Nevan when someone started hammering on the door to his apartments, so loud and insistent that what little mood there'd been was pretty much spoiled. I sighed and took his cock out of my mouth with what I hoped was a passingly apologetic grin, although truth be told, I hadn't much wanted to get on my knees in the first place. Not that he'd forced me, of course, him being far too polite for that sort of fun; it had just seemed the simplest, most efficient way to get him to stop asking what I'd been up to around the palace. Now that we'd been interrupted, though, there was no point in continuing. Some men enjoy being overheard, and I'm not averse to that sort of play, but Nevan preferred privacy.

We both took a moment to rearrange ourselves, the tips of Nevan's ears scarlet as he tucked himself into his nara, and then I went to open the door and see what had happened now. I don't know who I'd been expecting, but Tiern Ethin wasn't it, his pretty cheeks as flushed as if he'd been the one caught kneeling.

"Ru Kisian's been arrested!" he said, entering before I could even say hello.

"What? What for?" asked Nevan, alarmed. He leapt up and hurried over, his embarrassment forgotten. "What's happened?"

"They think he's responsible for the attacks on Tiern Velasin," said Ethin. He turned his big puppy eyes on me, oblivious to the sudden, ugly twisting in my stomach. "But that can't be right, can it? Kisian is one of their supporters!"

"Here," said Nevan, ushering Ethin to a chair. The young lordling sat, running shaky hands through his curly hair, and Nevan and I sat, too, on the settee opposite. "Tell us everything."

And Ethin did, though he wasn't the best narrator; he kept jumping back and forth whenever he remembered something he ought to have said already, so that we had to work to piece events into their proper order. All of his news, he said, had come from his grandmother, who'd had it firsthand in the asa's presence: Velasin had sent Yarasil and Irias to investigate Syana, and they'd actually succeeded; Velasin had been attacked by a Ralian assassin, now imprisoned in the palace cells; a deed had been found implicating Ru Kisian in the attacks on Velasin's life, and when he'd failed to account for it, he'd been locked up, too; Caethari had been released on new evidence; and General Naza had been stripped of his control of the investigation for having made too many errors in judgement.

The more I heard, the more on edge I felt. I didn't understand how the pieces fit together, let alone what it meant for me. The asa had asked Velasin outright if he thought the assassin had really been sent by King Markus—an easy thing to disprove if he'd exposed my role in things, to say nothing of amply demonstrating Ralian hostility, and yet neither he nor Naza had done so. Why? Velasin's silence made sense if he truly wanted me to investigate Naza, but at the same time, he'd given up the chance to show Asa Ivadi that the Iron Chair was withholding information from her, which would've been a far more effective way to strike at him than anything I could presently offer. In Velasin's shoes, I'd have sacrificed myself in a heartbeat. So why hadn't he?

But Naza's silence made even less sense. According to Ethin, the asa had been angry at his investigative failures, and specifically his fixation on Ralia and her sympathisers as culprits. Revealing me would've shown that his suspicions had a real basis, maybe even restored himself somewhat to the asa's good graces, and yet— nothing. It made no sunfucking *sense*. What possible use could I be to him? The night of the tierena's party, I'd done what he said and cozened Caethari into the maze, but even drunk, the fucking lovestruck fool hadn't wanted me—

You deserve someone who wants you, too.

I grit my teeth, the sting of it sharp in my throat. Why was I surprised? In all the sun-cursed world, there was only one person who'd ever wanted me, and unless Velasin was by some fucking miracle able to hold up his end of our bargain, my failures were about to get her killed. Who could he even have asked for help extracting my mother, anyway?

The answer came to me in the next breath, so bitterly ironic that I almost choked: Ru Kisian. The Velvet Chair, responsible for diplomacy and ostensibly committed to good relations between Ralia and Tithena, now languishing in a cell. *He* might've helped, but now he'd been taken off the board entirely.

Was Kisian guilty or innocent? Across from me, Ethin and Nevan were debating the question in anxious tones, but I didn't respect their opinions enough to listen. Whether guilty or innocent, a smart man would've denied everything, if only to stall for time: instead, Kisian had admitted to just enough to get himself arrested on the spot. What sort of a stupid plan was that? If someone had framed him—if he'd known he was being framed—he ought to have lied about buying the land; and if there was an innocent explanation to have given, he should've given it. So why hadn't he? Even if he'd been blackmailed or coerced somehow into getting involved, the smart thing would've been to confess the truth and throw himself on the asa's mercy. Unless whatever was being held over him merited a worse punishment than the one he'd get for being implicated in a political assassination, of course, but it was hard to picture Kisian as having those types of secrets—or unless the blackmailer had also been in the room.

Naza had been in the room.

I swallowed, losing myself in memory. The night of the party, when Caethari had rejected me, I'd stormed out of the maze and back to the gathering, bent on getting legless drunk. But Naza had

seen me come out alone; had taken one look at me and known that
I'd failed. I'd tried to avoid him, but I'd felt his eyes on me no matter where I went, and when I finally left the Mazepool Gardens, he
followed me.

"Leaving so soon?" he'd asked, in that deep, shivering rumble.

"I've got indigestion," I snapped at him. "Too much bad company."

He looked me over, smirking. "Too much, or too little?"

"Fuck you," I spat. "I tried, all right? The yaseran didn't bite."

The smirk deepened. "That seems to have hit a nerve."

Rather than answer, I'd stalked away—or at least, that was the
plan. Instead, he grabbed the back of my lin, and I jerked to a halt,
flushed and angry and mortified at how little he had to do, and
how meanly, to get my cock interested in the proceedings.

"The yaseran may not have bit," he murmured, crowding up
behind me, "but I will." He lowered his head, scraping his teeth
across the cords of my neck.

Soft sand slithered in my thoughts. The night air was cold, I had
no idea where Nevan had got to, and even though it had only been
a handful of hours since I'd staggered out of Naza's bed, Caethari
had left me primed for fucking, aching and hurt in a way I refused
to think about. Naza was dangerous, but that hardly made him
special. I didn't want to think. I wanted to be wanted.

"Bite, then," I spat shakily, and he did, squeezing my hips as
he sucked a mark high on the back of my neck. I made a truly
pathetic noise and went limp against him. He chuckled, nipped at
the bruise he'd left, and manhandled me back to the Iron Suite so
expertly that I was lost to that soft, pleasant space before we ever set
foot inside. He kissed me, stripped me, slicked me up and fucked
me facedown, arse up, my wrists pinned in the small of my back,
with such brutal, calm efficiency that I was sobbing before we were
halfway done.

"*Yaren*," I gasped, "yaren, yaren, *yaren*—"

I came twice before he was finished, so overstimulated by the end that I was yipping and yelping as piteously as a dog with a crushed paw. But though Naza's hands were blissfully cruel wherever they touched, his words were oddly soft.

"Kiensa did well," he murmured, kissing behind my ear, and shamefully, the pleasure of being praised was such that I passed out instantly. I stirred sometime later, dimly aware of being wiped clean, but when I groggily went to rise and leave, Naza pulled me back down again.

"Sleep," he said gruffly, and so I did, deep and dreamless, until I was roused the next morning in a ferocious jolt by the general shouting—not at me, as I'd automatically assumed, my body lurching straight into panicked wakefulness, but at the messenger who'd come to report Syana's death. While Naza swore and fumed his way through interrogating the hapless guard, I dressed as fast as I could, not wanting to stay and risk being a handy target for his anger. I was halfway to the bedroom door when he came back and saw me, his face darkening.

"I was just going," I said quickly.

"See that you do," he growled.

I fled, and bare hours later learned that not only had Caethari been attacked after I'd left him in the gardens, but Naza had suggested me as a culprit. I learned, too, that Caethari had been drugged when I approached him, and who would've done that but Naza? Sure, he fucked me as mean and sweet as anyone ever had, but given my historically appalling taste in men, that made his guilt more likely, not less. And on top of that, he'd made no bones about his dislike of Ralians, and he was a general, wasn't he? So how could a woman like Syana have gotten so close to Velasin, with Naza *right there*, unless he'd wanted her to succeed? If Caethari or Velasin ended up dead and Naza managed to blame it on Ralia—or worse still, on me, without the Shade's absurd jilted-lover story to hide behind—then I was absolutely fucked.

The realisation left me feeling cold and small and stupid, but worst of all, afraid. Too late, I realised that, even if I'd had the stomach for killing Velasin—and I didn't; I never had, though admitting as much to myself was still a wretched experience—I could no longer successfully pretend it was a matter of jealousy, because Naza knew the truth. I'd as good as killed my mother, and all because I'd been so hard-up for a decent fuck that I'd let a man I didn't, shouldn't, *couldn't* trust prise my secrets out of me in exchange for it, and now I had no cards left to play, and would in fact be lucky not to end up dead before the week was out.

Of course I'd gone to Velasin and tried to make a deal. What else was there left to do? I couldn't think of anyone else who'd help me, except maybe Nevan, and even if we'd had that kind of relationship, we both knew he didn't have the right connections. The slap had been unexpected, but not more so than his subsequent collapse and seizure. Half a dozen times as he lay in a healing stupor, I'd contemplated walking out—in his position, I wouldn't have pissed on me if I'd been on fire. But each time, I'd remembered Mama and forced myself to stay. For her sake, I could try. And yet, even then—*even fucking then*—I'd still struggled to voice my suspicions about Naza. I owed him nothing, and he'd made it abundantly clear that I meant nothing to him, but apparently that didn't matter enough to—

"Asri?"

I blinked back to the present moment, ashamed and cross to realise that Nevan had been trying to get my attention for some time. I plastered on an apologetic grimace, which under the circumstances seemed a better choice than a smile, and said, "Sorry, my thoughts were wandering. What is it?"

"I was just saying," said Ethin, still with that anxious note in his voice, "that I'm worried about Tiern Velasin. The asa released the yaseran on a technicality—what if he really is guilty, and he uses this chance to hurt him? I know he's your kin," he added to Nevan in a rush, "but you never met him before all this, and it's only by marriage—you don't know what he might really be like!"

For a moment, I thought Ethin was trying and failing to make a joke. But then I saw how earnest he was, saw the betraying flush on his youthful cheeks, and realised the poor little idiot was sweet on Velasin.

I couldn't help it: I laughed.

"What's so funny?" said Ethin, as close to being on his precious lordling's dignity as I'd yet seen him. "He's been through so much, it's only right to worry—"

"Ethin," said Nevan, with more gentleness than I'd have been able to muster, "Caethari loves him."

Ethin looked as shocked by this as if he'd been stabbed. "What?" he croaked.

"Caethari loves him," Nevan repeated. "I know they might seem awkward together at times—it's certainly what I thought at first— but after everything they've been through, a little public awkwardness is understandable."

"Velasin still deserves better," Ethin said staunchly, but there was a quaver in his voice that hadn't been there before. "He—"

I stood up, cutting Ethin off. I hadn't meant to; it was just that the thought of spending any more time listening to him prattle about his crush made me want to jump out a window, and as we were on the ground floor, it seemed like leaving would be the more effective option.

"Where are you going?" asked Nevan, surprised.

"Out," I said. There was an itch in my teeth and my skin and my bones. *You deserve someone who wants you, too.* I wanted to see Naza. I was afraid to see Naza. I wanted to get the truth from him. No—I *needed* to get the truth from him, to hold up my end of my tenuous deal with Velasin. "I just—out."

And so I fled, relieved and annoyed that neither of them called out or tried to stop me. A stupid contradiction; but then, *I* was stupid. Hadn't I learned that yet?

◆ ◆ ◆

I knocked on the door of the Iron Suite, damp and shivering. The wind had picked up as I came outside, and then it had started to rain, the sort of coldly humid drizzle that never seemed as bad as it was until you stopped moving and realised your fingers were numb. The nape of my neck was cold, and my hands, and my feet. I wasn't dressed for the weather; I'd been having so much fun experimenting with Tithenai fashion that a good winter coat was one of the few things I was yet to wheedle Nevan into buying for me. I felt an odd pang at the thought of him and didn't like it at all. Nevan was a means to an end: a good, boring, dutiful man who in Ralia would've probably married a woman and had good, boring, dutiful babies, but who in Tithena could afford to divorce his wife and spend his precious coin on trinkets for a superficial ingrate who openly slept elsewhere.

There's something wrong with you, I thought, the voice hissed and hateful, and bit my tongue to keep from laughing aloud.

The door opened suddenly, revealing Naza on the other side. He looked . . . I don't know how he looked. Some mix of anger and strain and weariness I wasn't best placed to interpret, sharpened to intensity at the sight of me. I expected him to ask what I was doing there, what I wanted or who'd sent me, but he didn't do any of that. Just stared at me for a moment, then said, "You're wet."

I blinked at him, nonplussed. "It's raining."

"I'm aware." He stared a moment longer, then stepped aside and gestured me in with a tip of his chin. I obeyed, still shivering, and shucked off my boots in the entryway, wriggling my socked toes on the floor to try and will some feeling back into them. The walk to the Iron Suite from Nevan's chambers wasn't so great, but despite the rain—or maybe on some level because of it—I hadn't gone straight there. My head was a tangle, and I'd wanted to try and walk it out, but of course that hadn't worked, and so there I was, staring up at Naza without the least idea of what to say to him, or of what he might do to me if I said nothing.

"I'm surprised to see you," he said at last. He cocked his head onside, thoughtful. "I'd assumed you'd have fled by now."

"Fled?" I asked, hating that my voice cracked. "I've got nowhere else to go."

Naza stared at me for a moment, his expression unreadable. Then he turned and walked into the main room—the room where he'd fucked me days ago, wringing my secrets out of me like water from a towel—and it would've felt strange to keep standing there, so I followed him, uncertain of what was happening. Silently, I watched as he pulled out a bottle of wine and two glasses from a sideboard, but was still surprised when he handed me one and motioned for me to sit.

"I didn't think we did this," I said, for lack of anything else to say.

He didn't answer; just poured the wine, then sat beside me on the couch. I stared at the cup. Was it poisoned? Drugged? He'd drugged Caethari easily enough—did he mean to do the same to me?

As if he could read my thoughts, Naza caught my eye, smirked, and took a meaningful pull from his own cup. He raised an expectant brow at me, and because I didn't know what else to do, I drank in turn. The wine was red and rich, smooth without being overly sweet, leaving behind a pleasantly acidic tang.

"You're an odd little thing," he said, watching me.

I bristled at that. "Odd to you, maybe."

"Maybe," he conceded. He was so much bigger than me, it felt ridiculous to sit beside him. One of his thighs was thicker around than both of mine pressed together. That shouldn't have been an arousing thought, let alone a comforting one.

I drank again, the wine a pleasant warmth in my gut. "Did you drug Caethari?" I blurted. "At the tierena's party."

Beside me, Naza stilled. I froze, heart rabbiting at the thought that I'd angered him, but all he did was frown, a strange look on his face. "No," he said at last. "I assumed he concocted that as a lie to appease his husband."

"He didn't," I said, the words gritted and fast. Over and over, I'd told myself I'd only thought Caethari was drunk, but even at the time, I'd known his behaviour was off. I just . . . hadn't wanted to think about why. Hadn't wanted to think that Naza thought a man would have to be addled to want to fuck me. "He was . . . off, that night. More than drunk. He kept babbling about the lights, and his husband, and how hot he was—and he *was* hot, even to the touch. Hotter than he should've been." I made a frustrated noise. "You told me to approach him there. I thought you must've done it."

"No," said Naza, a thread of iron in his voice. "Powders and drugs and poisons are the tools of cowards, not soldiers. And I am *not* a coward."

"Then—"

"Do I not get to ask anything?" he said, cutting over me.

Heat flushed through me, recalling the last time he'd questioned me in this room. "Haven't I already told you everything?"

"Some things, yes. But not all."

"A trade, then," I ventured. "A question for a question."

A bold and foolish request, and yet I blurted it out regardless. Naza had no reason at all to agree, not least because he already knew how to make me talk—and yet, after a moment's thought, he nodded his great, maned head in agreement.

"All right, kiensa," he said, the nickname so unexpected that I gulped a mouthful of wine to cover my whimper. "Answer me this: what is Ralia like?"

"In general, or for men like me?"

"Both. Either."

I stared at the floor. "I don't know," I said, pulse jumping oddly. "It's not . . . what else do I have to compare it to, really? This is the only other place I've ever lived, and I've hardly been here long." I fell silent, but Naza waited me out as I drained my cup, more swiftly than was sensible on a half-empty stomach, and eventually, without meaning to, I spoke, the wine-loosened words tumbling out of me like marbles from a pouch. "What's Ralia like? It's a place. It's home. It was never home. It's warm fires in winter, apples in summer, wine in spring, cider in autumn and dancing always. It's beautiful and clever and violent and cruel. I love it, and it hates me, and I wish I hated it too, but I don't. I'm not sure I can, without hating myself. I do hate myself. Ralia is a fist raised against itself in defence of itself. It's my mother. It's people, the same as anywhere else. Just people, and things, and the stories they use to justify treating the one as the other. I don't ever want to go back, and I hate that I can't. I do want to go back. Or maybe I just want to want to, I don't know. It's all the songs I've ever learned. It's the only place I know how to belong, and I've never belonged there once." My eyes stung, and I scrubbed at them angrily. "What the fuck kind of question is that, anyway? Ralia is Ralia. Leave it at that." And then, not wanting to hear what he thought of all that, "The assassin, Syana. You stood right there as it happened. Why didn't you stop her?"

Silence.

I was still staring at the floor, because that felt safer than the alternative. I didn't want to look at him; but then, I didn't want a lot of things.

I looked up.

Naza was perfectly still. He looked at me like a hunting hawk looks at a rabbit, and I had the strange, clear thought that, if he chose to snap my neck, it would at least be quick. But he didn't break my neck. Instead, he reached for the wine, refilled my empty cup and his own and took a long, slow pull of it, throat working as he swallowed. I flushed at the sight, then drank to distract myself from it.

"My predecessor," said Naza, then stopped. He moved his head, looking past me to the opposite wall. "The Iron Chair before me. General Teris Ko. He was . . . *political.*" He pronounced the word like a synonym for *untrustworthy,* or possibly *diseased.* "We thought him compromised. For years, Ralia provoked us along the border, insult after insult, and yet he refused to retaliate. We could defend ourselves, he said, but war was a different animal. We would not act as barbarians and start one. But we didn't start it!"

His fingers clenched around the wine-cup, and I tensed, half expecting him to dash either the contents or the cup itself into my face. Instead, he took an angry swallow and said, "When I was chosen to replace him—chosen because I am not political; chosen for being a soldier, not some addled courtier—I thought my mission obvious. Restore our pride. Reject Ralia and this farce of an alliance. What benefit is there to any of this? Nothing we need, or can't afford to lose." He made a soft, angry noise in the back of his throat. "Tiern Velasin is insolent. Maddening. Meddlesome. He makes me look a fool. He is *political*. And if I had known all that in the moment—if I had seen that woman for what she was, and known how he would humiliate me—then perhaps, yes. Perhaps I would have chosen to do nothing. But." His lip curled with disgust, and it took me a fearful moment to realise it was wholly self-directed. "But in the moment, I did not *choose* to do nothing. I saw an old woman dressed foolishly in ill-fitting clothes, and dismissed her the way a Ralian might: as unimportant. Unfit. Unthreatening. And ever since—" He broke off, jaw working soundlessly for a moment, before continuing: "*Ever since,* I have not been able to catch my footing, not once in this cursed palace. I have no soldiers here; the Iron Chair is not permitted them, lest the crown risk a military coup. The asa's guards may be sworn to her, but some take bribes; others are spies for different factions, other chairs and nobles. I do not know who to trust; whose coin is lining whose pockets; who says one thing and means another." He looked at me then, and the force of it was like a blow. "I did not let Syana strike at Velasin. But part of me wishes I had, if only because it would mean I had more control."

I stared at him, speechless. He didn't sound like he was lying, and yet the idea that he'd tell me the truth was nonsensical. It only made sense as a manipulation, Naza saying what I wanted to hear the better to use me later. I didn't believe a word of it. I *didn't*.

"My turn," he said. His gaze flicked over me, languid as a half-nocked arrow. "Now that you've failed your mission here, will the Shade truly kill your mother? It's just," said Naza, uncaring of how my guts had turned to ice, "I don't see how it benefits them. If the threat is fulfilled, they have no more control over you. Their leverage is gone forever. But if they leave it open . . ."

"Don't," I rasped. I slammed my cup down so violently that wine sloshed over the edges, puddling red on the table. "Don't say that."

"Why not?"

"Because I can't risk it. I can't, but I want to."

"Why?"

"Because I'm a bad son," I croaked. "Because I'm selfish."

"Selfish how?"

I laughed, the sound cracked and jagged. "Look at me."

"I'm looking," said Naza. He took my chin between thumb and forefinger, callused fingers tilting me this way and that like I was a colt he wanted to purchase. "What makes you selfish, kiensa?"

"Because I chose *this*!" I shouted, wrenching out of his grasp. "I never tried hard enough to be otherwise, I never—I was *always* like this, do you understand? My father beat her for it worse than he did me, and I still—I should've—I did try, I *did*, but I'm weak, I'm selfish and stupid and I hate, I *hated* him, I wanted to make him angry more than I wanted to keep her safe, and then he died and it wasn't supposed to matter anymore but of course it did, I got caught, and I thought it would only hurt *me*, but now—" I laughed hysterically, "—now, just once, *just this once*, my being like this could save her, and instead, no one wants me! The one time I could get fucked to a purpose, the one time that this could—that I could—and what the fuck am I for, if not for this? But neither of them wants me! Neither of them, so don't sit there—don't sit there looking at me like that and tell me it's fine, that I haven't—that I didn't—"

Naza grasped the nape of my neck and kissed me hard, tongue slicking into my mouth. I jerked against him, digging my fingers into his chest, and made a shocked, furious noise that he swallowed straight out of me. He tasted like the wine, but hotter, gripping my hip and hauling me onto his lap, the spread of his open thighs broad enough that I could feel the stretch in straddling them. I hung in his grip like a doll, then kissed him back, clawing at his lin half in anger, half in desperation.

He broke the kiss in favour of fitting his mouth to my throat, so I bared it for him, head tipped back.

"You don't want me," I panted. "You don't, I don't even like you—"

"I like you like this," he murmured into my neck—then froze, as though he was as shocked to have said it as I was to have heard it. Slowly, he tipped his head up. I trembled on his lap. My thoughts began to slide to warm, soft sand.

"Say it again?"

He squeezed my arse with both hands, nipping along my jaw. "Ask me nicely."

"Please, please say it again—"

"Say what?"

"That you like me. Please, yaren—"

He slid two fingers into my mouth; I moaned around them, wet and wanton, and shuddered as he lipped at the shell of my ear. "I like you," he whispered, pressing down on my tongue. I choked around his fingers, coating them with spit. "I like you like this."

I rubbed myself up against him like a cat in heat. Naza swore softly and withdrew his fingers, only to grab me with both hands and stand. I clung onto him with all four limbs, and he carried me into the bedroom, tossed me down on the mattress and crowded over me.

I should've pushed him away. Did I really believe a word he'd said? Of course he was lying—he must've known I'd gone to Velasin and was trying to throw me off the scent—

I have to stay, I thought, arching as he pinned my wrists. *If I try to leave, he'll know I don't believe him.* The fact that I wanted to stay was irrelevant. *Just stay. This is all you're good for. Who else would have you like this?*

"Kiensa," he murmured, and with a hitching sob, I gave myself over to him.

◆ ◆ ◆

Naza slept deeply, for a soldier. He'd worn us both out, but now, hours later, I was suddenly wide awake. I wasn't sure why. Maybe thanks to something in my dreams, though I didn't remember them. I sat up, the blankets pooled around my waist, and contemplated Naza, laid out beside me like a lion after a kill. I had actually seen lions before, years ago, at a private menagerie kept by a richer and more powerful man my father hoped to impress. After weeks of social grovelling, he'd finally been invited up for a hunting weekend, and wouldn't normally have brought me in a fit, except that he'd been told to. I hadn't known why at first, but that had changed soon enough. I'd like to say it was eye-opening, and that was partly true, but I'd hardly been blind to the world beforehand. Experience was just a different kind of knowledge. Learning had hurt, but at least I'd been useful. It was what it was. But I remembered the lions: huge and sleek, imported from Nivona at some wild expense, lounging bloody-muzzled over the carcass of a deer. They didn't know they were owned by someone; only that they were fed.

Naza's mane of hair was fanned on the pillow, the iron threads catching the moonlight. It wasn't really as late as all that, but darkness came quicker in winter in Tithena the same as it did in Ralia. Naza's face was half in shadow, a slight frown wrinkled between his brows. I wasn't fond of him; there was no point.

I looked away and rose, padding across the floorboards in pursuit of my clothes, suppressing a hiss at my various aches and bruises. There was a truly extraordinary bite-mark on my right shoulder, purple-red and blooming like a hybrid rose. I poked at it, pain-pleasure washing through me in ripples. Then I stopped. Breathed. Pulled on my smallclothes and nara, my undershirt and lin. I stared out the window, feeling the chill through the glass, and wondered what the fuck I was meant to do now.

I had no proof of Naza's guilt; I didn't even know where to start looking.

But Kisian might.

Slowly, my gaze travelled across the floor. Naza's clothes still lay where he'd dropped them. I slunk over, crouched, and rifled the pockets until I found what I was looking for: the general's palace token. It was cold in my palm, and felt strangely heavy. I looked up at Naza, half expecting to have been caught in the act, but he was still fast asleep. Was I really doing this?

Yes, I decided, and stole out of the bedroom before I could second-guess myself.

My boots were still by the entryway where I'd left them. I slipped them onto my bare feet, wincing at the chill, and eased the suite door open. Mercifully, it didn't creak, but once I was out, I didn't dare shut it all the way in case I got locked out. Instead, I pulled it as close as possible and crept out into the night.

The rain had stopped, but the air was frigid, and once again, I wasn't dressed for the temperature. I finger-combed my hair as I walked to the prison, trying to look more like I was on a legitimate errand and less like I was slinking home from a vigorous fuck. Markel had used a palace token to bluff us in to see Syana before; theoretically, I should be able to do it again. Even though the asa had taken him off the investigation, Naza was still the Iron Chair. That had to count for something.

Didn't it?

The guards at the prison let me in. My footsteps echoed loudly as I approached the desk, manned this time by a tired-looking woman. She raised an eyebrow at me, but straightened from her slump when I held out Naza's palace token and said, "On the Iron Chair's authority, I need to speak to the prisoner Ru Kisian."

The woman frowned. "He's no longer in charge—"

"I know," I said, fumbling for the excuse I'd concocted on the way over. "It's not about that. Ru Kisian was—is—the Velvet Chair. There are documents in his keeping that the Iron Chair needs, but he doesn't know where they are. I've come to ask their location."

The woman considered this, then sighed. "All right," she said, and took the palace token from me, scanning and recording it before handing it back. She gestured to one of the nearby guards, who straightened from his slouch and wandered over to us, look-ing more bored than anything else. "Cell twelve," she said. "Five minutes, no more."

"Thank you," I said, and bowed, shoving the place token back in my pocket.

Down the right-hand passageway we went, the nameless guard leading silently, until we stopped at a nondescript cell that looked much the same as the one in which Syana had been held. I frowned: from what Nevan had said, Caethari had been kept somewhere far more comfortable, so why was Kisian here? And where was the Ralian assassin, for that matter? I didn't know his name or what he looked like, but for a moment, I was tempted to push my luck and ask to see him, too, not because I thought he could tell me anything I didn't already know, but because, out of everyone in Qi-Xihan who wasn't Velasin, he might best under-stand my position.

"Five minutes," the guard intoned, oblivious to my chain of thought, and unlocked the cell door.

I entered. The room was lit by a single dim magelight, casting a bluish glow over the bare rock. Kisian was curled up on the platform bed, unshackled but asleep. I approached him warily, waited until I heard the guard move farther down the corridor, then gave his ankle a shake.

"Kisian!" I hissed.

He jolted upright like a snake had bitten him, eyes wild. "Asrien?" he stammered. "Have you—oh, gods—have you come to get me out?"

"No," I said.

"Oh." He knuckled the sleep from his eyes and stared at me, his expression haggard. "I suppose it wouldn't be you."

I perched next to him, the hard, cold rock of the bed base dig-ging into my thighs. "Listen, I don't have much time," I said, pitch-ing my voice low. "I want to help you, but I can't do that unless you tell me what's really going on."

Kisian looked as wary as a hunted thing—which I guess he was, under the circumstances. "You can't help me," he said. "I don't even know how to help myself. This whole thing is just . . . I want to say absurd, but that hardly covers it!"

"Has anyone else come to see you?"

"One of the asa's agents," he said darkly. "Qarrah, the one who brought that assassin in. She didn't even come to see *me*, not officially; just stopped by on her way to talk to *him*. It's probably absurd to find that insulting under the circumstances, but here we are."

Qarrah. The name meant nothing to me. "What did you tell her?"

Kisian looked bleak. "What I could. Not enough. There's someone—" He broke off, jaw working in frustration. "I have no proof, do you understand? It's why I couldn't defend myself. The documentation is all in my name, and if I tried to name them, it wouldn't—well." He let out a short, hysterical laugh. "Let's just say, if I die in this cell, it very much won't be suicide."

I suppressed a sympathetic shudder. "Start from the beginning," I said. "Why did you buy the land?"

"Because I had to," Kisian snapped. "I had—I have—gambling debts. I'm not proud to admit it, but there we are. A few months ago, I got a little too heavily in my cups at dice, became a little too convinced my winning streak was a function of natural prowess rather than luck, and I lost more than I could afford to. That was bad enough, but before I could figure out how to pay, I was told that the debt had been sold to a third party."

An unpleasant, anxious kinship swirled in my stomach. I'd had debts, too, and like Kisian, I'd had them used against me. "They sold your debt?"

"It's a common thing, here," he said bitterly. "Gaming houses prefer the certainty of cash over the promise of a debt, but for anyone rich enough to buy the debt outright, the leverage of holding it is frequently worth more than the actual money."

"But you're the Velvet Chair!" I protested. "How much could you have lost, that you couldn't afford to pay it?"

"My family are minor nobles," Kisian replied. "Historically, we do well with scholarship and art, but much less well with investment. I'm paid by the crown for my service, but as living in the palace covers my immediate personal expenses, most of that money goes to support the upkeep of our family estate. It's been in disrepair for many years, but my mothers refuse to sell it as a point of pride, and—well. It's complicated. But the damn place simply eats coin, which is why I attempted to supplement my income with gaming wins in the first place." He made a frustrated noise. "In hindsight, I was clearly rooked. The house invited me back week after week, and I kept winning; small, steady amounts that built my confidence, and each time they'd offer a little more wine, a few more inducements to stay at the table." He shot me a hollow smile. "We clever folk always like to think we're too smart to be caught with such tactics, but it only makes us more vulnerable, in the end."

I shivered: it was a truth I knew all too well. "What happened next?"

"Eventually, I was contacted by an agent of the person who'd bought my debt—this was when we'd first begun to reach out to contacts in Ralia about the potential for an alliance with Lord vin Aaro. Not many people were supposed to know about it, of course, but gossip has a way of getting around regardless. I was instructed to approach Cietena Alu Nyas with an offer to purchase her lands outside of Qi-Katai, bankrolled by my mystery debt-holder. It seemed harmless enough, so I agreed—no." He stopped himself with a tight, angry shake of his head, the gold beads on his braids chiming. "No, I knew it wouldn't be harmless in the long run—if it was, they wouldn't have needed me as a cat's-paw. It just wasn't obvious how I was being used. But I didn't have much of a choice; I did what I was told and signed what they gave me. That deed, that document Tiern Velasin found—they had me sign and seal a few blank pages, but I never knew what for." He gave a bleak little laugh. "Until today, obviously."

"I don't understand," I said. "They paid for you to buy the land, but then they just let you keep it?"

"No," said Kisian quickly. "I mean—no, that wasn't the plan—originally, I was meant to buy it and turn it over to them, but then we got word that Velasin had married Caethari instead of Laecia, and they—or their agent, rather; I've never dealt with them in person—had me hang on to it for the time being, in case the alliance fell through and the value remained low, so they wouldn't have to be seen reselling it."

"Who's the agent?" I said.

"Nobody important," Kisian said quickly—too quickly. "A man. A servant. It doesn't matter."

"It bloody does," I said.

A fraught pause followed. Then:

"He's a court functionary," Kisian bit out. "And that's all I'm going to give you."

I wanted to press, but there wasn't time to argue the point. "When did you last hear from him?"

Kisian swallowed. "I . . . after Velasin was attacked, after the party, there was a note waiting for me when I returned to my apartments. A reminder of my debt, and a—a suggestion, was how they worded it, that I continue to treat the matter with discretion, or else they'd demand the family estate be sold or turned over to them to make payment." He gripped my wrist, brief and fervent. "Understand, I very much want to live—I'd especially like to live and keep some semblance of my livelihood—but my family . . . as much as my being caught in this would shame them, losing the estate would shame them more."

I was struggling to come up with a reply when the guard rapped sharply on the cell door, startling both of us.

"Time's up!" he called.

"Please," Kisian whispered. "For your own sake, leave this alone."

"You know," I hissed back. "You know who holds your debt. Tell me! Or if not that, then at least the functionary's name."

"There's no point!"

The cell door swung open, revealing the unimpressed face of the guard. Desperately, I turned to Kisian.

"Just tell me this, then. Is it Naza?"

But Kisian didn't answer; just watched with a mix of fear and sadness as I was forced to stand and leave. His gaze followed me into the corridor, the memory of it haunting my steps as I was led back to the atrium, where I thanked the duty guard, shoved my hands in my inadequate pockets against the encroaching chill, and headed out into the night.

As I walked, I replayed the look on Kisian's face when I'd said Naza's name. Had he flinched? Nodded? Given some sign or other for me to interpret? I wanted to believe so, but try as I might, I couldn't find one. Cursing, I hunched my shoulders against the wind and began to make my way back to the Iron Suite. With any luck, Naza would still be asleep, oblivious to his missing palace token. I'd slip it back into his nara, climb into bed—no. If I slept in his bed, I'd only want to fuck him again in the morning, and that was a bad idea. He probably didn't expect me to stay the night, anyway, not after last time. I'd just have to be careful not to wake him sneaking in, or else he might want to know what I'd been up to—

Something hit me in the side of the head, so hard and unexpected that I was on the ground, dazed and smarting, before I'd even registered the blow. Pain and nausea jangled through me; I twitched on the flagstones like a poorly clubbed fish, burbling piteously. I saw boots near my head, and then someone hefted me up and over their shoulder like a sack of rotten apples. I tried to kick, but I was too cold and stunned—and, if I'm brutally honest, small—for this to be very effective, and as they began to carry me off, I was more preoccupied with not vomiting than fighting back. My churning stomach had a shoulder digging into it and my mouth tasted faintly of bile, but somehow I kept from disgracing myself as I was lofted away through the night, unable to track my progress through the palace grounds on account of being dangled upside down with hair in my eyes. At one point, we went up a flight of stairs—my captor cursed and grunted at that, jouncing me into a position that was presumably better for him, but still deeply unpleasant for me—but otherwise, I had no idea where we were.

Finally, we entered a building. My head had started to clear by then, the warm air a pleasant shock against my skin, but still, I found myself trembling. Too late, I recalled Ru Kisian's warning; part of me wanted to struggle, but I've never been a fighter, and as much as I enjoy certain types of pain in bed, I've a strong aversion to being hurt for unpleasurable reasons. So I just hung there, watching the floor underfoot change from marble to carpet, until I was carted through a set of double-doors and unceremoniously dropped. I landed on my hands and knees, which thanks to the carpet was less unpleasant than it might've been.

"This one snuck in to see Ru Kisian," said the man who'd been carrying me. "I thought you might want to conduct your own interview."

Slowly, I raised my head and saw who I'd been brought to.

"Oh," I whispered. "*Fuck.*"

Part Six

CAETHARI

26

C ae woke to the warmth of Velasin in his arms and wondered, for a muzzy, tenuous moment, if he was dreaming. Vel's head was pillowed on his chest, one leg tucked between Cae's thighs, an arm thrown over Cae's waist, but it was the scent of him that brought home the reality of the moment, bodywarmed and unmistakeable. Cae's heart thudded painfully. Hardly daring to breathe, he combed his fingers through Vel's hair and pressed a shaky kiss to his forehead. Except for that night at Ravethae when he'd been overtaken by foolishness and passed out in the stables, they hadn't slept apart since Vel's recovery from magical overextension back in Qi-Katai, but it felt like they'd barely touched in weeks. The trip from Avai to Qi-Xihan had been so fraught that Cae shied away from thinking about it, as though the recollection might somehow jinx the present moment.

Not wanting to wake Vel but unable to help himself, Cae gently thumbed his husband's cheekbone, drinking in the sight of him: the faint veins in his eyelids, the tiny lines at the corner of eye and mouth, the shape of his nose. And then his gaze dropped lower, to where the scar on Vel's throat was hidden against Cae's chest, and his stomach knotted up. He could've lost him so easily; almost had lost him, Vel bleeding out on a marble floor as Cae clutched at him, bereft and helpless. And then he'd been imprisoned, forced to pace behind bars while Vel exhausted himself doing who knew what, until finally he'd been released, and Vel had run to him, tumbling them both into bed with a fervent urgency that matched Cae's own.

"I love you," he whispered, and brushed a shallow kiss to Vel's mouth. He only meant to do it once, but couldn't resist the chance to kiss him again, and again, until Vel stirred sleepily against him and, before his eyes were even open, began to kiss back, the languid warmth of him pressing up against Cae with tantalizing promise.

As Vel finally woke, he made an interested noise in his throat and shifted to kiss Cae properly, tongue flicking into Cae's mouth. Cae was disproportionately undone by this: heat licked through him, cock filling against his thigh, and before he could really process his own actions, he'd taken hold of Vel's hip, squeezing against the bone. Vel made a sweet gasping noise and twined himself closer, shifting to nip and suck along Cae's jaw.

"Want you," he murmured, voice still thick with sleep. "Cae, sweetheart, please—"

Cae groaned and kissed him again, reaching down to take them both in hand. Just the idea of Vel was enough to make him hunger; the reality of him, sweet and pliant in Cae's arms, hips shifting as he rutted into Cae's grasp, was intoxicating.

They both spent embarrassingly quickly, Vel whining into his mouth as Cae worked their cocks beneath the blanket, shivering together through their aftershocks. Then Vel laughed, a warm, pleased sound, and bent his head to kiss Cae's collarbone.

"I missed you," he whispered shyly. "I really—I missed you, Cae."

"I missed you, too," he said hoarsely. His hand was covered in their joint spend; he needed to get up and wash it off, but didn't want to leave the bed, and was struggling to think of a compromise when, unprompted, Vel took hold of his wrist, guided his hand out from under the blankets and—Cae's softening cock gave a hopeful, electrified twitch—began to lick him clean. Cae groaned, suffused with heat at the sight. "Sweet saints, *Vel*—"

"Yes?" Vel asked innocently, pink tongue slipping between Cae's knuckles.

"You—" Cae broke off, breathing heavily. He couldn't get hard again so soon, but his body didn't appear to know that, and all at once he remembered what Vel had cried out the night before as he'd neared his climax: *I love, beloved.* He'd said it in Ralian, an exhalation as raw as if Cae had literally fucked it out of him, and recalling it now, with Vel's teeth grazing the skin of his wrist, his lips smeared shiny, made Cae feel feral. Swallowing hard, he watched Vel work for as long as he could, then dug his fingers into his hair and guided him up for a messy, desperate kiss. He tasted of them, salty and astringent; Cae pulled away, panting, and licked the remaining excess from his own fingers. Vel's eyes blew wide at the sight; he gripped Cae's shoulder, straddled his lap and leaned back down to kiss him into the pillows, again and again.

By the time they were done with each other, Cae had learned exactly how soon after an orgasm he was capable of having a second one, which was much sooner than he'd previously thought; he had a dim notion that this was a revelation he'd already had once regarding Vel, and yet in the moment it felt brand-new.

"We need to shower," he murmured, dropping a kiss on Vel's sweaty temple.

Velasin made a piteous noise and tipped his head, looking up at Cae through his lashes. "I can't. I'm too weak. You've ruined my legs."

"I'll just have to carry you, then," said Cae, and did so, slinging Velasin into his arms and taking them both to the bathroom. The hot shower was blissful, and not just because he'd gone without while being locked up; Vel leaned against him the whole time, his arms looped sweetly around Cae's neck, and made pleased, tired noises against Cae's throat as he soaped them both free of sweat.

It was only once they were dry and back in the bedroom to dress that Cae let himself think about what was going on outside their suite. Last night, after they'd first tumbled into bed together but before they'd fallen asleep, over a late dinner brought from the annex kitchens, Vel had brought Cae up to date on everything that happened during his brief imprisonment, including Rade's attempted assassination of Vel, his subsequent arrest and Ru Kisian's sudden downfall. This latter wasn't a pleasant thing to contemplate: if Kisian was guilty, then Cae had been fooled by someone he'd thought an ally, and if not, Cae's freedom had come at the expense of an innocent man's reputation. It was, however, easier to process than the idea that Vel had been attacked, again, by the same man who'd been hunting them since Etho. The fact that Rade was now behind bars did little to sap the anger Cae felt, the fear and helplessness that came from Vel being hurt again. In his telling of things, Vel had passed lightly over the fact that Rade had been sent by Nathian, and Cae hadn't pressed the point, because he knew a deflection when he saw one. Now, though, it hit him powerfully: that Vel's remaining brother had sought his death.

During his brief imprisonment, Cae had been haunted by thoughts of Laecia: of how, had events played out only slightly differently, she might've been arrested, sentenced to life in a cell much like the one he'd found himself occupying. He hadn't mentioned it to anyone, but in the immediate aftermath of her death, when Vel had still been recovering and Cae had been unable to sleep, he'd crept to the Aida's library and researched the means by which rogue mages could be safely contained. It wasn't something he'd had occasion to think about before then, but hunched in a too-small chair, a series of books and scrolls open before him, he'd learned that the problem had precedent. There were artifex devices, cuffs and collars and other such things, built to suppress an individual's magic, or to sever their connection to it. For a more permanent solution, however, there was also the option of something called *induced burnout,* in which a group of mages would channel so much magic through the condemned individual that they'd lose their affinity forever, in much the same way that exposure to a sufficiently loud noise could induce deafness. The whole thing had left him feeling sick; he'd shoved the knowledge aside, unwilling to contemplate any of it with reference to Laecia, but imprisoned, it had come back to him. Could Laecia have lived like that? Would she have wanted to?

He suppressed a shudder, pulling on his lin, and let his thoughts jump elsewhere. Unfortunately, this was less helpful than he might've hoped: in place of his sister, he recalled the ugly sight of his jade-handled dagger protruding from the body of Cietena Alu Nyas, the memory overlapping with the death of Killic at Velasin's hands. He found himself wondering where the blade was now. Had General Naza taken charge of it? Would it now be passed to the keeping of the asa's guards? Or had it already been discarded, lost to carelessness or stolen by some opportunistic soul?

"I can hear you thinking," Velasin murmured, wrapping his arms around Cae's waist and kissing the nape of his neck.

"I don't want to leave this room," Cae admitted with a gulp. He turned in the circle of Velasin's arms and pressed their foreheads together. "Or, I do want to leave, but only to take you home."

"I'm sorry," Vel said softly. "You never wanted to come here in the first place. I understand why, now."

Cae let out a strangled laugh. "In fairness, I didn't expect it to be quite this bad."

Vel squeezed his hips. "Do we have to stay?"

"What?"

"I mean, why can't we just leave? The asa summoned us and asked that we report on what we saw of Tithena, and we've done that already. It might be rude to leave unannounced, but rude is better than dead."

A surge of fondness tightened Cae's chest. He cradled Vel's face in his hands, thumbs stroking his cheeks. "Rude is better than dead," he agreed, "but you know—Vel. You know better than me why we have to stay."

"I know nothing," Vel lied, jutting his chin out adorably. "My head is empty. I haven't had a thought since the age of three."

Cae kissed his eyelids, his cheeks, his mouth. "If we leave, and someone comes after us again—"

"I know," Vel sighed, sadly. "I know."

Together, they finished dressing and headed into the lounge—where, to Cae's immediate shock and embarrassment, they found

Markel waiting for them, sitting at the table with an overladen breakfast tray and a studiously blank expression. Too late, Cae recalled that the morning's second round of bedroom activities hadn't exactly been quiet, and wished fervently for the floor to swallow him up.

"Ah," said Vel, who'd clearly reached a similar conclusion. "Markel. Good morning. We didn't hear you come in."

"That was extremely apparent," Markel signed, looking pained. "Breakfast?"

"Please," said Vel, and so they sat down to eat together, the combination of hunger and good food working very hard to patch over the shared awkwardness. Cae had been fed during his arrest, but sparingly, and he'd been too anxious to eat much in any case. Now, though, he found himself ravenous, and tore into the meal with abandon.

"All right," said Vel eventually, when they'd all done stuffing themselves. "Reality. Markel, what does the gossip say?"

"The gossip is confused," signed Markel. "Ru Kisian is—was—well-liked; the idea that he might've conspired in a murder-plot isn't being taken well. But a few people have started saying that he had gambling debts, and that he might've made some unsavoury connections among his gambling friends."

Cae frowned, a tickle of memory rising to the surface of his thoughts. "That night at the party," he said, slowly, "his assistant said something about him gambling with their plans. They were talking about Yasai Qiqa arriving unexpectedly and Ru Kisian not being concerned, so I didn't think she meant it literally, but—well. Maybe she did."

Both Markel and Vel looked perturbed by this possibility.

"What else?" Vel asked.

Markel glanced at Cae. "Opinion is split on whether Caethari killed the cietena. Some think Ru Kisian's arrest proves his innocence; other think they're both guilty, and a very few think it's neither of them." He hesitated, then added, "There's been some speculation about General Naza's role in things, too. The fact that he was put in charge of investigating but fumbled it so badly . . . some people are wondering if it's deliberate."

Vel sighed. "Which would accord with Asrien's theory that Naza is responsible for orchestrating the whole thing."

"It would," Markel signed, "but . . . to that point, there's also gossip that Asrien has been seen leaving the Iron Suite more than once, and at odd hours—late at night, or first thing in the morning."

Cae took a moment to parse this, thinking at first that he'd misread Markel's signing. "They think Asrien is bedding General Naza?" he asked incredulously.

"They do," confirmed Markel.

"Surely not," said Vel, but he sounded more intrigued than disbelieving.

"What is it?" asked Cae.

Vel rested his chin on his knuckles. "It's just . . . the way he was talking yesterday, when he told me his suspicions. It was like he didn't want to believe it even though he was saying it."

A complex mix of expressions flitted across Markel's face, so swiftly there and gone that Cae would've missed them if he'd been looking anywhere else. There was anger, and sadness, and something else, too, a sort of startled frustration that he didn't know how to categorise. He might've asked about it, but just at that moment, their conversation was interrupted by a knock on the door.

"I'll get it," said Cae, and rose to do so, feeling obscurely glad that he'd already dressed for the day instead of lounging about in a lin and robe.

To his surprise, Tiern Ethin was on the other side, a light flush accentuating the bridge of freckles across his nose.

"Good morning, tiern," said Cae, hoping he sounded suitably polite and not at all knowing. Velasin had, with a baffling degree of embarrassment, told him about Ethin's apparent infatuation with him, and while Cae was hardly in a position to pass judgement on the young tiern—frankly, it was astonishing that more people weren't besotted with his husband—it did leave him feeling obscurely smug.

"Good morning," replied Ethin, gaze darting towards Vel and back again. "Ah. I'm sorry to interrupt your breakfast, but I—we—my grandmother and I, that is, the Amber Chair—wanted to invite you both to lunch today." There was a slight, almost apologetic emphasis on the *both,* during which Ethin's gaze flicked minutely to Markel.

"Oh!" said Cae. He turned, looking over his shoulder to gauge Vel's reaction to the invitation and, on seeing that Vel looked receptive despite Markel's exclusion—and as Markel himself seemed more amused than hurt—replied, "Thank you, we'd be glad to attend."

"Good!" said Ethin, looking relieved. "We'll expect you at midday in the Mazepool Pavilion."

Cae frowned. "Is that the same as the Mazepool Gardens?"

"No, no." Ethin smiled. "It's a false heart within the maze itself. Don't worry, we'll set a servant at the entrance to guide you through." His flush intensified slightly, and without looking at Vel, he said, "As your husband wasn't able to attend the previous party, we thought it only fitting to give him a second chance to view the maze."

"We'd appreciate that," said Cae, both amused and touched.

"Wonderful! Then I'll see you later," Ethin said, and excused himself from the doorway with a parting bow.

Cae watched him go, then shut the door and returned to the table. "Well," he said. "That seems . . . encouraging?"

"It does," Vel agreed. He shot Markel an apologetic look. "If you'd prefer to come, we could probably—"

"It's fine," signed Markel, grinning. "As fond as I am of your company, I prefer to get my political gossip from the kitchens."

Vel pulled a face. "She probably wants to talk about the watchtowers."

"The what? Oh," said Cae, who'd put the matter completely out of mind. He winced. "Is that . . . a good thing, do you think?"

"I don't know," said Vel. "I mean, the rest of the Circlet is opposed to it, which suggests the tierena is, too, but maybe she's willing to negotiate? Though she more likely wants to talk us out of our position."

"Talk you out of yours, you mean," said Cae. At Vel's surprised expression, he rolled his eyes fondly and said, "I may be the yaseran, but I think the whole court knows which of us is the one to negotiate with."

Vel looked flustered by this. "But that's not—I'm not—Cae, you can't just leave all the politics to me, you'll—it'll make people think that you're weak, that I'm taking advantage—"

"I don't care what people think," said Cae. He reached across the table, twining their fingers together. "A good commander delegates to make best use of everyone's strengths; that's what Nairi does, and she's a *very* good commander. I've got many talents, Vel, but politics has never been among them, and I'm trying to learn, but that doesn't mean I'll ever have an aptitude for it." He swallowed, feeling abruptly shy. "I know . . . I know the yaserate isn't what you wanted or expected when you married me, and I'm sorry I didn't warn you about being my heir, but even though it's selfish, there's no one else I'd rather have at my side in this. I trust you. I trust your judgement."

A faint tremor ran through Vel's hand. "I wasn't raised to run a great estate," he said softly. "I was barely even taught to manage a small one. Nobody ever thought it was something I'd need to know. But I think." He swallowed, darting a glance at Markel. "I think, for you, I could try." He managed a laugh. "Just don't be surprised if I get things wrong."

"I could get it wrong, too," Cae pointed out. "In fact, most of the time, I'm not even sure it's possible to get politics completely right. You just have to—" he waved his free hand, searching for the right words, "—persist at understanding people, and what they want, and why, and how to talk to them about it, even when you'd much rather not. And you're good at that, Vel, no matter what anyone says. Our first day here, I didn't even remember we were meant to make a report about what we'd seen, but you did; you even knew to talk about the watchtowers. And, yes, I know you didn't know the full context for it, but still—" He broke off as Vel gave a sudden jolt. "What is it?"

"The watchtowers," Vel breathed. "The fucking *watchtowers.*" And then he started to laugh.

Cae shared a bemused look with Markel, who seemed equally nonplussed. "What about the watchtowers?"

Vel's expression was half-pained, half-impressed. "Cae, it was *Qarrah* who told me how Tithena would benefit from a watchtower system. *Qarrah,* who works directly for Asa Ivadi, who is trying to make the Conclave agree to institute watchtowers." He sat back a little and laughed again. "She played me. They played *us.*"

Cae took a moment to digest the implications, then frowned in disagreement. "I don't think they played us," he said slowly. "I mean, yes, it makes sense to think that Qarrah had an agenda in telling you about it, but that's literally all she could do; she couldn't guarantee it would be meaningful. You're the one who remembered it and thought to bring it up before the asa—I certainly didn't. And it's not like Qarrah knew that Rade was after us at that point; the fire came later, remember? She didn't know we'd be chased the whole way here, such that a watchtower system might seem to us an especially good idea by the end of it."

"Maybe so," said Velasin, but he sounded troubled. "I still don't know what the reseko means."

"The reseko?"

"The little statue, the one your grandmother gave me. Qarrah has a matching one, but beyond that, I don't know what it signifies."

Markel, who'd been listening quietly to that point, snapped his fingers to get their attention and signed, "I think it means that Yasa Kithadi and Asa Ivadi are closer allies than most people realise. Regardless of where the reseko came from, the fact that both the yasa and Qarrah had one—and that the yasa gave Velasin hers to make sure he'd recognise Qarrah as an ally—is significant."

Vel sat with this a moment. "You're probably right," he said, "and yet I still don't feel comforted."

"I don't do comfort," Markel signed tartly. "I do pragmatism and keeping you alive. And," he added, forestalling Vel's reply, "you already know *I* think you'll make a good yasan, but it matters, I think, that I'm not the only one."

Vel put a hand over his eyes. "Not listening!"

"Just accept it, Vel," said Cae, fondly amused. "Other people think you're competent."

"I'm not competent," Vel grouched. "I'm a scandalous reprobate." But he lowered his hand, a touch of heat in his cheeks.

With the serious business out of the way, the conversation shifted to the story of where, exactly, Markel had spent the night—in the Circlet Annex kitchens, as it turned out, with several amusing tales to be told of the experience that didn't relate to political gossip. Cae took a back seat to the conversation, more focussed on keeping up with Markel's signing than anything else: the new, condensed signing system they'd worked out was easier for Cae to use and follow, but with Velasin as his primary audience, Markel frequently interspersed it with the original, which made interpretation more of a challenge. Another time, it might've been frustrating, but after the events of the past few days, it was strangely relieving to be presented with a comprehensible problem, and even though he missed certain details of the narrative, the fact that he followed along at all left Cae with a feeling of accomplishment.

"What will you do while we're at lunch? Rest?" Vel asked eventually. "It doesn't sound like you got much sleep last night."

"I didn't," Markel admitted. "And even if she'd invited me, it's not as if I'd be able to talk to anyone other than you two."

"Stay here, then," signed Cae. "And . . . thank you, for giving us space last night."

Markel crinkled his nose in silent laughter. "You needed it," he signed. "Though if this morning was any indication, once we're back in Qi-Katai, I might think about moving out of your apartments."

The tips of Velasin's ears went pleasingly scarlet at this. Markel grinned, rose, clapped Vel on the shoulder and, with a parting nod to Cae, headed off to his chamber.

Cae waited until he'd heard the distant door open and close before turning to Vel and saying, as straight-facedly as he was able, "You know, if we're very quiet, he might not hear us—"

Vel threw a pear slice at him.

27

With the midday sun overhead, Cae told himself that the Mazepool Gardens looked less foreboding than they had the night of the tierena's party. The magelights in the hedges were inactive, the pale blue flowers standing out against the greenery like slices of wintry sky. Absent the crowds of guests and the attendant chairs and tables, the artistry of the gardens was more apparent, and he made an effort to try and appreciate it. There was a swooping, sinuous symmetry to the way the pebbled paths wound between the raised garden beds, statues and fountains, the tinkling of the water offset by the gentle rustling of leaves—all beautiful. And yet his skin still prickled with the memory of that drugged, unnatural heat, and he tasted again the mineral tang of the hot spring. It wasn't a physical response he'd expected to have, and the effect was profoundly unbalancing, as if one leg was suddenly longer than the other.

"Are you all right?" asked Vel.

"I'm fine," Cae said, then faltered, realising he'd come to a halt several feet behind his husband without having meant to stop at all. He swallowed, wanting to explain but also not knowing quite how to find the words for it. "Just." He waved a hand at the gardens, trying to summon a joke. "Not exactly my favourite place."

Instantly, Vel was by his side, a concerned look on his face as he grasped Cae's hand. "We can leave, if you'd rather," he offered. "Both of us, or I can stay and you go back—"

"No." Cae took a deep breath and smiled. "No, I'll be all right. Thank you, though."

Vel didn't look fully convinced, but he didn't argue, either. "All right," he said, and lifted Cae's hand up, brushing a kiss across his knuckles. Cae shivered pleasantly, his body refocussing away from the gardens and towards his husband. "Just remember, you're allowed to change your mind." Vel paused, considering, then said, "If you want to leave at any point, ask me if I'm feeling all right, and I'll fake a swoon and plead exhaustion. Agreed?"

"Agreed," said Cae, chest aching with how much he loved him. Thus fortified, he squeezed Vel's hand and squared himself against the gardens. "Come on, then."

As it turned out, there were multiple entrances to the maze proper from the gardens, only one of which was guarded by a waiting figure. To Cae's immense relief, it wasn't the entrance he'd taken with Asrien; even so, his pulse still ticked up slightly in anticipation, the way it only usually did before a battle or an ambush, and he made a point to breathe deeply, calmly, settling himself.

"Yaseran, tiern." Their guide bowed to them, and Cae realised belatedly that he recognised the man as one of the palace functionaries who'd greeted them when they first arrived.

"Ru Roya?" he asked, surprised. "I was expecting one of the tierena's servants."

Ru Roya smiled. "The tierena is borrowing the gardens with the asa's permission; my services are, as it were, a part of the loan. Now, If you'll kindly follow me—"

"Well, what's this?" a voice called out. "What a pleasant surprise!"

It was Yasai Qiqa, approaching with a foxish smile on thir lips, dressed in a single-sleeved lin of blue and gold brocade over a fitted blue undershirt, paired with golden brown nara. Half thir russet hair was braided back from either side of thir temples and tied together over the remaining mass, highlighting thir many earrings. Thei were an unexpected sight, but not, Cae was pleased to realise, a wholly unwelcome one.

"Yasai!" he said. "I didn't expect to see you today."

"Just Qiqa, please—I think we can dispense with the formalities after our little swimming adventure, don't you?" Thei smiled, inclining thir head to Velasin. "I'm glad to see you looking well."

"It's nice to feel well," Vel admitted. He tipped his head to indicate both the maze and Ru Roya. "Where were you headed? Tierena Keris has invited us to lunch at the Mazepool Pavilion."

"Has she, now!" Qiqa's smile brightened. "Do you mind if I tag along? I know I'm not invited," thei added, directing this remark to the servant, "but I promise to behave myself."

Ru Roya looked flustered by this, but was obviously in no position to refuse the Silver Chair anything, especially if Cae and Vel were amenable. Cae briefly considered declining, but the reminder that Qiqa had been the one to pull him from the hot spring was a comforting one, and as Vel's expression plainly said that the decision was Cae's, he saw no reason why not.

"We'd be happy to have you," he said, and Qiqa beamed.

"Wonderful! Lead on, then."

With a jerky bow, Ru Roya complied, stepping into the maze. As the greenery closed in around them, Cae felt a slight spike of panic, but the press of Vel's arm against his own and Qiqa's light, inconsequential chatter steadily worked to settle it, until he was able to assess their surroundings more objectively. The night of the party, he hadn't really understood how vast a construction the maze truly was: between the darkness and his drugged state, he'd lost all sense of time and space, stumbling along behind Asrien like a puppy after a butterfly. Now, though, he found himself awed by the place, and not just because his pulse still felt elevated. The maze was intricate, baffling and impressive, the scent of the blue flowers sweet without being overpowering.

"Every second year," Qiqa said, "the asa holds a contest for her courtiers to see who can solve the maze quickest—every *second* year, mind, because she changes the pathways each time, and it's not good for the hedges to have them moved and replanted too often, even with magical assistance."

Vel let out a low, impressed whistle. "I can imagine."

"I've heard of that," Cae said, trying to sound unaffected. It was disconcerting not to be able to see over the tops of the hedges: he was used to being one of the taller people in any given room or on horseback while in cities, and was therefore unaccustomed to having his vision obstructed. It brought back his earlier sense of imbalance, which was perhaps why he said, unthinking, "Laecia wanted to go one year, but Father said she was too young for it—oh." He swallowed against a sudden rush of grief, and added roughly, "I suppose she never will, now."

"I'm sorry for your loss," said Qiqa, thir voice softer than before. "Truly."

Cae shook his head, refusing his own sadness. He had problems enough to focus on in the moment without summoning yet more ghosts. "It is what it is," he said, and felt an immeasurable swell of gratitude as Vel squeezed his arm in sympathy.

Throughout all this, Ru Roya had remained silent, moving quietly and efficiently through the maze's innumerable twists and turns. Now, though, as they reached a new junction, he turned, offered a half-bow to the three of them and said, "Just through here."

Sure enough, the next corner revealed a mercifully open space, which at a glance looked large enough to have comfortably held a hundred-odd people—more, if the people in question were content to rub elbows literally as well as figuratively. A neatly paved path cut a curving line through soft, daisy-strewn grass from the maze entrance to one side of an elaborate, open-sided hexagonal gazebo, with two similar paths on opposite sides presumably leading to other routes through the maze. In the middle of the gazebo sat a long, high table made of a rich, reddish-brown wood that Cae couldn't immediately identify, the legs carved to resemble sturdy boughs wreathed with vines and roses. The table was laid with a vast array of dishes, the scents of which had his mouth watering the closer they drew, and at the head of the table sat Tierena Keris, with Ethin to her left. It was only when they mounted the steps to enter that Cae realised there were also more servants present—six, in fact, spaced apart from each other at the corners of the structure—plus another functionary, Ru Pyras. Two of the servants wore swords at their hips, which was unusual in the palace, but with the exception of the functionaries, all were posed as waitstaff, ready to help with the food.

The tierena rose as they entered, with Ethin copying a beat later. She looked pleased to see them, but frowned slightly at the sight of Qiqa.

"Yasai," she said, inclining her head. "This is an unexpected pleasure." Her gaze flicked to the table, which was laden with enough food to have comfortably served an extra three guests. "I'm pleased to be able to accommodate you, but—"

"I'm pleased, too," said Qiqa, cheerfully ignoring her attempt at a polite dismissal. "You always set a good table."

"I'm touched that you think so," the tierena replied, apparently resigned to thir presence. Sighing, she smiled again and gestured welcome to Cae and Vel. "Yasan, tiern; I'm so glad you could make it." She peered past them, as if looking for another guest. "Is your servant not with you? You've made such a habit of bringing him everywhere, I rather assumed he'd come."

"Oh!" said Vel. "Thank you, but no; he's run himself ragged the past few days looking after me, so I had him stay back." He hesitated, gaze encompassing the table's largesse, then ventured, "I hope you're not offended?"

"Not at all," said the tierena. "I hope he feels well again soon; you should take some food back for him, too."

"I'd appreciate that," said Vel.

They sat down together, though to Ethin's visible annoyance, Qiqa disrupted the seating plans by taking the seat opposite him at the tierena's right, putting Cae to Qiqa's right and Vel across from him at Ethin's left. To Cae's surprise, the functionaries sat, too, though at the other end of the table, leaving vacant seats between themselves, Cae and Vel—he hadn't anticipated their presence, but given the quantity of food and their apparent stewardship of the gardens on the asa's behalf, he supposed it made sense.

"I'm so glad to have this chance to talk," said Tierena Keris, lacing her fingers together on the tabletop. "Tiern Velasin, I was simply horrified by the attack on your life. The idea that Kisian would be involved in such a thing . . . I've known the man for years. It's simply unfathomable, and yet what are we to make of the evidence otherwise?" As she spoke, she motioned the servants forwards to start portioning out their plates. "Are you recovering well? I have every faith in the palace healers, but if you wished to minimize your scar for cosmetic reasons—which is not to say that you should, of course— I'd be happy to recommend a mage who specializes in such things."

Vel blinked, looking genuinely surprised by the offer. "I hadn't even considered that," he admitted. "I'll be sure to think about it."

"She does good work," said Ethin earnestly. "My sister had a terrible scar from where she was kicked by a horse, but—" He broke off abruptly, mouth falling open as he stared at Qiqa, who had just lifted Cae's entire, fully laden plate away from him and swapped it out for thir own.

"Please indulge me," said Qiqa, flashing Cae a bright, unrepentant smile. "I'm in a whimsical mood." And before anyone could respond to this, thei plucked a dumpling from his stolen plate— with thir fingers, Cae noticed amazedly—and popped the whole thing into thir mouth.

"By all means," said Cae, because what else could he say, really? He looked across the table at Vel, who was equally baffled, his eyes wide, and then at the horrified functionaries.

Tierena Keris sighed. "Qiqa," she said, in the universally weary tone of a disappointed teacher, "please. Must we have these theatrics? You're clearly here to a purpose: just say what it is and have done with it."

"Are you sure?" asked Qiqa, grinning as thei swallowed. Thei picked up another dumpling, fingers slippery with oil and water, contemplated it a moment, then slid it into thir mouth. "I didn't think you were fond of plain speaking."

The nape of Cae's neck began to prickle, and he looked again at Vel, whose posture had gone tellingly still.

"Qiqa—"

"It's just," said Qiqa, toying idly with thir unused kip, "that I had the oddest experience last night. There I was, taking an evening stroll to clear my head and enjoy the changing seasons, when suddenly I saw Lord Asrien leaving the prison in quite a hurry—badly dressed, I might add; he looked very cold—and I thought to myself, what business does Lord Asrien have with a prisoner at this time of night? It seemed like the sort of thing a conscientious chair would investigate, and so I followed him. But what do you think happened next? The poor man was coshed over the head by Ru Pyras here"—thei flicked thir fingers at the functionary—"and carted off who knows where like a bale of hay, which seems like pretty poor hospitality on our part, even if he is Ralian—no offence intended, of course," thei added, aiming a flicker of smile at Vel.

The tierena stiffened. "And this pertains to me how?"

"Did I say it pertained to you? I don't believe I did." Thei flipped and turned the kip along the backs of thir fingers, as if performing a coin trick. Then thei tilted thir head and smiled broadly, evidently unconcerned with the rising fury on the faces of Ru Roya and Ru Pyras. "Did it?"

Ethin, who'd been watching this byplay with his mouth hanging open, now turned to look worriedly at the tierena. "Grandmother? What are thei talking about?"

But the tierena didn't answer. Instead, she propped an elbow on the table and rested her chin in her palm, raking Qiqa with an assessing look. "You know," she said, almost conversationally, "you're a very puzzling person. Why did you eat the dumplings, if you knew what was in them?"

"For the drama, obviously," said Qiqa, cutting a quick, meaningful look at Cae. "And to prove that there *was* something in them."

A cold and unpleasant feeling slithered down Cae's spine. "Vel," he said, low and urgent, "we should—"

The armed servants moved with silent alacrity. One minute, they were standing at their posts; the next, there was a hand in Vel's hair and a blade at his throat—and at Cae's, although that felt far less important. He went rigid where he sat, pulse thundering in his ears as cold steel brushed the new scar on Velasin's throat.

"Grandmother?" Ethin asked shakily, voice cracking. "What's going on?"

"Politics, I'd imagine," Qiqa said faintly. Cae wasn't in much of a position to turn his head—whoever had a blade on him had also taken hold of his braid—but from the corner of his eye, he could see that Qiqa was sweating, thir warm skin looking ashier than it had just moments ago. Thei were slumped in thir seat, breathing shallowly through thir half-open mouth. "Business as usual."

"*Dramatics*," the tierena muttered. She closed her eyes for a moment, then opened them again, a rueful quirk to her lips as she looked at Vel. "My apologies, tiern," she said, and the horrific thing was, she sounded as if she meant it. "Please understand, the last thing I want in all this is for you to sustain further injury; this"— she waved a hand to indicate the servant, the knife—"is more for your husband's benefit, being as he is quite wretchedly fond of you." She flashed Cae a look of long-suffering annoyance, then turned back to Vel, her smile warm and coaxing. "You, though . . . your feelings are quite different, aren't they."

She said it as a statement, not a question, and even though he knew rationally that Vel did care for him, even if not in the same way and to the same extent, Cae still felt his guts turn to ice. He tried to cling to the memory of Vel crying out *I love, beloved* in Ralian, but that had been in bed, in passion, not a level-headed declaration, and even within his head, the words were drowned out by the memory of Vel in Etho, first struggling in his arms, then catatonic on the ground, reduced to trembling fear by Cae's idiocy.

"They might be," Vel said, not looking at Cae.

Don't assume he's telling the truth, Cae told himself, even as his stomach twisted. *Vel's smart; he knows how to play for time, how to get answers.* Back in Qi-Katai, when Ren Adan had held them captive in his cellar, it was Vel's quick-thinking decision to feign fear of Cae that had ultimately led to their escape. The same might well prove true now, if only Cae could keep his mouth shut and his fears in check.

"It's hardly to your discredit," said the tierena. "As I understand it, the circumstances of your betrothal to the yaseran were . . . fraught, let's say."

"You could say that," Vel said tightly.

The tierena's expression was sympathetic. "And owing to the nature of your marriage, am I right in thinking that returning to Ralia is no longer an option for you?"

"You are."

"Nobody mind me," Qiqa mumbled. Thei'd sunk a little lower in their seat, thir grip on the edge of the table white-knuckled. Thei flashed Cae a wan look. "I'm fine. It's all in service of making a point."

"Oh, do shut up," said the tierena, before Cae could even hope to think of a reply. "It's entirely your own fault."

A very belated gear turned in Cae's head. "You're the one who drugged me," he said, staring at the tierena. "You—"

"Technically, it was Ru Roya who did the honours," the tierena said, flicking her fingers at the glowering functionary. "Though it was me who tried to drown you—of which fact, by the by, Yasai Qiqa was well aware, having interrupted us right in the middle of things. And yet thei seemed quite unbothered at the time." She raised a querying eyebrow.

Cae's head was spinning. "What?"

"My apologies," Qiqa said weakly, smiling up at Cae through pinched, blueing lips. "I'd only just arrived, and I'd heard some rather confused gossip about you and the young tiern there"—thei gestured feebly at Ethin—"almost drowning in a river, and so I thought Amber might have been acting, if not sensibly, then at least understandably." Thei paused, shivering violently, then added, "Also, I owed her a favour, which I believe was fully repaid by letting her go about her business. But I did still save your life, yaseran, which I feel ought to count for something."

Cae had no idea what to say to that.

"All of that's as may be," said the tierena, returning her attention to Vel. "The point, tiern, is that your position is an unenviable one. The whole purpose of your marriage is a functional alliance with Ralia, but as you're married to a man, the Ralians won't accept it—which is why they sent poor Asrien to try and tempt you into infidelity, to say nothing of that awful business with your brother and the assassin. But even if you asked for a divorce, that same prejudice prevents you from returning home. For better or worse, you're stuck here—so why not aim for better?"

Vel's throat bobbed as he swallowed, scraping perilously against the edge of the blade. "What do you propose?" he asked faintly.

"Simple," said the tierena. "Marry me instead."

Cae wanted to laugh, but was beaten to his outrage by, of all people, Ethin, who shot upright as urgently as if he'd been poked somewhere delicate. "Grandmother!" he exclaimed, face red. "You can't—I mean, that is—"

"Sit down, Ethin," said the tierena—quite patiently, under the circumstances. "And let me explain." She waited until he'd done as he was told, then said, "I'm well aware that the tiern doesn't incline towards women; in fact, it suits me nicely. I've already had my children, and am quite happy with the results." She reached out, giving Ethin a grandmotherly pat on the cheek; this mollified him somewhat, but from Cae's perspective, the whole thing was bizarre. "To which point, Ethin, I'm quite aware of your affection for the tiern—now now, don't blush, it's nothing to be ashamed of. Quite the contrary." She straightened, addressing Vel once more. "At present, tiern, you are your husband's heir, which puts you next in line for the yaserate. Now, obviously, Yasa Kithadi is still alive, so in the event of the yaseran's death, you'd have many years left in which to learn the ins and outs of managing such a large estate—expertise which I, were we wed, would gladly share with you. Now, did you wish to take lovers, I'd have no objections to that, but once the yasa passes on, whenever that might be, I'll name Ethin my heir, and perhaps by then the two of you might have your own understanding, hm?"

"You," said Vel. Stopped. Flattened his hands on the tabletop, very clearly trying to contain himself. "The idea is to, what . . . share me with your grandson?" He bit back a strangled laugh. "And when you die, I'm to marry Ethin next?"

"Yes," said the tierena, calmly. "I'm not so arrogant as to think I'll live forever. The two of you will have years in which to get to know each other—" she broke off, frowning pointedly at Qiqa, who'd risen from thir poisoned slump sufficiently to let out a gargling burst of laughter, before turning back to Vel, "—as well as to learn the management of both territories. And in the interim, we'll have a marriage of alliance that will be diplomatically acceptable to Ralia, with all the potential for trade that entails, and years in which to cement that relationship sufficiently for it to withstand your marriage to Ethin. It's an ideal solution: everyone wins." She paused, lips quirking as she looked at Cae. "Well, almost everyone. I'm afraid the plan can't work while the yaseran lives—but one life, surely, is a reasonable trade for the security and prosperity the Ralian alliance will bring."

"If this plan *was* only about the alliance," Vel said levelly, "then Cae's death wouldn't be required. I could divorce him, marry you and achieve the same effect. But if we did that, I'd presumably no longer be his heir to the yaserate—which means, in turn, that Clan Talae wouldn't be able to claim it through marrying me. And that's what you really want, tierena—to expand your family's holdings and influence."

All at once, Cae found himself recalling the conversation he'd had with Tierena Keris at her party; it ought've come to him earlier, but the revelation that she'd been the one to drug him and hold him underwater had forced it from his mind.

"You told me this could've been avoided," he blurted, capturing her attention. "That night in the gardens. You told me, it would've been better if Yasa Kithadi had named my mother her heir, instead of waiting to name a grandchild."

"Of course it would've been better!" the tierena snapped—the first break in her composure thus far. "Better still if Inavi had never married Halithar in the first place, the pompous ass—she would've been far better off with my Seren. But no; she wouldn't entertain the idea, even though it would've benefited both our legacies for the families to merge—some nonsense about separate responsibilities and political balance that I'm sure she didn't believe for a second." She snorted. "Far better to let Inavi marry a wholly unsuitable idiot, move to Qi-Katai, delegate all her responsibilities and still fumble choosing an heir so badly that one of the candidates goes on a murder-spree and ends up dead. Just wonderful!"

Ugly heat rushed through Cae from head to toe. Without thinking, he went to push away from the table and stand, only to be brought up short by the hand on his braid and the blade at his throat, both of which he'd somehow managed to forget. Beside him, Qiqa made an unhappy wheezing noise, and for the first time Cae let himself process the fact that Tierena Keris had meant to poison him, only for the food to have been eaten instead by Qiqa.

"Will thei live?" he asked gruffly, jerking his head to indicate the yasai.

The tierena looked down her nose at Qiqa. "Thei might," she allowed. "Though I expect thei'll have an unpleasant time of things either way." And then, to Qiqa, "Honestly, *why* did you eat those dumplings?"

"I told you," Qiqa croaked. "For dramatic effect."

"And how would you have played that off, if the yasai hadn't been here?" Vel asked suddenly. "Was I meant to sit here and watch my husband die at your table, and not think anything of it?"

"Asrien," Qiqa panted, before the tierena could answer. "That's why you took Asrien, isn't it? To take the blame for this." Thei listed forwards, groaning slightly as thei clutched their stomach. "For the record, this is a *deeply* unpleasant experience."

"Do you have Asrien?" Cae asked, just as Vel said, "What have you done with him?"

"He's well enough," said the tierena. She blinked, clearly surprised by their concern. "Really, I find it hard to believe that you're fussed about his welfare—the man is a foreign agent sent to undermine you."

"As opposed to a domestic agent undermining us?" Cae asked tightly.

Two spots of colour formed on the tierena's cheeks. "King Markus thinks only of ending the current attempt at an alliance," she said, "not of how to replace it, or with what. No matter his personal feelings, he'd rather let his lords squabble and rage over whether or not to attempt a second union than negotiate in good faith—but if Tithena presents him with a palatable diplomatic solution, one he and his court can accept with minimal effort and maximum gain, well: that's a different story."

"And I suppose," said Vel, his voice impressively even, "that Asrien remains the chosen scapegoat for Caethari's death?"

"And mine," put in Qiqa.

"Of course," said the tierena, ignoring the yasai. Cae suppressed a flinch. "Ralia will accept his role in things, because it was their idea. Or didn't you know that?"

"Know what?"

"That, were his seductions to prove an inadequate temptation, Asrien was supposed to kill you, playing the part of a jealous lover spurned. His killing Caethari instead is rather more poetic, I think."

"Ralia might accept it," Cae said, fists clenched, "but what about Tithena? For a Ralian national to kill a yaseran—"

"It's scandalous, yes," said Tierena Keris, "but not insurmountable, especially with jealousy as the motive. In face, we might argue that it gives us a better position from which to negotiate—we can say to Ralia, *in recompense for the tragedy, despite which we are willing to continue this alliance in good faith, the throne might consider offering*, oh, for instance, financial aid to help rebuild the townships whose livelihoods were steadily decimated due to vin Mica's banditry, and whose restoration as part of a trade route would be of material long-term benefit to both nations."

Cae was still processing the idea of this as a positive outcome of his own murder when Vel said, with sudden, quiet intensity, "It wasn't Ru Kisian who bought the cietena's lands. It was you."

The tierena smiled. "I'm sure I have no idea what you're talking about," she said. "The purchases were all made in Ru Kisian's name, and if poor Alu was still alive to give testimony, she'd tell you the same thing. If he chooses to pass them on to me in the future, that's entirely his own decision."

"But—" Vel stared at her. "I don't understand. Your plan doesn't work if I'm dead. But if you were behind Ru Kisian, and Ru Kisian contracted Syana—" He broke off, fingers twitching on the tabletop. "But he didn't, did he? You framed him. You, what—had leverage over him? His gambling debts?"

"Clever boy," said the tierena approvingly. "Yes. And then I went to Alu—acting in my capacity as a good, concerned friend, of course—and told her that she'd been had: that her land was about to rise in value thanks to the alliance, and didn't she want to have revenge?"

"And did she?" Vel asked.

Tierena Keris smiled. "She did," she said. "And so I helped her find and contact Syana, and everything was set to work—and would've done, if that spiteful little virago had only done what she was supposed to and targeted Caethari." Her lip curled with displeasure. "But instead, she went after you and nearly ruined everything, for which she was given her due comeuppance."

"And so, when drowning Cae didn't work, you took his dagger," Vel said softly, "and used it to implicate him in the cietena's death.

Two birds with one stone." He swallowed, gaze flickering briefly to indicate the servants with their knives at his throat and Cae's. "I assume one of your fellows here was responsible?"

The servant holding Vel, a blocky-shouldered man with a single black braid coiled and pinned in a bun at the back of his head, gave a rasping chuckle. "At your service, tiern."

Throughout this recitation of guilt, poor Ethin had grown paler and paler. Cae would've felt sorry for him, except that, under the circumstances, it was increasingly difficult to feel anything at all. He was numb, and though a distant part of him was furious, more prominent was the cold, creeping guilt that had dogged him since the deaths of his father and sister. He looked at Vel, cool and composed despite the blade at his still-so-recently-opened throat, despite Qiqa sweating and gasping thir way through whatever poison thei'd ingested, and allowed a treacherous thought to consume him: would Vel be better off if Cae were dead?

It wasn't a rational thought. Tierena Keris was objectively terrible, and the idea of Vel marrying her made Cae want to rip the world apart with his hands, but that was a selfish, feral reaction, no more noble or defensible than the sudden despairing worry that not only Vel's life, but Tithena's diplomatic future, might be improved by his death. Cae was not a habitually morbid person, nor did he want to die, but as he sat there, his thoughts unspooled a litany of failure: Vel, first shaking on the cobbles in Etho, then bleeding out in the asa's hall; Laecia, screaming as she burned, an arrow sprouting from her forehead; his father, going rigid as his heart burst; even long-ago Mauri, pale in his arms and begging him for a quick death. How could Cae, of all people, hope to one day run a yaserate? Vel hadn't even been able to choose their marriage: if the whole point of Vel's being here was to cement an alliance with Ralia, and Cae's presence ruined even that, then what was the point of him?

"Vel," Cae croaked. "If you wanted—"

"Don't you fucking *dare*," Vel snapped. Cae's mouth fell open in shock. Vel had been so composed to that point that his sharpness came as a shock, and Cae was horrified to see that Vel was trembling. "Don't," Vel whispered again, and briefly shut his eyes.

When he opened them again, his gaze was as hard as Cae had ever seen it.

"Tierena," said Vel, turning to face her as much as the blade at his throat allowed. "Your offer is both flattering and well-reasoned. Ralia would certainly be more amenable to the alliance were I married to you instead of Cae, and I appreciate that you'd allow me to take lovers. You've gone to some lengths to arrange all this, and that effort should be respected. However, I'm sorry to say that you've founded your actions on a faulty premise."

"Oh?" said the tierena. She blinked, looking genuinely intrigued. "And what might that be?"

Vel smiled, the expression both hard and tremulous. "You think I don't love Caethari," he said. "But I do. I love him so much I hardly know what to do with it." Vel laughed, the sound so fragile and perfect that Cae's heart clenched in his chest. "I think I've been falling in love with him since the day I first rode into Qi-Katai. And if you hurt him—if you put so much as a scratch on him—so help me, I will burn your clan to *ash*."

28

For an endless moment, everyone was silent. Ethin looked frozen in place, his freckles stark against the shocky, ashen pallor of his skin; the servants were motionless and the functionaries slack-jawed, while Tierena Keris looked carved from marble, as still and foreboding as a mausoleum statue.

"Well," she said icily. "That *is* unfortunate—"

She broke off, leaping to her feet in alarm as Qiqa, who'd been lolling in thir seat like a drunkard, suddenly let out an agonized cry and began spasming violently, thir flailing arms knocking plates, cups and cutlery to the gazebo floor in a clatter of sound and motion—and in that moment, where even the servants were distracted, Cae moved. *Vel loves me.* Ignoring the blade at his throat, he grabbed his captor by the wrist and dug his thumb into the tendons, surging to his feet and pivoting around his hold while shoving the servant away. The man swore, caught off-balance, and as he stumbled backwards, Cae reached out with his free hand and drew the sword from his hip. Thus armed, he whirled back around—Ru Pyras and Ru Roya both leapt to their feet, alarmed—saw that Vel was half on his feet, struggling desperately to shove the second servant's knife away from his throat, and vaulted over the table, knocking yet more food to the floor in the process. Vel's captor swore and dragged Vel backwards, trying to get away from Cae, but couldn't draw his own sword without either releasing Vel's hair or dropping his knife, both of which he was reluctant to do.

"This plan works better with your cooperation, Velasin," the tierena said, standing back from the fray, the two rus rushing to her side, "but it will work regardless." She lifted her hand, signalling to the remaining servants, all of whom began to circle slowly towards Cae.

Ignoring his grandmother, Ethin chose this moment to scuttle around the head of the table and kneel at Qiqa's side, wide-eyed with fright. The yasai was on the ground by this point, twitching feebly; Ethin shot his grandmother a pleading look, but she shook her head.

"Thei knew what thei were doing," she said simply.

Cae brought his stolen sword into guard position, acutely aware that he needed to get Vel and get out before they were both boxed in. He could see the other servants approaching at the edges of his vision: five of them, including the man who'd escorted them through the maze, and he cursed internally at the reminder that, even if they broke free of the pavilion, he didn't know how to navigate the maze. *One thing at a time,* he told himself, and locked eyes with Vel, blood thrumming with desperation.

All at once, a stupid idea occurred to him.

"Vel," he said, injecting his tone with meaning, "are you feeling all right?"

For a split second, Vel looked at him like he was crazy; then he laughed in recollection, flashed a manic smile—and went limp, sprawling deadweight in his captor's hold. The servant hadn't been expecting it, but Cae had, and as the off-balance captor fumbled the grip on his blade in an effort to keep Vel upright, Cae swept in and delivered a clean, precise slash across the man's jugular.

Blood gushed out, a terrible rush of red. Reflexively, the guard released Vel and clutched at his neck, and Vel surged away from him, scrambling towards Cae, though not fast enough to avoid catching a spray of blood across one cheek. He grabbed Cae and they moved together, Cae's sword up as they tried to get around the table and out of the gazebo, but that was easier said than done. The servants—or guards, rather; the distinction felt increasingly apropos—had moved into position, and as alarmed as some of them looked to see their colleague bleeding on the ground, the tierena had evidently chosen her people well, as none of them backed off. More importantly, they were armed after all, although not with swords: each man or woman had pulled a knife from somewhere, and while Cae's blade gave him a superior reach, he had no shield or armour with which to counter-act their greater numbers. As soon as he struck at one, another might dart in under his guard, which meant he'd have to be clever as well as quick.

Cae's world narrowed to the awareness of Vel beside him, the blade in his hand, the servants closing in on them. *Vel loves me.* He didn't want to kill anyone else, but with Vel to protect, he wasn't sure what else he could do—

Beneath them, the ground shook.

For a disorienting moment, Cae didn't know what was happening—and nor, it seemed, did anyone else. Several guards shouted in confusion, all of them struggling to keep their balance as the earth twitched and rumbled underfoot. *A winter quake,* he realised, and almost laughed: just like the one that had spooked both Vel and the horses when they'd first ridden out from Avai. It was a saints-blessed bit of luck, and Cae was too pragmatic to ques-tion it: just grabbed Vel and bulled forwards before the shaking had stopped, taking advantage of the confusion and the guards' uncertain footing to kick one down and strike at the other, open-ing a gaping slash on his arm.

They ran out of the gazebo, stumbling forwards and nearly fall-ing as the ground continued to jump. Cae felt a pang of regret for leaving Qiqa behind, but even if he could've carried both thim and a sword at once, he had nothing with which to heal the yasai's poisoning, and so had no choice but to leave thim to whatever care Ethin was capable of providing.

"Which way?" he asked Vel, grasping his husband's hand. *Vel loves me.*

"Further in," Vel panted, already tugging Cae towards the most distant entrance to the maze. This made perfect sense to Cae: by virtue of having guided them in, at least one of the tierena's servants already had the main exit route memorised, which would put the two of them at a disadvantage, but it was much less certain that the guards knew the maze's internal routes, which evened the playing field. He ran alongside Vel, the guards already scrambling after them as the shaking stopped, and darted into the maze.

"You pick," he said to Vel, who swallowed and nodded, towing Cae towards the first turning and down the right-hand path, which curved a little before branching again. Vel led them left, then right again, swearing under his breath as he contemplated each twist in the path. Their pursuers seemed close, but there was no way to tell how accurate that was, as the hedges had a distorting effect on sound. One moment, it seemed like the tierena's people were right next to them; in the next, they heard nothing at all. Vel laced his fingers with Cae's and gripped him tight, proceeding through the maze with quiet determination. Twice, they hit a dead end and had to backtrack; both times, Cae expected the tierena's people to appear around the corner and ambush them, but they didn't.

A few turns later, Vel came to an abrupt halt. He was breathing heavily, hair disarrayed with dried blood on his cheek, his lin pulled askew from the struggle.

"Should we keep going?" he asked worriedly, pitching his voice low. "Or is it better to pick a spot and wait?"

Keep going, Cae meant to say. But what came out instead was a hoarse, "You love me?"

Vel bit his lip, that gorgeous flush spreading down his throat. "I do," he whispered. "I'm only sorry it took me so long to realise."

Cae cupped his jaw and kissed him desperately, wanting so much to lose himself in it but knowing he had to focus. Vel's mouth was hot and frantic against his own; if he hadn't still been holding the sword, Cae would've grabbed him and probably lost all sense of the world, but as it was, he forced himself to pull back.

"We should keep going," he said shakily. "For all we know, the tierena has sent more people after us."

"That would make sense," Vel said darkly, as they started moving again. "She's boxed herself into a corner with all this, and I don't see how she's planning to get out of it. If Qiqa hadn't shown up and forced her hand . . ."

"I'd probably be dead," Cae said softly, suppressing a shudder. Of all the ways he'd ever considered dying, poison was high on the list of things he didn't want to experience. To lighten the thought, he forced a cheerful tone and said, "Is it wrong that I'm still hungry?"

As if in answer, Vel's stomach grumbled, startling them both into laughter—and then Vel froze, a horrified look on his face.

"Markel," he breathed, and for a moment Cae didn't understand the connection, until he remembered the tierena's remark about sending him leftovers. "Cae, she thought we'd bring Markel with us—what if she's going after him now, too?"

Cae swore, his thoughts racing. "She won't want him dead," he said firmly, both because he believed it and because the alternative was unthinkable. "With her plan exposed, he's potentially the only leverage over you she has left."

Vel didn't reply to that; he didn't need to. They both knew Vel would do anything to keep Markel alive, and if the tierena succeeded in taking him hostage, she'd gain a powerful weapon.

They began to move faster, threading their way through the maze. From time to time, they heard rustling and raised voices, but were yet to intersect with their pursuers.

"Are we lost?" Cae asked, when they reached yet another dead end.

"Yes. No. I don't know." Vel rubbed his eyes, leading them back out. "I'm trying to keep track of where we're headed, but it's all getting tangled." He let out a short, mirthless bark of laughter. "The smart way to solve a maze is to only turn one way unless you've got no other options, but I thought, if I did that, they'd do the same and catch up to us too easily."

Cae nodded, shoulders hunched against the oppressive loom of the hedges. He'd been trying not to let the maze get to him, focussing hard on Vel and the urgency with which they'd been moving forwards, but now that they'd slowed down, his earlier claustrophobia was creeping back over him. He set his jaw against it, staring at the blue of the flowers, the glass of the magelights—dormant now, but sure to light up once darkness fell, illuminating the path—

"Wait," he said suddenly, gripping Vel's hand. "Wait a moment." He turned, scanning the hedges on either side of their current row, heart pounding. His memories of Asrien leading him through the maze that night were fragmented, made patchy and blurred by whatever drug the tierena had slipped him, but he remembered the glow of the magelights, leading them through the maze to the pool: and, more, how Asrien somehow never took a wrong turning despite his apparent unfamiliarity with the maze.

"The lights," he said, grabbing Vel's hand. "I think the lights are meant to keep night-time visitors from getting lost, which means they might not be in every path. So if we follow them—"

"—we find the way out," Vel finished. He looked Cae over with flattering breathlessness, but didn't say anything further; just bit his lip in a way that made Cae light-headed.

Together, they moved forwards to the next junction, scanning each hedge for the dormant globes, and found that, sure enough, the left-hand turn had magelights, while the right did not. Mutually giddy with this small success, they proceeded with renewed energy, Cae taking the lead, Vel close enough to brush against his shoulder. To his subconscious relief, Cae found that focussing on the magelights helped dispel the anxiety induced by the maze, as did Vel's proximity. He fixed his thoughts on Markel's welfare, trying to calculate the tierena's actions: there were several courses of action he might take in her position, but without knowing how many more people she had at her disposal, it was hard to gauge which was the likeliest. Her apparent arrest of Asrien meant that she had a scapegoat on hand for some of what she'd done, like the poisoning of Qiqa—assuming the yasai was dead, that was, and as such unable to testify otherwise—but how could she hope to play off the rest of what she'd done?

Please, let thim be alive, Cae thought, a silent prayer to whatever god or saint was listening. Qiqa had known the food was poisoned and eaten it anyway, providing swift, undeniable proof of the tierena's treachery at the potential expense of thir life. It would've been a safer thing to make verbal accusations, but much harder to prove: Vel and Cae might've been spooked, the subsequent escalation into violence avoided, but there also would've been nothing to force the tierena to lay out her cards in an effort to win Vel over. It had been a bold, dangerous move on the yasai's part, a terrible risk—

Cae's thoughts tumbled to halt. *Qiqa knew.* He'd missed the significance before, but now it hit him all at once: *how* had thei known? It wasn't just that thei'd seen Tierena Keris try to drown him, though that was certainly a piece of the puzzle that nobody else, presumably, had been privy to; it was that thei'd known to show up at the Mazepool Pavilion in the first place; known that the food was poisoned. The latter detail might've been guesswork, but the rest . . . was it a coincidence that Qiqa had witnessed Asrien's capture, or had thei already been suspicious? And if thei'd shown up fully prepared to be poisoned, had thei done so alone, or had thei cut someone else in on thir plans?

Cae was on the verge of voicing all this aloud to Vel when, without warning, the next turning led them onto the short, straight path that opened out into the Mazepool Gardens. Instantly, Cae stilled and slowed, catching Vel's eye. Jamming the sword awkwardly between his hip and elbow to free up his hands, he signed, "There might be people waiting for us. Let me go out first; you keep back, all right?"

Vel flashed him a stubborn look. "I won't hide in the maze while you get hurt," he signed fiercely.

"Not in the maze," he signed back. "You're unarmed; even if you came out a different way, you could end up cornered. If you have to run, run out into the palace and get help."

Vel's expression was pained. "I don't want to leave you."

"Helping isn't leaving," Cae signed. "Helping is *helping*."

Vel grabbed him by the collar and kissed him, so fast and slick it was a miracle Cae didn't drop his sword. He'd barely caught up to the fact that it was happening before Vel pulled away again, brushing their noses together.

"Just be safe," he whispered, and all Cae could do in response was nod, a terrible lump in his throat.

They separated, the sword back in Cae's hand as they moved towards the exit. *At least there's no magic this time,* he thought, and found himself grinning manically. It was a strangely steadying realisation: Cae wasn't good at politics, plots, assassins or magic, but he did at least know how to use a sword, and for once, that was all he had to do.

As he stepped out of the maze, he caught a flicker of movement in his peripheral vision and moved instinctively to block it. Steel rang on steel, and in the split second before he braced himself on his back foot and pushed forwards again, he assessed his opponents: the rangy, hard-eyed woman who'd struck at him, and another pair of swordsmen circling in from two other angles. Their stances spoke to professional training—soldiers, Cae guessed, or professional guards in the tierena's employ, though none was quite so foolish as to be wearing her livery—but they weren't fully armoured, dressed instead in thick leather vests over regular clothes. The leather was more protection than Cae had, but as he pivoted to counterattack, a strange, peaceful calm washed over him. Except for the night they'd spent at Ravethae, he hadn't managed a training session since they'd left Avai, and in that sense, he ought to have been rusty. Instead, the purposeful familiarity of it grounded him, as though he'd suddenly come into the warmth of the barracks after a long, cold stretch outside.

Back in Qi-Katai, what felt like a lifetime ago now, he'd run himself through the combat pattern called Needle Braid, a difficult sequence of moves used for fighting in close quarters, for the express purpose of impressing Vel. He hadn't practiced it since, but as the swordsmen closed in, he fell into its steps with the ease of breathing.

"Get the tiern!" someone yelled, but Cae was having none of it: as Vel slipped out of the maze and began to make a break for it through the gardens, Cae ducked, lunged and pivoted through his opponents, putting himself between them and Vel. One of them swore and tried to get past him; Cae stepped back and blocked his strike in the same motion, twisting to avoid the rangy woman's thrust. He couldn't hold the three of them off indefinitely, but he could hear Vel's footsteps crunching on the pebbled paths of the gardens and knew that, if nothing else, he could buy him a chance.

Except that, somehow, he *was* holding the three of them off, to their increasingly visible frustration. It wasn't that their swordplay was bad, although the fact that they clearly had no practice working as a coordinated unit wasn't helping; it was simply that Cae was better, and by an order of magnitude. Each of them telegraphed their moves so clearly that, even outnumbered as he was, it was thrillingly easy to dodge and parry, block and strike. He'd grown so used to sparring and running patterns against skilled opponents that he laughed aloud to realise that, from the outset, he'd been fighting to prolong the exchange instead of ending it.

"If you surrender, I'll accept it," he said, sidestepping a thrust while twisting to block an overhand strike. The nearest opponent swore as the miss overbalanced them, and childish as it was, Cae couldn't resist thwapping the hapless swordsman across the arse with the flat of his blade, a smarting rebuke his own swordmaster had delivered more than once in their childhood sessions.

"Fuck you," spat the man, and Cae laughed again.

"All right," he said, and moved.

As the second swordsman aimed a slash at his ribs, Cae turned and caught their blades together, slid the contact down to block him crossguard to crossguard, stepped inside his reach and, with his off hand, punched him hard in the throat. The man went staggering back, gargling; Cae flicked his blade free and sliced down cleanly, severing the man's sword-hand at the wrist. The hand dropped to the pebbles with a sad, underwhelming, wet-meat sound that was quickly drowned out by the screaming of its former owner. To their credit, the two remaining swordsmen didn't falter, but were still woefully unprepared for Cae to meet their subsequent thrusts with a counterattack of his own, forcing the two of them back. The rangy woman tried to stand her ground, but overextended in a way that left her vulnerable; Cae simply slid past and slashed across the back of her knee, and she toppled down with a cry. Panicked, the final swordsman raised his blade, but barely managed to parry twice before Cae feinted, found a hole in his guard and caught him across the meat of his thigh on a downstroke. He hadn't meant it as a killing blow, but by the quantity of blood that suddenly fountained up as the swordsman fell to one knee, he must've nicked the big artery in his leg. The man dropped his sword with a clatter, gasping as he fumbled to compress his wound; Cae turned away, not wanting to know whether he was successful—and froze.

"That's quite enough," said Tierena Keris. She was standing calmly some feet away, apparently indifferent to the twitching, bloodied bodies of her guards. Beside her stood Ru Pyras, and on his knees before them, his temple bleeding slightly, wrists bound roughly behind his back, one of Ru Pyras's hands dug cruelly into his hair while the other held a blade at his throat, was Velasin.

"Ru Roya is collecting your servant," said the tierena, still in that same level voice. "I advise you to submit quietly, or else—"

"Don't do it," Vel rasped, blinking a trickle of blood out of his eyes. His expression was somewhere between glazed and feral, fierce in a way that made Cae's heart turn over. "They can hurt me all they like; they're not having you."

Cae's fist clenched around the sword-hilt. "You can't possibly think this plan of yours will still work," he said to the tierena, playing for time. "You think that nobody will notice or care you've got Markel locked up?"

"Why would they?" she countered, lifting her chin. "Aside from his master, that is." She glared down at Velasin, kicking him lightly. "The way you kept bringing him with you to see the asa, I assumed he was really your lover."

"A common mistake, apparently," Vel said through gritted teeth.

"Markel does have a lover, though," said Cae. "Back in Qi-Katai. She's my grandmother's most trusted assistant. Believe me, she's going to notice if he suddenly vanishes."

The tierena waved a hand. "He's young. Relationships end all the time." But even at a distance, he could see the tic in her jaw.

"And for how long, exactly, are you planning to let Vel mourn me before you force him before the gods' witnesses?" Cae called, voice strained with the effort of not shouting. "To violate his consent like this goes against every civilized principle of Tithenai marriage—tierena, it's abominable, you must know that!"

For the first time, Cae saw something like shame in her eyes, a flash of it there and gone like distant lightning. "The violation happened when he was bartered to you," she said hoarsely. "He won't be forced to my bed like some blushing body-servant—"

"But he will be forced!" Cae snapped. "As surely as the asan once forced Asa Ivadi's courtiers to silence, so you will force him. Or do you think he'll never try to escape you—that, having been forced to you once, he'll be compliant thereafter? You say now that you won't threaten him—a bold claim to make, when you've rendered him bound and bloody—but who, by all the saints, would be foolish enough to believe you, when this is your starting point?" He laughed angrily, gesturing with his sword towards the distant Mazepool Pavilion. "Syana, the cietena, Qiqa—you've already killed three times; what's to stop you murdering Vel once he's served his purpose?"

"Not to interrupt," drawled a voice from Cae's left, "but for clarity's sake, you should know: I'm not actually dead."

Yasai Qiqa emerged from the maze exit, trailed by a shaken-looking Ethin. The tierena's ears flushed dark, gaze whipping to pin her hapless grandson.

"You told me thei were dead," she said, voice quavering.

"I lied," said Ethin, sounding near to tears. "But so did you."

"And about a great many things, it would seem," said Asa Ivadi, sweeping into view from around a curve in the gardens, flanked by Qarrah and General Naza and followed by a squad of royal guards. At the sound of her voice, Ru Pyras whirled and went to his knees—which, as he'd been the one keeping Vel in place, left him suddenly free from threat—while Tierena Keris turned more slowly, her earlier flush devolving into stark pallor. Cae, however, was paying little attention to this; instead, he lowered his sword and ran to Vel, hauling him upright and away from his former captors. Turning Vel, he sliced through the ropes binding his wrists and then stood in front of him, stroking worriedly up and down his arms.

"Gods, are you all right?" he whispered. He tipped Vel's chin up, inspecting the gash on his forehead—mercifully shallow, though the blood still dripping sluggishly from it made it look worse than it was—and only then realised he was shaking.

"I'm fine," Vel said, and managed a tremulous smile for all of a moment before flinging his arms around Cae and squeezing him, breathing wetly against his throat. "I'm fine. You're fine."

As Cae embraced Vel in turn, the asa directed her guards to take the treacherous functionary into custody. Ru Pyras was babbling apologies and protests, but nobody was listening, while four more guards moved to the swordsmen Cae had dispatched—two of whom were decidedly still alive, the other of whom was either dead or nearing it—and bore them away with all the silent efficiency of soldiers on a battlefield, taking Ru Pyras with them. Only then, as Qiqa and Ethin moved to stand a few paces from Qarrah—as Vel pulled back sufficiently from Cae to watch—did Asa Ivadi step forwards, assessing Tierena Keris.

"I didn't want to believe it of you," the asa said, a thread of hurt lacing the steel of her voice. "After all these years, Risi—why?"

"Why?" the tierena echoed bitterly. "Why not, after *all these years*? You know the depths to which Clan Talae had sunk by the time I inherited it; you know how hard I worked to restore us, make us better. You know what I want for my family. And yet, when you considered a Ralian alliance, you didn't approach me. Just as Inavi went to Halithar instead of Seren, so was Velasin sent to his children—and what do I get instead, Ivi? Scolded, for not supporting your ridiculous notion of watchtowers!"

The asa inhaled sharply. "For so little, you would threaten Tithena's peace?"

"Little for you, perhaps," the tierena said, voice strained with feeling. "Not to me."

The asa looked somewhere between grieved and angry. "Risi. You know I can't let this pass."

A strange sort of calm came over the tierena. "I suppose I'll be tried before the Conclave," she said. "Testimony given, voices raised. A debate about the future of Clan Talae." She cocked her head. "The Amber Chair? Would my heirs keep that, at least?"

"I can't promise that," the asa said, voice thick. "The Conclave would have to vote on it. Risi—"

"No. I know." Tierena Keris smiled, sad and strange in a way that made Cae's gut clench. "A different monarch might intervene on an old friend's behalf, try to soften the blow, but you didn't even do that much for your husband, did you? And I'm hardly more important to you than he was."

"Risi—"

"Just give me a moment, will you?" There was no sharpness to the request; only a sort of resigned exhaustion. When the asa nodded, Tierena Keris reached beneath the collar of her lin and drew out a fine gold chain, suspended from which was a carved medallion not unlike the one Yasa Kithadi had sent on to Cae at Avai. Sighing, the tierena pulled the chain over her head, the medallion resting in the palm of her hand. She smiled at it, thumb stroking across the engravings, then lifted her head and called to Ethin, "Catch!"

Medallion and chain sailed through the air with neat precision, and Ethin, though clearly startled, reacted in time to grab them out of midair. He stared at the medallion, uncomprehending, then looked up at his grandmother, face ashen.

"I formally acknowledge Tiern Ethin Talae as my official heir," said the tierena, smiling faintly.

Ethin looked overwhelmed. "Grandmother, I—"

"He had nothing to do with any of this," said Tierena Keris, cutting him off. She was fiddling with a large gold ring on her left hand as she spoke, the inset gem winking in the winter light. Looking straight at Asa Ivadi, she said, "I acted as I did to secure his future. He deserves to have one, still." And before anyone could stop her, she raised the ring to her mouth and swallowed the contents of a secret compartment set beneath the stone.

Swearing, General Naza dashed forwards to grab her, catching the tierena before she fell to the ground; Ethin cried out and tried to do likewise, but Qiqa restrained him. Cae wanted to look away, but couldn't, pulse loud in his ears as the tierena went rigid, convulsing in the general's arms. A froth of spittle appeared at the corner of her mouth; her limbs spasmed; and then, within seconds, she was dead, her body limp as Ethin screamed and Vel buried his face in Cae's neck.

29

They found Markel first, tied up in the Amber Suite and guarded by Ru Roya, but mercifully unharmed by virtue of the fact that the functionary had taken him sleeping. Had he been awake enough to fight back, Cae felt certain, the story might've been different, but as things stood, Markel was more annoyed than anything else—on his own account, at least. For Vel and Cae's sake, he was livid, though he steadily turned sombre as Cae relayed the details of what had transpired. The revelation of the tierena's guilt took him by surprise—*as it did all of us,* Cae thought grimly—but after his brief captivity, his main emotion was relief that they were no longer in danger. Even so, he still fussed over the cut on Vel's head until Vel, embarrassed, swatted his hands away and signed that perhaps Markel would like to go and finish his nap, as it had been so rudely interrupted.

"Should I?" Markel signed to Cae, a flash of concern in his gaze. The whole time they'd been talking, Asa Ivadi and the rest of the motley assortment of souls who'd followed them from the gardens—which was everyone except the grieving Ethin, who'd been gently led away to the care of Yarasil and Irias by one of the asa's guards—had been waiting outside, which lent the whole exchange an awkward, rushed sort of urgency. Not that the asa had been idle: once Markel's safety had been established and Ru Roya arrested, she'd started issuing orders to the various servants, guards and courtiers who, attracted by the commotion, had come to see what was happening.

"I think so," Cae signed back.

Markel hesitated. "Will Asrien be all right, do you think?"

"I hope so," Cae said aloud.

"You should rest," Vel put in, sounding very much as though he wanted to lie down, too.

"Just try not to wake me when you come back in," signed Markel, and with a parting squeeze to Vel's shoulder, he headed back to the Jade Suite, leaving Cae to put a mollifying arm around his husband's waist, savouring the pressure when Vel leaned into him. The tierena's suicide would've been an appalling thing to witness even without the events preceding it, but as shaken as they were, they didn't yet have the space in which to admit to it. Every so often, he'd catch Vel's eye and feel his throat close up with the enormity of what he'd almost lost—would see that Vel, too, was wrestling with deep emotion—and look away again, unwilling and unable to deal with it until they were alone.

As Markel departed, the asa handed her personal seal to one of her remaining guards and instructed them to go and release Ru Kisian. The guard saluted and hurried off, leaving behind Cae, Vel, Qarrah, Qiqa, General Naza and, of course, Asa Ivadi, who turned to the rest of them, grim-faced.

"All right, Qiqa," she said. "Show us where they took him."

"Your Majesty," said Qarrah, "you hardly need to concern yourself with this personally—"

"A member of the Conclave plotted murder within my palace," Asa Ivadi shot back, her voice steel. "If this doesn't concern me personally, what does?"

With that settled, Qiqa took charge, leading them out of the Circlet Annex and across the palace grounds in search of Asrien, who'd evidently been held elsewhere. As a trusted and regular face at court, Tierena Keris had held exclusive or primary access to several suites, and as they headed towards the room where Qiqa's spying of the night before had last placed Asrien, the mood became increasingly tense. General Naza in particular seemed quietly furious, his face like a stormcloud as they entered the building, terrified servants scuttling ahead of them to open doors for the asa.

They found Asrien exactly where Qiqa had thought he'd be, hog-tied and unconscious on the carpet, his face and arms mottled with fresh cuts and purpling bruises. Vel took a step to help him, but the general was faster, flicking a knife from his belt and slicing through Asrien's bonds with sharp efficiency. With more tenderness than Cae had expected, the general pulled Asrien onto his lap, murmuring his name and shaking him gently until, with a low, pained noise, his eyes fluttered open. For a moment, he didn't seem to know where he was; then he blinked, focussed on the general and made a scraped, wheezing noise that could almost pass for laughter.

"I'm sorry, yaren. I told," croaked Asrien. "She didn't ask as nicely as you, but I told."

Almost imperceptibly, General Naza flinched. "You're an idiot," he said roughly, and rose with Asrien in his arms as smoothly as if he weighed nothing. Turning to the asa, he dipped his head and said, "Your Majesty."

"A moment, General," said the asa. A firm note crept into her voice. "Don't think it's escaped my notice that you knew this man"—her gaze flicked to indicate Asrien—"was a foreign agent within my court, and yet you didn't see fit to inform me of it."

General Naza stilled. Swallowed. Looked at the asa, then down at Asrien, who burrowed his head against the general's shoulder and mumbled, "*Now* who's the idiot."

"I did know," the general allowed. His jaw worked soundlessly for a moment. "Asa, forgive me. I was—"

"I am not, at this point, interested in your excuses, although I certainly will be later," the asa said. "However, you may recall that I am not the only authority to whom the Iron Chair answers. As you were elected by the military council, it is they who will vote on your fitness to continue in your office, given your recent . . . choices."

For a moment, General Naza looked furious. His shoulders twitched. "If Your Majesty wishes me gone," he bit out, "it's within your power to strip the Iron Chair from me."

"It is," said Asa Ivadi dryly, "but that tends to upset my generals, and if they must be fractious, I'd rather it not be on my account."

General Naza shut his eyes, fingers curling more firmly around Asrien's limbs. When he opened them again, he looked tired. "We both know why they elected me," he said roughly. "Not because I'm any good at *this*"—he tipped his chin to indicate the palace and its politics, lip curling in disgust—"but to prevent the alliance from forming. A task at which I've failed."

"Makes two of us," Asrien mumbled.

A laden paused followed. General Naza stared down at Asrien, his expression unreadable. Then he looked up and set his jaw. "I resign the Iron Chair," he said. "Effective immediately. It has been an honour to serve, Your Majesty, but I think the post would be far better suited to . . . anyone other than myself." He barked a bitter laugh.

If Asa Ivadi was as stunned by this as Cae felt, she didn't show it. Instead, she inclined her head gravely and said, "If that is your decision, I am bound to respect it."

The general—or no longer a general now, Cae supposed; the title was ceremonial in his case, though ranked generals had held the Iron Chair before—looked oddly relieved. "With your permission, then," he said, gently readjusting his hold in Asrien, "I'll see to our Ralian's care."

"Do so," said the asa, but though her voice was tired, Cae didn't miss the speculative light in her eyes as she watched Naza carry Asrien out. He glanced at Vel, who looked equally struck by the whole affair, but neither of them spoke.

Silence fell.

Asa Ivadi contemplated the room, which the tierena appeared to have been using as an office: the walls were lined with shelves, and the space was dominated by a large desk surrounded by chairs.

Walking to the nearest of these, she sighed and sat down heavily, staring at the far wall while Cae and everyone else exchanged frantic looks about what they were meant to do.

"I should probably have this all searched," the asa said, to no one in particular. "Her estate, too. If she was willing to kill, what else might she have done?"

"At least she spared you the burden of a trial," said Qiqa, going to one knee by the asa's side. "That would've been worse for everyone."

The asa snorted. "Worse for Clan Talae, you mean," she said. "And worse for Ethin. There'll still be gossip implicating him, of course, but much less than if everything was dragged out in public." She blinked, looking at thim. "Incidentally, how did he save you?"

"With a panacea," Qiqa replied. "It was in my pocket. I would've taken it earlier, but the confessional dramatics went on longer than I'd anticipated, and by the time I had a spare moment, my hands weren't being cooperative." Thei shuddered, and for the first time Cae noticed how pinched thei looked. He felt a spike of guilt: when Qiqa had reappeared, he'd been so preoccupied with Vel that, on some level, he'd assumed the earlier poisoning must've been faked, or at least that Qiqa had exaggerated the symptoms, but evidently not.

"If I can ask," Vel said hesitantly, glancing between asa and ya-sai, "how did you know to come? Or that she'd try to use poison?"

Unexpectedly, it was Qarrah who answered. "Kisian's involvement never made sense," she said. "Or, well—it might've done, but the fact that he couldn't explain himself suggested he was being controlled or blackmailed somehow, and there's only a handful of people so powerful he'd fear to name them in self-defence. Still, I wasn't sure until after he was arrested; I was watching the prison, and every time someone went in or out, Ru Pyras would scuttle over to speak to the guards. I figured he was trying to see who was going to speak to which prisoners, so I did an experiment: I went in and asked to see Rade, then stopped by Kisian's cell unofficially.

494 · Foz Meadows

He was clearly afraid, but he told me the threat of losing his family estate was being leveraged against him by someone who'd used him as a front for buying Cietena Alu's land. He'd only interacted with them through an agent, he said, and when I gave him Ru Pyras's description, it was clear that was who he meant. So out I went, half expecting to be followed or otherwise importuned, but of course I wasn't, because there was no official record of me having spoken to Kisian. So I dropped by Qiqa's rooms"—she nodded at the yasai—"to ask thim to keep an eye on things, and went to see how Her Majesty wished to proceed."

"Which is how I came to see Asrien taken by Ru Pyras," Qiqa put in, "and how I knew to follow him here. And then I went and reported in, too." Thei winced. "In my defence, I didn't think she'd resort to torture; I thought she'd just offer a bribe, or maybe threaten him."

"How was he even allowed in to see Ru Kisian in the first place?" Cae asked.

"He had General Naza's palace token," Qarrah said. "Which is how the general ended up with us earlier—he'd realised it was gone and come to report it missing. He thought Asrien had stolen it and left the palace, though he was . . . cagey, let's say, about how that might've happened."

"I wonder why," Qiqa deadpanned. Thei smirked. "And here I was thinking that, out of everyone, Iron would be the most likely to tell you if he stumbled on a secret Ralian agent."

Asa Ivadi put a tired hand over her eyes. "I'd prefer not to deal with that presently, Qiqa."

Her tone was mild, but the yasai subsided instantly. "Yes, Your Majesty."

"But how did you know about the poison?" Vel asked.

Qiqa gave a lopsided shrug, thir long mouth quirked in an almost-smile. "She'd already drugged Cae once," thei said, "to say nothing of Syana's death. And it was a lunch invitation. What else was she going to do, challenge you to a duel?"

"Even with Qarrah and Qiqa's testimony, I didn't want to believe it," the asa said softly. "I'd already given her leave to use the Mazepool Gardens and Pavilion this week; it didn't feel incongruous in the least that she'd want to host a private lunch there, especially not with the two of you." She glanced at Cae and Vel.

"Hence my rather genius plan to show up unexpectedly, act like a nuisance, force her to reveal her schemes and in all respects save the day," said Qiqa.

Qarrah shot them an irritated look. "You're just lucky that whatever she put in the food was less potent than the poison in her ring."

"Well," said Qiqa, somewhat abashed by this. "Yes. True."

The asa sighed again, her expression bleak. "She named Ethin her heir, which means by rights he's the new Amber Chair. I could strip the chair from Clan Talae at my own discretion, or else call the full Conclave to vote on it—and of course they'd say yes, to say nothing of having plentiful suggestions about who ought to take it over—but if I do, then I need to assign it elsewhere, and that's more rigmarole than I presently care to contemplate, especially as I must also deal with a *new* Iron Chair." She blinked, then turned her sharp gaze on Vel. "What do you think, tiern?"

Beside him, Cae felt Vel tense at being directly addressed. "Do you want courtesy, asa?" he asked carefully. "Or an honest opinion?"

Asa Ivadi laughed. "The latter," she said.

Vel inhaled. Nodded. Thought a moment, then said, "If you want majority support to build your watchtowers, keep Ethin. He'll vote as you tell him to, and under the circumstances, the rest of the Circlet will know it for a loyalty test—they might not like the outcome, but they won't hold it against him once he starts to grow into the role. But if you reassign the chair on the condition that the new incumbent support you, the rest of the Circlet will close ranks against them—and that, I suspect, is a scenario you'd prefer to avoid."

Asa Ivadi huffed a laugh. "I fear you might be right," she said.

And then, to Cae, "You really have married well, yaseran. My compliments to your grandmother."

Cae flushed with pride, unable to resist curling a protective arm around Vel's waist. "My thanks, asa."

"The reseko," Vel blurted suddenly. Everyone looked at him, and though he was clearly embarrassed, he held his ground. "Where did the reseko come from?"

He'd addressed the question to Qarrah, but it was the asa who answered. "From me," she said, rising to her feet. "After what happened with the yaseran's sister, I was concerned there might be further reprisals, so I sent Qarrah to liaise with Kithadi and keep an eye on you. The idea was for her to remain anonymous, not revealing that she worked for me unless absolutely necessary, but in case that necessity did arise, I thought a token of trust might prove useful." The corner of her mouth ticked up in a tiny, private smile. "And I've always liked reseko. Delightful little creatures."

With that, she moved to leave. The pair of servants who'd unlocked the door were hovering out in the hallway, far enough not to be thought of as eavesdropping, but close enough to show they were waiting for further instructions, which they soon received, the asa instructing that nobody was to be let into the office until her guards had come to take control of it. The servants bowed low in acknowledgement, and then, like moons in orbit around a greater body, their small group followed the asa back outside. The sky had turned overcast since they'd been indoors, and a light drizzle was falling, stinging against their exposed skin and making the stairs to the courtyard slightly more treacherous than they might otherwise have been.

"What a mess," the asa muttered, seemingly to herself.

"With Your Majesty's blessing," said Qiqa suddenly, "I think I might need to go and lie down for a bit." Thei swayed on thir feet as thei said it, the sight alarming enough that Qarrah stepped in to put an arm around thim.

"Please do," said the asa. "You take thim," she added, in response to Qarrah's questioning look.

Bowing her head in acknowledgement, Qarrah took more of Qiqa's weight—a slightly comical sight, as she was the broader and shorter of the two—and led thim away.

Reflexively, Cae tightened his grip on Vel's waist. He thought again of Tierena Keris spasming in the general's arms and suppressed a shudder. Chill rain slicked the back of his neck, and as he exchanged another fraught glance with Velasin, he thought longingly of the moment when they, too, might excuse themselves from this draining aftermath.

As if she'd read his mind, the asa glanced at Cae. "The two of you will escort me back to the Little Palace," she said. Her dry tone brooked no argument, and so they were forced to comply, the pair of them flanking her like court functionaries as she led the way back to her private domain. It was a comparatively short distance to travel, but now that word about the day's events was starting to spread, they were stopped more than once by courtiers, guards and other nobles coming to either report or to see what had happened. The asa dealt with all of them, but though he was glad not to have to speak, Cae still felt the weight of their interest, stares scribbling across his skin like insect feet.

After a subjective eternity, they finally reached the Little Palace, where a small swarm of servants and courtiers, evidently alerted to the situation, were waiting for the asa. Cae briefly hoped this might mean he and Vel were dismissed, but after issuing a flurry of instructions, the asa said, "I require a private conference with Yaseran Caethari and Tiern Velasin," and herded them into a small, richly appointed side room.

"Sit," said the asa, gesturing to a pair of armchairs while seating herself in a third.

Cae exchanged a wary glance with Vel, who looked equally uncertain about this turn of events.

They sat.

For a moment, the asa said nothing: just studied them like a falconer scrutinizing a newly jessed bird. Then she sat forwards, her keen gaze flitting between them.

"Velasin," she said. "When I asked you whether Rade had been sent by King Markus, you knew about Asrien."

Cae went still, heart rabbiting. He looked at Vel, watching as his husband said, with admirable calm, "Yes, Your Majesty."

"As, we have seen, did Naza."

"Yes, Your Majesty."

"May I ask why you didn't tell me?"

"Because he'd already failed his mission," Vel said simply. "He was meant to either seduce us apart or kill me, and as he was unable to do the former and unwilling to do the latter, and had instead come to me for help, I decided he posed no threat."

"Help?"

"He was coerced," said Vel. "His mother's life was threatened. He asked me for aid in getting her out of Ralia."

"And were you able to provide any?"

"Not as yet," Vel admitted. "I was going to ask Ru Kisian about it, but. Well."

"Ah," said the asa.

A brief silence fell. Cae shivered, though whether from the conversation or the damp of his rain-wet clothes, he didn't know.

"It's a strange thing, this alliance," said Asa Ivadi. Her tone was mild, but her gaze was intense. "Many Ralian nobles were opposed to it even before you wed Caethari instead of Laecia, and yet King Markus pushed for it regardless. And when you *did* marry Caethari, he might easily have won favour with his court by arguing that, as your marriage isn't valid under Ralian law, it doesn't count for the purposes of alliance; and yet, he did not. He didn't call your marriage contracts into question, or propose a future alliance between, say, one of your female cousins and a lesser son of the Conclave. He didn't even send an assassin, although your brother's actions serve as proof that, had he done so, he would have found support for it, despite the inevitable ill-will and suspicion your death would've engendered in Tithena. No. Instead, he sent Asrien to try and tempt you away from each other—a gambit which roundly failed, and which, once it is known to have failed, will serve as proof that, contrary to the usual Ralian stereotypes, men like you are capable of faithfulness, and love, and duty."

Vel stared at her. "Are you suggesting," he said, voice deadly soft, "that King Markus in some way *approves* of me? Of what I am? That he is, in any sense of the word, supportive of my marriage?"

"I am saying," said Asa Ivadi, "that, of all the forms his disapproval might have taken, it has somehow taken the one which gives you the greatest degree of legitimacy while still allowing him to act as though he has no say in the matter. Perhaps he needs this alliance more badly than we've realised and is merely being pragmatic, or perhaps he considered your infidelity such a foregone conclusion that the alternative never occurred to him. Many people excuse their personal vices by assuming them to be universal facets of human nature, especially where that vice is enabled by power." Her eyes glittered, and Cae felt suddenly, chillingly certain that, when Asa Ivadi had confronted the former asan about preying on her courtiers, he had offered up a similar defence. She paused for a moment, fingers twitching on her lap, and when she spoke again, her voice was even. "We might speculate any number of things about his motives in this matter. I am simply observing, in my capacity as a monarch who must also weigh the moods of her court against her desires for the nation, that King Markus's actions speak more to compromise than to hatred."

"But if you had to guess which was most likely?" pressed Vel, a tense shake to his voice that made Cae ache in sympathy.

The asa sighed. "I think Asrien was a test," she said simply. "You would know better than I the light in which most of Ralia sees you, and why. The Doctrine of the Firmament is powerful, but I have heard it said that King Markus puts more faith in the material world than in the heavens. That being so, I suspect he saw your marriage as an opportunity to pit superstition against reality—to use your reaction in the latter to gauge the verity of the former. If you faltered, the bias would be confirmed, but if not, he'd have reason to believe your marriage might indeed prove stable enough to benefit the crown."

"And for this," Vel all but growled, "he blackmailed Asrien, uprooted him from his life and coerced him with the threat of his mother's death."

"I didn't say it was admirable or without cruelty," the asa replied. "Only that it was likely done to a purpose. And as I've said, this is all speculation; I might well be wrong."

"You are," said Vel, trembling. "You're wrong. You have to be."

"Why?"

"Because this isn't *better*!" he cried, anguished. "How could this ever possibly be better? To see us as tools—to use us without acceptance, to threaten and bully and coerce, and still to think of it as an improvement? What hope is there in that?"

"If you encountered a man with three hairs on his head, would you call him bald?"

Vel gaped at her, caught utterly off guard. "Would I—what? Excuse me?"

"A man with three hairs on his head," the asa repeated patiently. "Would you call him bald?"

"Of course, but I don't see—"

"What if he had four hairs, or five? Strictly speaking, so long as he still has one, we shouldn't call him bald, but we do. We say, *oh, it's close enough*—and in one sense, it is. But once the parameters have moved, what's to stop them moving again? Consider the problem the other way around. Baldness comes on in increments. The loss of a single hair is insignificant when you start with a full head, but little by little, the change becomes apparent. If a man lost three hairs a day for a year, at some point before he lost all of them, we'd start to call him bald, but would we agree on when that was? What's more important: to agree definitively on when baldness starts, or to recognise it as a process?" She spread her hands. "The loss of a single hair isn't baldness, just as growing one doesn't cure it. But both are, potentially, a starting point for greater change."

Vel took a moment to digest this. "Maybe it is a starting point," he said at last. "And maybe not. But either way, I don't have to find it meaningful. However this moment might look in a hundred years, there's no sense in trying to judge it now on the basis of an as yet unknown outcome. It's a single hair. It's nothing, not compared to my life, or Cae's, or Asrien's. We have to live in the present, and I can't—" His voice caught awfully. "Even if you're right, whatever good might come of it later, imagining a meal that my grandchildren might one day eat at a table that isn't yet built won't fill my stomach now. Fuck King Markus. I didn't say no to Asrien for him, or for you, or to prove some stupid point." He rose from the chair and held out a hand to Cae, who took it and stood in turn, overwhelmed. "Respectfully, asa, I think I've had enough politics and philosophy for one day."

Asa Ivadi didn't quite smile, but Cae thought he saw a spark of amusement in her eyes. "Go on then, tiern. Enjoy your present."

"I plan to," said Vel, and led Cae from the room.

"You just swore at Asa Ivadi," Cae said, feeling slightly dazed by the whole experience.

Vel smiled sharply. "Technically, I swore at King Markus."

"You know what I mean."

"I do."

"Vel—"

"Not here," said Vel, that shaky thread back in his voice. "Just wait. Please?"

"Anything," Cae said, and it came out raw.

Silently, they left the Little Palace. The rain was heavier now, a pattering, icy curtain as they crossed the palace grounds. Vel's hand was hot against Cae's palm—the only warm thing in the world, or so it felt—and by the time they reached the Circlet Annex, Cae was chilled everywhere else. Markel had left the Jade Suite unlocked, but was nowhere to be seen when they entered; Cae quietly prayed he was sound asleep and forced himself to remove his boots before his feet went numb. Vel did likewise, and then they stood and stared at each other, with only the distant, gentle sound of the rain to soften the cutting silence.

Vel moved first, stepping into Cae's space and looking up at him with gentle, gold-grey eyes. "Earlier," he said. "At the Pavilion, when the tierena listed all those horrible *benefits* to you being dead." He touched Cae's waist, fingers slipping through the slit in his lin to ruck up the hem of his undershirt, until his palm was curved against the damp, goosebumped skin of his hip. "You said, *if you wanted*, and I stopped you, I stopped you *right there*, because there isn't—Cae." He drew him closer, fingertips digging in slightly, sounding almost frantic when he said, "Even if I didn't love you, I would never have wanted that, *never*. But I do love you, and I know—I don't think I'm very good at love, and I'm certainly not very good at being a husband, but if I've ever done anything to make you think I'd—"

Cae kissed him, a desperate brush of mouths that deepened as he cupped Vel's jaw. Vel melted against him, slotting their bodies together, and for a sweet span of seconds, there was nothing else in the world that mattered; nothing that even existed. Then Vel pulled back and looked at Cae, his expression soft.

"Come to bed?"

Cae swallowed. The day's events were crowding out his head, a clamour of spite and ugliness; he wanted them gone. He remembered the night they'd spent in the garden in Avai, what felt like a thousand years ago now, and shivered as his whole body sang with longing.

"Can I kneel for you?" he asked shakily. "I just—I need—I don't want to think, I—"

Vel leaned up and kissed him, sucking Cae's bottom lip into his mouth. The pressure and the gentle sting of his teeth shivered through Cae, a pleasurable static, and when they parted again, Vel's eyes were dark.

"Come on," he whispered, and led Cae into the bedroom.

30

Afterwards, as Cae lay boneless and drowsing in the ruck of their sheets, his thoughts blissfully empty as Vel laddered sleepy kisses along his spine, something occurred to him: *we can go home.* The notion twisted within him, both sweet and barbed. Home meant Riya, Nairi, Liran and his other friends, the familiar space of his apartments, the beloved, curving streets of Qi-Katai; but it also meant grief and duty: the absences where his father and Laecia should've been, the pressure of his grandmother's inheritance. Not that there was a place he could ever go to escape the latter, but a part of him still quailed at the thought of meeting Yasa Kithadi again as her chosen heir; of taking up whatever sort of apprenticeship she thought fitting for his future. But he didn't want to linger in Qi-Xihan, either: even with Tierena Keris gone, the notion was stifling. He thought again of her death, the terrible, shuddering moment in which she'd gone limp forever, and tried to feel some satisfaction at having outlived the person who'd plotted his murder, but all he could hear was Ethin's grief, a mirror of the loss he felt for Laecia.

Behind him, Vel set his teeth to the meat of Cae's shoulder and bit down lightly, just hard enough to get his attention. "You're worrying again," he murmured, one arm slinking over Cae's waist as he crowded in closer, tangling their legs. "Did I not tire you out enough?"

"You did," Cae said, and meant it, body still tingling pleasantly from Vel's use. It was a new thing between them, this balance of give and take, but whatever uncertainties Vel had felt back in Avai were seemingly dispelled, at least for now.

"Are you sure?" Vel's tone was sly.

Cae laughed softly, turning within the circle of his arms. He pressed their foreheads together, savouring the heat of Vel's body, the salt-sweat scent of them together. He meant to ask about heading back to Qi-Katai, but a realisation hit him somewhere between the thought forming and the moment when he opened his mouth, and what came out instead was, "You're my home, now."

Vel stilled. "I'm what?" he croaked.

"You're my home," Cae said. He shut his eyes, palm sliding over Vel's ribs. "I was thinking I wanted to go back to Qi-Katai, but it's not . . . after Laecia, it doesn't feel the same anymore. Like I've lost it, somehow, or lost a piece of it, like something's been missing for years. Or, no—not like something's missing; like I am. Like I don't really fit, and maybe I never have, not since my mother left. And here, the palace, this isn't home, either, and I was trying to think where else I belong that isn't the revetha or the barracks, because that's . . . I belong there, but it's not *home,* it's different, you know? But you . . . I realised, wherever you are, whenever it's us, that's home. *You're* home."

Vel's breath hitched. "I think you are, too, for me," he whispered. "I didn't . . . I've missed Ralia, but Aarobrook hasn't been home since I was a child, and Farathel never was, not in the way you're talking about, and when I came to Tithena, I thought . . . I assumed on some level that I'd never find home again. Markel is my family, and that matters so much, I really would've been lost without him, but making him home would be selfish, I think, because he's so . . . he's his own person, you know? He's going to do so much more with his life than just look after me, and I'll probably be an absolute mess the day he leaves, even knowing I'll see him again, but you . . . if Qi-Katai ever felt like home, it's because of you. You're where I want to build."

Cae made a helpless noise and kissed him again. They fell into each other, a slow, teasing sweetness, and were on the verge of escalating to something more when they were interrupted by someone knocking on the distant door to the suite.

Cae groaned, burying his face in Vel's shoulder. "We're not here," he mumbled. "We've gone away, we're indisposed—"

The knock sounded again, louder than before.

"I'll get it," Vel said, starting to pull away. "Otherwise Markel will wake up and try to answer it, assuming we didn't wake him already."

Cae flushed. "No," he said, "I'll get it. You stay here."

He rose, pulling on his discarded nara and shrugging into a robe, which was all the concession to modesty he felt like making. The knocking was louder out of the bedroom, but Cae was relieved to see that Markel hadn't been roused by it.

He wasn't sure who he'd expected their caller to be, but General— no, *Commander*, now—Naza wasn't it. They stared at each other, mutually taken aback, albeit for very different reasons.

"Yes?" Cae said finally.

By way of answer, the former general handed him something. It was so unexpected that it took Cae a moment to process the object, but once he did, his breath caught.

It was his jade-handled knife.

"I thought you should have this back," Naza said stiffly.

It wasn't an apology, but Cae was too relieved to care. "Thank you," he said, unable to keep the feeling from his voice. "I—thank you." He swallowed, slipping his fingers through the ring-hilt, and tried to think of something else to say. "How's Asrien?"

It was hard to tell, but he thought perhaps the general flushed a little. "Recovering," he said gruffly. "Nevan is with him. I . . . it seemed better, that way."

Cae nodded, lips twitching. He hardly liked Commander Naza, but his awkward concern for Asrien was familiar enough that, just this once, he felt he could be magnanimous about it, though at the same time, he also felt a pang of annoyance. Of all people, he didn't want to feel any degree of kinship with the former Iron Chair, and judging by the look on his face, he was fairly certain the sentiment was mutual.

"Well then," he said, after a beat of silence. "Thank you again."

"Yes." But still the commander hesitated, hovering at the threshold like an unexpected relative. "Should you extend your stay in Qi-Xihan," he said finally. "If you wanted a sparring partner. I am available."

Cae blinked at him. "I . . . will keep that in mind," he said, feeling oddly flustered by the offer. "Thank you. Yes."

The commander inclined his head, a short, sharp jerk of acknowledgement. "Good," he said, and promptly turned on his heel and left.

Bemused, Cae watched him go, then shut the door and returned to the bedroom, the jade knife dangling from his fingers.

"Who was it?" Vel asked. "Did—oh!"

"The former general brought it back," said Cae, setting the knife reverently on the dresser.

Vel let out a startled bark of laughter. "He did? In person?"

"In person."

"Huh. That's unexpected." He propped himself up on an elbow, louche and so unconsciously lovely that Cae's breath snared in his throat. "I was thinking, though—it's probably a good idea to see how things play out at court over the next few days, just to know where we stand, but rather than stay on here, why don't we go to Ravethae? Your grandmother would probably be pleased at us taking an interest, and it's close enough to keep up with the palace without actually having to be here."

"Ravethae," Cae echoed. Something in him lifted at the prospect. He'd liked Ravethae, what little he'd seen of it. He thought of Ru Merit's kindness, the well-maintained grounds, the sociable invasion of Spoons and Son of Spoons, and found himself smiling. "Yes," he said, shrugging his robe off. "Ravethae sounds perfect."

Vel's eyes tracked him as he undressed, a spark in them that heated Cae's blood. "Good," he agreed, sounding slightly breathless. "I'm glad that's settled."

"Yes," Cae said, and shucked his nara, crawling back onto the bed. He prowled up the length of his husband's body, drinking in the way Vel yielded beneath him, tangled in the sheets like a half-unwrapped present. "Settled."

Vel laughed, arms stretching to twine around Cae's neck, that gorgeous flush warming his skin from throat to navel. "Come home," he murmured, his gaze full of love, and as Cae kissed him against the pillows, his heart beat in time with the truth of it: *I am. You are. We're home.*

Coda

ASRIEN

T his is it?" I asked dubiously, staring around us at what
was trying to pass for a town. Oh, the scenery was pretty
enough, especially with the Snowjaw Mountains looming
there in the backdrop, but as far as civilisation went, this didn't.
Half of it looked like a strong breeze would knock it over, and the
rest like one already had. And there were goats everywhere, which
is always unsettling. I don't trust goats, as a general rule. They always look like they're plotting something.

"Would you prefer a prison cell?" Naza asked dryly. "Under the
circumstances—"

"Yes, yes." I flapped a hand at him, abashed and not wanting
to be. The fact that Asa Ivadi had let me live in the first place was
bizarre enough; that she'd also consented to let me out of her sight
was downright miraculous. Whatever trade this stupid little town
might see in the future, it was presently nigh on unliveable, and in
a different life, I'd have turned up my nose at the whole endeavour
on principle. But as things stood—

"I am an ambassador to Vaiko's future prosperity. I'm *aware*."

Naza snorted to show what he thought of *that*, and I told myself
firmly that I wasn't the least endeared. Even having parted ways
with Nevan, whatever I'd had with Naza was a relic months dead,
ever since I'd woken from a healing sleep and learned he'd resigned
the Iron Chair rather than endure the likely rigmarole of the military council voting to strip it from him. I'd surprised myself by
feeling guilty about it, though that was perhaps due to shock that
Naza was yet to blame me for his disgrace. Sure, he'd been stiff and

angry when we first left Qi-Xihan, as snappishly stoic as a guard dog in his apparent humiliation, but he'd thawed as we travelled, and never once raised his voice to me over it, let alone a hand. Still, that didn't magically entitle me to the sort of saccharine happily-ever-after that Caethari and Velasin were so conspicuously enjoying—not that I wanted one, of course. Least of all with Naza, whose idea of happiness was probably swinging a sword around and then fucking about it.

"Where did you say she was meeting us?" I asked loudly, instead of contemplating any of this.

"Over there," said Naza, gesturing. "The Mountain Inn."

I followed his line of sight to the distant building, which was admittedly sturdier than anything else in the surrounding area, but still woefully underwhelming.

"Charming," I deadpanned. "Lead on, then."

Naza nudged his mount forwards, and after a moment, mine followed. I'd ended up with a quiet little mare for this trip, far better behaved than the biter I'd had in Qi-Xihan, who'd lamed herself taking an ill-aimed kick at a stable hand. She'd been a vexation and a nuisance whenever I took her out, and I told myself firmly that I didn't miss her.

The ground sloped up towards the Mountain Inn, which I could admit was well-named, if nothing else. A tethered goat bleated loudly as we passed it by, and I succumbed to a childish urge to stick my tongue out at it. The goat bleated again as if it were laughing at me. Wretched creature.

As we approached, a familiar figure emerged from the inn and waved to us: Qarrah. I hadn't yet spent much time with her—she'd been off travelling the last little while, some mission of the asa's—but still, I liked her despite myself. She was fat and frank and charming, and the last time we'd drunk together, she'd told me a joke so deliciously filthy that I'd near pulled a muscle laughing about it. I waved back to her, refusing to feel foolish, and watched as another two people emerged from the inn in her wake. One was a tall, slope-shouldered man I hadn't seen before, but who I assumed was the fabled Orin, Qarrah's partner in crime, and the other—

I stared, my heart pounding. Uncomprehending, I turned to Naza, but he wouldn't meet my gaze, which was its own kind of explanation. Hands shaking, I dismounted my mare while she was still in motion, stumbling as my toe snagged in the stirrup but somehow not falling, the added momentum shoving me forwards like some great, clumsy hand at my back. I ran, bracing myself for disappointment, to be wrong, for a trick, a mirage, but it wasn't. Her face was thinner than I remembered, her pale hair silvering where it fell around her shoulders, but it was her, she was here, she wasn't dead—

"*Mama,*" I croaked, and she flung her arms around me like I was a child again, not caring we had an audience. We dropped to our knees in the dirt; I was keening and she was crying, and she was so much smaller now than in my memories, bony where she'd once been soft, the only good kind thing in a world of teeth. "Mama," I said again, "Mama, *Mama*—"

"Asri, my Asri." Her voice was raggedy grief and joy, shaking as she kissed the crown of my head. "Oh, my sweet, strange boy. What a place you've brought us to!" And she laughed, as though my presence was the magic trick, not hers. I lifted my head and blinked wetly up at Qarrah, who beheld me with smug amusement.

"The Shade had some eyes on her estate," she said, grinning, "but not sharp enough to keep me out."

I made a hiccuping noise and looked at my mother, alive and whole and here. "I've brought you to the middle of nowhere," I said in Ralian. Relief flooded me, and embarrassment, and shame—always shame, so thick I could've choked on it. "I'm sorry, I'm so sorry—"

"Don't be," she said, and tipped my mouth shut with the edge of her knuckle, the way she'd always done when I was small. She wiped her eyes and sat back on her heels, smiling up at the mountains, her top lip pulled slightly askew by the old scar my father had left her.

"I feel like I can breathe, out here. What more do I need than that?" And then, more softly, "Who knew I'd ever come over the mountain?"

"A drink might be nice, at the very least." I scrubbed a wrist across my eyes and looked up at Qarrah, trying to summon a shred of hauteur but managing only hope. "Do they run to alcohol, out here?"

Qarrah laughed and extended a hand to help me up. "Lordling," she said, "right now, that's almost all they run to."

"Better than nothing," said Naza, who'd been standing there with the horses for who knew how long. I flushed, refusing to be flustered by his presence, and helped my mother to stand, her soft hand small in mine.

"It's a start," I said, and led the way inside.

Tithenai Glossary

Asa—a female monarch
Asai—a third-gender monarch
Asan—a male monarch
Asara—a female royal child/heir
Asarai—a third-gender royal child/heir
Asaran—a male royal child/heir
Ciet—a male child/heir of a low-ranked noble
Cieta—a female child/heir of a low-ranked noble
Cietai—a third-gender child/heir of a low-ranked noble
Cieten—a low-ranked male noble
Cietena—a low-ranked female noble
Cietenai—a low-ranked third-gender noble
Conclave—the governing parliamentary body of Tithena
Dai—a title given a low-level guard or soldier
Ghostfruit sap—sap from a tree that can be used as a poison
Halik—a single-piece garment that splits into panels from waist to
   ankle, worn by all genders
Kem—a third-gender person, plural kemi
Kesh—a strategy board game for two players
Kiensa—a form of address or endearment whose literal meaning
   is little pet, most commonly used for children and animals, but
   also used toward sexually submissive adults
Kigé—a third-gender parent
Kinthé—a third-gender sibling
Kip—a thin, two-tined eating utensil
Kiun—a parent's third-gender sibling, like aunt or uncle
Litai—a husband's husband; also used in Ralia as slang for any
   man who prefers men to women

Rahan—a military commander, in charge of a revetha

Ren—a polite title given to commoners or any stranger whose rank you don't know

Revetha—a garrison or fighting unit

Ru—a title given to scholars

Tar—a mid-ranked military title

Tiera—female child/heir of a mid-ranked noble

Tierai—third-gender child/heir of a mid-ranked noble

Tieren—a mid-ranked male noble

Tierena—a mid-ranked female noble

Tierenai—a mid-ranked third-gender noble

Tiern—male child/heir of a mid-ranked noble

Varu—a mid-ranked guard

Yaren—an archaic term originally used to address someone of superior rank, now used toward sexually dominant adults

Yasa—a high-ranked female noble

Yasai—a high-ranked third-gender noble

Yasan—a high-ranked male noble

Yasera—female child/heir of a high-ranked noble

Yaseran—male child/heir of a high-ranked noble

Yaserai—third-gender child/heir of a high-ranked noble

Acknowledgments

I started writing *All the Hidden Paths* in January 2021 and didn't finish the first draft until November 2022, which places it squarely in the category of Pandemic Book, at least in terms of the timeline. It's also true to say that it took me longer than usual—certainly longer than planned—to write, and while that's attributable in part to various life-altering events that took place during those two years, both globally and personally, there's one experience above all that colours my experience of writing it.

My original outline bears very little resemblance to the finished product, in large part because it was really just a selection of vibes and emotional beats very loosely joined together with mental string. I had a vague notion of Things I Wanted To Happen, but no underlying thematic or emotional arc to tie them all together, and as such, the more I wrote, the more I struggled to see what I was doing. And then there was—something. Annoyingly, I can't now remember what it was I watched or read that sparked the epiphany; only that something did, and I realised: *this is a book about what happens after you come out.*

In mainstream (which is to say, predominantly straight and cis) Western culture, so much emphasis is placed on the idea of a singular Coming Out as the triumphal apex of queer self-acceptance that it often elides the complexity of what comes next. Once you're Out, this logic says, the work has been done! What else is there to process? Never mind the fact that, even if every single queer person were to go about their daily lives constantly bedecked with rainbows, flag pins and pithily worded shirts declaiming our sexual and/or romantic preferences, there'd still be people who assume us straight until or unless they heard us say "I am—" to their faces; there's still a constant exploration of selfhood going on underneath. Coming out is something we do for ourselves, yes, but also to satisfy the curiosity of others. If the default cultural perception wasn't to assume that everyone is straight and cis until proven otherwise, there'd be no need for anyone to come out the way we do currently, because there'd be no "out" to come from. We would just *be,* as known or unknown as we wished in whatever setting—and perhaps we'll get there, one day. But until then, we have Coming Out: the process by which we let others know the extent to which we either deviate from or conform to their expectations in some semi-official way, so as to make our identities a matter of public record.

The problem with this, of course, is that it assumes the record need never be updated, let alone treated as complex. I came out as genderqueer in 2015 because that seemed accurate at the time, and I won't go so far as to say it's ever been wrong; but as I came to realise during the course of writing this book, it isn't completely right, either. Which is why, late in 2022, I started taking testosterone, and will hopefully have had top surgery by the time this book is published. I am, as the kids say, transitioning, and in terms of my personal well-being—and despite the present moral panic around transness—it feels wonderful. To quote comedian Mae Martin, "I'm not skipping around. It's truly just the absence of agony." Which isn't to say I was constantly in agony before now—or at least, not in the way you might be imagining, particularly given how compartmentalized I am. It was rather that, before, I would (for instance) routinely think to myself, *I'm not a person,* the words popping up at odd moments with a hollow, unpleasant sort of resonance; but since starting T, that hasn't happened once. It's hardly a panacea for the difficulties of existence, but it's helpful to feel like a person while facing them.

There's a lot more I could say about all this—and possibly will, at some nebulous point in the future—but this isn't the place. What matters here is that, once I understood what the book was doing, the process of writing it became indelibly intertwined with how I was coming to understand myself. As such, there's an added debt of gratitude to the people who made this story possible, and who've supported me both throughout its creation and in my newly articulated selfhood. To my agent, Hannah Bowman, and my editor, Claire Eddy, as well as everyone else at Tor: thank you. To my friends, both online and IRL, but especially Liz Bourke and the Bunker: thank you. And most of all, to my family: thank you, I love you, thank you. It's hard to explain exactly what your support means to me—to bastardize Jane Austen, if I felt it less, perhaps I could talk about it more—but please know, I value it beyond words. And on a more fannish note, I'd also like to offer a humble shoutout to Stray Kids, whose music, masculinity and friendship have had such a joyous, transformative impact on me at a time when I needed it most. Thanks, guys.

And, last but not least, to my readers: thank you for picking up this book. I wouldn't be here without you.

ABOUT THE AUTHOR

Foz Meadows is a queer Australian author, essayist, reviewer, and poet. They have won two Best Fan Writer awards (a Hugo Award in 2019 and a Ditmar Award in 2017) for yelling on the internet, and have also received the Norma K. Hemming Award in 2018 for their queer Shakespearean novella, *Coral Bones*. Their essays, reviews, poetry, and short fiction have appeared in various venues, including *Uncanny, Apex Magazine, Goblin Fruit, HuffPost,* and *Strange Horizons*. Meadows currently lives in California with their family.